9-2

FROM AWARD-WINNING AND BESTSELLING NOVELIST ROBERTA GELLIS COMES A FANTASTICAL ROMANCE OF MYTHIC PROPORTIONS

Persephone smiled at him and said, "I am no longer afraid that you will ravish me. You need not lie halfway across the cave to reassure me."

Hades straightened up abruptly. "Are you telling me you accept me as a husband?"

Surprise that she had barely bit back a "yes" kept her mute, but she managed to shake her head. He stared at her for another moment and then turned back to straighten the fleece he had pulled awry when she spoke to him.

"I have known you for one day, Hades," she said. "That is a brief time in which to agree to make over my life."

He looked over his shoulder. "We have lived through enough today to fill several lives and we have helped and sustained each other." Turning to face her fully, he added, "I do not see how time will show you better what I am. I am willing to pledge to you—my life, my honor, my heart—"

He swallowed and Persephone, who had been looking down, trying to find the strength to resist the logic of his words and the deep hunger in his voice, raised her eyes to his.

Hades closed the space between them before she even thought of retreat and caught her into his arms. His voice trembled as he said, "Oh, Persephone, my dazzling brightness. I have not felt such a light in my soul nor such a fire in my body since . . . I swear, not since my father drove me from Olympus. Be my queen, Persephone."

She did not answer, but she did not struggle against him as he then lifted his hands to the sides of her face, tilted it toward him, and brought his mouth to hers . . .

Please turn the page for rave reviews of previous works by Roberta Gellis:

ACCLAIMED AUTHOR

AWARD-WINNING NOVELIST

AND NOW TRAVEL BACK IN TIME TO ANCIENT GREECE AND THE FASCINATING TALE OF HADES AND PERSEPHONE . . .

Roberta Gellis

Dazzling Brightness

PINNACLE BOOKS
WINDSOR PUBLISHING CORP.

PINNACLE BOOKS are published by

Windsor Publishing Corp.
475 Park Avenue South
New York, NY 10016

First Printing: June, 1994

Printed in the United States of America

Chapter 1

A man waited in the tumble of boulders on the toe of a mountain intruding into the lush valley of Olympus. He was wrapped in a hooded gray wool cloak, so close to the color of the granite on which he leaned that to a quick glance he seemed only part of the irregular outline of the rock. In the pale light of dawn his face was shadowed by the hood, but the skin was so very white that a close examination might have made him noticeable—all but the eyes. The eyes were shadow within shadow, a blackness between brow and cheek.

A footpath curved around the toe of the mountain, leading from the temple of the Corn Goddess, which was on the very outskirts of the gleaming city that was home to the mages of Olympus, to a pool sacred to the Mother of Life. Four times a year, at the turning of the seasons, the lesser priestesses and novices of the Corn Goddess brought her ceremonial robes to that pool for a ritual washing.

The sun topped the shoulder of the mountain, setting the snow-capped peak aflame with rosy light. A bird raised a lilting paean to the morning. The man's head jerked up, but then he huddled closer to the rock, becoming briefly visible as he moved and then even less visible. He waited. Once a deep sigh stirred him. Then he was still again.

A sound, high and sweet but nothing like the intermittent birdsong that greeted the morning, drifted down the path. The man stirred briefly again as he took a deep breath and turned his head slightly so that he could see along the path. This time he did not have long to wait. The group whose singing had preceded them came into sight: First an older priestess, older but no crone, as evidenced by the lush curves filling out a gown the brown of a rich autumn; she was surrounded by a gaggle of little girls in white and older girls in green; then a more orderly group of young women dressed in the golden amber of ripened grain, all carrying baskets. As they approached, the sound of singing increased.

A very slight movement showed that the man had tensed as if he were peering forward, trying to see the second group more clearly. And then, a little way behind, a last young woman came into view, this one garbed in the tender green of early spring. She was obviously idling, in no hurry to catch up with her companions. The breath the man had drawn as he tried to see the faces of the amber-clad girls was checked. Had Zeus told her she was to be taken? Was she willing? If she were willing . . . but he did not dare take any chance. If he failed to take her, she would be immured in the temple in the future and guarded too closely for him to try again. He murmured softly and his hand moved under his cloak.

The older woman and the little girls had rounded the rocky toe and were progressing along the path, their backs now to the boulder against which the man stood. In another moment, the young women with their baskets also passed around the curve. The man gestured sharply and among the small rocks at the very edge of the path an exquisite flower of tiny, brilliant gems suddenly caught the light. His finger moved just a little—right, left. The jeweled flower rocked, throwing off glitters and gleams.

The young woman in the green gown paused as one and then another bright flash caught her eye. She searched the edge of the path, then hurried forward to kneel down and pick up the pretty thing. She stared at it, amazed. Around a golden yellow-diamond heart were ruby petals, and peeping from behind them emerald leaves—but the whole flower was hardly larger than her thumbnail and it was all one piece, as if diamond, ruby, and emerald had somehow been melted together and yet kept distinct.

While her attention was held, the man withdrew around the boulder and gestured again. There was a sharp, but not loud, snap. The young woman's head came up just in time to see a round piece of the boulder nearest her crack and fall. In the exposed hollow was just such a gem as that which she held in her hand. She looked at the flower in her hand and then toward the sparkling thing cradled in the rock hollow ten or fifteen steps up a sharp rise above the path. She looked right, left, and at the boulder again.

The man froze tighter against the surface of his shelter and clenched his jaws over the impulse to call to the young woman and a simultaneous but opposite urge to hide himself more completely. He resisted both silly notions but not without twitching at the hem of his cloak, which he was certain was visible. At the same moment that he yielded to that betraying movement, a voice floated back from around the curve in the path.

"Kore. Come along now. Kore!"

Although he knew what the young woman was called, the man's teeth set with outrage. Every person, even a slave, had a right to a personal name, but this poor young woman had to make do with Kore—*girl,* in the language of the mages. How dare her mother deprive her of that most personal possession, as if she were not a person at all. Furious, he moved again and then realizing he might have exposed himself, froze, holding his breath.

Just before the irritable voice demanding that she hurry came to her ears, Kore raised her eyes from a second suspicious examination of the gem in her palm to the twinkle in the boulder. One fine golden brow lifted. Despite what her mother often said, Kore was not a fool. She realized at once that, bright and beautiful as it was, the trinket in her hand was unlikely by chance to have escaped the notice of those who preceded her. And the rock shattering by accident while she was there? Nonsense, that was no accident.

Her heart beat just a trifle faster at the thought that someone had set a lure to draw her. Who could it be? She had seen several of the young men of the city look longingly at her during the procession that welcomed the spring. But only one of the greater mages could have wrought the gem or cracked the rock, and none of them had seemed interested . . . but anyone rich enough could buy the artifact and the spell too. Caution bade her drop the jeweled flower and follow the others swiftly, but then she heard the older priestess's impatient call.

Kore's soft lips hardened into a mulish line. No one

would harm the daughter of the high priestess of the Corn Goddess, and if someone desired a few words with her enough to make or buy so elaborate a lure, surely that person deserved a hearing. Her hand closed around the flower-gem and she began to climb the rise, calling out as she did, "In a moment, Dorkas. I wish to pick a flower. I will follow in a moment."

White teeth flashed momentarily inside the shadow of the hood. If Dorkas was the priestess in charge of the group, success was all but assured. Pebbles clattered down toward the path as Kore climbed. A moment later a cautious hand made a warding gesture, but no remnant of power remained, and the hand reached toward the gem in the hollow. In the instant when the girl's eyes were fixed on her prize, a part of the boulder seemed to separate itself. Kore's eyes lifted, her lips parted.

"Who—" she whispered.

A hand as hard as stone caught her head and drew her face into the folds of the cloak so forcefully that her cry was muffled. She tried to raise her hands to push herself away, but the cloak that had covered her captor had been wound around her and then around again, binding her arms to her sides, her legs together; the hood pressed against her mouth served as a gag.

"Forgive me," a deep voice murmured. "I mean you no harm. I swear I will not hurt you. There is no other way. Forgive me."

Kore twisted and writhed to no avail. She felt his other hand behind her thighs, lifting her, and she tried again and again to scream but the hand behind her head never loosened its grip, and she knew the sounds she made would be heard by no ears but her own and perhaps her captor's. She struggled to jerk her body up and down to break his grip, but she was wrapped so tightly in the cloak that her heaving had no effect. She could feel her captor walking swiftly and thought despairingly that he was strong as stone.

The word triggered a frightening memory. Just yesterday, when she had been complaining to her mother about always being the one who had to do the actual washing of the Goddess's gown, Dorkas, behind her, had laughed and muttered to herself that doubtless the Queen of the Dead would do no washing. At the time Kore had not wondered why the woman had used those words. Dorkas was always murmuring nasty things under her breath, just loud enough for only one person to hear so she could not be accused of illspeaking. Now Kore remembered and fear choked her. Had Dorkas *truly* ill-wished her into the power of the King of the Dead? Terror drove her to more violent contortions.

"Be quiet. Be quiet. I will do you no hurt," the deep voice soothed. "Your father has given me leave to take you."

Iasion, her father, was dead! In her effort to scream, to draw breath and scream, the woolen folds filled her mouth. Half suffocated and half mad with fear, Kore fainted.

She regained her senses lying on a low pile of fleeces, covered by the cloak that had imprisoned her. For a moment she thought she had fallen asleep in a storage shed of the temple where she had sometimes hidden herself from her mother's too-tender care when she was a child. But her eyes opened onto a roof of rough stone, plainly visible because each fleck of crystal in it glowed. It was so beautiful that for another moment Kore only stared, then memory and fear returned and her lips parted to scream.

"Please, please do not be so frightened. I will do you no harm. Only listen to me and I will explain what I have done."

Kore's eyes flew to the deep-voiced speaker. He sat, cross-legged, on another pad of fleeces a few feet from her, as if to give assurance that he would not touch her. She pushed herself upright, staring. Black hair, tightly curled, covered his head and curved around his ears. His mouth and chin were surrounded by a very short, neatly trimmed beard that left bare most of his cheeks. His skin was very white, paler than hers, which turned golden under the touch of the sun. The pallor only increased the darkness of his eyes, which caught and held hers. There seemed to be no bottom to those black pools.

"Persephone," the man murmured when he saw her eyes were fixed on him. "You are a dazzling brightness to me, so beautiful that you nearly stop my breath. I shall call you Persephone, if you will give me leave."

"Who are you?" Kore whispered.

"I am Hades."

For a moment her voice was suspended by fear, but then she forced out, "The King of the Dead?"

The man's lips twitched as if he wanted to laugh, but he did not, and said quietly, "That is what many call me."

"Am I dead?" Kore asked, eyes wide.

Hades burst into full-throated laughter. "No, of course not, my exquisite Persephone. Nor am I dead, nor do I expect to be, and I have a healthy appetite, which is why I seized you."

The laughter rang in the stone chamber. Stone of heart, stone of face, strong as stone, and black of eye—that was all she had ever heard of the Hades who was King of the Dead. Black-eyed this Hades was, and strong as stone; whether his heart was hard Kore did not yet know, but his face was alive with expression, laughter at the moment. Even in the laughter, however, there was admiration. She felt warmed by the glow in those black eyes and could not doubt that she was a dazzling brightness to him.

Nonetheless, she lifted her head proudly and said, "You may name me, but that does not make me *your* Persephone."

If the parents did not seize their right of naming at birth, anyone could set a name to a child for ill or good. The newly named Persephone could not and would not reject the name Hades offered, even though he had abducted her. All her life she had hated being called Kore—girl, only girl. She had begged her mother and others, too, to name her, but no one would dare oppose the chief priestess of the Corn Goddess on a subject so near her heart, and all her mother said was that she would be Demeter in her turn, after her mother died. Kore had been sick at the thought. She did not want her mother to die, but she felt crippled without a name. And Persephone was a name of beauty and power, all hers, hers alone, not a hand-me-down from the dead.

Hades had bowed his head. "Forgive me, Persephone," he murmured. "That is the truth. You belong to yourself and to none other. You are no slave though I have captured you and though your father has agreed that you should become my wife."

"My father is dead," she cried, her voice choked with renewed fear.

"Dead? Zeus?" Hades gasped, putting a hand down and starting to rise. "But I saw him hale and strong only—"

"My father was Iasion," Persephone snapped.

Hades settled back and smiled again. "Your blood father," he said. "Do you not remember that Zeus adopted you not long after he became the Mage-King? You gave me a fright, saying your father was dead. I am fond of Zeus. He is my youngest brother."

Her lips trembled but she firmed them. "I am not fond of him," she said. "And my mother never agreed to the adoption. Zeus has no rights over me."

"Demeter never opposed the adoption."

"Does one oppose the will of a conqueror?"

Hades shrugged. "Perhaps not, but that was many years ago, and Zeus has not proved to be so dreadful a tyrant. Demeter could have protested the adoption later, saying that she feared to deny him at the time. She never did. By the laws and customs of Olympus, Zeus is your father and has the right to give you in marriage. For many favors owed, he has given you to me."

"I thought a free woman had the right of refusal. I refuse. Take me home."

At first he was silent; after a moment he shook his head slowly and said softly, "You may refuse to be my wife but not my priestess. I cannot take you home. I must have a priestess who is fit to rule a temple of the Corn Goddess and who can teach the women of my realm to bring grain from the earth. If that mystery is not brought to my people, they will soon starve. My realm is rich, but not in such stuffs as folk can eat."

He gestured to himself and Persephone noticed for the first time the broad collar and wide armlets of beaten gold set with gems, the belt, so encrusted with jewels that it glittered and flashed with Hades's every breath and movement in the glow of the roof crystals. Even his boots had elaborate patterns of precious stones embedded in the worked leather.

"The dead do not eat," she said.

His lips curved but his eyes were sad. "The 'dead' of my realm must eat. There is some hunting in the caves and on the mountains, but it is very dangerous, and one cannot make bread from flesh. In the past we have traded our wealth for grain, but the supply is too uncertain. There are too many of us now."

She shook her head. "Even the Corn Goddess cannot bring forth grain from rock. A plant needs the sun and the rain." Her voice checked and then continued, trembling. "I need the sun and the sky, too. I cannot be buried under the earth and live."

"Do you fear this cave? Is this chamber too small for you? I can bring you to a place so large that it is hard to see the roof or walls, a many-pillared palace—"

"I fear never to see the sun," Persephone cried, shivering, "never to hear a bird sing or to see a rabbit hop or a lamb play. I do not wish to be the wife of the King of the Dead no matter how many cold gems you lavish upon me."

He sat with bent head, his hands open, palm up, in his lap. His sadness beat against her so that she had to bite her lip to keep back words of comfort. What comfort could she offer him when the only thing that would make him happy was to bury her alive? Nonetheless, a wave of sympathy flowed toward him.

His head lifted slowly, his eyes so big and black—so hungry—that Persephone's breath caught with fear. His cheeks were very slightly flushed, his mouth soft and full. He stared at her, seeking something, then gestured—and the glow of the roof grew so bright that she had to shut her eyes. She felt the light dim almost at once and looked at him again, prepared to defend herself, although she did not know how or against what, but he had turned his gaze down into his empty hands once more.

At last he said, "I will not force you into marriage. I have already told you that. Persephone, you are my sun. Will you not give light to my poor people, many of whom have suffered bitterly in the outer world? I promise you will see the sun and hear birds sing again, but there is life in the caves, too, some so beautiful and delicate that it can bring tears of joy. Will you not let me show you the glories of Plutos, give me a chance to win your forgiveness for stealing you away from your world into mine? We have a long way to go before I can bring you to an open place."

"Long way? You could not have carried me far. Take me back! That is not a long way."

The black eyes now raised to her were empty; the face might indeed have been carved of stone. Persephone shivered in the blast of freezing fury that flooded out of the man.

"I am sorry," Hades said. He did not sound sorry. "I will not take you back. You are only one woman, no matter how beautiful. My people are many and depend on me. I cannot let you have your way without regard for them. Your only choice now is to sit here in this cave, which you hate so much, or come with me to a place where you can sleep under the stars of the open sky and see the sun rise in the morning."

"I will sit here until I die," Persephone spat, "rather than go with you farther and farther from my home so that I am utterly lost."

"You are utterly lost already," Hades remarked, and his teeth flashed in what was not a smile. "But I have time. The valleys in which we must grow our grain are high. Spring has not yet come to them. There are several weeks before I must consider binding you and carrying you all the way." Suddenly his cold anger at her refusal seemed to melt and he uttered what seemed a genuine chuckle. "I am strong enough, but you are no wraith and I would really prefer that you walked."

"Point the way, and I will walk home quickly enough."

Hades sighed and pointed to the ceiling. "That is the way. While you think over how to find a path, will you not have something to eat? I would not want you to think I was trying to make my task easier by starving you to make you lighter."

"Having failed with words, you now think you can seduce me with spells?"

"Seduce you with spells?" Hades echoed, pausing as he unstrapped a sturdy wicker basket. "I wish I could. If I had a spell to seduce you . . ." His black eyes caressed her face, slid down her body to where the gray cloak masked it, then he laughed and shook his head. "No, I would not. When the spell ended you would hate me."

He had misunderstood her completely, but Persephone was momentarily silenced, shocked mute by her response to the desire he had offered up to her, almost like a sacrifice. Others had wanted her, but she had never felt so desperate a desire—perhaps because her mother had warded them away. She had resented that; she remembered being made curious by the whispered hints and inviting glances, but she did not remember feeling her skin tingle and her lips swell as if the man had touched her.

Meanwhile, Hades had opened the basket and taken from it something that smelled savory. Persephone could not tell exactly what it was because it was wrapped in vine leaves. He held the food toward her, bending forward so that if she also leaned forward and reached out she could take it easily from his hand.

"Here, take this while I get out a cup and pour some wine for you," he said.

Bemused, she had started to reach for the vine-leaf roll when his matter-of-fact tone startled her. The desire that had pushed everything else out of her mind was gone, as if he had closed the door of an oven and shut off the heat that had flowed from it. Fury at being so easily enticed—almost befooled—flooded her.

"I hate you now, you liar," she cried. "Do you think I do not know that to eat the food of Plutos or drink its wine condemns one to remain in its cold embrace forever?"

Hades's eyes widened and his mouth dropped open, but what came out was a roar of laughter, not a protest or another attempt to entice her. "Mother bless me," he got out between gusts. "I am trapped in a pit of my own digging."

"You mean that is only a tale you have set about?" Persephone's lifted brows spoke her disbelief.

Hades bit his lips as if there were words he was holding back by force, and he dropped his arm, allowing the hand that held the food to rest upon his knee. Finally he shook his head and said, "I will not answer your question, only say I am telling no lies about what I offer you. It will not bind you to Plutos."

"I do not believe you."

"You cannot escape me," Hades said, sounding both amused and exasperated rather than angry, "so what does it matter whether you eat and drink of the food of Plutos? Nonetheless, I will swear to you on anything you wish me to swear on, that nothing you eat or drink will bind you to my realm. I can and will hold you in different ways. The food"—he paused to chuckle and shake his head again— "will do you no harm, no, not even if you ate six pomegranate seeds . . . had I a pomegranate to offer you, which I do not, and could eating six seeds provide enough nourishment to keep a person alive, which they could not."

Since she was not very hungry and she was infuriated by the condescending amusement in his voice, Persephone turned her head away, nose in the air. Oddly, despite her protests, she did believe the food was harmless. Now, in the light of his laughter, she saw how silly was that cautionary tale of the maiden who had been trapped in Plutos by eating only six little seeds after being lured with sparkling jewels . . . Outraged, Persephone gasped.

That black-eyed demon had used the device in his own tall tale to catch her. By the moment it seemed more likely that he had set the lies about himself—or had them spread by others—to keep safe wealth beyond counting. A sidelong glance caught the sword that lay beside him. The scabbard was aglitter with gold wire and jewels; the guard and hilt of the weapon looked as if it had been a solid sapphire the size of a baby's head which had been carved into shape and holed in the center for the tang of the blade.

Now that she had turned her head and freed herself from the demands of his eyes, she saw that the walls of the cave glittered, likely with raw gems. There was reason enough to spread rumors that would keep the curious and the greedy out of Plutos. Thus the tales that circulated about fools who had entered the endless caverns, become lost in the maze, and finally been forced to eat and drink the produce of the dead and by contamination "doomed to join cold Hades's minions though yet alive."

The words of warning rang in her mind—only she knew Hades was not cold. She pushed the knowledge away, drawing on her resentment, which was increased by the sound of chewing and the glug-glug as the contents of a wineskin were transferred to a cup. Her mouth watered and she set her teeth. She would not give him the satisfaction of asking for what she had just refused. She sat still, staring at the wall, waiting for him to plead with her to eat and drink.

A scritch on the stone floor brought her head around, a hand outstretched to ward him off, but he was only pushing the laden basket closer to her.

"I will leave the basket where you can reach it." His voice was dull and he did not look at her. "I have been hard at work for many days—the food and fleeces did not come here by chance— and I am tired."

He made a gesture and lay down. Persephone looked away again, uncertain whether she should be angry because he had not urged her to eat or seem concerned about whether she did or grateful because he was pretending to need sleep so that she could salve her pride and eat without asking him. She glanced at him, but the hypnotic black eyes were closed and she could not tell from where she sat whether he was truly asleep. She looked away, knowing from her own experience that one could feel watchful eyes, but she could not resist stealing another glance at his face. Was it still handsome when the eyes did not bind her?

To her surprise, she found she could not make out the features clearly. She glanced around. The walls showed no sparkling gems now. Heart pounding, she raised her eyes to the ceiling. The glow was dimming. Even as she watched, what had been golden dimmed to a dull orange. Her lips parted to cry out to Hades to bring back the light, and then she clamped them shut. She was no child to be afraid of the dark. If this was his way of punishing her, he would get little satisfaction. He was the one who had places to go, things to do. She could outwait him, even in the dark.

Chapter 2

Hades had not the slightest intention of punishing Persephone. He had completely forgotten that she might react differently than those accustomed to the loss of light. He had dismissed the power that caused the crystal to glow out of habit, because he was not thinking clearly and because he had spoken somewhat less than the truth when he said he was tired.

The truth was that he was totally exhausted by the mixture of physical effort and emotional turmoil he had suffered over the last few weeks. His doubts over what he was doing had drained him, and this day had brought him to the limit of his strength. Because there was no cave that opened to the surface near enough, Hades had brought his prize down through the rock itself into this small bubble.

Weariness dragged at him, setting the weight of mountains on his eyelids, and he put aside a small anxiety about the openings he had noticed. There was no passage to the surface. He had told Persephone the truth, that the way home for her was up through the roof. Even if she found a passage, Hades thought, she would not dare to leave—and if she did, he could find her.

Yet even when the last glow faded beyond his closed eyes and the comforting dark enwrapped him, Hades could not sleep. The emotional battle he had fought was more exhausting than his physical exertion. Disappointment was like a knife, pricking him into spasms of regret. Perhaps if he had not taken Persephone by force. . . . But Zeus had said she would not consent, even if she desired to accept what he offered, because she feared her mother, who dominated and oppressed her. And that much was true; she had not even had a name when he had taken her.

Disjointed scenes of what had driven him to act flicked through Hades's mind. The plot had its beginning in midwinter, when he had learned that the supplies of grain would not last until spring and no more could be expected because of the bad crops in the outer realms. He had realized then that Plutos must have its own grain, its own goats and sheep and cattle—which meant fodder to feed them; that is, more grain. The time had come to call in the favors that Zeus owed him.

That scene came back, playing itself out behind Hades's closed eyes as if he were living it. Zeus had not been pleased to see him appear unannounced in the inner rooms of his palace—an unspoken warning that Zeus's triumph over Kronos was largley due to Hades's opening the way into Olympus—a feat he could accomplish again. Nonetheless, no particular expression changed Zeus's handsome face. They scarcely looked like brothers, Hades had thought irrelevantly. Although they were both tall and strong, Zeus was as blond as their mother Rhea, with glorious, softly curling golden hair and blue eyes as light and keen as the bolts of energy he could gather and throw.

All Zeus said, however, when Hades announced he had come to call in long-due favors, was, "So long as you do not ask my life, my kingdom, or my honor, I will do all in my power to grant any favor you desire."

"Could I get some advice first?" Hades had asked, grinning.

Zeus had laughed aloud and clapped him on the shoulder, exclaiming, "What? You expect me to tell you how to get the most out of me? Is that fair?" But Hades had noticed that the blue eyes were wary despite the laughter.

Still, when Hades made it plain the desire for advice was not all in jest, Zeus had led him to a small, private chamber off the back of the great hall, waved him to a seat, and poured wine. He had listened seriously to Hades's explanation of his problem, but when Hades finished, "So I must ask of you a priestess of the Corn Goddess so that I can build my own temple and Plutos can partake of the mystery of raising grain," Zeus sighed heavily.

"That was what I feared you would ask."

"Feared?" Hades echoed. "I do not think it so great a difficulty for you to convince the high priestess to send one of her consecrated women to me. Her mystery would not be allowed to pass out of my realm. And you know well enough that there would be nothing for her to fear in Plutos. My people would welcome her. She would have her choice of acolytes—"

"The problem is not with Plutos," Zeus interrupted sourly. "The trouble is between Demeter and me."

Hades closed his eyes for a moment. "Another cast-off mistress?"

"No. I have more sense than to toy with the high priestess of the Corn Goddess. In fact, to give assurances of my good will, I offered to take her to wife and make her equal with Hera. How should I have known that her lover, Iasion, had been killed in the fighting when we took Olympus and that she would be infuriated by my offer instead of flattered?" Zeus snorted with disgust. "*I* did not kill the man. Why blame me?"

"I suppose because he would have survived if you had not started a war," Hades remarked dryly. "And perhaps after she refused you, she became afraid you would drive her out as you did Kronos's favorites."

"I thought of that, and I tried to assure her. I went to all the trouble of formally adopting her daughter by Iasion, so that Kore—" Zeus stopped speaking abruptly.

"What girl?" Hades asked.

Zeus lifted his eyes, which he had dropped to stare at the dark wine in his golden cup, and they were bright with intention. "Kore is what Demeter calls her daughter. She has forbidden the naming of the girl. And it is all of a piece with the way Kore is treated. Demeter never lets the poor creature out of her sight, not even to visit me—her own father."

Unaware of what he was doing, Zeus touched his lips with the tip of his tongue. Although he said nothing, Hades thought that Demeter might be wise to forbid her daughter to visit Zeus. At the same time, he found his own body responding to Zeus's sensual gesture, thinking that the daughter of the chief priestess—Hades could not bring himself to call her Kore—must be a luscious morsel to stimulate Zeus even in her absence.

"The girl," Zeus was saying, "is allowed no congress with men, and she is more than twenty years of age . . ." He hesitated, then smiled broadly. "I *am* her father. I have the right of giving her in marriage. And she is a beautiful creature, all golden—hair, eyes, skin—beautiful! Take her to wife, Hades. You will be doing her a great kindness to free her from her bondage to her mother."

"I need a priestess, not a wife, however beautiful," Hades pointed out. "I do not need another mouth to feed—and one who is in no danger in her native place—"

"But she is!" Zeus interrupted. "Not in danger, her mother loves her well—too well, I think. I meant that Kore is a full priestess. Dorkas was complaining to me the other day that Demeter neglects her duties, pushing all the preparations and prayers onto Kore. The only trouble will be getting hold of her, for Demeter would never let her go. Why should she, when it would mean she would have to perform her duties herself? You will have to abduct her in secret."

Hades's eyelids quivered, but he did not permit himself to open them or to turn his head to look toward Persephone. He had argued with Zeus over the idea of abduction, but not very hard, perhaps not hard enough. He had been stirred by Zeus's half-concealed excitement. He had wanted to see—to have—Demeter's daughter; he had wanted to be convinced.

Now Hades recalled Zeus's enthusiasm with a sinking heart. He knew Zeus was a manipulative devil, and he should have suspected such eager compliance. At the time, he had only been relieved that Zeus had not denied him with the very reasonable protest that the corn mystery was not his to give or to withhold. He had been content, thinking that Zeus was eager to fulfill his pledge with a favor that cost him nothing. But that was true, Hades thought, the cloud of despair that had been covering him lifting a little, and Zeus had obtained the additional advantage of revenge on Demeter.

Nor was Zeus's tale all lies; Persephone had no name until he named her—and she had accepted the name, accepted it eagerly. And then, to cheer him further, Hades heard a small sound as the basket moved. A little while later he smelled the spices of the meat roll as she opened the leaves. An enormous relief eased the tension in his muscles. She had taken food. She believed he wished her no harm. If she had come so far in a few hours, surely he would be able to draw her the whole way—into trust, perhaps into fondness. Lifted on a wave of hope, Hades slept.

Unfortunately he slept in ignorance of the truth. Persephone was eating and, when she found a full cup of wine propped in the corner of the basket, drinking, not because she was becoming reconciled to her fate but because she hoped to escape it.

She had sat at first with closed eyes, because it was easier to endure the dark with her eyes closed; she could tell herself that when she opened them it would not be so black, it would be no darker than her own shuttered room at night. It seemed to her that she sat for hours and hours without moving, although she suspected less time had passed, knowing well how time could drag when there was something unpleasant waiting.

She listened intently—after some time she could have sworn that her entire body had become one open ear—but heard nothing from Hades beyond a soft sigh now and again. The last breath she heard was longer and deeper. He *had* fallen asleep, she thought resentfully. He does not care whether or not I eat, and he does not fear that I can escape him. She was so angry that she forgot the utter lack of light and her eyes popped open as she turned her head to look at him.

He could not see her reproach; his eyes were closed. But lacking the amused laughter in them, his face was less hard and much sadder than she remembered, the fine lips turning down at the corners. Black lashes swept pale cheeks, the skin so white it showed almost bluish until it disappeared under his black beard. Faint gleams showed from the jeweled clothing and his hand lay slightly away from his body, stretched toward her, palm up as if begging for her hand to be laid in it.

He really does want me, Persephone thought, and had to clench her hand to resist the appeal. She tore her eyes away from him, looking down as if to be sure she did not betray herself. Her hands were pale against her dress, which appeared black in the dim light. Dim light? Persephone drew a short, hard breath. How could there be any light? Her eyes flew up, but the roof was utterly black. Yet there was light lower down. Her glance swept the walls and stopped at a narrow fissure from which came a dim ice-blue glow.

Persephone almost laughed aloud at the accidental frustration of Hades's attempt to discipline her. Clearly he had lighted the cave as he entered it and had never noticed that his path from the outer world was betrayed by a gleam of light. Her teeth caught her lip hard to repress a cry of joy. His path from the outer world would be her path to it.

She grasped the cloak that still lay warmly over her knees, and started to pull it aside and rise, but then she paused. She had better be certain he was deeply asleep, not just drifting on the surface. It might not be possible for her to cross the cave and get into the narrow passage in absolute silence. If he were deeply asleep, a small noise might not waken him, whereas anything might alert him out of a doze. However, she found it very hard to wait, now that she had seen her escape route, and she tended to keep watching Hades, in case he should wake and see the light.

Realizing that watching him might disturb him, she sought another target for her eyes and soon found the basket. Since she was hungry, she decided she might as well eat. If he heard anything, the sounds of her unwrapping and chewing might well reassure him and send him into deeper sleep. She found several of the leaf-covered rolls immediately, and beside them a large wedge-shape that she thought must be cheese.

The light was too dim to see what was below the edge of the basket, so she explored lightly with her fingers. A round form she decided from the feel must be bread, although the loaf was much smaller than any with which she was familiar, and beside it—Persephone had to bite her lip again to keep back another cry, this time of surprise. Beside the bread was a knife. She hesitated before she explored that. Would a man who had abducted a woman leave a knife for her to find?

Resentment flared in her again. Why not? If he

thought her weak and silly, he would believe her incapable of using a knife. Could she? She fingered the hilt and glanced at him sidelong. But he had done her no harm, and he had named her—a beautiful, powerful name—Dazzling Brightness, Persephone. No, she would not hurt him, at least not unless he tried to stop her from escaping. Nonetheless, she took the knife from the basket very carefully, making sure it did not touch or catch on anything that would make a sound and betray her, and set it in her lap.

Her further exploration of the basket had led her to the full cup of wine. Anxiety had dried her mouth, and she lifted that and drank, then set what remained beside her while she unwrapped the meat roll inside the vine leaves. It was very good, delicious, in fact. She ate another, sipped the wine, thinking that Hades did not stint himself although he said his people were hungry.

Honesty made her revise that statement while she ate still another meat roll. He had said they needed grain, that the numbers of his people were growing and they would face hunger in the future if she did not teach his womenfolk the mystery of raising corn. And the loaf of bread in the basket *was* very small. Was she doing wrong in planning to escape?

Persephone's lips thinned. No, she was not doing wrong. If Hades wanted a priestess, he should have approached her mother and asked, not seized her and carried her off without a by-your-leave. Even if Zeus had agreed . . . But Hades was Zeus's brother; if her mother knew that, she probably would not have sent a priestess with him, and certainly she would not have allowed her daughter to go.

Suddenly Persephone smiled. This was the most exciting thing that had ever happened to her, and the way Hades looked at her—The smile froze on her lips. What was happening to her? The food! It was sapping her will, twisting her mind. Being abducted was not exciting! It was a violation of her rights as a free woman. Hades had lied to her! She must escape now, before the poison took a greater hold on her.

She seized the knife and got to her feet, kicking the cloak out of the way. The cup overturned with a small clink, but Persephone did not hear it. Nor did she see or hear Hades turn and sigh. Her eyes were fixed on the dim bluish glow, and she hurried toward it, uncaring of the scratch and scrape of pebbles under her feet.

The light did not look so inviting now. There was a sickly tone to the blue. And she remembered suddenly that Hades had pointed to the ceiling and said that was the path out. But if he had lied about the food, he had lied about everything. Fighting her reluctance, she squeezed her way into the crack and inched toward the light, struggling, as she forced her way forward, with an ever-increasing terror that the rock would close in on her.

As a rough piece of stone tore Persephone's gown and scraped her shoulder, it occurred to her that Hades could never have come through this passage carrying her. Then this was not the path he had taken. She hesitated, then firmed her trembling mouth and pushed on. This was light. Light meant the sun in the open sky. Perhaps this was not the way Hades had come, but if she followed the light she would find a way into the outer world and from there she would somehow find her way home.

As if her determination had broken the resistance of the passage, it widened a few steps farther along, letting her walk easily. She hurried forward, shivering, suddenly aware that she was bitterly cold—yet it had been warm enough in the cave. Hades. It was Hades who made light and warmth. He was as great a mage as Zeus. To be priestess/wife to so great a mage, would that be so terrible? She hesitated, looking back, and then remembered that her desire to return was not her own but caused by the bespelled food. She had to reach the outer world. When she did, the spell drawing her back to Hades would be broken.

The clink of the wine cup that Persephone overturned rang louder in Hades's mind than in his ears. Exhaustion, however, lay upon him like a thick blanket, weighing down his limbs, and regret blurred and distorted his thoughts. He turned his back on the sound, sighing with reluctance to determine the cause. He did not want to know; he did not want to act, only to sleep. Beyond the oblivion of sleep lay misery.

The scrape of leather on stone disturbed him again. Still he clung to sleep. Quiet returned soon, but as he drifted down the memory of that sound troubled him, prodded at him. He tried to sink below the meaning of the grating of pebble against stone—that someone was walking about near him—tried to sink into the black depths of sleep, but a constant prick of responsibility kept drawing him up, demanding his attention.

In his own chamber, none would harm him. Why should he care who walked and where? And with the question his eyes flew open. He was not in his own chamber but with Persephone in— The blue light struck his eyes, and he sprang to his feet staring around wildly. She was gone! He opened his mouth to call, then clamped it shut. If she heard his voice, she would run, perhaps headlong into what dwelt in the blue light.

Hades snatched up his sword and leapt to the fissure. He thrust a shoulder in, but realized even before the fabric of his tunic caught against the stone that he could never pass in the normal way. For a moment he leaned into the rock, his shoulder and breast beginning to blur and slide into the stone, but then he drew back. He did not know how long the narrow passage was. It would take too long. He backed out, strapped on his sword, and laid one hand on each wall.

"Mother help me," he whispered, and then began to press outward. "Open," he demanded through gritted teeth. "Open!"

Persephone soon realized that the light was growing stronger. Hugging her arms around herself for warmth, she began to run. Soon she did not feel the cold so bitterly. The air that wafted into the passage was warmer and felt damp, she thought, but it had a strange scent. Priestess of the Corn Goddess, Persephone knew growing things and what she smelled was not of the land she knew. Her step faltered. The light was wrong too. It was not like sunlight but like moonlight, only much brighter and with a strange blue tinge.

Suddenly Persephone was afraid. What was ahead was not the world she knew! But it must be, she told herself. She was bespelled, bedazzled into thinking the outer world alien and repulsive. Likely the light seemed strange because she expected it should be high noon; instead, more time had passed than she realized and it was really twilight. Setting her jaw, she began to run again.

Despite her determination, her steps lagged slower and slower as the tunnel she was in became enormous, dwarfing her. The blue-white light was now so strong that she could see the rock that surrounded her clearly. Here and there were oddly smooth patches in the walls and floor. She paused to look at a protrusion of the smooth rock; it was clear. She could see through it. How curious. Hades had promised he would show her marvels.

A moment later she realized she was standing still, half turned to the passage behind her. She jerked her head around, forcing herself to look forward. This way was freedom she told herself. Hades's promises were all lies—and then, as if to confirm the thought, she saw green ahead. Grass, it must be grass. Persephone forced herself forward, trying to ignore the regrets that dragged at her, holding her back. But where the passage ended, triumph and regret alike were forgotten as was the danger of waking the captor she had left behind. She stopped short, crying out in amazement.

At first she thought she had emerged from Plutos into an entirely unknown realm, cold, and barren of tree or bush, where as far as the eye could see the tumbled rocks were covered with a strange green moss. Then she saw that she had not emerged at all, only entered a cavern so huge that the farther walls were almost lost in the strange blue light. That, like the light Hades had summoned, came from the roof, but not in glittering points. The blue light poured steadily from wide swathes and rough patches in the ceiling and in the upper walls.

Persephone stood still, tasting the bitterness of defeat and wondering what she should do. Go back to Hades? He loved to laugh, and now he would have good cause to laugh at her. She stood irresolute; the faint sound of her footsteps now stilled, she heard the even fainter burble of running water. The wine she had drunk was sour in her mouth. She would like a drink of water. The source could not be too far. If Hades wanted her, let him come after her. He could not be in any doubt as to where she had gone. She need not run back to him like a whipped bitch.

The floor sloped sharply from the lip of the passage toward the center of the cavern. Persephone had to watch carefully where she put her feet lest a moss-covered rock turn and unbalance her. And the moss itself was slippery and unlike any she knew. Near the passage it had been low. As she walked, it grew taller. The odor she had noticed in the passage, which was strange to her but not unpleasant, came from the moss rather strongly when she crushed it under her feet.

By the time she was at the bank of the stream, the moss was knee high, and beneath it nearest the water grew a tiny forest of round white crowns—surely mushrooms. Persephone bent to look closer, shadowing the water. As she did, a creature rose out of the stream and flung itself at her, hissing like a too-tight covered pot boiling over.

She reared upright, shrieking with alarm and thrusting out her hands to ward the creature off. The knife, which she had been clutching all the while she walked, caught the thing in the middle. The hiss rose higher, almost to a scream, and blood stained the soft, pallid flesh of its underside. It fell back. Persephone scrambled backward too, but it twisted around lithely and found its feet to rush forward again, opening a broad mouth with too many teeth.

The creature was waist high and quick. Persephone did not dare turn her back and try to outrun it. Its forepart rose slightly, as if it were preparing to leap. It could easily bear her down. With the courage of desperation, Persephone stepped forward and struck downward with her knife, screaming, "Hades! Help! Hades!"

The dagger scored on the snout, tearing a nostril. Blood poured down into the thing's mouth and it backed away, a long tongue coming out to lick at the blood. Persephone tried to run backward, knife ready. The creature's skin was moist and shining. Perhaps it would not go far from the water and she could escape it. But that hope died as it started forward again.

"Hades!" she shrieked. "Help me!"

She tried to go back faster. A branch of moss caught in her skirt and tugged her sideways. Countering the pull, she leaned the other way, and a rock rolled under her heel. There was a sound like thunder, grating and crashing, and through it came a voice like a brazen bell calling her name. Hades was coming—but not soon enough.

Chapter 3

Persephone screamed for Hades again, windmilling her arms as she lost her balance and fell backward. The moss cushioned her so that the rock did not bruise her badly, but the long stalks, incredibly strong for moss, tangled her arms. She struggled wildly, trying to push herself upright and free the hand that held the knife. She saw the beast coming; from behind a long shadow loomed over her.

Legs were suddenly astride her hips, legs in boots so bright with jewels that she blinked. In that blink the creature was beheaded. Persephone saw the sword only at the end of its swing, red running down the silvery blade.

"Are you hurt?" Hades cried, twisting to look down at her.

Persephone swallowed. His face, always pale, now had the gray-white look of a corpse and was streaked with rivulets of sweat. The hand that held the sword trembled so violently that red droplets scattered from the blade.

"No," she gasped, pushing back with her heels so that she could slide from between his legs. From his look she feared he would collapse atop her. "I am not hurt," she assured him more steadily, hoping it was fear for her that had drained him and that knowing her safe would restore him.

"Thank the Mother," he sighed, setting his sword point into the ground and leaning on the weapon. "Can you stand?"

"Better than you, I think," Persephone replied, getting to her feet.

"I do not doubt it." He smiled at her. "You are a marvel. Most outworld women would be in screaming hysterics—and many of the underworld folk also, to speak the truth, those who never leave the home caves."

Even as he spoke the praise, however, his head was turning to look over his shoulder. Persephone was torn between pleasure and pique. His acknowledgement of her courage and common sense—what good would hysterics have done her; had she not fought the beast it would probably have torn her to bits—made her feel strong and proud. On the other hand, his distraction irritated her; it was entirely too possible he was mouthing a polite formula while he was thinking of something else.

Before she could speak, however, he had turned back to her. He drew a deep breath as if it could restore him, but to Persephone he looked even grayer and more drawn when he said, "Go back the way you came as quickly as you can. There are worse things in the caves of blue light than this hudorhaix."

Persephone drew a sharp breath and started away, but a fearful glance over her shoulder showed that Hades was not following. He was facing the stream again, the lines of his body tense with watching and listening. Worse things? Panic drove her a few steps farther before common sense stopped her dead in her tracks. If Hades were hurt or killed, would she not die of cold and starvation, even if the beast that he fought did not soon follow her?

"Be strong," she whispered, turning and coming back the few steps she had fled.

He whipped around to face her, black eyes wide, but there was color in his cheeks and lips. "What did you do?" he asked.

"Nothing." She drew herself up. "I wished for you to be strong to defend me, and I came to stand with you. Perhaps I could distract the thing so you could strike at it more easily."

"You *must* be my queen," he breathed.

She shrugged, although the intensity in his eyes and the near-awe in his hushed voice made her know she was worth more to him than gold or diamonds—or even bread in this strange world—and that brought blood to her cheeks.

"I am only trying to save myself," she said tartly. "What safety could I find in these caves with no guide and no light if harm came to you?"

"You wished me to be strong," he repeated, as if he had heard nothing else she said, then turned away abruptly.

"What comes?" Persephone whispered.

Hades shook his head and knelt to wipe his sword clean with handfuls of moss. "Nothing at the moment. I was only wondering whether I could take the time to cut some meat from the hudorhaix. It is very good eating. But it would not do to carry the bleeding flesh with us, leaving a trail. Better to leave the body for the sauraima to feast upon." But he kept his eyes on his weapon as he spoke.

"Eat it?" Persephone looked at the pallid thing and shuddered.

When Hades glanced up, he was grinning. "Most likely you have eaten some already. I am not certain what was in the meatrolls, but it is as likely to be hudorhaix as wild goat. If you do not like it, you should be eager to teach the women of Plutos to grow grain. When we have fodder for them, we can have herds and will no longer need to hunt in the caves."

"Perhaps I might have been willing—though I cannot think I would be eager—if you had asked me. But to snatch me and force me . . . I would rather eat hudorhaix myself."

Hades shook his head, then with lifted brows asked, "Would your mother have let you come with me if I had begged her for you?"

The answer was obvious, and for some reason Persephone did not wish to suggest that her mother might have been more sympathetic if he had asked for Dorkas or another priestess. She turned her back and started up the slope toward the mouth of the tunnel without reply. Fortunately, she did not need to wonder whether Hades was following; she could hear him. Twice he came even with her and she increased her pace, hunching a shoulder to show he was unwelcome, but she was furious when he did not try again, even though she told herself she would have given him no different response.

Just as they arrived at what had been the crack through which she entered the tunnel, it occurred to her that Hades's restraint might be a mark of courtesy and good will rather than the irritated patience with which her mother ignored or denigrated her attempts to strike out for herself. Hades, after all, *had* praised her courage, and again had said he wished to make her his queen, but before she could really consider the idea, shock pushed it out of her mind.

The wonder of seeing the opening that she had escaped through with some difficulty now wide enough for her to pass easily without sidling was considerable, but that became insignificant when she noticed, sunk into the rock on either side but smooth and still glowing hot, the mark of a man's hands. No wonder Hades was gray with exhaustion when he came to kill the hudorhaix. He was a great mage, indeed, to widen that tunnel against the weight of rock holding it. It was a wonder such an expenditure of power had not crippled him or stopped his heart, and he had recovered so quickly

. .

Persephone blinked. Hades had the power to crush her as an ordinary man crushed a louse if she offended him, yet he had not scolded her for her foolish attempt to escape, he had come the moment she cried for help, and he had not offered one word of reproach over the dreadful expenditure of power it had cost. She stopped before entering the small cave where she had first wakened and turned to face him.

"I am ungracious not to thank you for coming so quickly to save me," she murmured.

"You are kind not to blame me for not warning you, but I did not know there was a blue-light cave so close."

She could not resist glancing up at him under her lashes and chuckling. "I cannot blame you for that. Warning me would not have done the slightest good. I would only have believed that you were trying to frighten me away from a path to the outer world, as I believed—"

She stopped abruptly and Hades cocked his head. "Believed?"

"The foolish tales you set about to deceive those who would seek to steal the riches of Plutos."

Persephone flushed slightly as she spoke. What she had almost said was that she believed he had lied about the food, that the food she had eaten was bespelled, because she had been so reluctant to leave him. That would have explained why she would have believed he was lying about the cave of blue light too, but she had no intention of confessing that she was not nearly as eager to return to her mother's care as she kept insisting.

"But you will believe me now, will you not?" Hades asked anxiously. "The tunnels themselves are dangerous. There are sinkholes and sudden drop-offs that end in lakes so clear the image of the ceiling looks like a solid floor. The caves are worse. In many black ones, pillars grow from the floor and the ceiling and some are armed with sharp crystals that can cut flesh to the bone if you blunder into them. In the light ones—I swear to you the hudorhaix is the least of the dangers. There are worse beasts and worst of all, the truly dead—those whose hearts are stone and whose minds are black sinks of foulness. Persephone, I beg you not to run away from me. There is no path from here to the outer world, I swear it."

"You could carve a path for me if you wished," she said perversely.

His dark eyes slid away from hers, but then his mouth hardened. "I could, yes. But I will not. My people need you, and though you do not wish to believe me, it is for your good also that I keep you."

Then suddenly he laid his hands on her shoulders

and kissed her forehead. His lips burned, but before she could jerk away or even remember that she still clutched a knife and turn it on him, he released her and stepped back. She stared, eyes wide. There had been no desire, not a flicker of passion, in that kiss, but Hades did not offer an explanation, only gestured for her to enter the small cave. When she did not respond, he did speak but in a quiet, indifferent voice, urging her again to go ahead and cautioning her to be careful of the rubble that lay on the floor.

Confusion made it simpler for Persephone to obey without protest, and she did need to watch where she put her feet because there was barely enough of the faint blue light from the great cavern behind them for her to see her way. As she stepped into the relative darkness, however, her forehead tingled, and the ceiling came to life. She looked back over her shoulder, but Hades had not yet entered the small room.

"What have you done to me?" she called out to him.

"You are too brave and too unwary," Hades replied, stepping into the cave. "You will have light now wherever you are."

Although she was actually grateful, recalling how frightened she had been when Hades fell asleep and the light died, his bland expression made Persephone very suspicious. "So that I will not be tempted by false gleams?" she asked.

"That, too." Hades smiled.

Persephone was annoyed; Hades's answer had confirmed some unspoken purpose in the spell he had set on her and apparently she had guessed only the least part. However, a second sharp question died in her throat as his head turned abruptly toward the tunnel. She, too, heard what had drawn his attention, a sound of thrashing and thin, high whistles. Hades's lips thinned and he went at once to pick up the fleece he had been lying on. He dropped it atop the one on which Persephone had lain, rolled them swiftly together, and tied them with cords that had been sewn to one end of their undersides. To these he looped two padded straps, through which he slid his arms and lifted the bundle to his back. The cloak Persephone had dropped on the floor he pulled across the top of the rolled fleeces and tucked firmly under the sides.

"Take the basket and come," he said softly but urgently.

"Where are you going?" Persephone asked in return.

"Come now and come quickly," he said. "We do not have time to talk and it is dangerous."

There was a bleakness colder than the stone that surrounded them in his voice. Her mother would blame her for following him farther from where he had snatched her up, Persephone thought, but something about his manner terrified her. Without another word she dropped the knife she had been carrying into the basket, caught it up, and hurried to where Hades stood.

"There." He pointed to a black opening over his head. "I will lift you up. Crawl in and go ahead. In three or four body lengths the passage will broaden enough for you to turn. Wait there for me."

Almost before the words were out of his mouth, he had gripped her around the waist and lifted her. Persephone thrust the basket into the passage, but she could not lift herself in. Hades set her down, moved his hands down to her hips and lifted again. She got enough of her upper body into the passage that time to squirm in, but he did not release her entirely. One hand slid lingeringly down her leg until his fingers could not reach her any more.

As she entered the passage, its utter blackness was relieved by a small glow here and there in the sides, floor, and ceiling. It was not really enough to see by, just barely enough light to give her an awareness of size and direction. Persephone found herself ridiculously disappointed. The spell Hades had set on her was a poor thing to fade so quickly. He was not, apparently, as strong a mage as she had believed.

She was a fool to be disappointed, she told herself fiercely. She should be glad. The stronger he was, the less chance she would have to escape him. Persephone picked up the basket, but found immediately that the passage was the most awkward size imaginable. It was just about high enough for her to sit up in but too low to walk in, even bent over, and as Hades had said, not wide enough to turn around. She would have to crawl, and it was very difficult to crawl in a long skirt with a basket in one hand. She gave the thing an ill-natured shove and followed it to clear the way as she heard Hades grunt with effort. A soft thud told her that he had arrived.

"You had better will more light in here if you wish to be able to see," she said over a few lower grunts as he levered himself fully into the passage. "I am afraid your spell has already faded."

"Not that," he said, between hard breaths. After a moment he went on, "I can't get any more light than you have unless I melt the rock behind the walls so it glows—and I'm not going to do that. The walls might collapse and, of course, narrow as this tunnel is, we would roast. Not enough crystal in here. Go ahead. Don't stop. We want to gain some distance before the hudorhaix is devoured."

"Is there no passage through which we could walk?" Persephone protested as she moved painfully ahead.

"You will be able to walk soon. I did not choose this way to annoy you. The passage I intended to take was walkable, but it is at floor level and would make it too easy to follow us."

The threat implicit in those words drove Persephone forward without any further complaint, but she was soon gasping with effort. A moment later she whimpered softly as the lights above her began to recede and she thought she was becoming faint. At the same moment Hades told her she could stand, and she realized that the light had grown fainter because the ceiling was farther away.

They moved faster then, Hades's hand on her shoulder propelling her ahead more quickly than was really safe in the dim light. The effort not to stumble took all Persephone's attention until Hades's hand closed on her so hard she cried out.

"Quiet!" he whispered. "Hold your breath."

She was so frightened, she did not consciously obey him, but instinctively she listened as intently as he did; one does not breathe when one is so intent upon listening. Then she heard his breath sigh out, and his hand fell away from her shoulder.

"I could not hear anything," she whispered.

"You do not yet know for what to listen," he said quietly, but no longer as if he was afraid that their voices, echoing back through the passage, would betray them. "I could barely make out the noise myself— it is like a soft rumbling, very soft, with a very thin high overnote. It means they are still feeding at the hudorhaix and that means the pack must be small. In a larger pack, the weaker would have been driven off and they would have smelled our trail and followed it. I would have heard them much more clearly, because they would have been in the cave just below the opening, leaping at it and squalling with rage."

Persephone shuddered. "Take me home," she breathed. "In Olympus people are not followed by ravening beasts."

"Nor would we be followed by them if you had not sought to escape me," he snarled, but then he said more gently, "It was my fault. I should have explained the dangers to you more clearly."

Since Persephone knew she would have acted in exactly the same way no matter what Hades had said, she acknowledged neither his accusation nor his apology. Instead she asked, "Are we safe now?"

"Only the home caves and the valleys upon which they open are safe—and they are as safe as Olympus with all those lecherous mages about and that merry, light-fingered devil Hermes ready to thieve any loose bauble for amusement. You were too protected, hidden in the temple, to know what Olympus truly is. But we can go more slowly now. I do not think there is any immediate danger. If the pack is small enough, the hudorhaix may sate their appetites and our scent may be obscured by the odor of the moss before they hunger again."

Persephone found Hades's last remark somewhat less than completely reassuring, and she shivered again. Hades must have noticed because she saw him move and then the cloak he had used to envelop her was placed over her shoulders.

"You are cold," he said. "I am sorry. I forget that you are not accustomed to the caves."

She said, "Thank you," before she remembered that

she should be angry over the reminder of her abduction and only after she spoke realized that she had been cold.

The wool was very soft and the cloak surprisingly light, considering that it fell to her ankles. At that, she was fortunate she was so tall or it would have trailed on the ground and been a hindrance. She found the warmth soothing. Insensibly her fear diminished and she became more aware of her surroundings.

First she noticed that the light changed, sometimes brighter, sometimes dimmer according to the changing patches of crystal. Then she saw that the passage was sometimes broader and sometimes narrower. Once, when it grew steadily narrower until Hades had to stop and remove the bundle from his back so he could sidle through, she feared it would close too tight for them to pass or that the passage might end altogether. Recalling that Hades could open the way or even carry her through the rock, if what he had told her about how he had brought her into the little cave was true, she was momentarily soothed.

That memory, however, woke another less comforting. Had not Hades said this wasn't the way he had intended to go? She looked back over her shoulder, but it was not light enough to make out an expression on his face. All she could see was a white blur with its dark markings of eyes and beard.

"Do you know where we are going?" she asked.

"No. Does it matter?"

"It matters to me," she replied indignantly. "This is your realm and you say you love it, but I do not. And I certainly do not desire to be lost in the dark."

"We are not lost. I cannot be lost. I thought you were asking whether there was a particular place I was trying to find. All I want right now is water, and I know there is water somewhere ahead. I can smell it."

"If you are thirsty, there is wine in the basket," Persephone reminded him.

"I am not thirsty. If we cross water or can wade through it for some way, they may lose the scent even if they do follow us."

Although Hades's voice was calm, almost casual, Persephone found herself frightened again. "Who . . . what . . . are they?"

"A pack of ponpikoi—they are like rats, only larger and they run in packs like wolves. If I had seen any sign of them, I would not have wasted time talking back in the cave."

"Why do you not close the passage behind us?" Persephone asked, shuddering with horror. "Surely that would stop them."

He laughed softly and said, "I am a mage, not a god. My strength has a limit, and I am near that limit now."

He paused as if waiting for her to say something, but Persephone had no idea what he expected from her. She looked questioningly at him and asked, "What can I do?"

He came closer, peering down as if her face was the most important thing in the world. After a moment, he shook his head and said, "Go forward. I can feel the passage widens ahead."

Now Persephone was not so sure she wanted the passage to widen. In the confined space she felt the creatures could not surround them and Hades might have been able to kill them one by one. On the other hand, the faster she went, the farther away they would be. She hurried forward, but in a few minutes the receding walls made the way so dark that she stumbled. Hades caught her before she could fall and put an arm around her shoulders.

"I am more accustomed to the dark. Let me steady you," he murmured. Pride bade her twist away, but the warmth and security of his embrace was too desirable. "I am afraid," she whispered.

"You need not fear. I will not let harm come to you. To comfort you, I would go back and close the way, no matter the cost, but there are other reasons not to seal that passage. If a hunting party should be attacked by the ponpikoi, it might be their only escape. There is danger enough for my hunters without closing their lines of retreat."

"But if there were grain to feed herds you would not need to send hunters into danger," Persephone said, her voice light. With his arm around her, she was not afraid and could not resist teasing.

He chuckled. "You are accusing me of having a mind that runs along a passage without side entries. Sometimes I fear you are right, but I swear this time I am innocent."

Persephone laughed, too. "I must confess I am surprised that you credit me with sense enough to understand anything, after the way I ran off."

His arm tightened around her. "That was ignorance, not lack of ability to understand—and it showed a high courage, which I admit I did not guess you had. Zeus said you bowed always to your mother's will without protest—"

"That is out of love, not fear," Persephone snapped.

"I believe you," Hades said. "But I could not know that before I met you. And Zeus could not tell me much about you, beyond your great beauty and that you were able to perform the full rites of the Corn

Goddess, because he does not know you either. I do not wish to hurt you by speaking ill of one you love, indeed, I do not think ill of your mother, because I am certain what she did was done out of love. But too much love is not healthy."

She stiffened under his arm. "How can there be too much love?"

"Perhaps I said that wrong." His grip relaxed just a trifle, as if to show she was free to break loose if she wished. "I mean a love that cages and cripples its object, forbids it to be fully everything it can be—"

He stopped abruptly, pulling Persephone back against him and gripping her so hard that she was lifted to her toes for a moment and the basket dropped to the floor, fortunately landing on its flat bottom so that nothing spilled. A sharp gesture of Hades's free hand instantly killed the little glittering points that had provided light. From the blackness that now surrounded them, Persephone could see in the distance a faint shimmer that might be golden light.

"The sun," she breathed, but she did not struggle to free herself to run toward the light, and in the next instant terror turned her cold because Hades, who had faced the hudorhaix with near contempt and the ponpikoi with no more than caution and distaste, shuddered.

"No. It is not the sun," Hades whispered, and looked over his shoulder as if he were considering going back, as if facing the giant rats that ran in a pack like wolves might be a lesser evil than what lay ahead.

Chapter 4

When Dorkas and her maidens reached the pool of the Mother, Kore was still not in sight. Dorkas allowed herself to smile, as if at the antics of the little girls who now began to pick flowers, chase one another, and search the banks of the pool for newts and tadpoles, but she was riding a crest of hope that the flowers Kore had called out she wished to pick were of Hades's devising. Dorkas remembered no flowers of special beauty or profusion along the road.

If Hades did take Kore, Dorkas intended to be the next high priestess, and it was not likely that she would have to wait for Demeter's death before she held the wand. She was Zeus's favorite; it was she who had told him when Kore was allowed to leave the temple. She knew that Zeus's purpose in relinquishing Kore to his brother was to obtain a priestess who would be more malleable than Demeter and willing to support him. Her smile broadened a trifle. When she had the wand, Zeus would indeed find her malleable and supportive—but for a price.

She became aware of the young priestesses in golden gowns placing their baskets in a semicircle around the pool. The rock above it was already bathed in rosy light. When the sun touched the water, the garments must be washed. She did not dare trifle with that rite. Turning from the pool, she frowned and walked back along the road a little way, as if she were looking for Kore, then came back to the waiting priestesses.

"I cannot think what is keeping the girl," she said. "How long can it take to pick a few flowers? Aglaia, see that the little ones are gathered and ready to sing. I will go back and fetch Kore."

She ran as long as she believed the young women could see her and then slowed to a crawl. She was torn between her desire to be sure that Kore had been taken and her fear of Hades. She had only one glimpse of him, as she was leaving Zeus and he was arriving to learn what she had told his brother, but he looked as black and cold as the caves in which he lived. Hades, she thought, stopping altogether, was not like Zeus, who could be beguiled with a few sweet words. To her it seemed all too possible that if he saw her spying on him, he would open the earth and bid it swallow her.

Despite her fear she started forward again. The temptation to be certain that Kore was gone was too great to resist. At the edge of the outcropping of rock, she stopped again. She could not see Kore on the rising slope, and there was no sound beyond the soft sigh of the morning breeze. Slowly she rounded the strewn boulders, peering cautiously ahead. Her heart leapt when she saw the crushed sprigs at the edge of the road. Kore had climbed up toward the largest of the rocks. Her eyes scanned the ground eagerly, picking up a few more signs of the girl's passage, but the trail did not go farther up the hillside.

Dorkas sighed with relief. Hades must have been

waiting, hidden by the rock. He had snatched Kore and carried her away. Curious now that her fears of meeting the King of the Dead were allayed, Dorkas followed Kore's footsteps and examined the area. It did not take long for the jeweled flower, still lying in the hollow of the rock, to catch her eye. She caught it up with an intake of breath.

Perhaps, she thought, what she had done was for the best, as Zeus had said repeatedly. Perhaps there even was a Great Mother and She approved Kore's delivery into Hades's cold hands and his possession of her. She fingered the tiny gem. If she had not seen it, one of those who would be sent to search for Kore would surely have found it, and the fact that Hades was her abductor would soon become known to all. That would be a disaster for her own plans to become high priestess; Demeter would surely insist that Zeus demand her daughter's return, and Zeus would be forced to do so because he could not admit that he had suggested the abduction.

Dorkas tucked the exquisite bauble into her sash and frowned thoughtfully while she bound the thongs that held her purse around it so it could not slip or drop out. It would be better, she decided as she secured the jewel, if no one suspected an abduction at all, and that was possible enough because Kore was known for disappearing for hours in the temple's extensive grounds. A quick glance at the sun told Dorkas that she still had some time. No one would question her if she came back breathless at the last moment. All would believe she had been searching for Kore. And no one would see what she was actually doing because the road and the whole area around the pool were forbidden to all except the priestesses during the sacred laving.

With a broad smile, Dorkas returned to the road in a meandering path, actually picking a flower here and there. She crossed the road and wandered about on the other side until she came to the bank of the small stream which had its beginning in the pool farther along the road. She picked a few more flowers, then dropped the whole handful into the water to be carried away. Finally she retraced her steps, taking care not to bruise any more plants in returning than she had marked on her way. That took a little longer than she expected, and she ran all the way back to the pool, arriving pale and out of breath just as the sun touched the edge of the pool.

"I could not find her," she gasped. "She picked flowers all over the meadow and I think the lazy girl was hiding from me. Just the other day she was complaining about always being the one to have to wash Our Lady's clothing, as if it were not the greatest honor."

"But it is time *now!*" Aglaia cried.

"Lay out the garments," Dorkas said. "I will do the washing. I am sure the Lady of the Corn will accept my good intentions and not punish us all for Kore's carelessness if I do not perform the ritual perfectly."

She looked over her shoulder at the novices and saw that they were in their proper half circle, the littlest centered with taller girls on each side, the tallest at both ends so they formed a horned crescent. Dorkas lifted a hand and looked back into the pool, which was now flushed with diffuse light. A moment later, the bright edge of the sun showed in the water. Dorkas gestured sharply and the girls' voices rose in a paean of praise. She hurried to the first garment and began the ritual washing. Aglaia took the wet garment from her hand, laid it on the grass, and all the other priestesses knelt to fold it into the elaborate pleats in which it must dry in the sun.

Although she knew the ritual as well as or perhaps even better than Kore, Dorkas deliberately faltered twice. She had decided it would not do to allow anyone to guess that she had been studying it in private. She realized that she need not have been concerned about that when one of the attending priestesses hissed at her for handing one of the washed garments to Aglaia with the wrong hand. Her mind had wandered from the ceremony she knew too well to Demeter's reaction when they returned without her daughter.

When her part in the ceremony was over, Dorkas grew more and more nervous and several of the other priestesses clearly shared her discomfort. Instead of playing with the novices or laying out the food that had been covered by the Goddess's garments in the baskets, they kept running to the edge of the road to look for Kore. Finally Dorkas stood up.

"I am very worried about that foolish girl," she said. "Since my part of the ceremony is over, I am going to walk back along the road and look for her again. If I cannot find her, I will return to the temple and tell Demeter what she has done. You must keep a close watch on the little ones, Aglaia, and see that the others fold the garments correctly."

Until she was well out of earshot of the others, Dorkas called out to Kore as she went, bidding her return at once, telling her they were all worried and she should not play such cruel tricks. By then she was suffering such pangs of anxiety about what Demeter would do to her, that she was really sorry when Kore did not answer. Her distress was easy enough to read by her pale face and her shaking hands when she arrived at the temple and sought the high priestess.

"I am so sorry," she cried, after breathlessly relating what had happened. "It never occurred to me that your daughter would actually miss the ceremony. I thought she was teasing us. I looked for her, but there are so many places to hide if she wished to hide. I almost came too late myself, and none of the others knew the rite."

Demeter stared at Dorkas, her blue eyes cold as deep ice. "You should have watched her better," she said. "You know how restless she has been."

Dorkas bent her head beneath the rebuke and bit her lip, but that was more to hide a smile of relief than because of the blame. Demeter was angry but not worried, and it was only fear that would make her vicious. She had no suspicion that the mischief was not of Kore's own making.

"But what should we do?" Dorkas asked. "Should I go into the city and ask for men to make a real search?" She widened her eyes. "But then Zeus will hear that she has run away, and he might say—" She clamped her mouth shut.

"Kore has not run away," Demeter snapped. "She is very childish sometimes, and takes a delight in making me worry. No doubt she was watching you rush about frantically looking for her and thinks I will do the same. I will teach her a good lesson this time and ignore her. She can come to no harm in the valley. When she is hungry enough or it starts to get dark, she will come home." She paused, staring hard at Dorkas and taking deep breaths. Then she slapped her hand on the carven arm of her chair. "As for you, you have been derelict in your duty and have doubtless offended Our Lady with your clumsiness in performing her ritual. You may spend the next two days fasting and kneeling to her, begging her pardon."

"I am sorry, so sorry," Dorkas murmured, but she thought the punishment a small price to pay for the success of her ploy. Even if Demeter did begin to worry about her daughter, she would wait a long time before she admitted to Zeus, who had often complained that Kore was too much confined, that the girl had fled her control.

"You will have company in the shrine when Kore returns," Demeter said. "Go!"

When the offending priestess was gone, Demeter slumped in her seat and let the tears she had fought against rise to her eyes. Ungrateful child, she thought, she does not care a bit that I have spent half my life smoothing her path and guarding her against pain. She wants "freedom"; she wants "love." How often have I told her that love only opens a door to misery. Men! If they do not leave you, they die. Did I not hang on Iasion's neck and beg him to stay safe beside me? No, he would defend his city! Idiot! Cruel idiot not to care that I would be left to grieve.

She rose and paced restlessly. If only she could be certain that Kore was being spiteful and had hidden herself to avoid the rites and to wander freely outside of the temple. It might be so, Demeter assured herself. The child had complained about performing the rites over and over and about being held a "prisoner." Demeter sighed. She had explained again and again that there would be much less chance of anyone challenging Kore's accession as high priestess if she were the only acolyte who had performed the rites. Not that the explanations had done much good. All the silly girl had said was that she did not want her mother to die. Naturally not, but one must look ahead, even many, many years ahead.

As far as being held prisoner . . . Demeter stood still and bit her lip, staring sightlessly ahead. It did not matter what Kore felt or wanted. After this escapade she really would be a prisoner. Never again would she leave the temple grounds. Demeter sighed. She had tried to temper necessity with mercy, but Kore was unreasonable in her demands and it was impossible to yield to those. She did not dare allow the child to mingle freely with the people of Olympus. Aside from her beauty, which drew far too many eyes and would make half the men in the city into seducers who would only break Kore's heart, there were far too many mages. Sooner or later one of them would discover that Kore had that most precious of all Gifts, the ability to enhance the power of others. They would tear each other—and her—apart to own her.

No, Demeter thought, moving blindly forward in the direction in which she had been staring, she would *not* throw away the treasure the Goddess had given her to guard. She needed Kore's strength herself. Why should she share it with others? She had given the child life with her own agony, and despite Kore's whimpers, Demeter knew that what she had planned for her daughter was the best life a woman could have.

When she stopped, sensing something in her way, Demeter found herself beside a window. Although she knew she was being foolish, she murmured, "Open," to release the spell that kept out everything but light, and leaned out, hoping despite knowing better that she would see a graceful form in spring-green silk running across the temple grounds to beg pardon. Twice she tensed and stared as green-clad forms caught her eye, but not for long. She could not deceive herself for more than a moment about the spindly, barely pubescent girls dressed in green. Even at this distance she knew they could not be her tall, richly curved daughter.

Lips tight, Demeter snorted and turned away. A mature body did not tell the whole tale. Some children developed physically long before they were ready to take up the burden of being adults. Kore *was* only a child, but her lush body was the source of a fear Demeter could not push out of her mind any longer. She had seen the young men ogling her daughter during the celebration that welcomed the coming of spring; worse, this spring she had seen Kore look back. She is only curious, Demeter assured herself. The child could not yet know desire; nonetheless, curiosity could lead to trouble.

Demeter turned her back on the window and resumed her restless pacing. For years she had warned away every man she had seen who showed any interest, made it plain that Kore was consecrated to the Goddess and that severe punishment would befall any man who touched her. But a man driven by lust seemed blind and deaf to warnings and to fear, and she had not been able to watch Kore every moment. If the ungrateful girl had yielded to some fool's pleas and managed to make a tryst . . . Biting her lip with vexation, Demeter shook her head. It did not matter. Restless and rebellious Kore might be, but her daughter did love her. She would return.

But the slow hours passed and there was no sign of

Kore. Demeter thought again of the option she had so swiftly dismissed—demanding that Zeus order a search of the valley so her daughter's seducer could be caught and punished—but she quickly rejected the idea. Perhaps the search parties would find Kore and her lover, but Zeus would be far more likely to insist on marriage than on punishment. That would be a disaster. Racked by fear and helplessness, Demeter wept and cursed the spirit in Kore that she did not dare try to break.

As high noon passed, however, she began to feel more hopeful that Kore was simply idling away the day in freedom, wandering alone. Surely if she had met a man, she would have hurried home after their love-making. With any luck, she would have been disgusted by the actual happening compared with her dream and eager to conceal what she had done under the small mischief of evading her part in the laving of the garments. Even if she was thrilled with her lover, she should have been willing to confess in the expectation that her mother would then agree either to her marriage or to bringing her lover into the temple as other priestesses did. So compelling was Demeter's hope that for the first part of the afternoon she was able to turn her attention to the order in which the ploughed fields were to be blessed with seed.

Later still, as the sun sank in the western sky, it occurred to Demeter that her daughter might not have run away willingly. Her initial reaction to the idea was denial. No man in Olympus, not even one of the great mages, not even Zeus himself, would dare take by force the daughter of the high priestess of the Corn Goddess. Zeus would certainly have done so years ago if he dared. For all his handsome face and merry laugh, he was the cruelest and most lecherous of all of his kind, she thought—and caught her breath.

The connection in Demeter's mind between Zeus's lechery and the term "years ago" had suddenly become significant. Years ago lust had not been involved in their contest over Kore. When Zeus had adopted Kore and had the audacity to ask that she come to him freely as a girl might to her father, the child would not have appealed to his lechery. She was gangly and awkward then, her body all hard angles and her nose too big for her face.

Demeter had not suspected Zeus of designs on Kore's body but of wishing to control her heart and will. Once he had cozened Kore into affection, Demeter suspected he would have arranged for an "accident" to take her mother's life. Probably he would have fastened his ultimate chains to Kore's soul by comforting her for that loss. Then the temple of the Corn Goddess would have been as much his to command as the city of Olympus.

Recalling that she had won that contest of wills, Demeter, who had stiffened in her chair, relaxed a little. Zeus had not mentioned Kore in years. Then she pushed away the scribing tablet she had been working on and rested her chin on her clasped hands. She had been a fool to forget how Kore had changed. Zeus might well have been inflamed by seeing her during the rites of spring. Demeter cursed herself for allowing the child to play so prominent a role and promised herself that when she had her back Kore would never again leave the temple grounds. It was for her own good, she thought bitterly. Zeus, like other men, would only notice the ripe body; no man would care that Kore was really still a child. And lust was the one thing that could blind Zeus to consequences.

Rising slowly to her feet, Demeter smiled. No other mage in Olympus would dare take Kore by force because Zeus would be forced to help find his "daughter" and add his power to her mother's to recover her. Ergo, if Kore had been abducted, it could only be by Zeus himself. No doubt lust had added a spur to the arrogance that had been growing in him since he had overthrown his father and become Mage-King of Olympus. Probably he had thought she would not dare confront him now because she had feared to object to his adoption of Kore. Demeter drew a deep breath. How wrong he was! How very wrong!

She had started across the room when the door opened and a little novice stuck her head around. "They are serving the evening meal, Mother," she whispered. "Will you come or should I bring something to you here?"

"Evening meal!" Demeter echoed. Her eyes widened as a Goddess-inspired answer was granted to a problem that had not yet occurred to her. It was now clear how to prevent Zeus from suppressing her complaint. "No, I do not wish to eat," she said to the novice, her voice soft with awe, "but I will come down."

In the refectory, she stood before her seat at the head of the priestess's table. The chair at the foot of the table, where Kore sat, and Dorcas's place on the bench at her right, were vacant. Tears sprang to her eyes at the sight of Kore's empty chair, but she forced them back and struck the brass wheat sheaf that lay beside her plate against the bowl that symbolized the earth.

When the compelling bell tone had shimmered into silence, Demeter said, "Kore has been stolen from us. When Dorkas told me she had run away to play like a spiteful child, I was fool enough to believe her. If harm has come to Kore, I will be justly punished, for I should know my daughter better. She might complain or tease me, but she is devoted to the Goddess and would not willingly offend her by failing to perform her rite."

A murmur of distress, particularly from the younger girls who were not jealous of Kore, rose and fell.

"Dorkas is praying to Our Lady to be forgiven her sin," Demeter went on, "and I am going to Zeus's palace to demand the return of my daughter. Even the Mage-King must know that the servants of the Lady must not be offended. No seed will be blessed nor sown until Kore is returned to us. Aglaia, come with me."

The room was so silent that the brush of Demeter's skirt against the leg of her chair was clearly audible. Shock held the forty-seven girls and women frozen, their breath suspended. Never in the history of the temple had the blessing and sowing been withheld. Even the year when Zeus had overthrown the Mage-King Kronos, when the ploughing had all too often turned up half-rotted corpses and the ploughers and the sowers alike had been racked with grief and fear, the seed had been blessed and planted.

"Aglaia!"

The voice was like a thrown javelin. Aglaia leapt to her feet, banging her belly against the table. Breaths were drawn, but no one spoke and only the heads of the very little novices turned to stare wide-eyed at the high priestess. Indifferent to the silent disapproval,

Demeter hurried from the refectory and from the building, Aglaia panting in her wake. The priestesses might be horrified; but they were powerless to rebel.

Only the high priestess and her three acolytes knew the spells for blessing and sowing, and Dorkas and Aglaia had never actually cast the spells. Demeter had always enlivened the seed and the earth herself, supported only by Kore, or let Kore perform the rite, because in that rite lay the real power of her Goddess. Zeus had forgotten that. He might rule Olympus, but the lightning he cast killed only one at a time. If her power did not bring the corn in manyfold richness from the earth, thousands would die unless the secrecy that protected Olympus from the native tribes were breached and her wealth expended to buy food. No, Zeus would not dare hurt her or deny her demand for her daughter before the many dinner guests in the great hall.

Eager for the confrontation because Zeus was so well known for his womanizing that no one would believe his denials, Demeter passed the wide-open doors that offered welcome and hospitality to all who wished to enter the public rooms of the palace of Olympus. A huge corridor ran crosswise to the entrance, its painted and gilded roof supported on silk-smooth walls of white marble veined with gold. Three great arches opened into the corridor, of which only the one on the far right showed light. A murmur of many voices came from the chamber beyond the lighted arch but no loud shouts or clashing of serving dishes. The perfect moment. Demeter ran the last small distance, leaving Aglaia utterly breathless, clinging to the pillar that defined the arch.

"Zeus, where is my daughter?" Demeter shrieked.

"You have laid your hand on one sacred to the Goddess—"

"Not I," Zeus replied, pushing back his carved and gilded chair and standing up.

He had not needed to raise his voice in the sudden silence that had fallen after Demeter's accusation. Hera, still in her chair beside his, raised furious eyes and then frowned slightly, rage dissipated into puzzlement by what her seer's eye saw behind the innocent and righteous expression on Zeus's face, which she knew all too well. The great mages seated at two long tables just below the dais had all turned to stare at him also.

"Liar!" Demeter cried.

"She is my daughter also," Zeus continued, shaking his head, "and I would not foul myself with such pollution. If Kore is not in the temple, I will swear by your Goddess, avatar of the Great Mother, that I do not know where she is." He shook his head again. "I am not perfect in chastity—" A roar of laughter greeted that miracle of understatement and Zeus smiled briefly, but the laughter died abruptly as his face grew grave and he gestured for silence "—and Kore is a ripe and beautiful woman, but I would not soil my own daughter."

Demeter swayed with shock and Aglaia crept forward to support her. Demeter had expected Zeus to claim innocence, to protest on his honor that he had not seized *her* daughter—which might even be true if he had set Hermes, who could flit from place to place, to snatch her. But she had not expected Zeus to call Kore *his* daughter and to speak of pollution—that rang true in her ears and she feared in all others—nor did she believe Zeus would swear an oath on the

Mother with such sincerity. Yet he *was* lying. She knew he was!

"You thought her safe in my keeping!" Zeus exclaimed, and swallowed hard as if to suppress more words.

The eyes that had been staring at him shifted to Demeter, and Zeus had all he could do to suppress his satisfaction. They all believed him now—and why should they not? Every word he had spoken was the truth. He had no idea where Hades had taken Kore, and, attractive as Kore was, she had become taboo to him once he had adopted her. But mostly they believed him because everyone knew how much Demeter hated him; they also suspected that she brought her accusation to the dining hall of Olympus—although the girl might have been missing for hours—to make the greatest trouble for him.

"But I do not have her, Demeter," he added, frowning as if he were worried. "Foolish woman, how long has the child been missing? She might be lying out on a hillside with a broken leg."

"No," Demeter whispered. "I would know that."

"Does Kore have the Gift of speaking mind to mind?" Zeus asked, subduing a sharp qualm.

"No," Demeter said hastily. "She has no Gift beyond the link with Our Lady that lets her quicken the seed. But I am her mother. I would know—"

Hera snorted. "Did I know when Hephastus fell into that ravine and broke his hip so badly the healers could not mend it? He was there two days. Mothers may think they are so closely bonded to their children that they feel their hurts, but it is wiser not to trust too much to that."

"Ares," Zeus said, "call out the young men so we

can send out search parties." As Ares rose and hurried out, Zeus looked down at his wife. "Hera, will you scry for us? I know one bit of hillside looks much like another, but perhaps something will be recognizable and Ares would *know* she was out there, so the men will search more carefully."

"She has been taken!" Demeter insisted. "I *know* she is concealed somewhere, held by force."

"I will scry for her in the city as well as on the hills," Hera said. Then she rose and stared at Zeus. "But there are spells that can blind any scrying, even mine."

"Then let Demeter conduct a search herself or direct the search of others as she pleases," Zeus said promptly. And then to Demeter, "I will give you a sigil that will carry my authority to enter into any place for the purpose of searching for Kore. And that authority will include the private rooms of this palace and the public and private rooms of any home or workshop in Olympus. It will entitle you to command a force of men, or search with your priestesses. Can I do any more?"

"Hermes hid her for you outside of Olympus!" Demeter cried.

"Hermes," Zeus commanded.

The tall, slender mage rose. For once his hazel eyes were not sparkling with laughter and his mouth was solemn. "I swear I have not seen, spoken to, transported, or hidden your daughter anywhere, Demeter. Nor do I know where she is now, nor have I known her whereabouts at any time today."

Demeter scarcely glanced at Hermes. He was known for his love of mischief, for slyness, and for his clever lies. If he had been involved, she would not catch him nor catch Zeus through him. She had only wanted to remind those whom Zeus had convinced of his innocence that he had more ways to work his will than direct abduction. And then she remembered another problem.

"You will move her from place to place as I search," she sobbed.

"I do not *have* her, Demeter," Zeus repeated, his voice soft, his eyes steady on hers. "Nor do I know where she is."

"So you say and so you swear." Demeter's voice grated like chalk on slate. "And perhaps the words are even true, but the spirit behind the words is false. I will neither bless seed nor sow it—"

"Demeter!" Zeus's eyes blazed and blue light hissed and sizzled between the fingers of his raised hand. He did not roll that light into a ball, however, nor even point a finger to send a little stinging arrow. Instead his voice rang like a brazen gong. "You may not starve a whole people because you blame me for the death of your lover more than ten years ago. *I did not take and do not have your daughter.* Your temple is sacred *because* you bless and sow. If you do not, the temple is sacred no longer and I will not lift a hand to protect it—or you—from the just rage and revenge of people whose own children are starving."

"Zeus." Hera, who had risen to her feet when she agreed to scry for Kore but had not moved away, laid a hand on his arm. "She does not mean it. She is mad with grief. She loves her one child too much."

Zeus sighed. "You are right. But the spells that quicken the seed are in the Goddess's giving and Demeter has no right to withhold Her bounty because of a private grief or rage. If she will not do the Goddess's will, the Lady will empower another."

As he spoke, a terrible weakness washed through Demeter from her head down to her feet as if some warm strength that had upheld her was draining away. She clung to Aglaia to keep herself upright, and in another moment the strength had returned. Had the Goddess warned her, or was she just frightened by Zeus's threat?

"We will see," she gasped. "But in the end I will have Kore back."

"It may be so, Demeter, but I will tell you plainly that if Kore is not lying hurt somewhere, then I think she went because she wished to go—to find a little freedom. Hera spoke what all know. You love her too much and hold her too close. Even a daughter must breathe. However, since I have no proof that she is where she is by her own will, I say here and now to all assembled—and order that my word be carried to all those not present—that if Kore is anywhere in the valley of Olympus she is to be brought to a public meeting where she may answer for herself whether she wishes to return to her mother's keeping."

"I will have her," Demeter repeated. "I will never give up."

Chapter 5

"If that golden light is not the sun, what is it?" Persephone asked softly, all her suspicion reawakened.

It had occurred to her, as her mind sought a refuge from a horror that could cause Hades to shudder, that he would certainly wish to keep her away from any exit from the caves, and that sunlight might be abhorrent to him. That would account for the shudder and the way he looked back, as if facing the danger of the ponpikoi might be preferable to giving her access to the surface world. Yet somehow those thoughts did not comfort her.

Although he had released her, they were standing close enough that she could feel him shake his head. "I do not know what it is." Hades's voice was quiet, but not as if he feared detection from whatever lay ahead. "We call it chrusous thanatos, the golden death. It grows on the soft black rock that we cut for burning. It is slimy and stinking and if it touches you, it eats you, slowly, inch by inch. If you can come to a healer in time, it can be cut out, but the roots grow deep and fast. Sometimes it will grow inside the body without any outward sign until the pain begins. One healer cut to find the cause. She could not even recognize what was within. It was all golden slime. The healer also died."

Persephone swallowed hard. What he had described seemed an untraversable horror. So untraversable as to be a made-up reason to avoid an exit from the caves? "Must we go back then?" she asked.

"We cannot," he said, and she felt the movement of his body as his head turned to look back again. "I am almost certain that the ponpikoi are in the little cave. I do not think they have yet entered the passage we took, but there is no way we could travel downward and take a different passage safely. And there have been no side passages to this tunnel. We will have to go through. I would have to sooner or later, for the place must be cleansed."

Persephone's heart had sunk like a stone. What he said made impossible her hope that he was lying to keep her from finding her own world again. But the final words wakened hope once more.

"You can cleanse it before we pass?" Persephone sighed with relief and then found she had hoped too soon.

"I could have if the ponpikoi were not behind us and we had food and drink enough. It will take many days for the natural waters to cool the rock which I must set afire." Suddenly his arm went around her and he pulled her close. "I have frightened you. I am sorry. You will not be in any danger. I will clean a passage for us and find you a safe place to stay while I return and burn it all."

"But you are afraid," Persephone whispered, burying her face in Hades broad chest.

His other arm joined the first around her and she felt

a pressure that must be his lips against her hair. She brought up her hands, but she did not use them to push him away as she knew she should.

"Only a fool does not fear that kind of danger," he said against her hair. "But I hate it more than I fear it because it has killed so many for whom I cared."

One part of Persephone was terribly afraid, but another part was tempted to raise her head and see if his lips would find hers. Shocked at her impulse to invite a caress when his abduction had not only violated her rights but placed her in terrible danger, she did push away. Hades lifted his head and let her go. Persephone was so annoyed she snapped at him.

"Because they had to pass through and did not have your power?"

"I do not think so," he answered calmly. "All carry fire and can burn a path clean. But the torches are both salvation and the greatest danger. We are fortunate that there is so little crystal in this rock and I was able to see a hint of the yellow light ahead. Had there been more light in the tunnel, we could have walked right into a patch before I smelled the stinking stuff. What often happens is that the torchlight and odor of burning mask the first signs of growth, and a hunter brushes it unknowing or steps upon it. It will eat, not only flesh, but also leather, anything that lives or once lived."

"Then we will have to walk in the dark," Persephone said.

"If you will again give me leave to steady you, you will not fall."

Persephone could hear in Hades's voice that he was smiling, and she began to wonder again whether he was telling her tales of horror to bend her more easily to his will. Even if he were not, why could he not use his power to avoid the danger?

"You told me you brought me down through the rock," she said. "If the danger is so great, why do you not bring us back up through the rock?"

"One does not rise through rock as through water," he replied, laughing. "And how do you suggest we reach the roof? Can you float through the air and carry me with you?"

"I have no Gift aside from the Goddess-lent ability to quicken seed," Persephone snapped. "But I am not a fool either. Is it not possible to begin at the wall and climb?"

"You are not a fool," Hades agreed, approval and admiration in his voice. "It is possible, but unfortunately there is nowhere to go. There are no caves or passages near enough to either side or above or below us. It would take a week or more to find the surface, and I cannot sustain us for so long, even with—" He stopped abruptly and then continued, "Besides, there would be the chance of passing through a seam of black rock that carried the chrusous thanatos. In any area where it appears, one is safest in the open, where one can see it and avoid it."

Hades's acknowledgement of her objection and his earnestness in giving a reasonable explanation bolstered Persephone's self-confidence. That he could laugh at all eased the sick fear inside her.

"Then let us go," she said, "before I sink down weeping and am a useless danger."

"Queen of my heart, light of my eyes, that is not in you," Hades murmured, finding her hand and raising it to his lips. Then he chuckled. "It might be that when the danger is past you will weep, but not before we are safe.''

She knew she should pull her hand away and reprove him for speaking words of love to her if she wished to continue to insist he return her to Olympus, but strangely, with each dreadful danger, she became less sure she wished to go back to her protected existence and her mother's coddling. Allowing him to retain her hand, she drew a deep breath and bent her knees to pick up the basket she had dropped when he first pulled her against him. That she had remembered their food in the face of danger made her feel strong and competent, and when she straightened she merely repeated, "Let us go."

Hades brought the hand he had kissed to his belt. "Take hold and come behind me," he said. "We must stay in the center of the passage in as narrow a space as possible. Wrap the cloak close and keep the basket between us if the passage narrows so that neither brushes a wall."

He set out at a slow pace, which he increased when she did not falter. Soon Persephone wrinkled her nose as the cool smell of earth and rock was tainted by a putrid-sweet mustiness. Another few moments and Hades stopped. Peering around his broad shoulder, she saw a bright thread of sickly yellow-green creeping along the right-hand wall. Hades reached back and patted her hand comfortingly, bringing his other hand up to point at the thin end of the yellow-green glow, which thickened into a rope farther back.

The bright thread hissed, then darkened, and the stench of burning flesh mixed with the smell of rotten sweetness making Persephone gag. Hades's finger moved and the hissing increased as a thicker portion of the putrid growth blackened. Slowly Hades moved forward, following the still broadening band of yellow-green, heating the rock as he went and killing the growth. Now the band was so broad that it lit the passage dimly. Persephone could see the stuff had an oily sheen, which gave an irridescent quality to its phosphorescent glow. It should have been beautiful, but somehow it looked slimy and somewhere in the distance she heard the slow drip of liquid. Persephone's stomach churned.

The passage curved a little, blocking their view for a few steps, and when they rounded that curve Hades stopped abruptly, drawing breath. They were in a small cavern, which was lit from one side—brightly to Persephone's dark-adjusted eyes—by broad seams and thick branching trees of the growth that crawled up the right-hand wall and swathed the roof almost to where they stood, hanging down in glistening strands. Directly below the thickest growth was a little pool of water edged by what appeared to be large rocks fallen from the roof.

Persephone instinctively looked upward, and was distracted for a moment from her sick fear of the growth by a new fear, a forest of threatening spears of naked rock that hung from the roof, protruding through the chrusous thanatos. A single drop fell from one rock point, larger and thicker than the others. The finger of rock itself was clean of the growth, as was the cone that rose from the floor where the drop landed, but around the base of the cone the yellow-green slime grew in thick folds, brighter above and darker below as if it fed on itself.

Suddenly Persephone became aware that Hades was standing with closed eyes slowly turning his lifted head from left to right and then back again. Following him she looked all around and then, more anxiously, around again. When the second survey did not show what she sought, she drew in a breath that trembled with horror and began to shiver. She could see no other opening, no way out.

When he heard her gasp, Hades reached back to grasp her wrist. "Do not fear, I have found a path, and it is safe, I think, but we will have to climb." He pointed. "There."

About a third of the way around the cavern to the left, up near the roof, were several jagged openings. She could barely make them out because it was dark there—and then she sighed with relief. It was dark there because the rock was clean. On that side of the cave there was no growth she could detect as, she now realized, there had been no growth on the left side of the passage.

Only one thick finger of the yellow-green stuff intruded between them and the sheltering blackness near the left wall. It grew out of the dense folds around the base of one of the cones that rose from the floor. Hades moved toward it, turning slightly to point at the far end of the growth so that Persephone could see his profile. She noticed the muscles in his jaw beneath his short, curly beard move with effort and did not need to wonder why. Not only did the chrusous thanatos blacken immediately but a sullen red glow showed beneath it. A moment later, flames began to lick up through the ash and crawl backward toward the living stuff. When they reached the unburned growth, there was a whoosh as fire ran over the surface toward the little pool.

"Come quickly," Hades said, taking Persephone's

hand. "I do not think the whole cave will begin to burn, but the nearer we are to a refuge—"

Suddenly a gout of water flew from the pool to douse the approaching flames. It was not magic. Someone had scooped up and flung the water. A flicker of movement showed behind the largest boulder and before the hissing died, a voice shrilled from among the rocks near the pool. "Burn me, will you? I know you, Hades! As you were 'merciful' to me, I will be merciful to you. Leave the woman and I will let you go. If you do not leave her and go, I will throw rocks at you, rocks covered with chrusous thanatos."

Hades swept Persephone behind him so that she was sheltered by his body, but his eyes remained fixed on the rocks. He did not draw his sword. If the infected man came close enough to strike, likely they would be lost anyway and the sword would certainly have to be abandoned.

"I did not intend to burn you nor did I sentence you to die the golden death, whoever you are," Hades said slowly, his voice steady and without anger. "If you know me, you know what I can do. Do not be a fool."

"You exiled me for nothing!" the outlaw shrieked. "For using a woman! What have I to fear from anything you can do? It is your turn to fear me, so now I will use *your* woman."

Howling laughter burst between the words. Persephone had clutched at Hades in her terror, which had been intensified when she felt the stiffening of his body each time the outlaw laughed. Still clinging to him, she backed away from the threat. To her relief he moved back with her. One step, another.

A glowing yellow pebble flew at them, blackening before it fell to the floor.

"I can throw faster than you can burn!" the mad voice yelped, howling between the words again.

A form rose from the rocks and Persephone sobbed with horror. It was all patched with the yellow-green slime, which had grown completely over one eye.

"Man!" Hades bellowed, "Turn your back and I will go my way and let you live what is left of your life."

More pebbles covered with chrusous thanatos flew, a handful, but one cannot aim a handful of pebbles and most scattered wide. The two that showed a small promise of coming in their direction Hades blackened.

"You are the fool!" The thin shriek rose so high it hurt Persephone's ears. "You cannot escape me. I can run faster than you can climb. As soon as I touch you, you are lost."

The outlaw started toward them, shambling around the edge of the pool, and Hades stood still as if he acknowledged the horrible truth in the threat. Persephone drew breath to scream, but no sound could get past the iron grip terror had on her throat. Hades raised his head.

"Wish me strong, Dazzling Brightness," he muttered.

Heat rose in Persephone, gathered between her breasts, and poured outward. She heard Hades cry out, but the words were lost in a terrible grinding roar as the ceiling of the cavern shook and spears of rock broke loose and plunged downward. She heard one dreadful shriek that rose even above the shattering crashes, and then Hades turned and thrust her back toward the wall behind them.

Her knees were suddenly so weak they nearly buckled, and she could barely keep her hand closed around the basket, but Hades did not let her fall. He lifted her off her feet with one arm around her waist and plunged along the wall in the direction of the black mouths that yawned near the roof.

Below them he stopped, letting her feet touch the ground but clutching her to him. She felt him gesturing with the hand that did not hold her, but she was shaking with weakness and did not try to turn her head to see what he was doing. The roar of falling rock had diminished to a distinguishable medly of individual sharp cracks and crashes as one and then another of the spears broke loose and fell. Persephone listened fearfully for cries or groans, but no sound of a human voice was intermingled in the noise.

"Can you stand alone, beloved?" Hades asked. "I do not know how to give back what you poured into me. I have made hand and footholds in the rock. Can you climb up?"

His voice was strange and when she lifted her head to look, Persephone saw his eyes were glaring, the pupils glittering with red sparks. His face was set, too, like a man fighting great pain, but before she could speak he turned her in his arms so that she faced the wall. She realized then that some of the noise she had heard were holes being broken out of the rock wall just as he had broken the boulder to expose the second flower.

"I have seared the wall and the inside of the central opening, so it is safe for you to go up and wait for me."

"Wait for you?" Persephone echoed faintly, turning her head to look at him over her shoulder. "But where are you going?"

"I must burn this cavern clean."

"Now? This moment?"

"Persephone, I must rid myself of the power you bestowed upon me or I will burst or burn myself. Go up." He touched her forehead. "It will be light for you, but do not go too far into the tunnel."

He pushed her forward, less gently than his usual handling of her, and she went, too bemused by what he had said to protest further. The power she had bestowed upon him? What power had she to bestow?

Persephone staggered the few steps to the wall and began to climb slowly. She felt less weak, but it still required a far greater effort than she expected to raise a hand and foot and then the other foot to rise from one set of notches to the next. The basket, to which she still clung, hindered her too. If the wall had not slanted somewhat so that she was more crawling upward than climbing, she could not have progressed more than a few feet.

Her sudden weakness puzzled her. She thought at first it had been caused by fright, but then she remembered that she had felt strong enough to pick up Hades and carry him backward with her when the outlaw had first threatened them. She had not felt drained then . . . Drained!

The word brought back to mind the knot of heat between her breasts, heat that had run out of her and into Hades. But that was not a Gift. Or was it? Her mother said she had no Gift except her link to the Goddess, and it was true she could not initiate any spells; she had tried hard enough in the past, hoping to find a niche of life for herself that did not leave her a simple alter ego of her mother. Yet did she not remember when she went with her mother to bless the corn that a kind of gentle warmth flowed out of her? She had to pause and cling as a wave of distress washed over her. Her mother would not lie! Not to her!

Then Hades bellowed, "Burn!"

The sound filled and echoed around the cavern like a physical force and struck her a violent blow. Worse, it was followed by a roar that all but flattened her against the wall. Next came a blast of heat that seared her back and drove out of her every thought except that of a need to escape. She mounted upward again at a pace she would not have believed possible, hardly aware of reaching the tunnel mouth and creeping forward into it until the searing heat on her back and the red glow of fire that glared from the tunnel entrance were lost in the cool, dim twinkle of the crystals lit by Hades's magic.

The near dark calmed her fear of the holocaust behind her and simultaneously renewed her fear of the chrusous thanatos. She stopped abruptly and stared around at walls, ceiling, and floor. All glittered with little sparks, but none had the sick yellow-green tinge of the deadly growth. That fear dispelled, another seized her and she jumped to her feet, whirled around and started back toward the burning cavern, screaming, "Hades!"

"I am coming," he shouted.

She heard him running and in a moment he was beside her. He clutched her to him just as the tunnel went almost black. Behind them was the faintest red glare; ahead, Persephone could see nothing no matter how she strained. Then the crystals lit again.

"You went farther than I told you to go," Hades said, his voice sharp. Nonetheless, he gently took the basket, which had begun to feel like the burden of Sisyphus, from her numb hand.

Despite the kind gesture, fear and relief demanded an outlet and Persephone protested indignantly. "I was blown half the way, and it was too hot to stop at first."

"You were a little overgenerous in your giving," Hades snapped back. "I asked for strength, not to be filled with the power of a volcano."

That remark came so uncomfortably close to answering her own thoughts that Persephone was struck dumb. Hades made an indeterminate wordless noise, as if he were choking back words—or was about to speak again—but he said nothing, simply starting forward. When they had walked about fifty paces he stopped and killed the light again. Now it was black as Persephone had never seen blackness before—and she did not mind a bit. Black was clean, and the strong arm around her made it safe and comforting.

When the crystals lit again, Hades was smiling. "We are safe now," he said. "This tunnel is pure stone, no black rock, and the ponpikoi will not come through that chamber." He uttered a snort of laughter. "Nothing will. It will be years before it cools."

"Will that not be dangerous to . . . to those who travel through your realm?"

"No, the smell of burning will warn men as well as beasts, but it was kind of you to think of my people."

He started onward, helping her when the passage narrowed or flattened or the footing became rough and uneven. Most of the previous passages had been smooth, like rocks long washed by water, and they often had a layer of soft sand on the floor, which made for good footing. In this one, the sand was pierced by ribs of rock—hard crystal, Persephone thought, because each rib glowed. But though she tried to concentrate on the passage, her mind kept going back to the subject of power. And, in spite of the last few pleasant words they had spoken, the new silence between them was not comfortable.

At last Persephone asked, "Are you sure the power came from me? Could it not have been your own desperation . . ."

Hades looked down at her as her voice drifted away, then sighed and shook his head. "You know now. It is too late to go back to unknowing. But you are still tired and we both need to eat. I am almost sure there is another chamber ahead where we can rest—and talk, if you wish."

She nodded wordlessly, less because she wanted to rest, although if not for Hades's supporting arm she might have slid to the ground, than because she did not know what to say. They walked in silence for some minutes more until Persephone became aware that the light in the passage was growing brighter. She hesitated, but Hades reassured her, explaining that the rock was changing and there was more crystal in it. The chrusous thanatos appeared only where there was earth mixed with black burning-rock.

Soon after, Persephone heard running water and hesitated again, but Hades drew her on, smiling rather wryly this time. "You need not fear to travel the caves when I am with you."

"Oh no?" she answered smartly. "Was it not you who led me into that yellow-lit garden of delight?"

He laughed but his lips had a wry twist. "What you have seen is not the kingdom I wished to show you. I had hoped to enchant you with the beauty of my hidden land before I warned you of its horrors. I had also hoped you need never actually meet or see any of those, but you had to go your own way."

"If you had not abducted me—" Persephone had begun, and then stopped speaking as they came to a dead end.

The passage was so full of crystal that it was as bright as day, and she could see Hades smiling down at her. He pointed to a narrow crack in the rock. "On the other side is our haven. The wall is not more than an arm's-length thick. I do not wish to break it, so I will carry you through."

"Through the rock?" Persephone breathed.

"Are you afraid?" he challenged.

"Of course I am afraid. Do you think me an idiot? What if we get stuck?"

"I never have yet," Hades said, grinning. "And if we do, I have enough left of what you gave me to turn that wall to dust."

He took her in his arms, one behind her back and the other under her knees so that she touched nothing but his body, and told her to set the basket into the curve of her belly and hold it there as he advanced on the wall. She watched in mingled horror and excitement as Hades's arms flowed into the glittering rock, darkening it where they touched. As her body came into contact with the wall, pressed forward by his behind her, Persephone drew herself in, expecting to feel crushed. To her amazement, she felt only the slightest resistance, as if she were slipping into mud. Nonetheless, when her head touched the wall, she cringed, drew a deep, deep breath, and buried her face between Hades's neck and shoulder.

In fact, it seemed she did not need to breathe while they were in the rock, which was fortunate because the passage took much longer than she expected from the slight resistance she felt. After a time she grew more curious than afraid and lifted her head. It was not hard, but she could not see. It was not dark, but there was before her eyes only that kind of light one sees with one's lids closed. Later she thought she might have unconsciously kept her eyes shut, but Hades told her he could not see with his eyes either, only with the Gift that let him sense almost everything in or below the earth and carried him slowly toward any goal he set.

She remembered as they passed that this was the way he had abducted her, and she honed one or two remarks to finish the sentence she had begun. However, when Hades came into the open and set her on her feet, she just stood, open-mouthed. If he had not abducted her, she would never have seen the wonder that opened before her eyes.

Chapter 6

Olympus was beautiful, with its wide, tree-shaded streets and its glorious, shining white buildings, Persephone thought. But this—this was fairyland, lit with a white crystalline light that came from a myriad of glistening white lacy nodules attached to the low roof and from several stone pillars, down which ran many, many, thin, coruscating ribs of light. A clear, narrow pool lay on one side of the cavern, fed by a tiny tinkling waterfall that burst from the far wall. And the rock that made up the wall! Persephone stared, scarcely breathing, at cascades of stone that ended in billows of frozen foam, all glowing and rippling as the power that lit them ebbed and flowed.

Hades moved and Persephone was able to tear her eyes away from the marvel of stone carved into lacy billows and streamers. The next thing she saw was that near the pool were large, flat, knee-high rocks. If they had had backs, Persephone would have sworn they were chairs set deliberately to allow comfortable viewing. She looked suspiciously at Hades only to find him looking at her. He seemed to read her face because he shook his head, laughing.

"No, I did not first bring you through all the horrors and then try to make you forget them by bringing you here," he said. "I have never seen this chamber before. As I have told you, I did not mean to come this way."

He wriggled out of the rolled sheepskins, which he had replaced on his back after they escaped from the cavern of the chrusous thanatos, and untied them. Doubling one, he laid it on the largest of the flat rocks, one large enough to seat them both, then gestured her to join him and took the basket from her hand. When he lifted the cloth that covered the food, Persephone's mouth began to water. She sat down at once, took a meat roll, and bit into it hungrily. Hades took one too, but he did not sit. He wandered toward the end of the cavern, staring down one after another of the tall, thin cracks in the wall behind them.

Persephone paid no attention. She could not remember ever having been so hungry in her life. By the time he returned, she had eaten two more rolls, had a cup of wine, and was eyeing the small loaf of bread and a little covered pot, which she thought might contain fruit preserves.

"I left you two meat rolls," she said, "but all that is left beside those is some wine and the bread and that pot of something."

"That was supposed to serve for breaking our fast." Hades chuckled. "I thought I was capturing a delicate lady who would be too terrified to eat much. I did not expect to need to fill the equal of a farmer in reaping season."

Persephone sniffed loftily. "Some people eat when they are sad or frightened to comfort themselves."

Hades burst out laughing. The sound leapt merrily

from wall to wall and Persephone found herself laughing too.

"Very well," she admitted. "I suppose I should be frightened to death, but all I feel is hungry. And I do not see why you are laughing. Unless you expect to reach your home caverns tomorrow, we are going to starve."

"I had other caches of food, but I have no way to reach them from here," Hades said reproachfully. "And we have two days more of travel than I intended too. I will have to hunt or fish."

"Not hudorhaix," Persephone wailed.

Hades cocked his head at her. "There may be fish in the stream. I have not yet looked. That might do for tonight and for a midday meal tomorrow, but after that it will be hudorhaix or something you might find even less inviting to look at, although I swear that most things I can catch are tasty when well cooked. Unless—"

"Unless?"

"Unless you will stay where I put you and not try to run away while I hunt in the open. I swear you will be nowhere near Olympus and that the reason I want you to stay is that you will be in danger in the wild country, not because I fear you will find your way home."

Persephone busied herself with cutting a small piece off the bread, opening the pot, and spreading the dark brown paste. She was very ready, too ready, she told herself, to give Hades the promise he asked. What held her silent a few moments longer was her fear that Hades would sense that readiness and read into it light-mindedness or wantonness. She was tossed on roiling waves of contrary emotions—shame at her eagerness to remain with this man, utter delight in the beauty that surrounded her, wonder that that beauty should so diminish, almost wipe out, the terror of the dangers she had experienced, an astonished pride in her own ability to withstand such terror, and an even greater astonishment when she realized she did not wish to give up forever the looming possibility of facing new dangers.

"I will promise not to try to escape you," Persephone said at last, "only if I do not recognize any landmark that could guide me back to Olympus."

She almost smiled when she said it. Having been out of the temple so little—only into the main squares of the city and to a few sacred places within the valley— Persephone was almost sure she could not recognize any landmark.

To her surprise, Hades's lips thinned with anger. "Did you think I would not realize that is as good as saying you intend to run away the first chance you get?" he retorted. "I do not like to be taken for a fool and lied to slyly."

"If by now I still took you for a fool, I would be one," Persephone said. "You are wrong about my intentions. I do not even understand of what you are accusing me."

It was Hades's turn to look surprised, but he said, "One mountain peak looks much like another. I thought you intended to convince yourself that you were seeing a peak you recognized. I tell you it will not be so. We will be outside of the valley of Olympus entirely. There is no way you can get there from where we will come out, except by climbing the mountains between."

Persephone lifted the bread toward her mouth, barely choking back a promise that she would not run away under any circumstances. The scent of the spread, apple and spices, should have made her homesick, but instead it brought her the assurance that no matter how different Hades's realm was, it was also much the same.

By the time she had chewed and swallowed the bite, she had found what she considered a safe answer. "I will except mountain peaks from my list of landmarks," she said, and took a second most satisfying bite of bread and tangy spread. Then she recognized the odor of the spice, and she raised shocked eyes to Hades. "This *is* apple butter? It is not some concoction of hudorhaix and cave moss is it?"

Hades stared at her for a moment, then laughed, stuck a finger in the pot, and tasted what he brought out. "Not hudorhaix, certainly. No one, not even my cook, has ever discovered a way to make goat taste like apples—and hudorhaix tastes like goat. We do have apple trees, so I imagine the spread is mainly apples, but I think the spice is blue-light cave moss." He paused and added with cynical politeness, "I hope you do not dislike it. It is widely used."

Persephone lifted her arched golden brows into an even higher arch, and the twist of her lips implied "What good would it do if I did not like it?" while the words she spoke, with equally false politeness were, "I do not dislike the taste or the scent of the moss, but I cannot say I like to think of what was walking on the ground from which it grew—"

"You mean you prefer bull's shit to hudorhaix shit for manuring the earth?" Hades interrupted, choking on laughter.

For one moment Persephone stared at him, her mouth—full of another bite of bread and spread—

inelegantly open. She had been thinking of the pallid, slimy creatures walking on the moss. Then she shut her mouth and almost strangled, trying to laugh and swallow at the same time. Hades kindly pounded her back until she could breathe again.

"That was a low blow," she said with what dignity she could gather. But as the real sense of what he had said penetrated through the jest, she drew a shocked breath and asked sharply, "What do you know about manured fields? That is a mystery of the Goddess."

"Not among the natives," Hades replied. "I had heard that digging manure into the earth brought richer crops and so I went to see. I did not wish to call in the favors Zeus owed me. But even though their land is far better than our thin-soiled valleys, their crops cannot be compared with those of Olympus. I knew manuring would not yield grain enough to feed my people, and I had already tried everything that I remembered seeing when I was a boy before my father drove me from Olympus—everything except asking for a priestess of the Goddess. Can you truly bring richer crops to our fields, Persephone, or is there something holy to the Goddess in the earth of Olympus?"

She did not even consider lying to him and saying that Olympus was holy soil so that he would take her home. She said, "How can I answer that? I have never been out of Olympus. I know the rites and have performed them. I know that when a field is cursed by Zeus's command or for some insult to the Goddess, and the seed is not blessed nor sown by a priestess, little grows. Thus I believe it is the Goddess's blessing that makes the stalks thick in the field and the heads of grain heavy on each stalk." She looked up at him and then down again. "My mother says I can bring from the Goddess the power—"

The word caught in her throat and brought back a vision of Hades, his eyes sparking red with power and his face steeled against pain, and she asked the question that had been in the back of her mind all the time.

"What is my Gift, Hades?"

For a moment he did not understand the question. First he had been appalled at having given Persephone the opportunity to say she would be useless to him in Plutos and that keeping her there would be for nought. When she did not seize the opening, his joy was so much more intense that he only filled his eyes with her, not really paying attention to what she said. The change in her expression warned him, however, and he gathered his wits.

"I am not certain I know it all," he said, "but what you did for me the first time was to restore the strength I had drained to open the passage. In the cave of the golden death, you made greater—much greater—my own Gift."

"Is that a Gift?" she whispered, searching his face.

"To another mage, the greatest that can exist," he answered honestly. "To you, yourself . . . I do not know whether it can serve any direct purpose of yours, Persephone."

"But my mother must have known of it, and she told me I was not Gifted. I asked more than once." Her voice trembled near tears. "She lied to me. My own mother."

Hades looked down at her bent head, wondering whether it would serve his purpose better to let her believe the worst or to comfort her. But he knew what feeling betrayed had done to others, even to Poseidon, who had his own great Gifts, and beside that, he could not bear her sadness. He knelt down before her and took her hands in his.

"If she knew, and I am not certain she did know because what you gave—if you gave to her when you blessed seed and sowed it—may have felt like a God-dess-granted burgeoning of her own Gift. But if she did know, I think it likely she kept silent for your own good."

"For my good?"

Her eyes met his again, and her expression was a mingling of anger and hope—and trust. And the trust was in him, Hades thought with warm satisfaction.

"Can you not see that if knowledge of such a Gift spread abroad in Olympus, every mage would have striven to have control of you? They would have torn you apart among them. To speak the truth, I am not at all sure I would have told you myself if I had not been driven half out of my wits by the power you poured into me. Nor am I certain my silence would have been for your good. I cannot swear that I would not have wished to keep what you had all to myself. But I am sure that whatever other motives drove your mother, her first was a desire to protect you."

"She is *always* trying to protect me," Persephone said, exasperation rather than grief and bitterness in her voice, and after a moment a little smile pulled at her lips. "You, on the other hand, bring me places where goats, rats, and yellow slime try to eat me. Since you have decided on noble confession, will you not admit that it is unfair to expose me to one danger after another?"

Swallowing a shout of joy, Hades rose from his

knees and looked haughtily down his nose at her as he said, "Ah, but I do not think you need protection."

Her eyes widened with suprise at first, and then she stuck out her tongue at him like a naughty child. Hades very nearly bent and seized it in his lips, but she had pulled it back and taken the last bite of bread. He stood a moment longer, clenching his fists behind his back while he restrained a desire to push her back on the fleece and love her at once, which would have ruined all his good work in being "fair" to her mother. That she trusted him now and did not want to run back to Demeter's protection was clear enough from the way she joked about the horrors they had survived and dared him to offer to return her to the temple. Should he take the dare, just to see how she would avoid accepting his offer?

A chill slid over his skin. "Let me remind you," he said severely, "that the confrontation with the hudorhaix was all your own idea—and all the other dangers grew out of that."

Hades sat down and reached for one of the meat rolls, telling himself it was an errant breeze from one of the tunnels that had chilled him. He did not wish to admit to himself that there was even the smallest element of doubt in the certainty he felt that Persephone would be his. The sudden rush of desire he had subdued was not important, more a mark of his swelling delight in her than an urgent physical need. And it was easy to control because he knew she would be his in the end. He knew it as surely as he knew his naming of her had been perfect. Only a dazzling brightness of spirit could have poured that power into him.

Persephone sniffed again, this time clearly implying that she accepted no responsibility for their troubles.

"You mean I should have sat there like a ninny waiting for my abductor to finish his nap when I believed I saw a way out?"

Hades sighed and took a bite of the meat roll. When he had swallowed, he remarked, "That is just what I thought you would do, or perhaps cry a little—but as I have said before, I did not know, neither you nor that a blue-light cave was so near." He laughed suddenly. "What we both need is to be better acquainted with each other—much better acquainted."

He leaned toward her, his eyes fixed on hers, and held his breath as she seemed to sway closer, but before he was sure she had been tempted to respond to his wordless invitation, she dropped her eyes to the basket.

"You are not going to like what a closer acquaintance with me shows if you do not find me more to eat," she said tartly, eyeing the last meat roll.

"Take it. Take it," he offered, gesturing toward the basket. "It is a small sacrifice when I was just about to offer you my whole heart."

Persephone's eyes sparkled even more brightly as she looked up. "Were you planning to bake it or broil it?" she asked eagerly, and then when she saw he was dumbstruck, added thoughtfully, "Too bad we do not have a pan. If we did we could fry it, which would be best because heart is very tough and it is most edible when sliced thin."

Hades, who to tease her had hurriedly taken another bite of his meat roll as soon as he stopped speaking—pretending he feared she would demand that too—had been caught totally by surprise. His eyes bulged as he struggled not to laugh and spray her with half-chewed food. This time she pounded *him* on the back, and when he had finally conquered his need to cough, and swallowed, he put down the remaining portion of the meat roll and made a gesture of defeat.

"Very well. You win. I will put filling your belly ahead of my desire to win your—no, I will not say 'heart.' I can imagine what you would answer to that. I will see if there is anything in the pool."

Persephone pushed the basket a little toward him, smiling faintly. "Finish your meal," she said. "Filling your belly is as important as filling mine."

He smiled back but shook his head. "Mine does not need so much filling just now. All jesting aside, take the last meat roll. You are hungry because you drained yourself and need to be restored. I am not hungry because I still hold some remnant of what you gave me."

"I never thought of that," Persephone said with a note of relief. "I have never been so greedy in my life. I pretended to be joking, but to my shame I begrudged you every bite you took." She put out her hand and touched his gently. "Are you sure you do not need the last of the meat rolls? There is only a little bread and apple butter left for tomorrow if you cannot find any fish."

"I am sure," he said, and was glad that it was true, because he was afraid she might sense a lie, but he would have said the same if he were famished. Then he laughed and added, "And you will not be so hungry tomorrow."

They chewed together in companionable silence until the meat rolls were gone, then Hades said, "I will spread the other fleece. Lie down and sleep. That will do you as much good as more food, I think."

She lay back when the fleece was adjusted, but caught at Hades before he turned away toward the pool. "If you had not been so strong a mage, I could have killed you by pouring too much into you. Is that not true?"

He hesitated, wanting to soothe her but knowing that simple soothing was too dangerous. In fact, he thought the only reason she had not killed him, accustomed as he was to gathering and storing power, was because he had been so depleted by his earlier striving with the earth. However, he was not going to admit that, which would be as dangerous to him in another way. He thought now that he could make her love him, but if he could not or love should change to hate, he dared not place such a weapon in her hand.

"Perhaps," he said at last.

Her eyes were huge, magnified by unshed tears, which also lent a glistening brilliance to their gold. "But I do not know what I did, not the first time when it was safe nor the last when it was not. I do not know how to judge or measure or even prevent myself from giving. Hades, do you think my mother locked me in the temple because I was dangerous? Is my Gift wild and untameable?"

"No Gift is untameable," Hades replied. "Yours only responded to the need. You were frightened by the chrusous thanatos and the outlaw and poured out too much. As to your mother, you know she did not really *lock* you in the temple, nor did she forbid your mingling with the other priestesses, so she did not believe you to be a danger to anyone. Do not create horrors for yourself. Demeter kept you close, as I said, because she feared some mage would seize you." He paused, looking down at her, his dark eyes lighting. "And some mage has."

"Most wrongfully," Persephone murmured, glancing away from him and then up again, provocatively, from under her eyelashes.

"Not wrongfully at all," Hades protested, keeping a sober expression, although he was delighted that his abduction seemed to be turning into a source of teasing. "Your father gave permission . . ."

He had let his statement trail off, expecting a smart rejoinder, but she did not respond at once. She must be working on a gem, he thought, quite content to wait and watch the way the gold irises glinted through the gold lashes, but in another moment her eyes had closed completely, and Hades realized she had fallen fast asleep.

The sudden slumber made him feel somewhat more confident that she would not burn him alive accidentally. Her hunger and exhaustion implied that she had expended nearly all her strength, and he remembered she had nearly collapsed after passing power to him. Long practice had taught him ways to draw more power than flowed naturally, tapping his lifeforce to near extinction if necessary. But he did not believe Persephone could do that, at least not now, and he need not teach her that technique. When she was recovered, they could examine her Gift and he could show her how to bind it within her and dole out the flow.

Smiling, he pulled on the cloak gently, until the cloth was no longer bunched under her and would cover her more completely. He stood looking down for another moment, wondering whether Demeter had truly been ignorant of her daughter's power or merely selfish in keeping it secret. That Demeter had told Persephone she had no Gift for her daughter's own good was unlikely. Persephone's advantage would have been best served by explaining the danger of exposing her ability to give power to another, and teaching the girl—

The word checked the flow of his thoughts and brought conviction. Demeter had known, Hades thought, turning his back on Persephone for fear she would feel his anger and be disturbed. Demeter had been silent because she did not want her daughter to have anything of her own—not even a name. Demeter had seen "Kore"—girl—only as an extension of herself and had used her daughter's Gift as if it were her own.

Then Hades's grim expression relaxed. Demeter had done him a very good turn by her selfishness. He would teach Persephone how to control her power, how to withhold it, even from him. Thus, he thought cynically, he would demonstrate his "nobility" and prove that he wanted her for herself, not for what he could drain from her.

He glanced back at her, considering that thought, and decided it was by no means a lie. The priestess was necessary to his people, but he, as a man, certainly wanted the woman who was a dazzling brightness to him as much as, no, more than, he wanted the mage Persephone. As he started to walk to the pool, he chuckled softly. Of course, teaching Persephone to bind her power within her would also ensure that no other mage in Plutos would become aware of what she was, and stick a knife in his back to get her.

In the pool, darting shapes soon caught his eye and he smiled at them. He had expected some life, because they were nearer the surface than he had admitted to Persephone, but the size of the fish pleased him. In fact, he had smelled the growing things of the outer-world in the air coming in through one of the tunnels, although he did not know whether there was a usable entrance. Sometimes a crack opened onto a sheer cliff, but he did not need to worry about getting out and hunting now. Now his only problem was catching the dinner and breakfast he could see but not reach.

Although he still hunted sometimes for pleasure or to kill an overbold predator in a blue-light cave for the safety of his gathering parties, he had not fished since he was a boy. He shivered once, remembering that raw fish were all he had to eat when he used to hide for days from Kronos in the caves behind the slave prison. He had always gone back, his bitter loneliness overpowering his fear of his father. Each time he would convince himself that he had misunderstood Kronos's frequent brutality. For a long time he had been unable to believe that his own father really intended to *kill* him—until his mother had warned him one night, just in time for him to escape Kronos's freezing blast.

He shivered again and then laughed. Nothing is ever all bad. He had thought it the ultimate horror when Kronos was not satisfied to have driven him out and set out to hunt him to the death. It was his need to defend himself against the sucking out of all warmth, which was Kronos's Gift, that had taught him to use his own, the moving and heating of rock and earth. And, he thought, chuckling again, surviving before he had discovered his Gift taught him just what he needed to know now.

He lay down and extended a hand into the water, slowly moving his fingers as if they were responding to the current. The fish were blind, of course, but either the warmth or smell of his hand or some sensation from the movement of his fingers was an irresistible attraction. He did not catch at the first, which was small. Soon a larger one darted in to nip at his hand. Hades managed to stroke the creature's side as it passed and it turned and slid back over his hand. The third pass it made was slower. On the fifth, Hades's hand closed. He always felt a trifle guilty about beguiling the poor things, but in the past he had been hungry, and now Persephone was hungry.

Chapter 7

Persephone did not sleep for very long. She was wakened by an urgent need to relieve her bladder, a need that had been suppressed earlier by fear and excitement. The urgency was too great for shame or politeness, and Hades's casual response—first he had handed her several broad, still-pliable leaves on which the meat rolls had rested, and then pointed to a modest crevice at the far end of the cavern into which ran a small stream from the pool—eliminated any embarrassment she might have felt. She returned to the fleece-padded rock feeling much better, but still hungry.

Hades intercepted her look at the basket and laughed. "There is only fish for now," he said, beckoning her to another of the flat, raised rocks.

He used the corner of a thin slab of stone to pry off another slab, which had hidden a cavity holding two large fish. They were already headless and tailless and had been baked in their own skins. With the knife from the basket, he flipped one of the fish onto the slab of stone he had used for prying and the other onto the cover of his improvised oven.

Gingerly, but with considerable haste, Persephone pulled away the blackened skin and picked out a piece of the flesh. It was soft and moist and, even unsalted, delicious.

"I must say," she remarked, teasing at another strip of flesh, "that your Gift is much more useful than Zeus's. All he could do would be to char the poor fish to ashes with his lightning."

"I thank you," Hades responded gravely, working on his own fish with an alacrity almost equal to hers, "but I fear you are not thinking the matter through. He could use the lightning to make a fire and cook fish that way."

"And what would he burn in here?" Persephone mumbled through a large mouthful.

"Alas," Hades replied, "that is one of the drawbacks of my realm. But I must admit, I have more trouble imagining Zeus cooking fish at all than wondering how he would do it. Between his looks and his charm, he manages to get someone else to cook his fish even when he wanders among the native people."

"What are they like?" Persephone asked with bright-eyed interest, recalling from their discussion about manured fields that Hades also went among the people who lived on the coast below the mountains that sheltered Olympus.

"They are very much like you and me. Most are not so tall and strong as Olympians, and—they know different things. For instance, they know little of working stone and they can only work the soft metals, but they are much better hunters and many can live off the land, an art Olympians have forgotten. Most of my people are native folk."

Persephone's hand hesitated on its way to her lips. "But they are dead—I cannot forget that."

"They are dead to their own people," Hades replied. "They cannot go back to the outer world. But in Plutos they are not dead. They eat and drink, laugh and cry, work and sleep, just as you and I."

"What does that mean?"

"It means exactly what I have said, no more, no less. I cannot explain further to you, not yet."

"Will they be cold to touch?" Persephone's voice trembled slightly.

Hades laughed. "Of course not—at least not unless they have been swimming in a cold pool." Then he sobered and his eyes grew very sad. "Some are very twisted and broken. Do not be afraid of them or turn away from them. Those are often the most Gifted, and they were cruelly abused because the native people fear the Gifts of the Mother. Be kind, Persephone. They have suffered enough."

"Is my father there?" she asked.

"But you know Zeus—ah, you mean your blood father. I keep forgetting."

"Iasion, my father," Persephone repeated stubbornly.

"No, he is not in Plutos. I have never seen the man and never heard his name before Zeus said he was not guilty of his death."

"How can you be sure he is not in Plutos? How could you possibly know every person who has died in Olympus and among the native villages?"

"Thank the Mother I do not," Hades said, smiling. "That would be hundreds and hundreds and hundreds of thousands. We are not nearly so many. In fact, I do not know every single person from the native tribes, but I have made it my business to know every person from Olympus."

Persephone knew that smile was significant, but his last remark distracted her from thinking about what he had said first. "Why do you need to know everyone from Olympus?" she asked.

"At first because Kronos was trying to find a way to kill me. Later, after Zeus drained Kronos and he killed himself, I had to assure myself that those who came from Olympus did not desire to avenge Kronos's death on his rebellious sons, starting with me." He shrugged. "I have never come across any who loved Kronos enough to wish to kill me for his sake, but some blamed me for the loss of their privileged status under the old order and wished to reestablish the order in Plutos." He paused thoughtfully for a moment and then went on. "Most have settled down well enough. A few are even less trouble than those who settled into the ways of Plutos."

Although she was certain that something dreadful had befallen those who now made "less trouble"—befallen them at Hades's hands—and she knew she should be horrified, instead Persephone felt a rush of pride in Hades's calm voice and half-smiling expression. He was a man who knew how to rule.

If Hades was aware of her approval, he gave no sign, his half-smile changing to a frown as he continued. "The malcontents are a different matter. Most are just a nuisance, like an itch one cannot scratch. I know they try to stir up trouble, may even succeed some day, but there is nothing I can do."

"Why not?"

"My realm would be no better than those they escaped if I punished without cause. And I might be mistaken. A grumbler might be just that, one who has a complaining nature but intends no harm."

Persephone uttered a giggle. "But Hades, you would be considered a public benefactor if you rid the realm of those."

He laughed too, but the crease between his brows did not disappear. "The danger, not to the realm as a whole but to a man or woman here and there, is not from those who live in Plutos and whine and complain. There are outlaws who roam the outer caves and valleys. Some I exiled, some committed crimes and fled before they could be taken, some refused to accept the conditions I require to enter Plutos—"

"You would turn a man away because he had not two obols to pay your ferryman?" Persephone asked, shocked.

Hades blinked and then laughed more heartily. "No, my ferryman is not really so niggardly, but," he added conspiratorially, lowering his voice as if someone could overhear, "you must not spread that word around or Plutos would soon be utterly ruined."

The laughter made the bejeweled collar around Hades's neck and the gold and gem work on his belt flash. Persephone sniffed and said, "You need not make a jest of two obols because of your wealth. I have known those who dripped as much gold and as many gems as you do to be far from generous to the temple."

"You are right, but that tale of Charon collecting obols is a strange one. I wonder where that started?" He stared past her for a moment and muttered, "I wonder if someone is pretending to be a doorkeeper and collecting obols before they come to Charon . . . Hmmm. I must look into that."

"But why should anyone want obols?" Persephone

asked. "You just pointed out that Plutos is rich in gold and gems."

"Those are worthless in the outer world because they are bespelled. They turn to dross when touched by daylight, unless I myself have released the spell. So someone might want to collect a hoard that would not crumble away."

"Who?" Persephone did not ask why Hades had bespelled the wealth of Plutos. It was clear enough to her that if a few escaped the caves and brought back gold and gems, the caverns would soon be invaded by armies of gold seekers.

"I would suspect someone who 'died' for a real crime rather than for being Gifted. A person can be both, and my judges might not look farther than the Gift for a reason a man or woman is sent to Plutos. Even those who have committed crimes are given a chance to redeem themselves, and a twisted soul can be hidden." He shrugged. "Obols are a small matter. It would take a very long time for anyone to collect enough obols to buy his way into a place where he could do harm."

"And enough obols for that might be too heavy to carry," Persephone said.

Hades laughed again but then the troubled look came back. "In Plutos what folk hoard is food, not coin. Within the home caverns, every man and woman has a share. Their labor and what they produce is exchanged for food and cloth—those things we cannot yet make in Plutos. Food is what those who live outside Plutos's shelter seek. Most do not survive more than a few days or a few weeks, but a few have mage power. Some have formed outlaw bands. All the outlaws are desperate and dangerous, Persephone."

"You do not need to warn me, after our meeting with one of them where the chrusous thanatos grew."

"Not about someone so far gone, but if I bring you, as I promised, to where you can see the sun and feel the breeze you must not think because you are in the outer world that any party is trustworthy. They may be; they may be my people hunting, but if they should be outlaws and take you, they might use you very ill before I could find them and take you back. I do not want you to feel you can safely roam alone just because you are outside the caves."

"I will not." She put out a rather greasy hand and took his, no less greasy. "I swear as I hope my Goddess continues to favor me that I will not run away nor show myself nor speak to any if you bring me to the outer world."

On her last words, the light went out of Hades's face. Up to that moment whether he was laughing or troubled, there had been an underlying joy in him and it was suddenly gone. He stood up abruptly, his hand slipping from hers.

"Very well, we can go now if you wish. I cannot promise we can actually leave the cave, but there is some opening to the surface beyond one of the tunnels. You will be able at least to look out, and if I can do it, I will get you out."

Understanding came to Persephone. Hades thought she had been pleading to leave the cave. She barely bit back the assurance that she would stay in the caves forever to be near him. Too sweeping assurances would be a mistake, perhaps binding her to more than she wished to concede so soon. Surely she could bring back the light to Hades's eyes without giving him all the advantage.

"We do not need to go now," she said, sitting where she was and idly picking at the bones of the fish to glean a scrap of flesh here and there. "It must be near dark outside, and it will be cold at night so early in the spring. This place is beautiful and comfortable." She glanced toward the pool and back at the improvised oven. "And there are fish for supper. We can look at the opening to the surface tomorrow."

"I thought what you just ate *was* supper," Hades said, plainly trying to sound exasperated, only the relief in his voice was so clear he must have heard it himself, because he began to laugh and admitted, "I am glad you do not hate the caves—and I already have two more fish ready for baking."

"How long does it take?" Persephone asked.

"Not long enough for you to begin again considering how parts of me would taste," he rejoined, still smiling. "But perhaps we should see how far the opening is and whether we can get out. We could come back here to sleep, but a few spices to bake with the fish would be pleasant, and if I can find a tuber or two—"

"They will be very dry and woody at this season," Persephone remarked without much enthusiasm, much surprised to find that she was not pretending— she really did not care whether they left the cave or not. And then she cocked her head curiously. "But how would you know which plants can be used as spices and which have tubers that can be eaten?"

"Did you think I changed from a fugitive child to King of Plutos overnight? I lived no short time on raw fish, and then by hunting and gathering, both in the caves and in the valleys. It has been many years, but I think I would remember the look of the plants."

"I might be able to help," Persephone offered somewhat doubtfully. "I was taught the lore of growing things as part of my studies to be priestess. I had to remember long lists of blessed and accursed plants. But most of what I learned will be useless. Many of the plants do not even grow in this part of the world. My mother told me that many grew to the north and west, far past the mountains, from where Kronos brought his people. However, there are a few I know I would recognize, because I have seen them in the wild places around Olympus."

"Then if you are not still tired, let us go."

Persephone thought his voice was tight, as if he were again wondering just how much she wanted the outer world, but she did not feel it wise to offer more assurances. He would see how she felt—she was not certain herself just how she would react—when they came to the opening. Thus she merely rose and followed him to one of the irregular crevices in the wall behind them, larger than the one she had used as a privy but not far from it.

As in the passage leading to the cavern with the pool, there was much crystal close to the cavern and the light was bright. That diminished as they walked until Persephone stumbled. She reached for the wall to steady herself, but could not find it, and she realized the passage had become much wider. Hades put his arm around her as soon as she reached out, and she did not need to stumble again. Before much longer, however, a gray light appeared. Now Persephone could smell earth and growing things. She was surprised when she felt no urge to quicken her pace and she held steady beside Hades, although he dropped his arm when the light strengthened as if to allow her to hurry if she wished.

It was as well she had not, because the passage ended abruptly in a sharp drop to the floor of another cave with a very wide, low mouth. The light came in from the opening, around which Persephone could see a carpet of green. Although she had been startled when Hades's arm flashed up to block her way and protect her from the edge, in the next moment she saw that the drop was only about half a body length deep. Hades swung down and reached up for her, making the descent easy, but the roof slanted down toward the entrance so that they had to bend over and finally crawl outside.

Less time had passed since Hades had seized her that morning than Persephone had expected. The sun was still up, although barely above the western peaks. A glancing light gilded the delicate alpine flowers at the foot of sheltering outcrops, but snow still lay in many hollows. She looked around at the hillside, which dropped away from them in gentle undulations to a valley floor far below. In several places water broke out of the ground, forming small rivulets, most of which were swallowed up before they went any distance, but around which was a lush growth of plants. It was a pretty scene. Persephone smiled—and was suddenly aware, although she did not know how, that Hades had stiffened.

"Tsk!" she exclaimed. "We should have brought the basket. How are we going to carry back what we find?"

"We could stick some things through our belts," he said, and his voice was easy as she had hoped it would be when she made plain her intention of returning to the cave. "But what I would suggest is that you allow me to cut off the bottom of your gown. It is torn with all the crawling, and you tripped on the hem once already. If you let me make a bag of the cloth below your knee, I promise you five gowns as lovely when we reach the home cave."

"And where would an unmarried man come by women's gowns, one or five?" Persephone snapped before she realized that she was exposing her jealousy.

Hades lowered his eyes. "I am the king," he said too gravely. "I can take what I desire."

Persephone knew the gravity was assumed, but she was too furious to consider what that meant. "Thank you for your generous offer," she said disdainfully, "but I think I prefer my torn dress to the hand-me-downs of your bed partners."

"Never would I do so crude a thing!" Hades exclaimed, struggling with the corners of his mouth. "I assure you, the gowns would be all new." But the struggle became too much and he burst out laughing, rocking back and forth. "Persephone, Persephone, I am a man and not so young. Did you think I was a virgin too?"

She turned her back on him, and he put a hand gently on her shoulder and turned her back.

"I have lain with more than a few women," he said, now completely serious, "but none has shared my bed in the sense you mean for many years now. I have taken a little easy pleasure, and given it too, I hope— but you need fear no rivals, not from the past and not in the future."

"I know what such lies and such promises are worth," she said, turning her face away. But she did not pull free of his grip and, although she had no intention of admitting it, she was mollified.

He snapped back sharply, "I do not lie nor make any promise lightly."

Oddly, Persephone did not think he was angry, despite the sharp tone. Something told her he was really flattered, and she was further soothed. His manner toward her was certainly not of a man seeking a little easy pleasure. She did not know much about men, she reminded herself—and then she thought, *but I do know the tales about Zeus, and myself have seen the way he looks at and speaks to a beautiful woman.* Nonetheless, she understood the advantage of reserving any sign of belief or acceptance.

"Five *new* gowns for two handspans of cloth?" she said slowly, as if she were adding advantage against price. "That is a good bargain. Now let me see . . ."

"Persephone!" Hades barked. "If you are considering deliberately forgetting the basket each time we go gathering so I will carve up your gown and offer you new ones, put it out of your mind. I have no intention of bringing you to my palace stark naked. It is bad enough that you will doubtless tell everyone I abducted you and not admit it was with your father's permission. I do not intend to let you make my subjects think I tore off your clothes too."

She looked at him sidelong and shrugged. "If that is already your reputation . . ."

"No, that is *not* my reputation, which is why my people would be—" he began hotly, then drew a sharp breath. "Persephone, if you do not stop teasing me I am going to murder you."

The remark had been more in the nature of a test than a tease, but she was satisfied with the answer and

she laughed. "Not before I bless your seeds and fields,
I hope. I do not think Zeus will give you permission to
abduct another priestess if you kill the first one."

He made a strangled sound and Persephone laughed
again, but she had been looking away from him teas-
ingly and suddenly her mind "saw" what her eyes had
been resting on idly. She pointed eagerly to the left.
"Oh look, Hades, are those not the young shoots of
asphodel? And there, beyond that trickle of water,
surely that is askolonion?"

Now Hades looked out at the surrounding area with
more attention and nodded. "You are certainly right
about the askolonion and I think about the asphodel
too. And in the water above where the askolonion is
growing is winter cress. I know that one. I have eaten
enough of it at this time of year. And look beyond.
Those are shoots of some kind of lily, which means
bulbs below. I do not believe this valley has been
gleaned in many years—if ever. I suppose no one
would pass the chrusous thanatos to find the passage
that led out. We will have a more tasty second supper
than I expected, and for little labor."

Without more words Persephone started toward the
plants she had recognized, but she was not thinking
about them. She was thinking that Hades had confirmed, all unaware and thus truthfully, his assurance
that she could not find her way back to Olympus even
though she was now in the outer world. Had there
been any passage from one valley to another outside
the caves, his people, who were plainly in want of the
fruits of the earth, would have gone around the cave
of the golden death and gleaned this valley. She
stepped along light-footed, not quite smiling as she
bent above the nearest patch of winter cress.

They did, indeed, eat well, and there was sufficient food to quell at last the hunger that had gnawed at Persephone more or less constantly since she had poured out her power into Hades. Having returned scraps and bones to the pool where they would feed its living inhabitants, she turned to find that Hades had spread his share of the fleeces on another flat-topped rock, although there was room for both on the large one where she had been lying.

She smiled at him and said, "I am no longer afraid that you will ravish me. You need not lie halfway across the cave to reassure me."

He straightened up abruptly. "Are you telling me you accept me as a husband?"

Surprise that she had barely bit back a "yes" kept her mute, but she managed to shake her head. He stared at her for another moment and then turned back to straighten the fleece he had pulled awry when she spoke to him. His head was bent too far over what he was doing and he was taking too long over it to hide his disappointment.

"I have known you for one day, Hades," she said. "That is a brief time in which to agree to make over my life."

He looked over his shoulder. "We have lived through enough today to fill several lives and we have helped and sustained each other." Turning to face her fully, he added, "I do not see how time will show you better what I am. I am willing to pledge to you—my life, my honor, my heart—"

He swallowed, and Persephone, who had been looking down, trying to find the strength to resist the logic of his words and the deep hunger in his voice, raised her eyes to his. Both choked on surpressed laughter.

"Oh, I wish I had not said that about your heart," she murmured, and bit her lips.

"I wish you had not too. I am going to have to find some other part to offer you, something less tasty." Hades swallowed hard again and there were tears in his large black eyes, but Persephone did not think they were of grief.

"But I am not hungry anymore." Both lip and voice quivered, Persephone being racked between mirth and disappointment.

Hades closed the space between them before she even thought of retreat and caught her into his arms. He was shaking with laughter and his voice trembled as he said, "Oh, but I am hungry, Persephone, my dazzling brightness. I have not felt such a light in my soul nor such a fire in my body since . . . I swear, not since my father drove me from Olympus. Be my queen, Persephone."

She did not answer, but she did not struggle against him when he stopped laughing, then lifted his hands to the sides of her face, tilted it toward him, and brought his mouth to hers. The pressure of lip on lip was very light, hardly a kiss. Persephone knew she had only to step a pace back to be free of him. Instead she closed her eyes, partly to avoid the strain of looking at his face, which was too close, but more because there was a very strange sensation in her body.

The teasing, light tickle of Hades's lips and the bare touch of his chest against her risen nipples seemed to be the source of the trouble. Persephone circled his back with one arm to pull him tighter against her and used the other hand to press his head forward. Surely the firm pressure would put an end to the tickling, which was generating an insidious warmth that was turning her limbs to jelly.

As if he understood and intended to cooperate, Hades released her face, sliding one hand around her back and the other down to her buttocks. He pressed her firmly into his body, but Persephone found it did not help at all—and she realized that he did not intend to help. The fingers of the hand around her back were running gently back and forth over the side of her breast, which made her nipples even more sensitive to the pressure of his chest against them. And the hand on her buttocks—that was rubbing her against a hard bulge between Hades's thighs.

Between her own, she could feel the nether lips full and slick with moisture and a sense of emptiness that needed to be filled. She knew that was desire for coupling. She had felt it before, once most strongly when she had by accident come upon Dorkas and a man locked together. Yet that had been only a shadow of what she felt now, as had been the interest she felt in those who cast admiring eyes on her in Olympus. And why should she resist, she thought, letting her lips part for Hades's exploring tongue. She was promising him nothing by yielding her body. Many priestesses of the Corn Goddess had lovers; that only fulfilled another aspect of the Great Mother's worship.

Although he held her tighter than ever, Hades's tongue withdrew and his head lifted. Persephone opened her eyes. To her amazement they were no longer standing by the spread fleece but lying upon it, she on her back, Hades poised above her. He lowered his head and kissed her, then raised it again, looking troubled.

Persephone felt an additional spurt of warmth at

this evidence that he was waiting her permission, and she smiled and whispered. "Let us celebrate the Great Mother's gift that there be male and female and joy in their coming together."

"So do I wish," he murmured, "but this time I may not bring you joy but pain. A maiden's first piercing is not always easy, and I do not wish you to hate me or to think it will always be so."

Of the pain, Persephone had heard *ad nauseum* from her mother, who made no pretense about wishing to spare her daughter that pain—and the pain of bearing children too. She was grateful, nonetheless, for Hades's warning and quite certain that his final words were equally true. She had, after all, seen and heard Dorkas's satisfaction and knew that some of the other priestesses went willingly, eagerly, to meet their lovers.

"Would it be easier for me with another man, Hades?"

His mouth thinned to a hard line and his eyes glittered like polished jet. "No, not easier nor sweeter, I promise you that."

He unhooked his broad belt and cast it aside, pulled the pin from the cloak she wore and spread it apart. The movement opened his kilt, no longer held by the belt, and it slid away. Persephone had seen naked men in plenty when they wrestled, cast the discus, or performed other exercises in the games of the solstices or the rites of passage, but she had never seen a man aroused. Her breath drew in, and then in again much harder when Hades lowered himself and took her nipple in his mouth.

The wanting had diminished when they talked, had been further dampened by the shock of wondering how she would engulf what she had seen. It flooded through her again, a mindless urge that made her lift her hips before thought or fear could restrain her. But Hades did not respond by thrusting into her. He only slid himself between her thighs and rubbed against her while he sucked one breast and fingered the other.

Vaguely Persephone wondered whether she should be hurt because Hades had not taken what she offered, but in a very few minutes she could not think at all. She moaned and writhed, pressing his head closer, squeezing his hand, releasing that to clutch his buttocks and struggle to change his position to fill her emptiness. In the end her need was so great that when he did impale her, the shriek she uttered was as much of satisfaction as of pain.

Without instruction, her legs clutched him to her, eased when he rose to plunge anew. They urged him faster, deeper. She cried aloud, feeling that she would split in two, but driven by a spiraling pleasure that fed off the pain, the almost unbearable sensations in her breasts, and the feel of Hades's body touching and releasing hers. She gasped for breath as the pleasure grew and grew, and shrieked again when it burst in spasms. Those faded and then pulsed anew as Hades lifted his head and howled like a beast, his body arched backward, locked in its moment of climax.

Chapter 8

Persephone woke slowly, aware she was being watched. With her eyes still closed, she frowned in irritation. It had been years since her mother would sit by her bed and gaze at her as if she expected her to break out in spots or disappear. Then she became aware of an ache in all her bones and between her thighs and began to wonder whether she had been sick. Simultaneously she realized that her bed was strange, a fleece atop something hard as rock and she was covered with a woolen cloak rather than her own smooth blanket. A man's deep voice touched with exasperation caused her eyes to snap open and brought her to reality.

"You need not frown. I am very sorry that I fell asleep at once," Hades said. "I am not usually so thoughtless, but I had a rather strenuous day, and that—that coupling was a little out of the usual for me."

He was sitting beside her on the edge of the rock, his body turned so he could look at her. Below the end of his short tunic, which came barely to his hips, he was naked. He should have looked ridiculous—he did, and

Persephone giggled—but nonetheless she could feel a ripple in the muscles of her belly.

"I have no idea when you fell asleep," she said, blinking in confusion. "I think I was before you." Then the exasperation in his voice irritated her. "After all," she went on, "my day was no easier than yours. I was abducted, not you."

"But that cost you no effort," Hades pointed out, trying to sound indignant but laughing. "I did all the work of the abduction. I had to half strangle you, carry you—and you are no wraith—and bring you with me through the rock, which is hard labor, I assure you."

"What happened to me," Persephone pronounced in as high and mighty a tone as she could manage when she wanted to laugh too, "was very exhausting."

"Tell me about it!" Hades exclaimed, the corners of his mouth quivering. "I thought I would fly all to bits."

She shuddered, suddenly sobered. "I am sorry. I do not know how to control myself."

"Mother forbid you ever try," he said, giving up the struggle and grinning from ear to ear.

"But you told me it was dangerous, that I could have killed a lesser mage."

"A lesser mage," he echoed, laughter gone, his face hard with fury. "What do you want with a lesser mage?"

Persephone shrank away from eyes flat as polished obsidian. "Nothing," she cried. "I did not even know I had a Gift. How could I learn how to use it?"

The rage disappeared as quickly as it had erupted. He laughed again, full throated, throwing his head back. "Your Gift. I thought we were talking about

. . ." He hesitated and then with a secretive half-smile said delicately, "our worship of the Mother."

Except for the small flick of desire when her eyes had fallen on his bare lower body, Persephone had been distracted from that memory. Now it returned and with it the explanation of Hades's sudden anger. He was jealous! The knowledge gave her intense satisfaction and recalled a more immediate memory—the way he had said their coupling was "out of the usual" for him. Her fair skin colored.

Hades had been silent, watching her, but he made no direct comment about her flushed face. "You are so enchanting that I have lost all common sense." He smiled and touched her cheek gently. "But you are right and I a fool. We have far to go and may face other dangers. If you are willing to add to my strength, you had best know how—and you had best know how to seal what you have within you so that no mage can sense your Gift or draw from you without your consent."

"You also?" she asked softly.

"Yes." His reply was short and hard.

She sat up and kissed him on the lips, holding the cloak so that it covered her upper body, which was as bare as his bottom. Although she completed the movement, she squeaked with dismay before he could respond. "Oh, I ache and I am all sticky."

"I hurt you," he said softly. "I did not mean to. I meant to be gentle. You drove me out of my wits."

Again memory brought a flush to her skin, part shame but more a flash of recalled pleasure. She shrugged. "You are not alone to blame. I am very ignorant and hurt myself too."

Hades shook his head. "I cannot believe you are

real. I cannot think of any other woman alive who would face the dangers you have faced without complaining, and share the blame—"

"Not without complaining," Persephone pointed out, looking up at him through her lashes. "I have complained in the past and reserve the right to do so—loud and long—in the future." She laughed. "Do not make me into some perfect ideal or you will be sadly disappointed." Then she shook her head. "And sharing the blame does not absolve you of quite shocking behavior."

"You did not appear to be at all shocked—" Hades began, and then rolled his eyes up. "I wonder if I will ever learn not to snap at the bait you cast for me. Persephone, how is it that no one has murdered you?"

She began to laugh again but stopped and looked down at her hands. "I do not believe I ever had anyone to tease before. One cannot tease someone who will be hurt and cry."

Hades did not respond to her remark. He bent and groped around the base of the stone, afraid his face or his voice would betray his satisfaction. She was his, all his, forever his—not because she responded to his lovemaking but because she trusted him and could laugh with him; that was a rare and precious bond. Still, he knew it would be a mistake to let her see his certainty. That might breed resentment. Let her believe she was still free.

When he sat up, his kilt in hand, he said, "What we both need is a hot bath."

"Oh yes!" Persephone agreed, then she frowned. "But if you heat the pool, the fish will die. I think we have done enough damage to them already, poor things."

Hades stood, wrapped the kilt around himself, and tied it in place. "No, no. There are natural hot pools," he said, but he spoke absently and swung his head, muttering when he found what he was looking for, "There it is. I wonder how it got all the way over there."

He went almost to the flat rock where they had eaten to pick up his belt, and closed it over kilt and tunic, turning his head and raising a brow when Persephone giggled. They both remembered him flinging the belt away, but she said nothing and Hades shrugged and went to pick up the empty flask that had held wine. While he rinsed it and the remaining cup and filled both with water, Persephone pulled her gown up and reinserted her arms into the sleeves. She found her girdle on the other side of the rock and simply wound it around her waist until it was short enough to tie fast, making no attempt to recreate the elaborate folds and crossings of the previous morning. By the time Hades carried the filled cup and some sprigs of mentha to her, she was able to drop the cloak and still be decent.

The refreshing taste of mint chewed and rubbed over her teeth with a frayed twig somehow seemed to ease her aching muscles, and she was hungry enough to make movement to the "table" rock the lesser evil. An excellent breakfast—cold baked fish and lily bulbs and cress kept fresh in the pool—made her feel even better, so that when Hades rolled up the fleeces, she packed the basket and made ready to go with only a few grimaces to mark her twinges.

The path Hades chose was an easy one. It led away from the outer world at a sharp angle to the passage from which they had entered. Persephone thought

Hades was wary as he indicated their path. Perhaps he expected her to cry out against going deeper into the caves, but she felt no reluctance, being utterly content to go anywhere so long as she was with him. Since she was not prepared to admit that, she merely remarked that she hoped there would be no climbing or crawling.

Hades said he could not promise, he only knew the way was open. When she groaned dramatically, he promised to carry her if the passage became difficult, and she rejected his offer with a show of indignation, commenting that he had already insulted her by saying she was heavy. He assured her blandly that he liked well-fleshed women, and she had turned to him, quite cross, until she saw the gleam in his black eyes, whereupon she said, equally blandly, she was glad of it, since she did like to tuck into a meal. Hades threw up his hands like a fencer who acknowledges a point, and she giggled and asked a perfectly inoffensive question about how Hades lived in Plutos.

She found his answer so interesting and so evocative of further questions that she was quite surprised when Hades stopped and said they would go down through the rock and be within a short walk of the hot baths. Persephone found sinking into the stone floor more terrifying than passing through it in the passage. It was quite dreadful to see Hades's feet and legs swallowed up, and she bit her lip and hid her face. Hades patted her comfortingly and, surprisingly, admitted he did not like the look of sinking either.

They were so long in passing that Persephone would have screamed or wept when she discovered she could not ask Hades if anything were wrong, but she could not scream or weep either. Her mind was a black pit of horror, and she prayed to the Mother for death, which would be far, far preferable to being entombed forever alive, able to think but not to see or hear or feel. That last word saved her from despair and madness because she realized she *could* feel; a soft pressure slid upward over her body as if she were sinking into mud. Hot mud, too, she thought, and found something new to worry about: whether Hades had misjudged the place and would bring them out into a cavern full of molten lava.

They came out quite safely, but not as Persephone had begun to imagine, after realizing the heat was growing no more intense, feet first into empty space. Hades laughed for quite some time over that idea when she told him of it, chuckling over a vision of them hanging from the roof with their heads in the rock and dropping, who knew how far, to the floor below. What did happen was that when the sensation of sliding downward stopped, Hades took a single long step sideways and they were out into . . . Tartarus?

The great cavern certainly looked like a place of torment. It was barely lit by Hades's power, except immediately around them, because the roof and walls were so far away, and gouts of steam billowed up with giant hissings from basins worn into the floor by water spilling from cracks in the ceiling. The place smelled of sulfur and hot metal too.

"Mercy!" Persephone exclaimed. "I said I wanted a hot bath, not to be boiled alive."

Hades only laughed and took her free hand, leading her surely past the steaming basins to where an overflow had carved a quiet stream. She could choose her own temperature, he told her, hotter near the center, and cooler, though never cold, as it approached the wall of the cavern, where it disappeared into a jagged crack in the rock already worn smooth near the base.

He left her to drop the cloak, remove her gown, and enter the knee-deep water, returning a short time later with the cup full of sand as fine as powder. Persephone's hand half rose to hide her breasts, but she used it instead to take the cup from Hades, who was extending it blindly, his head politely turned away. She did not look around to see where he was but used the sand vigorously to rub away the stains of earth on her hands and more gently on those on her thighs. She was smiling a little when she rose from the water and did not attempt to hide her body while she reached for her gown to dry herself with its cleaner parts.

That done, she pulled the cloak around her almost regretfully—and not because it was really too warm in the cavern for a cloak. But when she looked around, Hades was nowhere in sight, and she wrinkled her nose, not sure whether she was annoyed or relieved. It never occurred to her to be afraid she had been abandoned, and after a moment's thought, she knelt beside the stream and washed her gown, slapping it on the rock border as she had been taught to do with the garments of the Corn Goddess.

Persephone laughed when she thought of her complaint about always being the priestess who had to do the washing, and then again when she remembered Dorkas saying she would need to do no washing when she was Queen of the Dead. But then she sat back on her heels. Surely that remark implied that Dorkas knew she would be taken by Hades. And how had Hades known she would be on that road at that time? Not by chance. No, it was not by chance, because

Hades had told her he had caches of food and probably of other essentials like clothes and blankets too. Almost certainly it was Dorkas who had told Hades—no, not Hades, Dorkas was afraid of Hades. She had told Zeus and Zeus had told Hades.

Absently, Persephone wrung the gown as dry as she could and then sat staring down at it. Dorkas and Zeus had wanted to be rid of her? No, Hades had told her he had asked Zeus for a priestess of the Corn Goddess. But why had Zeus chosen her and suggested abduction? He could have asked her mother to send Aglaia or Dorkas herself—no, not Dorkas. Persephone wrung the gown again. Dorkas was warming Zeus's bed. In any case, Zeus had not raised the question with her mother at all. He had deliberately exposed himself to the deepest fury of the high priestess of the Corn Goddess by suggesting Hades take her.

Because he wanted Hades to have a suitable wife? Persephone remembered Hades saying more than once that he was fond of Zeus, and that regard might easily be returned, for Hades, surprising as it might be, was a man easy to love. For a moment Persephone lost the thread of her thought while she considered just how easy she found it to love Hades.

Zeus, however, was not a woman, and there were many suitable partners for Hades in Olympus. After all, the priestess and wife did not have to be the same woman. Zeus would need more than a desire to see his brother well wed as a reason to incite her mother's wrath. Which brought Persephone around to her first thought: Zeus wanted to be rid of her, and Dorkas had been willing to help him.

It was an unsettling notion, and Persephone was grateful when Hades suddenly loomed over her. His hair and beard sparkled with water, and he was carrying his damp tunic in his hand. The wide collar of gem-studded gold looked even more exotic against his pale skin. He caught her eyes resting on it and smiled when they moved away to examine more carefully his well-muscled body, but all he said was, "I can lay your gown out over some hot rocks nearer the center away from the water. It will dry fast there."

She started to hand it to him and had a vision of the poor thing all creased and crumpled in ways that would make her body appear thick and ugly. "I would rather lay it out myself," she said.

"It is hot," he warned, but unlike her mother did not continue to caution her when she rose to her feet.

He wore an odd little smile that Persephone did not entirely like as he watched her fold the gown into careful, long pleats, but he made no remarks about it, although he only dropped his own tunic over some nearby rocks. She tchked at his carelessness and smoothed the garment carefully. When she was finished, he led her back into a passage that was brilliant with lit crystal, set the rolled fleeces against the wall so they could sit in comfort, and began to teach her how to grow a layer inside her skin that would allow no energy in or out.

At first it was surprisingly difficult. Even when she caught the concept of growing an inner skin, she forgot to cover parts of herself and Hades would send out a Need that leapt upon her Gift wherever it was exposed and sucked at it. The gown was dry long before she learned the lesson, and they set out on their way along the crystal-lit passage. Oddly, Persephone found it easier to concentrate on her inner body when her outer was occupied in a rote task that required no thought. And at last Hades found an image—repulsive though it was—that made the feat possible.

"It is like a wet bladder in an uneven crock," he said. "When you fill the bladder, it bends and creases into every irregularity. When it dries, you could create another crock with the same holes and cracks and lumps by pressing clay to the outside of the bladder."

She saw it hanging limp, wet and slimy inside her. She filled the bladder with power and felt it expand; filled it fuller, and it snapped into place, sealing her off, heart and mind, from everything. It was a horrible feeling, as if there were a thin wall cutting her off from life. She saw Hades blink, as if he had seen something that shocked him, and then she felt him open his Need into a yawning maw. Previously he had waited for her to say she was ready, but the suddenness of his attack did not affect her.

Nothing poured out of her wrists, as it had when she had forgotten to include her hands in her protective envelope, or trickled from behind her eyes or from inside her ears. She was aware of everything; she could see, hear, touch, smell, even taste the typical musty coolness of the water-carved passageway through which they passed, but she felt no response to those stimuli. She knew Hades was trying to draw power from her. She saw his black eyes narrow, his brows knit, his lips thin, but she did not feel his Need. Whatever was within her lay quiet, untouched by his effort. Hades smiled and nodded.

"You have it," he said.

His approval brought no pleasure. "Hades," she whimpered, catching at him, "I am locked inside myself. Let me out. Let me out!"

He clasped her to him. She could feel his arms

around her, feel the warmth of his body, but she *felt* nothing.

"Softly, love, softly," he murmured. "You closed yourself in, only you can unlock yourself. To be open is the easy part." And he began to suggest images she could use to be rid of the wall inside herself.

What he said was not necessary. His calm assurance was enough. She had shed the inner skin before he was done talking—emptied it first, then made it thinner, like fine tanned human skin, and finally crumpled it into a little leathery lump, which she stored below her heart. Hades stopped explaining abruptly and Persephone realized he was aware she was open and vulnerable again. Before he could urge her, she had drawn out the crumpled leathery bag, refilled it, and retreated within herself. As before, he knew without telling that she was protected and launched first a most persuasive plea and then a violent assault.

After she was content with her mastery, they talked about nothing and laughed a great deal, until Hades led her outside again. There was little to be gathered in this valley this early in the spring, although there would be berries and nuts in the autumn. Seemingly in the past it had been gleaned too thoroughly of plants with edible roots and bulbs for those to restore themselves, but Hades brought down two thin hares with his sling and they ate the rather stringy meat with some of the remaining cooked arum.

"You would eat better if you were willing to let me hunt hudorhaix," he said when she remarked that her jaws were tired of chewing.

"We will see," she replied, but this time she did not shudder at the thought.

She enjoyed being out, but she did not mind going

in again. By now she looked forward every moment to seeing some new marvel of beauty when a passageway opened into a cavern, and she was not disappointed. The shapes and colors into which the rock was carved were infinite. In one small open space, a clear pool held what appeared to be perfect pearls of all sizes, and in another there were huge white crayfish.

They had those for supper that night, and after eating, Hades began to instruct her on how to control the flow of her power. She found that, which he had apparently thought would be the most difficult, very easy. She had only to imagine little holes in the skin gloves inside her fingers through which the power could ooze and be directed and which she could even shut off temporarily by clenching her fists.

Nonetheless, she was very tired by the time she had each detail of management perfect and said so. Instead of eagerly spreading the fleeces, Hades looked away. Persephone had just begun to wonder, sick at heart, whether he had found joining their bodies distasteful, when he looked back, his brow furrowed with anxiety.

"I must tell you—not because I care but because it will be dangerous to you—that when you close off your power . . ." He looked down at his hands which were tightly clasped in his lap.

"What?" Persephone breathed. "I saw you look strangely at me when I first did it, and I saw that you knew when I had freed myself from my inner wall. What makes you so uneasy?"

"You lose much of your beauty," he said flatly.

"I see," she said, equally flatly. "But that is your problem, not mine. Do you want a wife and priestess who is no beauty and shows no trace of a Gift or one who is falsely lovely and might make other mages envious?"

Hades grinned broadly. "I want a wife and priestess named Persephone no matter how she looks. Beauty is a good thing, but there are many beautiful women, more beautiful than you even when you are enhanced by power. What I have never found is a woman of your charm and wit and courage."

"You are a most skillful flatterer," she said, pleased—until her eyes widened with the realization that he had trapped her into an open admission that she would accept his offer to make her wife and priestess. "Ooohh," she breathed. "That was a sly trick. Was any of that tale true?"

He laughed. "Well, the change is slight, but I felt it at once, so another mage might also notice and find a clue to your Gift. Since you cannot live all the time with your power sealed off—" Persephone huddled in on herself at the thought of living totally cut off from life, and Hades put an arm around her. "There is no need for that. Your Gift is only apparent when you give or someone draws from you, apurpose or by accident. Tomorrow, you can try to retain the enhancement of your beauty while binding within you all else. Now we must sleep. You must be very tired."

Persephone sighed agreement but roused from her troubled thoughts to ask why Hades was separating the fleeces by a substantial distance—unless, she said, her new ugliness had given him a distaste for her.

"Do not be a fool," he snapped. "If I lie with you, I will keep you awake all night. I thought you would want time to heal."

"Have you so little self-control?"

"Yes," he said rather grimly. "You have only a choice of a hard bed or a hard man."

Whereupon they both burst into laughter and Hades piled the fleeces together. As he had foretold, they had a restless night—about which neither complained—and slept late into the third day. Not long after they finally started out, Persephone caught at Hades's arm and told him that she smelled the moss of a blue-light cave. After some argument, she agreed to let him go ahead and look for trouble. He was soon back, assuring her she would be safe if she stayed near where the passage entered, away from the water.

Then Hades hunted while Persephone gathered the topmost, tenderest shoots of the spicy moss and a whole basketful of mushrooms. She did not see and did not ask what he had killed. The dripping slabs of meat he unwrapped from layers of moss when they reached a good place to sleep looked no different than those that were carved from cattle by the slaughterers of Olympus, and they tasted delicious when broiled on a bed of red-hot stones.

More than enough remained for the next day, but proved to be unnecessary, which annoyed Persephone, who would have gladly left the basket behind if she had known. The passage they started into in the morning grew more and more difficult. Twice they had to climb sheer walls by handholds and footholds and once they needed to crawl. Although she made no complaint, Persephone was starting to worry when she had to flatten herself to her belly.

Then Hades, who had been staring at walls and floors in an abstracted fashion all morning, took them sideways and possibly farther down through a mass of fractured rock. That was, Persephone found, a more horrifying experience than the long descent to the cave of the hot pools because of the intermittent flickering through reality and the non-world of being inside stone. She was somewhat dazed when they came out in a cave of exquisite fluted pillars and crystal-laced walls, but it was not the beauty of the place that fixed her wandering wits. Her eyes had found the one unnatural thing in the place—bundles stacked against the walls.

A hasty unpacking exposed well-wrapped meat and cheese and bread held fresh by spells, blankets and grass-stuffed pallets, a packet with a fine silver comb and brush and scented creams and oils and fine pumice stones for grooming, and two gowns that made Persephone's eyes stare with greed.

"I owe you three more," Hades said, looking at her from the corner of his eye as he spread them before her.

Persephone could not help licking her lips, but she did her best to seem indifferent and answered coolly, "Yes, but I do not think either of those will be very practical if we have much more climbing and crawling to do."

One gown was a fine rich purple wool with long sleeves bordered in gold, the collar and hem set with pale topazes and bright amethysts. The other was a very dark blue, held with bright pins on each shoulder, of so thin a fabric that Persephone could see her hand as a pale blur though it when she lifted the skirt. It was quite stiff, being embroidered in wide bands with silver thread, but between the bands the wearer's body would show, barely veiled.

"I assure you your trials are ended," Hades said. "This would have been our first night's stop if we had gone the way I planned. From here, all the passages are easy and all the caverns safe and beautiful. I intended to make my home palatable to you, you know."

She looked up from the rich gowns. "In honesty—I will give you my promise to quicken your fields and seed no matter what you tell me—how palatable will Plutos be to me?"

"How can I answer that?"

He looked around at the delicately ridged columns, polished smooth and gleaming by the water that built them and ate them, at the intricately branched formations of crystal that grew from the walls and glowed with power—white and pink and blue and pale green.

"To me it is more beautiful, more desirable, than any other place. I love it—both dark and bright, the silence, the purity of sound when there is a sound"— he put fingers to a small cut in his shoulder that had sent a trickle of blood, now dry, down his arm—"even the unexpected knife of crystal that flays my skin. The sun and the wind I enjoy, but they are too changeable, too restless. After these many years in the unchanging caves, the constant movement of light and shadow, the constant whine and whisper, make me uneasy. But I cannot speak for you."

"That is not what I meant," Persephone said. "Will I like your people? Will I find friends?"

"If you are asking me sidelong whether you will find yourself the target of hatred by a bevy of beauties who have been supplanted in my affections, I will tell you again there are none such. I have taken my pleasure with several women in the past year or two, but all of them live by that trade."

"No, you vain man," she said, smiling slightly.

"That is not what I meant either. I meant exactly what I asked."

"A queen cannot afford to have many friends. It will be best to choose carefully among those you learn you can trust. To open yourself to all—"

"I have sense enough not to do that. I suppose what I want to know is whether I will be welcome or only tolerated as a hated necessity."

Hades smiled. "In that sense I am sure you will find Plutos palatable. You will be welcomed with open hearts, deep respect, and high hopes. It will be harder to ward off those who wish to be your friends than to discover those who find you acceptable."

"I have never had to do that," Persephone said. "My mother often warded away even those I would have liked to know, and I never understood why. Do you think my judgment was at fault?"

"Oh, no. You will not catch me in the snare of criticizing your judgment. I think it very likely your mother was overprotective. On the other hand, I suspect you have too tender a heart—and you are young. You should be on guard against letting your heart be too easily touched. However, I will not pick and choose your companions. I will only tell you of a few men and women you must learn to accept because they live and work in my palace and are dear to me. Even so, you need not feel those folk must be your friends."

Over the next three days, between times when Persephone worked on perfecting control of her Gift, Hades told her much about Plutos and its people and how he ruled them. Those who were his chief helpers were Koios, his steward, who had made plain to him that a priestess would be necessary if the people of Plutos were not to starve; Sisyphus, who was in charge of the

mines that provided ores for smelting into metals and
black rock for burning; Arachne, who oversaw the
womenservants of the palace and had woven the cloth
for the gowns Persephone had found so lovely; and
four or five others whose names did not stick in Persephone's mind.

Those three she remembered because she had heard
of them before. All had been considered criminals,
Koios by Kronos and Sisyphus and Arachne by other
powerful mages favored of Zeus. They were now—
dead.

Chapter 9

Persephone did not mention to Hades that those whom he named as his servants were dead. She knew he would only laugh and speak again that puzzle—that they were dead in the outer world but alive in Plutos—but it made her uneasy. Thus, despite Hades's assurances and the improvement in her spirits and appearance provided by the supplies, Persephone found herself fearful and shy when he told her they were near the home caves. She put a determined smile on her face, but perhaps he felt the hand she had slipped into his tremble or sensed her quickened breathing.

"I will take you to the palace first," he said. "You can rest and make yourself ready. Then you need only stand beside me, as you are accustomed to standing beside your mother in ceremonies. I will show you to my people and tell them of the treasure I have brought to Plutos. You need not speak. You will then be able to meet singly with those you wish to meet, in my presence if you like, or alone."

"Thank you," Persephone said. "I am sure I will soon grow accustomed."

They turned aside from the tunnel they were following into a narrower way. Eventually Hades carried her through a thick dividing wall into a chamber of such exquisite beauty that for a moment she forgot her fears entirely. In another moment her fears were supplanted by renewed wonder when she realized that this was no natural beauty. The room had been carved into solid rock, and gems had been set into the walls to make pictures. Here was a hunting party in a blue-light cave, there a party of men by a river. She looked away with some effort. Chandeliers of bronze hung from the ceiling, each arm cupping a glowing crystal the size of a man's fist.

"This is my bedchamber—*our* bedchamber," Hades said.

"I will never be able to sleep in here."

"You do not like it?" Hades tone was carefully neutral.

Persephone laughed. "Oh, Hades, how can you ask such a silly question? Who could not like—love—such work? I will not be able to sleep because I will be too busy looking at the pictures."

"Ah, that need not trouble you. I think I can distract you. Or we could release the spell and lie in the dark."

He led her past the huge bed that gleamed like gold to a curtain-hung doorway; smiling, he lifted the curtain. Persephone stepped in and gasped in surprise. There was a woman facing her, also looking shocked. She stepped back hurriedly, treading on Hades's toes. He yelped and hopped back out of the room, lifting his foot to rub it.

"How dare you!" she gasped, turning on him. "You told me there was no woman in your household." And then, more furiously, when he began to whoop with laughter, "How dare you laugh at me."

"It is not easy," he said, still grinning. "As I have said before, you are no wraith and I think you have squashed my toes."

"I wish I had squashed something else!" Persephone hissed.

"Oh no, you do not," Hades got out between gasps. "You would be very sorry because I am totally innocent."

"She is not your woman?"

"Yes, indeed she is, but—" He caught Persephone's hand, which she had raised to strike him. "I am innocent, I say," he repeated, still chuckling. "Go in and look the woman in the face. Then if you still wish to be rid of her, I will arrange it."

"I will arrange it myself," Persephone snarled, and flung back the curtain.

To her astonishment, the woman was still in exactly the same place. It was not reasonable for her to stand there, neither to come forward to listen nor to retreat, considering the conversation between herself and Hades. Then she saw that the woman's color was not natural. A strange gray tinge covered her face, arms, and gown. She must be one of the dead, Persephone thought, and felt shocked by Hades's laughter. And then she saw behind the woman the curtain she had just passed, and then Hades, who had lifted it. A mirror!

First she laughed and then she gasped. Her mother had a small, unusually flat round of silver, polished so fine she could see her face. However, Demeter had seldom allowed Persephone to look in it because it needed such careful handling. A brush with a fingertip soon created a dark blemish that required long, careful polishing to restore the brightness without creating distortion. Persephone had sometimes used the reflection in a quiet pond or a dark bowl filled with water, but she had never seen her whole self and seldom seen her face upright instead of bent forward.

"Am I forgiven?" Hades asked.

Persephone smiled. "Of what is it made?"

"Rock, but I am not sure what kind. We tried this and that. I melted the surface until it ran all together and then we polished it smooth. It is a little darker than I wanted, but the best I could find to have ready for you. I did not adorn the chamber. I thought you should choose what you liked for your private room. And you will have the temple too, of course."

"I will have my own apartment in the temple?"

"Yes, of course."

"Why?" The question snapped with suspicion.

Hades smiled and shook his head. "Not because I wish ever to be rid of you, Persephone. But I do not know what mysteries you practice. If there are rituals congress with a man would profane—"

Persephone laughed. "There are rituals that must be performed in the absence of men, yes, but My Lady watches over the quickening of life, and congress between male and female is necessary, not profane."

"I will do all in my power to aid Her," Hades said and kissed her. "You can give the chambers in the temple to your chief acolyte."

Not until I know her well, Persephone thought, curving her lips into a meaningless smile, which soon became truly warm and approving. It had occurred to Persephone that she need not fear her position might be usurped. She would be not only high priestess but queen.

Meanwhile, Hades had led her through another doorway in the bedchamber into a very long, narrow room crowded with tables, upon which were many tools and heaps of bright gems and what looked like dull pebbles. She realized that this must be Hades's workroom, where dull pebbles became precious stones, and began to ask questions, which he promised to answer another time, since he wished to show her the whole of the private apartment in the palace.

A third door led to a bathing room, with a sunken tub of bright-veined marble. Removing one stone in the wall above it released a stream of warm water, which filled the tub if another stone were dropped into a hole in the bottom. A waist-high basin of the same marble and a similar arrangement of fitted stones provided a place to wash face and hands if one did not wish to bathe. Beyond the washing room was a much smaller chamber with a privy stool. In the small space, the sound of running water—doubtless a stream below the stool—was apparent.

The last door—a real door of wood with a thick metal bar to keep it locked—led out into a square corridor that opened into three audience chambers: one was quite large and as gorgeous as Hades's bedroom, but in place of the bed was a long polished stone table and many chairs, the one at the far end a magnificent, gilded throne, while that at the near end, if not quite as high, was even more magnificently gilded and set with gems; the second room, also strikingly adorned, was only suitable for a few people to sit comfortably and talk; the third was a lived-in room furnished with thick-cushioned couches, sagging leather chairs, and a small round table at one side.

"This is where you live," Persephone said, looking around and sinking into a chair.

"Yes, where my friends come to talk at ease."

Persephone smiled. "How like you, Hades, to make the greatest mark of your affection an invitation to a shabby room."

"If you wish it to be furnished anew, you need only give the order."

She laughed at him. "I would not change a stick— oh, yes, I will have to ask you to add one straight chair so that I can sit at my embroidery . . . Oh, that was left behind."

"You need only say what you want, and you will have it. If you were doing some special piece, I can retrieve it for you if you can tell me exactly where it is."

If he were caught, her mother would discover where she was. She shook her head and put out her hand to him. "You are too indulgent to me. I will gladly start anew. It was a veil for the Goddess and it would be very wrong to steal that, even to adorn Her in a different place."

He took the hand she had held out, but before he could answer there was, distantly, the sound of a door opening, a soft thud, a dragging scrape, another thud. Hades bent down and said softly, "That is Koios. If you wish, I will go out and tell him to wait in one of the other rooms." He hesitated and then said, clearly reluctantly, "If you prefer, I will tell him not to come into this chamber without invitation."

"No, let him come," Persephone said, although she had to force out the words. She felt sick and guilty, although what had happened to Koios had happened before she was born. Still, Olympus had been the home of his people before Kronos drove them out, and the sound of the stick and the dragging leg made a vivid picture of what Hades had said about Koios being crippled by Kronos. She lifted frightened eyes to Hades. "He will hate me if you forbid him what I am sure has always been precious to him."

"He will not hate you, but . . . it would hurt him, and he has been too much hurt already."

Persephone found a smile and Hades kissed her swiftly, murmuring thanks before he straightened and went to the door. She heard a grating voice, one that sounded as broken as the body, utter a cry of surprise and then an anxious question.

"She is here," Hades said, "and we are both unhurt. I am sorry we are late and worried you, but my lady is no meek slave. She did not take lightly being abducted without first asking her permission."

"An abduction presupposes lack of permission," the gravelly voice stated with great earnestness. "It was unreasonable for her to expect you to apply for permission."

Quite without volition, Persephone giggled. She had not the smallest doubt that Koios intended to be funny. That was just the straight-faced kind of jest Hades favored.

"Perhaps," Hades replied dryly, "but not unreasonable for her to be angry. Owing to her determination not to yield tamely to having her will crossed, we had to take a roundabout path."

"As long as you are both here and safe, all is well," Koios said. "But now I will go back to my chambers. It would be better, I think, if *you* came to *me* in the future, or sent for me when you are alone so that sight of me will not offend the queen."

"No friend so dear and so loyal to Hades can offend me," Persephone said from the doorway.

Her voice was steady and her face calm, but that was because the first shock of seeing Koios had been absorbed while the men were still talking. She did not think she would ever get over the terrible wrenching pity she felt when she stepped softly to the doorway and looked out, but she hoped she did not show it. He must have been broader and taller than Hades before he was broken to bits. Now one leg was short and too thick; the other, more like its natural length, was oddly twisted and trailed behind. His arms were bent unnaturally too, and his head leaned almost to his shoulder, the nose smashed flat and one ear missing.

He shrank into himself and swung his crutch as if to turn away, but Hades put a hand on his shoulder and said, "This is our priestess and my queen, Persephone."

"A dazzling brightness you will be in Plutos, Queen Persephone," Koios said. Then he took a deep breath and added, "And if you are still angry at being brought here, the blame should fall on me. I am the one who convinced King Hades that Plutos must have its own crops and flocks."

"If I wished to lay blame," Persephone replied, smiling, "it would be upon Zeus, who despite his claims, has no right to dispose of me like a parcel of goods. However, your king is a most persuasive person. I am no longer angry. Come in and join us. I was just saying to Hades that I would like to have a straight chair and a frame for embroidery here. Do I apply to you for such things?"

"The queen gives an order," Koios said, starting forward by placing his crutch, then lifting the leg he could stand on and swinging it forward, dragging the other behind. "The queen does not apply to anyone."

Persephone turned and stepped into the room, but then she turned to face him again so he would be sure she was not afraid to watch his painful progress. In turning, her eyes met Hades's and she saw such gratitude and relief that she was repaid many times for controlling her revulsion. She felt strong and sure of herself, no longer frightened of meeting the "dead" of Plutos. If Koios had died in Olympus, which she thought not impossible from the injuries he had suffered, he was nonetheless truly alive here. The thump of the stick that supported him, the scrape of his dragging leg, were proof of his solidity. There was nothing of the cold, thin shade about him.

She smiled at him when he had dropped into the nearest chair. "Do you want the dazzling queen to put her big foot in her mouth?" she asked. "In Plutos, strange things are precious, like bread, and others, precious in Olympus, like gold and jewels, are near worthless. I suppose what I was really asking was whether you or another would warn me if I was making an unreasonable demand before I gave an order."

"You can have anything you want," Hades said. "It is my purpose to make you happy here."

"Yes, and if what I desire is important to me, I might insist, even if it cost high, but—" Persephone turned toward Koios and made an exasperated gesture. "Hades is far too indulgent. I do not wish to make enemies or wake envy by asking for what is difficult to obtain out of ignorance when the thing itself is of little importance to me."

"That is reasonable—and generous—my queen," Koios said. "And I will be glad to warn you, and to obtain even what I warn you against if you still desire it, but you will have your servants and your acolytes—"

"But I will not know which among them to trust at first."

"No one will try to hurt you here," Hades said.

She smiled at him. "Not apurpose . . . perhaps. But people will lie for many reasons: because they think they would be pleasing me, because they fear to tell an unpleasant truth. I know I can trust Koios because— forgive me, I do not mean to hurt you, Koios, but I know you *cannot* aspire to Hades's place, nor could any selfish act give you more power than you already hold through his affection. Thus, I am sure your first interest is Hades's welfare, and you will not let me damage that."

Koios stared at her for a moment then twisted himself around to look at Hades and broke into a gargling laugh. "The queen is already wiser than the king, who has too great a trust in the goodness of men . . . and women."

Hades shrugged. "It is too late for that warning."

"Do not think me that kind of fool," Persephone said, looking at Koios with a mingling of amusement and admiration. It took tremendous courage to utter that challenge when Hades had indicated plainly enough that he was too enslaved to struggle. "I have not the smallest desire to wield the king's power. For one thing, I could not. I have not his Gift. For another, I have power of my own as high priestess of the Goddess."

Koios bowed his head as much as was possible in its

twisted position. "You are wise beyond your years, my lady."

"It does not take many years of serving in a temple to learn what ambition can do."

As the words came out of her mouth, Persephone felt like a fool. How many times over the past days had she wondered why Dorkas and Zeus had wanted to be rid of her? Zeus's reasons were still a mystery, but in Dorkas's case, Persephone now understood. Dorkas wished to be high priestess, and that would be totally out of her grasp as long as Persephone—no, not Persephone, Kore—was in Olympus.

Persephone had to put her thoughts aside at that point and pay attention. She needed to do no more than nod to Koios's further complimentary remark, but then he asked when she wished to meet the other high servants on Hades's staff, and she decided it would be best to be done with it at once. She found it less a trial than she expected, none of the others having been as harshly used as Koios and none being as dear to Hades. She needed only to be polite.

The next day cryers were dispatched to tell all the dwellers of the underworld that their king had chosen a queen and that the queen was also a priestess learned in the mysteries of the Corn Goddess. The people were summoned to acknowledge queen and priestess. Audience would be held in the great cave every day for a ten-day period. In particular, every female must present herself to be tested for a place in the temple.

Persephone worried that she would not be able to find enough women with the urge to serve the Goddess, and in the privacy of their bedchamber asked Hades if his people would obey. He laughed.

"None can live without bringing the fruit of their

toil, be it cut gems, dug ore, smelted or hammered metal, or whatever else they make to me or one of my deputies. Most food and cloth or wool or linen comes from the outer world, where they cannot go. The worth of their labor is exchanged for what they need to live. No one would dare disobey."

He saw the trouble in her eyes and laughed again. "Dear love, most will not wish to disobey. Some have enough brains to look forward to a day when the fields will bear enough to make bread plentiful and provide fodder for herds and flocks. Most will be curious and hope for a festival to celebrate my handfasting. A few will grumble that possession of an Olympian woman is making the king arrogant."

"The men," Persephone said. "But some of the women will be terrified. For this reason or that, some will think being chosen for service in the temple a dreadful fate."

"Then do not choose them," Hades said.

"I will not if there are enough with the touch of the Goddess on them. But what if there are not enough? Only about one in ten in Olympus are fit for temple service. What if many fewer—or none—of the native women can serve?"

"I do not know," Hades said. "But many of my people are Gifted. Hatred and fear of their Gifts is what sent them here to Plutos. Why worry before trouble comes?"

He kissed her lips and then her throat. A gesture extinguished the crystals in the chandeliers. Only a single gem-picture on the wall remained glowing softly, that of a fall of water over a low cliff. It was a waste of power, for Persephone's eyes closed as

Hades's mouth traveled downward. She did not need to see, only to feel.

She had a flicker of guilt over how easily he was able to divert her, but it had no chance to grow because he proved to be right over the next ten days. At the time alloted to them, even those who grumbled and feared came to an immense cavern lit not with powered crystals but with common pitch torches. These circled rows of white stone columns, not natural artifacts but worked until smooth so they reflected the light.

When the people were gathered each day, Hades and Persephone came through the great gates of worked brass that closed off the wide passage out of which the palace had been carved. They stood on the dais while Hades made Persephone known and restated the purpose of the summoning; then they seated themselves, Hades in his immense throne and Persephone in a chair somewhat less massive but as ornately and richly decorated. The people came forward in twos and threes and family groups.

On the very first day, Persephone knew she would not need to force any woman to serve her—every third showed the golden shimmer that betrayed the touch of the Goddess, and even more of the children were gifted—so she left the choosing until she could summon the women to the temple itself. She asked to see it on the eleventh day of her sojourn in Plutos, the eighteenth since Hades had thrown his cloak around her and carried her off.

To her surprise, it was no great distance. At the far end of the cavern there was a steep chimney into which a curving stair had been carved. At the top was a passage through which a fierce wind blew from one of those wide, low mouths she had seen before. Beyond the mouth was a lovely valley, and to the right, built into the slope of the mountain so that it overlooked all the open land, was a glistening white temple. A path led from the cave mouth to the building.

"There is nothing inside except the image of the Goddess," Hades said. "I did not know what else was necessary. I did not even know whether it was permitted that a man make the image, but I wanted to do it. And since the temple is not yet consecrated, I thought it could be moved or destroyed if it was not suitable."

"Did you wish for Her help when you made the image?" Persephone asked.

"With all my heart and soul," Hades replied. "Even if the crops in the outworld are better next year, there is a limit to our ability to trade, and the number of my people grows. If the Goddess does not bless us, we will soon face starvation." He hesitated, staring at the temple ahead. "I do not know what you will think. I had an image in my mind of such delicate beauty, but . . . It is not what I planned. I swear that the stone formed under my hands of its own will, and I was afraid to try to change it."

They said no more until Persephone stood before the image. Then she touched Hades's hand and whispered, "It is She." And before her courage could fail—for she suddenly knew her mother could not hand down the place of high priestess as a man handed down his chattels to his child—she lifted her arms and cried, "Mother, bless us."

With the words, her power poured out in a flood far beyond what she had passed to Hades in the cave of the golden death. Her vision dimmed and her limbs grew weak. She heard Hades cry out but could not respond, and then as she felt her life drain away with the last of her power, a great golden wave enveloped her, supported her, and what she had poured out was restored with a new, shimmering strength in addition. Then Hades caught her to him.

"Beloved, what befell you?" Hades voice was trembling, his black eyes wide with foreboding. "I thought you would fall, and tried to catch you but I could not touch you."

"I was in the Mother's hand," Persephone whispered, clinging to him.

"I was afraid." He bent his head and kissed her hair. "That face . . . I carved it with my own hands, but I cannot read it. One moment I see the loving kindness of a mother and another I see the inexorable judgment of fate. And do I not deserve punishment? Did I not take a virgin from Her temple? Partly it was to bring Her presence here among us, but, Persephone, partly it was because I lusted for you. I wanted you for myself and I took you without asking Her leave."

Persephone lifted her face and smiled. "The Mother does not frown on lust. Men may set value on virginity, but the Goddess values the fruit of the union of male and female." She turned her head to look at the image. "The danger was not that I am a woman instead of a maid, but that I had some flaw of heart or mind that made me unfit to serve Her. But that is passed. I offered Her what I am, and She accepted me."

She stepped out of Hades's embrace, took his hand, and walked to the portico of the temple, where she looked out over the valley. "There is much to be done."

"Command me, priestess, and whatever you need

will be brought; laborers will be assigned to do your bidding."

Persephone's eyes gleamed with enthusiasm. "The earth must be turned, and then turned again. And I will need seed." She frowned. "Seed is stored in the temple in Olympus. Where will I find—"

"I will obtain seed," Hades said.

"From the temple? Oh, be careful, Hades. If my mother hears of it, she will guess where I am and demand my return."

He touched her face, gently, uncertainly, with none of the assurance he showed when they made love. "Persephone—"

"Yes, Hades?"

He stared at her a moment longer and then burst out, "I cannot bear that you should think yourself a prisoner, that you should be bound to me against your will. You must be free to choose your own world. If you still want me to take you home—" He swallowed hard. "I will."

She laughed and took his hand. "I must choose, indeed. Two women, six maidens, and ten girl-children for the temple. They must be trained, at least partly, by the time the earth is turned and you bring me the seed. The temple must be furnished and formally consecrated. I will be too busy for a long time to talk nonsense."

Chapter 10

In a warm, sunny glade quite near the pool where the garments of the Corn Goddess were washed, Dorkas lifted her head from Zeus's shoulder and said, "Demeter is quite mad."

Zeus sighed. "About the disappearance of Kore, yes. She was back searching my palace again only last week, even though Hera has sworn to her that she would not indulge me in that way and has scryed for Kore more than once."

He was beginning to regret having arranged the disappearance of Demeter's daughter. For one thing, the unremitting grief of the mother distressed him. He expected fury and spite, the emotions she had shown—although she had called them grief—when she accused him of her lover's death. And she had been angry and spiteful, but beneath that was real fear for Kore. Moreover, he had been sure that Dorkas would be able to convince Demeter that the reason Kore could not be found was that the girl did not want to be found, and that if Demeter ceased searching and made clear that Kore could be free to do as she pleased with her life, the girl would show herself.

If he had been able to get such a promise from Demeter, he would have asked Hades to bring Kore back or to allow Demeter to visit her. Hades . . . Zeus had a sudden memory of his brother, who had come about midsummer to assure him that Kore—no, he had named the girl Persephone—was well and happy. There had been something different about Hades, a kind of . . . contentment. Recalling his brother's look, Zeus suddenly felt dissatisfied and—although he wished Hades no ill—thoroughly irritated.

Dorkas was running her fingers around his ear, which he ordinarily found stimulating. Her attentions were so calculated, however, that more and more they left him as unmoved as he was sure they left her. He pulled his head away.

"She is not fit to serve the Goddess," Dorkas said, sitting up, her voice now sharp. "You know she is not. The whole city is complaining about the way she invades their houses without warning and accuses everyone of being in complicity with you."

Zeus looked away from her bare breasts, eyes half hidden under lowered lids. He was tired of Dorkas; she was like a lute with only one string. His eyes had come to rest unseeingly on the brush and small trees that edged the little glade. When the color of the foliage reached from his eyes to his brain, he was reminded that six moons had waxed and waned since Hades had taken Kore.

"I suppose I should have put a limit of time on my agreement with Demeter," Zeus said, his indolent voice a bad match for the hard gleam of his blue eyes under their sheltering lashes. "But, after all, you promised you would be able to convince her that Kore desired her freedom and that she would return when

Demeter was willing to agree that she live her own life."

"She will not listen. She says Kore loves her and was happy. When I remind her of how often Kore would hide herself on the temple grounds, she slaps my face and calls me a liar and sets me penances. But all the priestesses know that Kore was straining at the leash on which Demeter held her. I tell you, Demeter is mad and is not fit to serve the Goddess."

The shrill voice put the cap on Zeus's irritation; he wondered, not for the first time, whether Dorkas had tried to soothe Demeter or instead tried to intensify her grief and loss. He realized he did not trust Dorkas at all, and that he had made a mistake when he allowed her knowledge of his plot with Hades. She was too selfish and too ambitious to be a suitable high priestess.

Demeter might hate him, but could do little harm because her prejudice was now a laughing matter in the whole city. And if it was true that he could not use Demeter to apply pressure to those he wished to bend as he had hoped he could use Dorkas, he now saw that that was all to the good. At least when Demeter agreed to withdraw the Goddess's blessing from a wrongdoer at his bidding, all accepted her decision. Demeter might be considered mad on the subject of Kore's disappearance, but she was recognized by all to be scrupulous, even Goddess-inspired, in her service. Zeus drew away from Dorkas and also sat up.

"You know I have nothing to say about Demeter's fitness to serve. The Goddess is well able to accept or reject her own priestesses. The crops were good—perhaps not so good as they have been in the past, but good enough so it is apparent the Goddess has not rejected her."

"You mean the Goddess has not rejected me! Who do you think did all the work of blessing? It is time for Demeter to be removed from the temple."

Zeus did not believe Dorkas's claim that she had performed the blessing. He was quite certain Demeter would never allow anyone to perform the rites in her place as long as she believed Kore would hold that place in the future.

"Be reasonable, Dorkas," he said, shaking his head so that the golden curls she had smoothed back fell forward onto his brow. "You know I cannot 'remove' the high priestess of the Corn Goddess. If she had continued to refuse to bless the seed and sow it as she threatened in her first madness, the other mages and very likely the Goddess herself would have supported my suggestion that she be supplanted. However, she did not; she did her duty. I do not see that I have any right to complain of her, even if she does search for Kore long after reason says hope of finding the girl should be gone."

"You mean I must wait until she dies for the place you promised me?"

Zeus looked at her in silence for a moment, his eyes clear and steady. "I promised you nothing. That does not mean I am against your succeeding to the role of high priestess when that place is vacant. All it means is that I will not make a promise I cannot be absolutely certain I can fulfill. If I promised you the place, and one of us should die before that promise could be honored, it would be a mark upon my soul."

There was nothing threatening in his face or voice, but Dorkas rapidly reconsidered her intention of hint-

ing he would be better off satisfying her demand than
having all Olympus know he had contrived Kore's
disappearance. She forced a smile and said, "I trust
you to do your best for me, but I am concerned for the
reputation of the temple. And it is not easy to live with
Demeter these days."

"I am sorry for that, but—" Zeus stopped abruptly
and let his head swing slowly until it stopped on a
direct line with the palace in the city. He jumped up,
gathering his kilt, tunic, and cloak. "Hera is scrying, I
think," he whispered, and ran off into the woods.

Dorkas shivered as she watched him go, but she
pulled her gown over her head without haste. If Hera
had seen them, it was too late already, but if Hera had
only started her spell, it would follow Zeus and never
touch her at all. Dorkas felt somewhat comforted,
knowing that that would have been his purpose in
running away, not cowardice. Hera was very strange.
She seldom quarreled with Zeus, but wreaked her
anger on the women with whom he lay. She shivered
again but then sighed gently. Mostly Hera punished
those who had born children or gotten with child by
her husband. Dorkas knew she had not conceived.

Then she frowned, lifted her head, and with closed
eyes turned it back and forth. Although she was not
strongly Gifted, she could usually sense sorcery, and
there was no taint of it in the glade, no faint breezless
breeze that might betray the use of power. Suddenly
she remembered that Zeus had told her it was safe to
stay and enjoy each other, because Hera was attending
a childbirth. Dorkas's teeth ground together. He had
not fled to protect her but had only used that excuse
to get away quickly.

What a fool she had been! He had been using Hera's

jealousy as an excuse for weeks, and she had not realized it. He had only lain with her because he had nothing better to do and had come upon her by accident. Dorkas swallowed hard. Zeus never had any intention of helping her to be high priestess. He wanted Demeter to go on acting mad so that the temple would fall into disrepute and Zeus himself would be the only authority in Olympus.

Dorkas sat there a long time, until the chill of autumn crept into the false summer warmth that the high sun and the sheltering foliage had kept in the glade. Twice she wiped tears from her cheeks, but when she pulled her cloak up and over her shoulders, her mouth was hard. If she wished to be high priestess, Demeter must be driven from the temple soon. Not the next day or the next week, but before the next spring solstice, when two of the younger priestesses would be ripe for elevation to acolyte.

Once that happened, Dorkas knew her chances of taking Demeter's place would be lessened. Now she was the only possible choice, Aglaia having already voluntarily yielded the position to Demeter when Dorkas was a novice. She *should* be the obvious choice even if two new acolytes were chosen, but her new revelation about Zeus made her unwilling to take the chance. The Goddess was supposed to choose, but Dorkas had an ugly suspicion that the "Goddess" would choose the priestess Zeus preferred, likely the youngest and most malleable.

Dorkas bit her lip. She must make it impossible for Zeus to endure Demeter. She would have to arrange that Demeter accuse him again, with the jewel-flower as evidence. Everyone knew Zeus had gifted Hera with similar pieces when he was trying to make peace with her. Likely Hades had made those too and given them—or sold them—to his brother. Yes, that would send Demeter off to confront Zeus, screaming like a virago and demanding—if Zeus denied he had used the gem as a lure—that he begin an inquisition among the mages and other rich and powerful families to discover who had bought the piece from Hades.

Eagerness to show Demeter the gem she had found in the hollow of the boulder made Dorkas jump to her feet and start out of the glade at a near run, but by the time she was close to the temple her pace had slowed. Her first impulse, simply to thrust the gem in Demeter's face, had been dismissed almost as quickly as it arose. Then Dorkas had tried to think of a way to present the jewel-flower, and realized she could not simply say, six moons after the abduction, that she had found it near where Kore had disappeared. Demeter would remember she had said she searched the area for Kore and would ask too many questions about where and how she had suddenly come across the bright jewel.

In fact, Dorkas reluctantly admitted to herself, it would not be safe to show Demeter the jewel-flower so soon after Zeus had virtually told her he had used her and discarded her. Whatever else he was, Zeus was no fool. He would at once connect Demeter's evidence and knowledge with his discarded mistress's dissatisfaction.

At the winter solstice, the Goddess's garments would be washed again. What could be more natural, Dorkas thought, than that she should go with Aglaia to look—not because she expected to find anything but as a sad tribute—at the last place she had seen Kore. Aglaia was easy to manipulate. If Aglaia found the jewel-flower by the foot of the rock, she would certainly bring it to Demeter. There would be no way for Zeus to connect his rejection of her with Demeter's presentation of the jewel as evidence that Kore had been lured into his power.

Dorkas was sufficiently afraid of Zeus to use the six weeks before the winter solstice to plan every detail, including what she would say to Demeter if the high priestess was too thick-headed to connect the jewel with Zeus on her own. Even if she could avoid that, she knew she would have to "confess" to Demeter in private that she had mentioned Kore's excursion out of the temple grounds to make the connection between jewel, Zeus, and abduction absolute. She could extract a promise that the confession be under the seal of secrecy. Demeter would not ordinarily break that seal, but if she did in this case—Dorkas shivered, then smiled—she would simply deny she had said it and say in public that Demeter was mad.

Several days before the rites, Dorkas set into Aglaia's mind the idea of climbing to the boulder where she had seen the print "of Kore's dear little foot" (never mind that Kore's feet, commensurate with her height, were not little at all). On the day, when they neared the boulder on the way to the Mother's pool, Dorkas slyly twisted the hand of the child novice nearest her. The little girl of course cried out. Dorkas busied herself with the child's tearful complaints and did not climb up to the boulder with Aglaia.

Of course the jewel-flower was there already, just tilted up above a little pile of dirt so the sun would hit it and bring forth its most brilliant gleams. Dorkas was around the curve of the road when Aglaia cried out with surprise at her find and took care she was not even present when Aglaia brought the jewel-flower to Demeter.

Dorkas had remained to perform the rite and wash the Goddess's gown, sending Aglaia back with no more than a sigh and a shake of the head over the possibility that the jewel was a lure Kore had dropped when she was surprised and taken. She said nothing directly about the similarity of the jewel-flower to the gems Hera had. Aglaia knew as well as anyone else who had the most exquisite jewelry in Olympus.

Dorkas's plan worked perfectly in the sense that Demeter did not suspect that Dorkas had picked up the gem at the time of Kore's abduction; unfortunately, neither did Demeter associate the jewel-flower with Hera's pieces, and through Hera, with Zeus. And Aglaia, who was trusting but not an idiot, did not—as Dorkas hoped she would—point out the connection. Thus, Demeter, whose mind was half elsewhere, only looked at the gem with indifference and returned it to Aglaia.

"It can have nothing to do with Kore," Demeter said impatiently, "even if it was found where Dorkas last saw her."

Aglaia's expression of intense relief focused Demeter's attention. She became aware that her acolyte must have been too afraid not to bring the piece to her but almost equally afraid that it would catch her interest and renew her efforts to find her daughter. Mingled despair and fury tore at Demeter.

"Out!" she screamed. "You do not care if grief drives me mad! You want me to be mad! You want my place!"

Her voice checked on those last words as her eyes

caught the horror in Aglaia's face when she turned to flee. Demeter swallowed hard. She knew Aglaia did not want to be high priestess; in fact, the older woman had held the office temporarily before Demeter had been chosen and consecrated, and she had hated it. Now Aglaia thought she was mad. Demeter uttered a bark of laughter. There was no "now" about it. Everyone already thought she was mad. For the last few moons when she searched for her daughter, doors had been opened with laughter and jeers. The mages she suspected of being willing to help Zeus hide Kore had passed beyond irritation to contempt. Demeter covered her face with her hands.

It was too late for searching, Demeter knew. It had been too late for a long time, but what could she do? Accept the loss of her daughter? No one wanted Kore to be found. They were all completely convinced now that, as Zeus had said, Kore had run away of her own free will and was hiding from her mother. Demeter knew that was a lie. Kore was a loving child who would not do such a terrible thing; Kore knew how much grief and sorrow had filled her mother's life and knew she was her mother's one solace. The priestesses had spread the story that Kore wanted her freedom, that she wanted her *own* name, that she did not want to be high priestess. All lies.

"They want me to seem mad because they all want to be rid of me," Demeter moaned softly to herself, weeping with self-pity.

When she heard the words, she blinked away the tears—having shocked herself into awareness of a truth she had not previously faced. She had not a friend in all of Olympus; even her priestesses had turned against her. *Even* her priestesses? The lesser priestesses were the last to want Kore back. While Kore was with them, they had accepted the fact that Demeter would always be high priestess, that Demeter would live again in her new-named daughter after her old body died. Now that Kore was gone, ambition had wakened in them.

Gone where? Demeter uttered a sob. She was not in Olympus, not in the city, and not in the whole valley. For a moment ice trickled down Demeter's back as she once again grappled with the fear that her daughter was dead, raped and finally murdered to enforce silence. Then she shook herself. The Goddess would have warned her of that. Yet the comforting thought had a twinge of discomfort in it. Why had the Goddess not aided her search?

For some reason the jewel-flower, almost certainly Hades's work, came into her mind, and ice ran up and down her spine again. Then she shook herself. Kore was not dead, and Hades had nothing to do with the living. Demeter's memory of Hades had been seared into her mind and heart when she had met him again and again as she searched for Iasion after the battle in which Zeus had conquered Olympus. Hades had stalked the streets with his scarred, crippled minions, turning over every body, gathering up the dead. And his knife had run red with the blood of those not quite dead to whom he had given grace. Demeter sighed. At least the screaming and moaning had stopped. And Hades had been just. He had not gathered in those wounded who could recover. Those his walking dead had placed in the carts of the healers that also followed him. He would not touch Kore, who was young and healthy.

That assurance notwithstanding, the icy *frisson* that

had crawled along Demeter's spine seemed to have settled around her heart. She could no longer bear to be alone, but she did not desire the company of her cruel and scornful priestesses. She rose and hurried from her apartment to the oval chamber at the front of the temple that was sacred to the Goddess. Sun poured in through the slices of crystal set in lead that circled the dome over the image, bent the light from whatever angle it came, and bathed the effigy in light. Demeter turned right, walked around the statue, and stood facing it. She felt no particular touch from the Goddess; nonetheless, she was comforted. She had just raised her hands to speak an invocation when she heard weeping.

For a moment Demeter was tempted to ignore the sound. If it was one of the children, Aglaia would soon be there to comfort her. But almost as soon as the thought was defined, Demeter realized that the sound was too harsh and heavy to be a child. If a priestess was weeping that desperately, Demeter wanted to know why. She walked to the other opening in the back of the sanctuary and found Dorkas crouched just outside in the corridor that led to the acolytes' chambers and the dormitories.

Demeter was so surprised to see Dorkas weeping so bitterly that she was frozen in place. Dorkas, who was as hard as any person Demeter had ever known, had never been a favorite, and Demeter had developed an active distaste for the woman when she heard rumors that Dorkas lay with Zeus. Moreover, Demeter had grave doubts about Dorkas's real devotion to the Goddess. She had come from one of the least important families among the Olympians and had likely chosen the temple as a way out of poverty. Before Demeter could back away, Dorkas looked up.

"Oh, forgive me my lady," she sobbed.

"Forgive you?" Demeter had some difficulty commanding her voice. For some reason Aglaia's find leapt into her mind as she forced out, "For what?"

"That jewel, it must have been the temptation that drew Kore from the path when we were around the curve and could not see her. She called out to me that she wished to pick a flower. *A* flower, she said, not some flowers. I never thought it was a strange thing for Kore to say until after Aglaia showed the gem to me."

A wave of relief that Dorkas's "crime" was so innocent swept through Demeter, impelling her to answer with grudging kindness, "Well, I might not have thought it strange myself. I do not see that your mistake is anything to weep over, particularly since I cannot believe that pretty trinket has been there all this time."

"But I fear it has," Dorkas cried, beginning to sob again. "I did not believe you when you said that Zeus had taken Kore, but that jewel-flower is so like those Zeus gave Hera, so like . . ." She bent her head to her knees, hiding the expression on her face as Demeter put a hand to the wall to support herself.

"Mother," Demeter breathed. "I knew I had seen that kind of jewel before, and that where I had seen it could not have anything to do with my Kore. Of course! I had seen Hera wearing those gems—and Hera would not take Kore. But it was Zeus who gave the gems to Hera."

"Yes, and that makes me guilty of worse," Dorkas wailed, lifting a tear-streaked face. "But I did not know! I did not know! I told him."

"Told him? Told who? Zeus? What did you tell him?"

Dorkas closed her eyes and tears ran down under the closed lids. "We were lovers. You knew that. I did not try to hide it. Often he would ask questions about the temple—" She opened her eyes and for a moment her old defiance flashed in them. "I always told him what I knew and what I thought." She brought up her hands to hide her face—and also to shelter it if Demeter struck her. "How could I guess he would conceive such an abomination against his own daughter? He asked me whether you ever let Kore go without you outside the temple grounds. I thought he was only curious or that he wished to meet her, speak to her. I told him . . ." Her voice sank to a whisper. ". . . that you did not accompany Kore when she washed the Corn Goddess's garments in the Great Mother's pool."

Demeter stood staring down at the hunched and trembling Dorkas. Her eyes were blank with the shock of comprehending her own blindness. How could she have forgotten that few people knew Kore ever left the temple grounds without her mother? The question was obliterated by fury. Had she remembered, she would have known that Dorkas had told Zeus of Kore's vulnerability at that time and place. It had to be Dorkas and Zeus, because no other priestess had a liaison with a great mage. She could have dragged Dorkas with her and demanded a public confession. Even now she could force Zeus—

"My lady," Dorkas sobbed, catching hold of her skirt. "Do not tell him I told you. He will blast me."

There was fear in those words, real fear. The thought "real fear" echoed through Demeter's confusion, and she realized that the genuine fear had exposed the false regret. Tears and trembling and confessions were completely out of character for Dorkas.

"Then why did you tell me—now, when it is too late for the knowledge to do me good?"

"Because he cast me aside," Dorkas spat.

That was genuine, too, Demeter thought, but Dorkas was still speaking.

"It is not too late," she urged. "Take the gem. Show it to all. Aglaia will go with you and tell where and how she found it. Demand that Zeus bring Kore back from wherever he took her."

"Back from . . ." Demeter echoed.

Half stunned by a new revelation, she pulled her skirt from Dorkas's grip and walked past her into the short corridor that opened into the apartment she had once shared with Kore. "Back from" . . . the words echoed again in her mind. What had ailed her all these moons to search and search again places where she knew Kore was not held? First her mind shuddered away from her own question as a brief fear that the Goddess had clouded her thinking lashed her. But she knew Her Lady could not be so cruel, and she soon realized that she wished to blame the Goddess because fear had made her shrink from a truth she dreaded.

She had known since the first harvest that Kore was not in the city or valley of Olympus, but she had refused to acknowledge it because that would mean she would have to leave her temple, her home, to search for her daughter among the native people. She had really known it from the beginning, known that none of the mages would try to conceal Kore in Olympus. Most of the great mages visited the native towns. They purchased a spell from Hermes that would take them from Olympus to some particular place among the native folk, often to a temple in their honor.

Demeter shook her head, distracted for a moment from the enormity of the task before her. Poor little people, they were so simple. They feared even the weakly Gifted among themselves and worshipped the great mages as gods—mostly Zeus, who took special delight in their praises . . . and in despoiling their virgins.

Suddenly Demeter's eyes opened wide. Fool! she mouthed silently. Fool! Kore would be in one of those temples—but which? There were so many. She would have to force him to tell her. She would take Aglaia and the gem . . . The familiar ring of those words brought her mind up short. There was a little stink about them, something, a warning of falseness. Of course! Dorkas had said those words.

Demeter took a deep breath and walked from the doorway, where she had been standing absorbed in thought, to her favorite seat. Now that she had swallowed the unpleasant medicine of knowing she must leave Olympus, she must think carefully about what to do. If Zeus guessed what she had learned, he would stop her.

"Oh!" she breathed, sinking down into the chair before which she had been standing. Dorkas had told her to go to Zeus and confront him. "That sly bitch!"

So Dorkas thought her confession would be a double-edged sword. One cut would revenge her on Zeus and the backhand stroke would . . . But how would Demeter's accusation revenge Dorkas on Zeus? More than six moons since Kore was taken, he could claim anyone had dropped the gem. No, of course not. He would admit he had lost the gem, possibly even confess

he had brought it to give to someone . . . someone?
Dorkas! And she would support his "confession."

Demeter gripped her hands together tightly. It was
a plot between them to be rid of her. No, Dorkas's
hurt and fury when she said Zeus had cast her aside
were genuine. And her fear of Zeus was genuine—but
her advice to confront Zeus was false. So the plan was
Zeus's. Demeter knew Zeus was aware she hated him
and had never trusted her; it was no surprise that he
wished to be rid of her—*and of the daughter she had
trained to dislike and distrust him.*

Then suddenly all the different thoughts settled into
a clear pattern. Dorkas and Zeus had one purpose that
bound them together: He wanted a high priestess he
could bend to his will, which meant he must be rid of
Demeter and the daughter who would be another
Demeter, and Dorkas wanted to be high priestess,
which meant she must be rid of Demeter and Kore
also. Although Demeter knew it was foolish not to
have seen that obvious fact sooner, she was not as
disturbed as by her earlier blindnesses, which had been
owing to fear and an avoidance of the truth. Her blindness with regard to Dorkas was a result of Goddess-
given knowledge.

Demeter suppressed a small pang of guilt. She knew
that Dorkas could not be high priestess, that the Goddess would never accept her. Because she had known
that, she had dismissed the problem of jealousy of
Kore as a source of her disappearance. Aglaia had not
the strength to hold the place—her short tenure as
high priestess had drained her power so deeply that she
nearly died—and she had willingly retired; Dorkas
was unfit. Demeter sighed. She had chosen Dorkas as
acolyte for that reason, so that there would be no older

candidate to challenge Kore's claim to be high priestess. Perhaps that was wrong. Perhaps Kore's disappearance was a punishment for that selfish act. She
should have trusted Her Lady more completely.

Oddly, that thought made Demeter much happier.
Kore was so perfectly fitted to serve the Corn Goddess
aspect of the Mother that Demeter could not doubt
she would be safely returned to the temple. Perhaps
she should do nothing, just wait until the Lady sent
Kore back to her? No, that was not right either. One
did not wait for the Corn Goddess to plough the fields
or sow the grain. To accomplish a purpose, one must
act. Demeter took a deep breath and began to think
out those actions.

Chapter 11

When Demeter appeared in Poseidon's great hall three days after the winter solstice, the King of the Sea was not particularly overjoyed. He was a frequent enough visitor to Olympus that he was well aware of Demeter's increasingly comical search for her daughter.

"Kore is not here," he said, "and being less guilty than Zeus, I do not need to indulge you by allowing you to turn upside down my house and those of my subjects."

"I have not come for that," Demeter said.

Poseidon raised his brows to express silently a doubt he was too polite—at the moment—to voice. "Then to what need do I owe the honor of this visit?"

"A refuge for my grief. The temple is a constant reminder of my loss. All Olympus is a constant reminder of my loss. Your realm, surrounded by the sea instead of with mountains, with the waves beating at the foot of your palace, is so different. I wish only to rest here for a time." She held his eyes steadily and added, "I beg you not to answer me at once, but to give me a private audience so I can explain my need more fully."

That steady look was a far cry from the distraught woman who sought what she herself knew could not be found. Poseidon bowed his curly head in agreement and lifted a small shell from the arm of his irridescent, pearl-studded throne. When he blew across it, an exquisite horn-tone sang gently through the room. A very lovely young woman and an old man emerged from behind a curtain that apparently covered an opening in the wall.

"Go with Nerus and Neso," he said. "They will show you to a chamber where you can rest. When I am finished with my duties here, I will listen to all you have to say."

At that command Nerus led the way to a room where a wide window gave a view of the ocean through rough squares of a substance so clear that Demeter had pulled her cloak tighter around her as they entered in the expectation of a cold wind.

"What is that?" Demeter asked, staring in amazement. The panels were clearly not crystal. Crystal was never more than a few inches wide and always distorted what one saw through it because it bent the light.

"I do not know, madam," Nerus replied. "It is not a fruit of the sea nor of Aegina. The king trades boats full of salt fish for it to King Celeus. One of the sailing men told me Celeus gets it from Hades himself. If so, the king of Plutos seems to have a great appetite for salt fish."

"Appetite?" Neso said, with a bubbling laugh. "You could feed all the dead with the amount of fish Poseidon has sent to Celeus—although what the dead might want with fish I cannot understand. Just be careful, madam. Do not tap it or lean on it. It is very fragile, and though fish are plentiful, I think the king would not be pleased to send more boats full to replace what he has paid for already."

Demeter nodded, but she paid little attention. Now she remembered that she had seen the substance in the private rooms of Zeus's palace and been told that Hades made it himself, from white sand. She stood looking at the sea, comforted because she was certain some signal had passed from Poseidon to his servants to make them take her to a place that satisfied the request she had made. And when Nerus gently guided her to a seat that would let her continue looking at the sea, and the girl asked whether she should bring wine and cakes to refresh her, she was further assured.

She was thus perfectly calm when Poseidon joined her some time later, and smiled as she said, "Thank you, my lord, this is a beautiful place."

"Demeter," Poseidon said, seating himself in a chair opposite to hers, "I do not believe a woman who has cherished a hatred for Zeus all these years and believes she has been hurt anew by him—whether rightly or wrongly—has come here to rest and look at the sea."

"You are very wise." Demeter smiled again. "And you need not protest anew that you do not hold my daughter. I know Kore is not here, but I have proof now—something that was dropped in the place where she disappeared—that Zeus did take her. I am still not sure how he contrived to do it. Perhaps some servant of his carried her off—"

Poseidon shook his head. "I know Zeus's faults," he said, "but I have heard that he said he would not violate his own daughter—and I believe that."

"I do too," Demeter assured him. "That was not his purpose. He wished to control the temple of the Corn

Goddess and knew that he could not bend me to his will nor my daughter after me. Well, my daughter is more precious to me than my place in the temple. I have reason to believe that she is hidden among the native people, perhaps in one of the many temples where Zeus is worshipped."

Demeter dropped her eyes and bit the inside of her lip to hide her satisfaction. Poseidon had, without saying a single word, given her the best piece of news she had had since Kore had been taken. One brief unguarded expression had exposed to her Poseidon's resentment of the worship accorded to Zeus.

Quickly, before he could guess what she had learned, she continued. "I wish to search for my daughter, but I need a safe haven for myself and help in gathering news of her. I know you do not desire any quarrel with Zeus—" A quick glance under lowered lashes showed Demeter how Poseidon stiffened at what might be innocent but also might be an implication he feared his brother, but her voice continued unchecked—"so I will promise to make no outcry against Zeus, even if I find Kore in one of his temples. And I will gladly pay for your help by making your land more fertile. If it is your pleasure, I will train such maidens as I find fit to the service of the Goddess."

"You will teach the mystery of the Corn Goddess here in Aegina?"

Demeter raised her eyes to his and held his gaze. "On the mainland also," she said. "But only by your order and in such places as you command." Then she shrugged. "Or not at all, if you will."

Poseidon was not as skilled as Zeus at hiding what he felt—he had less need, for he had fewer great mages as subjects—but Demeter saw at once that he was no stupider than Zeus. He had immediately recognized the increase in his influence over the native population if he could grant this or that petty ruler a richer harvest. He saw just as quickly that the increase in his power might bring him into conflict with Zeus. What he did not see, Demeter was certain, was that once she had established a temple, taught a few Gifted native women the rites, and introduced the worship of the Corn Goddess—which would reinforce their half-buried memories of worship of the Mother—there was no way he could undo what she had done.

Demeter felt a pang of anxiety when Poseidon rose from his chair without any reply, but she continued to meet his eyes and he nodded. "There are too many mixed goods and evils in such a proposal to decide at once. However, you will have no need to wait for me to untangle all of those before I send out for news of what maidens are come into Zeus's temples since the spring solstice. Meanwhile, you will be welcome to this apartment and to whatever else you need to . . . ease your heart."

In fact, Demeter's heart was mostly at ease during the weeks that followed. She was in no hurry for news of Kore, since she had convinced herself that driving her from the temple had been the object of Kore's abductor, rather than harm to or ravishment of her daughter. Poseidon's messengers were out, she told herself one afternoon when she felt as restless as the heaving sea outside her window. Meanwhile, no harm could come from Kore being confined to a temple of Zeus; doubtless she would have even less freedom than she had had in Olympus and would come to appreciate her mother's light rein.

As for Zeus—Demeter smiled slowly, with enormous satisfaction—what a surprise he was about to receive. Doubtless Aglaia and Dorkas would bless the seed and sow it. Aglaia knew the rites and Demeter had taken particular care to instruct Dorkas—to show she had been forgiven for her transgressions with Zeus. But Aglaia, who had the true Gift for enlivening seed, had not enough power. After doing no more than lending a little strength to her high priestess, Aglaia was exhausted. She would kill herself if she tried to fully quicken more than a field or two. And Dorkas had some weak, undefined Gift that Demeter could tap, although not with the sweetness and rich result of feeding off Kore's Gift. But Dorkas's Gift could not of itself quicken seed. The crop that would spring from the earth in Olympus would be so sparse that half the herds would have to be slaughtered for lack of winter fodder, and the people would be belly-pinched. Demeter smiled again and sighed a soft, contented sigh. Zeus would call her back and give her anything she desired to make her come.

As the time of planting approached, however, Demeter was grateful that she had employment more taxing than looking at the sea from the window. If she had not the task of seeking out Gifted women among Poseidon's people and teaching the strongest among them the rites that enlivened seed, despair would have been creeping upon her, inducing in her a kind of madness like that which had afflicted her in the last moons in Olympus. A few of Poseidon's agents had returned to his court and they carried disturbing news. There were no priestesses in Zeus's temples. Of the four who had come back, three reported no women at all, not even servingwomen. One temple was not so strict and employed a very few old crones who did the washing and suchlike.

Fortunately, Demeter was finding more difficulty, and more satisfaction, than she had ever expected in instructing the native women. She was surprised at how few women were Gifted until she saw the fear in those in whom she felt a Gift. Then she remembered a conversation she had heard between Hermes and Athena about how stupid the native folk were because they feared and drove out their Gifted.

It was a nuisance—but also a challenge—to have to teach the women in secret, but all were so fearful of having their Gifts become known that even the promise of assured plenty would not draw them to her openly. Still, Demeter took pleasure in thinking of the many hidden altars to the Goddess. Perhaps when the rich crops were garnered, the women would grow bolder.

When the blessing and sowing was over, however, Demeter woke one morning, realizing she had had no news from Poseidon for many weeks. Feeling weak and weary, her power depleted from heavy use with weak support during the urgency of planting, she sent word to Nerus with the girl who brought her breakfast that she wished to speak to Poseidon immediately. Nerus urged her to wait, saying that Poseidon had duties, but when Demeter cried she had been used and would depart if she were no longer welcome to Poseidon, Nerus bowed.

"Come then," he said, shrugging. "Wise words seldom change what will be. The king is still abed, but he has given orders that you are welcome to him at any time."

Demeter was so sure she would be led to some antechamber and bidden to wait, that her anger was much diminished when Nerus brought her directly to Poseidon's bedchamber. The sheer astonishment she felt at the appearance of the room also left little room for rage. Fully one half of the floor was a pool of water, out of which rose a wide set of curved stairs that seemed to be made of mother-of-pearl of a remarkable luminosity, all washed with pale pink and blue and green and gold. A graceful chair of polished bone inlaid with varicolored coral stood at one side of the topmost step, which extended into a platform.

Facing the pool but back from the low wall that surrounded the top step and kept out the water, stood Poseidon's bed. He was, in fact, still in it, propped up by pillows against the inner curve of what looked like an enormous conch shell. Its interior, of gleaming blue-green nacre, made a dramatic background for his dark curls and warm brown skin. Beside the bed a confusion of bright garments betrayed that there had been another occupant who had left with more haste than dignity.

Shock and appreciation of the truly unusual beauty of the room notwithstanding, Demeter could not be polite. "What has become of your messengers?" she asked.

"They have all returned," Poseidon replied calmly. "I am sorry, there is no good news. There is simply no possibility of any girl even distantly like Kore hiding in any temple of Zeus. It seemed useless to break your heart each time one of my men returned."

"None of the temples have priestesses?"

"None. We should have realized that. It is perfectly logical that Zeus's temples should not have priestesses. To gather women together would only attract Hera's attention and make it impossible for him to enjoy them. Why should he bother with priestesses anyway? He has the Gift of disguise and can approach any woman he desires in any form. Women in his temples would only be a temptation to him and to his priests and give them a reputation for lasciviousness."

Demeter's hands rose and clasped beneath her bosom. "I was so sure," she breathed. She shuddered and her eyes widened. "Where is she? Where? I was not afraid for her before, but if Zeus does not have her—but he must! I have proof . . ."

"Sit down, Demeter!" Poseidon's voice was sharp enough to check her rising hysteria. "There are other places to look, but my men did not confine their questions to temples and I am beginning to have doubts about whether Zeus does hold your daughter. What is this proof you say you have?"

"A flower-jewel, just like those Zeus gave to Hera, was found where Kore was last seen. No one else in Olympus has ever had—"

This time it was Poseidon's eyes that widened. Demeter stopped speaking when she saw the effect her words had on him.

"No one in Olympus," Poseidon said. "But Hades himself might have as many such toys as Zeus or more."

"No!" Demeter cried. "Hades would not take a living girl into the realms of the dead."

"But Hades is not himself dead," Poseidon pointed out. "Perhaps he does not like, or cannot be satisfied by, the embraces of spirits."

"No! No! I will not believe it. Kore is *not* dead!"

"I did not say she was dead. Did I not just point out to you that Hades is not dead? Unfortunately."

"I will not believe that my poor Kore, my bright and beautiful Kore, has been imprisoned among the cold shades for a whole year," Demeter wailed.

Poseidon snorted with contempt. "You can refuse to believe that Hades holds her if you like," he said, "but I am beginning to think that is the only answer. Moreover, two of my men brought back hints that Hades has taken a bride, a tall, golden woman called Persephone, which in the old language means Dazzling Brightness."

"You never told me that!"

"I did not think much about it before you mentioned the jewel-flower. Why should I think that Hades was in any way involved? And the woman did not sound anything like what you told me of Kore. The only thing they had in common was being blonde—" He hesitated and pursed his lips, then added, "But that is a real rarity among native women. I should have realized Hades's bride must be an Olympian. Beyond the fact that she is almost as tall as Hades and blonde, what is said of this Persephone is that she is truly Queen of Plutos and that Hades bows to her will."

Demeter wrung her hands. "That does not sound like Kore. I cannot imagine her ruling the harsh King of the Dead. But—but she is tall." Her voice faltered. "I think of her as little, because she is my little girl . . . only a little girl . . ."

Poseidon frowned. "Little girl? But Kore must be more than twenty winters of age."

"Not so much as that!" Demeter exclaimed. But then she burst into tears. "That was why Zeus said I could look for her where and as long as I pleased. He knew! Dorkas told him when my poor Kore would be alone and vulnerable and he told . . . Hades . . ." She shuddered. "Poseidon, you must go to Hades. You are his brother. Ask for my daughter back. I will do anything for you. Anything!"

"I cannot do that, Demeter. That is the bond among Zeus, Hades, and me. We each have our place and our power and we do *not* interfere with each other. Kore is Zeus's daughter as well as yours. He has the right to demand that Hades return her. I have not."

"But Zeus helped Hades take her. You know he would not ask for her return. What can I offer you—"

"Nothing!" Poseidon would not meet her eyes. "I will give you what help I can—a ship to take you where you will, silver or even gold to buy servants and favor—but I cannot myself approach Hades."

"Who can approach Hades if you cannot?" Demeter sobbed. "What can gold buy from Hades, who has possession of all the gold and jewels under the earth? Where can I go in a ship?"

"That I can tell you," Poseidon said. "You can take a ship to Eleusis. The king, whose name is Celeus, claims there are caves not far from his palace where the dead can be called and will answer if sacrifice is made. Ask there for your daughter."

"Ask!" Demeter cried, eyes wild. "What good will that do?"

"The dead do not lie," Poseidon replied, his voice hard. "You will at least know whether or not Persephone was once Kore. I have done all I can for you, Demeter. I will do no more."

Self-absorbed as she was, Demeter had an excellent sense of self-preservation. Something in the tenseness of Poseidon's body and the quality of his voice pierced through her anguish and warned her that she was treading very dangerous ground. She suspected that if she pressed him further to deal with Hades on Kore's behalf that he would send her away and dissociate himself from her completely. Poseidon was jealous of Zeus and cautious of arousing his ire, but he had been willing to send his own men to make inquiries about the workings of Zeus's temples. Hades was apparently far more threatening to the King of the Sea.

"Very well," Demeter said. "If I must go alone, I will. When—"

Her question about when a ship could be ready to take her was interrupted by an eruption of the water in the pool. A huge bubble formed and burst to show the sleek black head and crazy smile of a sharp-nosed porpoise. It chittered at Poseidon and he cocked his head and rose from the bed.

"I must go now," he said hurriedly, striding across to the pool. Poised to dive in, he said over his shoulder, "I may be long away. Nerus will provide you with whatever you think you might need."

He was long gone and Demeter eating a midday meal with small appetite when she realized that Poseidon had left her without any way to prove who she was or that he would approve any help given her. Nerus might have money for her and the right to order a ship to sail to Eleusis, but Nerus could not give her any personal token from Poseidon that would identify her as one it would oblige Poseidon to help. What appetite she had vanished, and for the first time since she had left Olympus, she had the urge to fling herself to the ground and scream.

Her despair was intensified when she sensed a subtle pressure on her to leave. No one was rude, the service accorded her was just as gracious, but baskets for packing the possessions she had accumulated appeared, and she was told whenever a ship crossing to the mainland near Eleusis was ready to leave. She resisted for half a moon, but then realized it would only annoy Poseidon to be denied his own palace by her presence in it and if she annoyed him enough, he would simply give orders that she be removed.

This was a battle, Demeter reasoned out one sleepless night, that she could not win. She had no weapon to use against Poseidon. He had helped her because he enjoyed spiting Zeus and because if it could be proved Zeus had taken Kore, Zeus's reputation in Olympus would be badly damaged. It was a source of mild amusement among the Olympians, except perhaps to Hera, that Zeus stole native girls. It would be far less amusing that he stole the daughter of the high priestess of the Corn Goddess, particularly after he had sworn a mighty oath before them all that he had not. However, Poseidon could gain no points with the Olympians if Hades had taken Kore—and Poseidon was afraid of Hades, so afraid he did not want to be associated in any way with anyone who crossed the will of the King of the Dead.

In the morning Demeter told Nerus that she would take the next ship to Eleusis. Although she was not urged to stay longer than the three more days before a ship would sail in the direction of Eleusis, sufficient gold and fine gowns were pressed upon her to mark her as a person of importance, as well as bracelets and necklets and earrings—but not of nacre or of pearl or of any substance that belonged to Poseidon's realm.

The rich garments and accoutrements accorded her a very civil welcome in Celeus's city, but when she asked whether someone would take her to the caves that opened the way into Plutos, she met a stone wall. The townsfolk denied any such place existed. One told her it was a confusion of Eleusis with Eutresis, far inland. Another said it was a foul calumny propagated by a neighboring kingdom that hoped to spoil their trade by giving them an evil reputation. When she went to the palace with her request, she was turned away. King Celeus was not in Eleusis, she was told, and his servants did not know when he would return. She persisted, asking in shops where she saw displayed metal bowls, fine weapons, or other fruits of the underworld. The merchants indignantly denied that they dealt with the dead. The townsfolk became less friendly and accommodating. Again she saw the winks and nods, the sly smiles and pointing fingers that marked her as a madwoman.

Distraught and despairing, Demeter took to wandering in the countryside searching for the place on her own, but there was nothing close to Eleusis that could hold the entrance to a cave, except some blue shadows off to the west that hinted of hills. Days passed into weeks. Having exhausted all nearer possibilities, Demeter decided to look in the hills. But she had never traveled so far, even in the valley of Olympus, and there she was accompanied by priestesses and servants who saw to her comfort.

Beside that, Demeter was reduced to near witlessness by her terror of confronting Hades. Her mind was completely filled with memories of his stone-hard face with its down-turned bitter lips, his heavy-muscled arm rising to strike, and his dripping, bloody knife. And each time she tried to throw off those memories and assure herself that Hades's actions had been merciful, that he would have only prolonged the agonies of the dying by passing by the mortally wounded, she remembered Poseidon's fear of any conflict with the King of the Dead. Frightened into thoughtlessness, clinging only to the fixed idea that she must have Kore back, she set out without food or even a cloak.

Near evening, hungry and footsore, she sat weeping by the side of the road that led west. She heard the voice of a girl and started upright at a familiar tone, but caught her heel in the ragged hem of her gown and fell.

"Oh, poor lady," a gentle voice cried while two pairs of hands helped her upright. "What are you doing here all alone when it is so near night?"

Beyond caution, Demeter said, "I am seeking my daughter, and the only one who can give me news of her is Hades."

One girl's breath caught. The other said softly, "But if she is dead, Hades cannot send her back even if his stone heart should be touched and he should wish to help you."

"She is not dead." Demeter sighed, too worn to do more than weep quietly. "I have sought her from fabled Olympus to the isles of the sea. In King Poseidon's palace I saw a clear, stiff substance that can be set into a window and will keep out the wind and rain, although it is so clear one can hardly believe it is there. I have seen that stuff far away and I know it is made by Hades himself. And King Poseidon told me he traded salt fish to King Celeus for it. But the townspeople say they know nothing of dark Plutos and King Celeus will not receive me. So I will seek in the hills myself until I find the cave where one may speak with the dead."

The girls had been examining her while she spoke.

Both saw her fairness and the set of features that appeared on the statues in the temples of the gods. Also, under the dust her garments were of the finest cloth and the richest embellishment. She spoke their language well, but with a strange accent. They glanced at each other. Both had heard cautionary tales about terrible punishments meted out for lack of courtesy to beautiful foreigners, who were gods in disguise—and the woman had spoken of fabled Olympus.

"Why do you say King Celeus would not receive you?" the smaller of the girls asked.

"I went to his palace and they said he was not there and did not know when he would return."

"His palace in Eleusis?" the taller girl asked.

"Yes."

"But he is not there," she said, touching Demeter's arm almost pleadingly. "He is here. We came here two moons since because my mother, Queen Metaneira, was heavy with child. She was lightened of son three weeks ago, and we will stay where the air and water is pure until little Demophoön has a strong hold on life."

Demeter smiled faintly. "You are Celeus's daughters?"

"Yes, great lady." The smaller girl's voice shook. "Do not be angry with my father. He did not know."

So they recognized her as one of the mighty. Demeter felt hope and fear in equal proportions. Now the way to confront Hades was open to her, she would have to find the strength. Then she realized her silence and her rigidity had frightened them even more. Touching gently first one anxious face and then the other, Demeter smiled again.

"No. I will not blame King Celeus. If he will tell me where I may call forth the King of Plutos, I will swear never to tell another where the place is or that King Celeus knows of it, and I will go my way and trouble you no more."

That, however, was a promise Demeter discovered she would not be able to keep. King Celeus came out to her in the porch after one daughter ran in to tell him who she feared had been walking his road dusty and neglected. The other girl seated Demeter and called a slave to wash her feet. The king nodded approval of his daughters' courtesy. He had had dealings in person with Poseidon, Demeter guessed, seeing the way his eyes touched her and dropped, and he recognized her kinship to that Olympian. When she asked him flatly for the way to the entrance to Hades's realm and told him why she sought it, he did not withhold the information she desired. He told her, however, that she would have to wait about half a moon for an answer to any question or demand.

"Unless, of course, you have a way to enforce your will that we have not," he said. "But if you do not wish to use your power to that purpose, we would be honored, madam, if you would be our guest while you wait."

Two weeks, Demeter thought. She would have two weeks before she must face Hades's dripping knife. She shook her head. "Who can force proud Hades?" she replied and began to say, "I am grateful for your kindness—" but she breathed in sharply and looked down at the slave who was untying her sandal thongs.

The touch had communicated the woman's Gift, and it was a well of fertility. Demeter laughed aloud. "What is this woman's name?"

"Iambe," Celeus said uncertainly.

Demeter laid her hand on the slave's bowed head

and stroked her hair. "I will repay you richly for your hospitality," she said to Celeus, stroking the woman's hair. "I will teach Iambe certain rites, and in the coming years you will have such crops as your land has never seen before."

King Celeus bowed. "At your will, great lady."

His respect for her was so profound that Demeter thought of demanding that he send a servant to ask for Kore, but she put the notion aside, knowing it would accomplish nothing. Hades could simply ignore any demand by a messenger. However, a mother's curse in the Mother's name delivered in person might give pause even to the King of the Dead.

The very next day a guide took her to the cave entrance, leading—of all unlikely sacrifices—a sow in farrow.

When Celeus had told her of the sacrifice demanded before the dead would reply, she had asked, "Is there some special knife I must use to kill her?"

Demeter had barely managed to keep her voice steady for she had never in her life killed even a dove. On the altar of the Corn Goddess she had laid the first fruits of the ploughed field and the tended garden. Her Lady desired no living sacrifice—unlike the blood-thirsty Maiden, also an avatar of the Mother, that Artemis worshipped—and Demeter did not believe she could kill the sow.

To her enormous relief, Celeus had replied, "You do not kill her at all. In the cave there is a trough graven in the stone across the mouth of a dark passage. Do not cross that. One messenger did, and he did not return. Call out that you have brought a sacrifice. If there is no answer, you must wait and call again. Eventually the passage will begin to glow. Drive the sow over the trough. She will pass through the glow and then disappear, and one of the dead will appear to speak to you."

Even with the assurance that she would not have to kill the sow, Demeter hardly managed to maintain her dignity when the guide pointed to a black mouth in the side of the hill they were climbing. She was so frightened that she took the sow's lead and sent the guide away. Go she would, she knew, even if her legs would not hold her and she had to crawl into that open maw, but she did not want King Celeus's guide to see her weeping and trembling.

From the outside, the black of the cave seemed impenetrable, and Demeter stopped some ten steps away from the entrance, unable to drive herself closer. It was the pig, whose nose had started to twitch and twist, who bumped into her and pushed her the last few steps.

Inside, the cave was not nearly so black as she had thought because it was a shallow place and the daylight behind her illuminated a fan of the floor and wall above it. Demeter was able to see a black mouth in the wall and the gouge in the stone that marked the forbidden territory. In fact, the sow would have dragged her right over the trough, which was closer to the outer entrance than she expected, had horror not locked her muscles tight. She stopped in time, hauling back on the ringed nose so that the animal squealed in pain, but it was her shriek of terror that summoned the dead rather than any intended call.

The sow was making angry grunts and squeals, pulling on the lead until pain halted her again, when a sickly pale light rose from the floor and a ruin that had once been a man—a terrible creature, in tattered rags besmottered with black stains that Demeter knew were long-dried blood, black hollows for eyes, and what seemed like a ragged hole where its mouth and chin should have been—seemed to ooze from the wall. The lead slipped from Demeter's nerveless fingers, and the sow charged forward—and disappeared beyond the lighted area.

"Wait."

The word echoed softly. The dead thing passed back into the wall. Despite the determination that had driven Demeter to defy Zeus, ignore the scorn of her fellow Olympians, and even leave the safe haven in which she had spent her life, she would now have fled—except that her feet would not move. She stood frozen, panting with fear, mind-blank except for the screams that burst in her head but would not come out of her mouth. And then—nothing happened.

The pale light was steady in the corridor, no shrieks of an animal dying in pain and terror came out of the dark, no worse spirits came to afright her. Such fear cannot last with nothing to feed upon. The peak of her terror passed and with it her paralysis. Her knees gave way, she sank to the cold stone floor, and her eyes closed. How long she sat she did not know, but moment by moment the resolve that had nearly been routed by fear strengthened. The horror she had seen was not so terrible as black-eyed Hades with his bitter mouth and red-stained knife.

"The sacrifice is accepted. What do you desire of the dead?"

The soft hollow voice brought Demeter to her feet. The question lashed her into fury, bringing back the agonies of the whole year past. "My daughter!" she shrieked.

For a long moment, that which had once been a man was silent, as if it were thinking. Then slow words, almost reluctant, came. "The dead do not return to the outer world."

"But my daughter is not dead!" Demeter exclaimed, drawing herself up, and went on, her voice ringing in challenge. "I am Demeter, high priestess of the Corn Goddess. Tell your master Hades that he had no right to steal Kore. I demand that he return my daughter to me. King of the Dead he may be and master of the riches of the earth, but the Mother reaches even into his realm and She will not endure this abomination. By the law of the Mother, he must deliver Kore up to me, her mother."

Chapter 12

Spring was turning into summer. Returning from a day at the temple, Persephone gave a last look over her shoulder at the valley below the cave entrance. The bottom of the valley was almost dark in the shadow of the mountain, which blocked the last rays of the evening sun, but she knew the grain grew so thick that it was like a solid mass of green. This second spring she had ruled as Hades's queen, there were two smaller temples in two other valleys presided over by fully trained priestesses, and in those valleys the crop was as rich.

Persephone did not resent that. She was high priestess, but unlike her mother she did not want to keep the blessings of the Goddess in her own hands and herself quicken the grain for each small valley. The Goddess had given her two surer ways to hold her place: At each solstice all the priestesses gathered at the great temple, and Persephone fed their Gifts so they could perform their duties in full. Fortunately, it was not her strength she gave; she was only a conduit from the Goddess, who filled and refilled her with a shimmering power that lifted her spirit and garbed it in a golden joy. And the Goddess had given her Hades's heart.

She stopped and turned, looking gratefully toward the gleaming temple. There would be more bread in larger loaves this autumn. Perhaps next spring it might be possible to take some cows in calf as sacrifices or capture some of the very young calves of wild cattle and tame them. She looked up to the flanks of the hills which were too steep for planting, but no wild cattle would browse there. Instead, squat dappled bodies moved under the gnarled mountain oaks.

Chuckling aloud, Persephone turned back and walked on toward the cave. Nothing could better define Hades's wish to please her—and his good sense—than his reaction when she first urged him the past autumn to demand sows in farrow as a sacrifice.

"Sows?" he had said, black brows climbing almost into the black curls on his brow. "Sows are not dignified. To demand that an ox's blood be spilled into the trough to summon the dead . . . that is right, an action full of mystery and magic. The dead come, they listen to the suppliant and send him away. Then when the natives cannot see them, they dismiss mystery and magic, drag the ox back into the cave and butcher it, set the spells of keeping, and send the meat back to Plutos. But a sow? If you must have pork, there is more meat on a boar—but that is still less meat than on an ox."

"Do not be so silly. I do not want the sow slaughtered. There are ten to twenty piglets inside a farrowing sow. And there are lots of acorns on the mountain oak trees, even if they are dwarfed, and other nuts and berries and roots that we do not favor but pigs will eat gladly as they will eat the mushrooms in the blue-light caves. Soon there will be many full grown pigs to slaughter, whereas it will be years before we have grain enough for cattle fodder and years more before there are cattle enough to use for meat, because they breed so slowly."

Hades had frowned. "How can my folk maintain a sense of terror if they are seen chasing a squealing sow?"

"You will need to open a chamber behind the lighted place in the passage and put in it huthnon. The suppliants will not smell it, but the pigs will. They will run past the light and seem to disappear. That will have to be mystery and magic enough. If you are so worried about your dignity, say that the pig is sacred to the queen of Plutos." She remembered licking her lips as she said, "Roast crackling is worth more than dignity."

Persephone's smile broadened again as she remembered Hades's sigh and the shake of his head and twinkle in his eyes when he said, "I do not understand why you are not too fat to waddle. All you think about is food."

"Is that not why you brought me here?" Persephone had asked with a giggle.

Hades had seized her in his arms and kissed her. "It is not why I keep you here," he had murmured, pushing her back toward the big bed.

Remembering that kiss and what followed, Persephone quickened her stride toward the cave. She stepped into the dark eagerly. A strong arm reached out and steadied her against the gale that always blew. She smiled at the man as he helped her to the stair down the sinkhole. So many now passed through the entrance because of the need to care for the growing crops and the herd of pigs that Hades had ordered guards to be on duty, some to be sure the wind and steep stair caused no accidents, but others to watch across the valley for any stranger who, hunting or traveling, might stray into the valley. Those folk must "die" so that Plutos would remain inviolate.

In the great cave, all made way for her, standing out of her path and bowing respectfully, but there were many smiles, many soft murmurs of praise and gratitude. Persephone drew warmth and strength and pleasure from the love and honor shown her. She did not find the dim light in the huge cavern gloomy. It was soothing to her, quieting after the glare of the sun.

She walked the length of the cavern, lightfooted with happiness, and saw with surprise that the bronze gates to the palace were open. Persephone hesitated just a trifle as she passed through, past the bowing guards. She had not known that Hades was giving audience today and the messengers from the caverns where trade was conducted were not yet due.

Usually Hades told her and asked her to sit beside him while he gave orders or made plans; indeed, it was sometimes she who gave the orders if the decisions had to do with the crops or temples or who should serve in the outer world and who be restricted to the caves. Hades dealt with questions regarding the deep mines, trade, and . . . justice. Persephone shuddered slightly. If some evildoer had been caught, Hades would wish to spare her hearing his crime and seeing justice done.

She flicked a sidelong glance at the large arch opening into the lesser throne room, but it was dark and the corridor leading into the rock from the arch at the opposite side was quiet. On the right of that corridor, Koios's door was closed. To the left, light spilled out of Arachne's apartment. Persephone could not see beyond, so the doors of Hades's other high servants must be closed. She heard the weaver's voice chastising some poor novice and recalled that Arachne had asked her to stop in and look at a new length of fabric, but she continued straight ahead, entering the square corridor through the central arch. A servant was just stepping out of the open doorway at the back where a warren of small chambers housed the palace staff.

Persephone hesitated again in the corridor, hearing voices from the formal reception room entrance on the right, then turned away. She told herself that Hades had a right to conduct private business. He did not follow her to the temple or ask what she did there. She opened the bedchamber door on the left and walked in. The gem-set walls and crystal globes in the chandeliers came alight. She had just taken hold of the door to shut it when she heard Hades say, "Myron, ask the guard whether the queen has yet returned."

She stepped out of the doorway at once, smiling, and saw Hades at the entrance to the reception room. "I have just come in, my lord."

His face did not light up as it usually did when he saw her. Nor did he invite her to enter the reception room. He waved the servant away, came across, and drew her back into the bedchamber, shutting the door behind them.

"I have a messenger from the caves at Eleusis there," he said, gesturing toward the reception room. "He came ahead of his usual time because a woman who looks like you and said she was Demeter, your mother, came to the cave and demanded that I send back her daughter, Kore."

She stared up at him, dumbstruck. Hades looked as

if he were sitting in the judgment seat. His black eyes were hooded, his face like carven stone, his voice cold and harsh.

"But it is more than a year," she breathed. "I had hoped she would have given me up for lost by now."

Hades reached out and stroked her arm. "She loves you." His voice softer, but with a slight tremor. "You do not wish me to yield you?"

"No, of course not," Persephone said, her own voice stronger now that he had given evidence that he still wanted her. She had had a moment of horror, wondering whether he was so stiff and cold because he was trying to hide his relief that her mother had found her and he could be rid of her with honor. But she still could not see his thoughts past the black of his eyes, and she said nervously, "There is so much to do. Women come every day to the temple to ask to be priestesses. There are the crops to oversee, new valleys to be opened, the folding of the herds to be considered—"

"A husband to be loved?" Hades asked, smiling.

Persephone threw one arm around his neck and kissed him.

He cocked his head when their lips parted, but she did not speak. She wanted to beg him to lie and say he had not taken her and did not know where she was, but over the year she had lived with him she had learned that what he had told her that first day—that he did not lie—was true. He did not even like to bend the truth and would scowl and look black when she suggested a necessary evasion in dealing with contacts with the outer world.

Also, she was ashamed to admit she was afraid of her mother. She did not know how to explain that her wider experience, with his love and her observation of others who loved, had taught her how unnatural her mother's hold on her had been. She thought she could resist Demeter, but recalling her mother's obsessive hatred of Zeus over Iasion's death, she feared there were no limits to what Demeter might do to get her back.

Hades cleared his throat. "I am sorry to have to tell you that your mother was much frightened by the appearance of the messenger."

"That is his purpose," Persephone said, but she felt sick. Normally Demeter avoided ugliness. That she had not fled the horrifying spectacle a messenger presented but had persisted in demanding the return of her daughter boded ill.

"What I mean is that such a sight might make her more frantic to 'rescue' you from the horrors of your life among the dead."

That was true. Persephone's spirit lightened and she chuckled. "All those horrors, like a golden bed with a warm man in it, and clothes befitting a goddess, and enough jewels to crush me flat if I decided to wear them all at once. Oh, how I suffer!"

"Yes, but your mother does not know that," Hades said, smiling but shaking his head. He hesitated and added slowly, "Do you wish to go with the messenger and assure her that you are well and happy?"

"No!" Persephone exclaimed. "Hades, you do not know my mother. If she saw me, she would try to seize me."

Hades put an arm around her and drew her close, leading her with him to a cushioned bench just beyond the gem-picture of the waterfall. They both sat, he with one arm still holding her while the other hand tilted her face up to his.

"None can take you from me if you do not wish to go."

She sighed. "You do not know her persistence. How did she learn where I was? How did she get to Eleusis? She has never before left Olympus as many of the great mages do. She said she never would. I fear she has been seeking me for the whole year."

Hades shrugged. "I cannot really blame her. I would seek you for a hundred years if you should be lost to me and tear the earth apart until I found you."

Comforted, Persephone snuggled closer. "That is different. It is natural for a man and wife to cling together. A mother must let go of her daughter."

"True enough, but Demeter does not know that you have found a husband who loves you. We have been foolish, and unkind too, I think. Likely it is her terrible fear that you are frightened and unhappy that has driven her to search so long and so hard."

"Perhaps," Persephone agreed, feeling guilty about her mother's grief but still reluctant to have any contact with her.

Hades shook his head. "She will never believe any message we send her. It is best that she see you and see that you are happy and do not wish to leave Plutos. I will send a different messenger—Ixion, who is a smooth-tongued rogue—dressed all in jewels and gold, and I will invite her to come visit you—with a promise that she may return to Olympus or any other place within reason."

After a silence, Persephone sighed again. "I suppose that would be best," she said. She heard the flatness in her voice and found a smile. "That is very kind of you,

Hades, but is it not likely that she will learn more than you wish her to know about our land and our people?"

"She will see very little and certainly not come close enough to touch any of the 'dead.' " His lips thinned into a grim smile. "We have visitors from the outer world from time to time and have ways to deal with them. None of them have shown any inclination to linger or return."

"If you are sure her visit will do Plutos no harm . . ."

His smile warmed to gentleness and delight. "I am glad you have found my land and my people so"—he chuckled—"so palatable. Do you remember when you asked me if you would? Palatable! As if Plutos was something to eat." He laughed again, louder. "That was not long after you wanted my heart baked or broiled!"

Persephone changed another sigh to a chuckle. Clearly he did not recognize her reluctance to have her mother as a guest. In any case, she was being very silly. Demeter could not drag her out of Plutos against her will. And Hades was quite right: It would be best to convince her mother, who did love her, that she was content—more than content—happier than she had ever been in her life. Dear Hades, he probably would give her his heart baked or broiled if she wanted it.

"I have changed my mind," she said, stretching up to kiss him. "I will take your heart any way you want to offer it, but I like the *boom, boom* it makes by my ear when we lie together, so I hope you will keep it where it is."

Hades looked somewhat startled but immediately bent his head to return her kiss. A moment later his hand slid up her arm to pull the pin that held her gown at the shoulder. His mouth followed the cloth downward as it fell. Every touch was a delight, but Persephone found time before his lips reached their goal and completely bewildered her to undo the clasp that held his broad collar. That fell, too, slipping down his chest and then off his thigh onto the bench—which was just as well, for he rose to his feet a moment later, lifting her so that his lips could cling to her breast, and he would surely have trodden on the collar unaware if it had dropped to the ground.

He stood arched above her after he had laid her on the bed, his mouth moving to the other breast when he had that bared, his fingers keeping the first nipple hard and erect. His other hand teased open the knot of her girdle and then began to work her gown down. She lifted herself toward him, and the gown slid past her back and hips and was gone.

Her breath was coming hard and fast through parted lips, but she was not yet lost to all beyond the sensations of her body. She still knew what she needed and she did not want to wait while he pulled off his clothes. Resisting the urge to press his head tighter, she used her hands to unbuckle his jeweled belt and pull loose the tie of his kilt, catching both and flinging them away, grasping his hips and pulling him toward her. He needed no further invitation, but set a knee on the bed and straddled her. Before he could lower himself, she ran her hands, fingers curved to scratch—oh, so lightly—along the hollow where the thigh meets the groin. Hades flung up his head and groaned, groaned again when her hands met and drew him into her.

Nonetheless, he lowered himself slowly, beginning to tremble as her hands slipped out of the way, up along the path they had previously taken. Still, when he was lodged he lay quiet. She would have none of that. She writhed beneath him, wrapped her legs around his hips, pressing him deeper, relaxing and pulling away, and then pushing upward again. He could not resist that; moaning, he began to move with her.

"Stop, love," he gasped after a few minutes. "Stop. I cannot—"

The warning was unnecessary. Persephone was not listening and her voice drowned his as she heaved against him more violently, precipitating the explosive climax he had been struggling to control. Emptied, Hades lay flat, unable for the moment to do more than breathe.

After another few minutes Persephone said faintly, "You are forever telling me I am not a wraith. Neither are you."

"Sorry," Hades muttered. "I am too tired to move. Just give me a push and I will fall over." He did, however, lever himself up and roll onto his back. After another few moments of silence, he asked, "What brought that on?"

At first Persephone did not reply. Then she said, "I just wanted you. When you said that about baking or broiling your heart I—I remembered how good you have been to me."

"A very fitting expression of gratitude," Hades said.

He was smiling, and he closed his eyes as if to sleep, but despite the effort he had expended he did not now feel sleepy. The brief explosion of passion was not at all like Persephone's usual behavior. Not that she was reluctant in his bed, but she had developed a taste for refinement in lovemaking. She did not grab and rush to climax, as a child seized and devoured a sweet it thought might be denied it. His teeth set when he realized he had inadvertently defined his sense of unease.

Once it was clear in his mind, however, he was certain the explanation of her haste was correct. But it was impossible that Persephone should fear he would be snatched away. That she might be snatched from him? The tenseness that had crept into his muscles eased as he recalled that she had warned him several times that her mother would persist in trying to get her back.

Hades drew a deep breath of pure satisfaction. She had become all and everything to him, so much so that he was often racked with senseless fears. Every now and then she seemed to look inside herself or away into nothing and he would begin to wonder whether she really cared for him or had only accepted her state as captive with good grace. His eyes opened and he smiled. Good grace did not include what had just happened between them.

The strength was coming back to his limbs and he was suddenly eager to meet and overcome the last threat to his happiness. He turned his head to tell Persephone what he intended, but she had not recovered as quickly as he and seemed to be asleep. Then he thought better of his notion. Her trouble was that she was used to Demeter always getting her own way.

Well, Demeter might be high priestess in Olympus, but she had no power in Plutos. Still, she would make less trouble once she had seen that Persephone was happy and had every luxury any woman could desire. But he need not distress Persephone by talking about her mother. He would arrange Demeter's visit as a surprise, and when Persephone saw first that her mother was powerless in Plutos and second that she recognized her daughter was safe and well, Persephone's fears would be removed.

Hades eased himself from the bed gently, drew the cover over his wife, and picked up his kilt, belt, and collar. Decently clad, he went out and sent a servant for Ixion, to whom he explained the situation.

"So you must dress as richly as a king, as richly as you can without looking ridiculous. You are to say these words exactly to Lady Demeter: Hades, King of Plutos, has, with the permission of her father Zeus, taken to wife the Lady Persephone—not an unnamed Kore—and Persephone is now Queen of Plutos and high priestess of the Goddess in her own temple."

"Will that pacify her?" Ixion asked. "Just words? No matter how richly I am dressed?"

"I do not expect it, which is why you are to use your own words and your best powers of persuasion to invite her to visit her daughter for as long or as short a time as will please her." Hades took a magnificent ring, a gold-set cabochon-cut ruby dark as blood, from his finger and passed it to Ixion. "Give her this as my pledge that she may enter Plutos, stay safe in Plutos, and be escorted out of Plutos to any reasonable place, including Olympus, at her own will."

"I doubt she will reach for it across the blood trough. Shall I step over? She may know me from that little . . . ah . . . disagreement I had with Zeus. She always watched closely anything to do with him."

The black of Hades's eyes was suddenly bottomless. "Do not try the little game you played with Hera with Queen Persephone. I do not have Zeus's bad conscience to make me equally merciful."

Ixion swallowed hard. "Queen Persephone would not waste spit on me," he said.

"Perhaps not," Hades replied with a smile that brought cold beads of sweat to Ixion's brow. Then the rictus of his lips softened. "However, if you can tempt the Lady Demeter, I would not mind at all—and Zeus would probably forgive you your trespass and invite you back to Olympus."

Relieved, Ixion laughed. "I will do my best," he promised, "but I am not sure I wish to return to Olympus. I would rather have my own valley for crops and herds—that one beyond the blue-light cave—" He stopped because Hades had raised a finger.

"There is time to consider that," Hades said. "First accomplish your task." He was silent for a moment, then added, "You cannot step over the trough or your fine clothes will turn to rags and your jewels to dry turds. However, you can reach your arm across to her. She will see the change in your sleeve and your rings, but *my* ring will remain what it is and your hand will also remain strong and healthy."

"That will help," Ixion agreed.

Hades nodded. "Say anything you like to calm her and assure her. My only purpose is to convince her that Persephone wishes to remain here. That means Lady Demeter must not be exposed to any horrors. I will furnish you with crystals that will provide light, and it is only a candlemark of walking to the river. You will have to take her north in one of the boats that carry the trade goods, drug her so she will sleep during the passage between the rivers, and then bring her up the Styx. I will have watchers to warn me and I will meet you in the lower cave, making sure it is all alight. I can bring her up to the palace myself."

Once Ixion was on his way, Hades put the problem of Demeter at the back of his mind. It would be almost a moon before she could arrive in Plutos and a hard life had taught him not to look for trouble before it arrived on its own. He was not surprised that Persephone never asked him what message he had returned to her mother's demand nor that she seemed a trifle uneasy for the first few days. Her reactions seemed to confirm what he had decided about her feelings.

As time passed, however, he was puzzled when she did not grow calmer but instead began to cling to him as she had not done since her first few days in Plutos. Instead of going to the temple or discussing and planning with Koios the winter accommodation for the pigs or other such matters, she would often sit in his workroom, just watching him. At night she would creep back into his arms to sleep after they had made love or sometimes wake him to couple a second time.

He did not mind her watching him—in fact, nothing delighted him more than to see her pleasure and amazement as precious gems and exquisite jewelry took shape under his hands—and he would have been glad to satisfy her five times a night. Unfortunately, he could not believe she only craved his company and his body. This was something like the snatching at him just after he had told her of her mother's demand, but not exactly the same. It was a kind of long farewell, as if she were trying both to store him up within herself and fill him with her against the famine of a long parting.

Hades told himself it was all nonsense. He was master of the underworld, and no force could wrest Persephone from him. Unless she demanded the right to leave . . . He always pushed that thought down deep

and smothered it with memories of her kisses and
fondling, the way she would take his hand for no
reason at all, the way she would look around their
bedchamber or the great cave. The love she bore him
and the place was plain. And if she did not ask to
leave, no one could force her.

Nonetheless, Hades was well pleased when Ixion
returned alone. Angry and abashed at his failure, the
man said, "She would not come. She insisted that you
were trying to trap her among the dead so that she
could not bring her daughter back to the outer world."

"All know that my promise to return a person to the
outer world is good."

"The woman is mad. She knows only what she
wants to know and has the fixity of purpose of the
mad. She would not listen to a word I said. When I
told her Kore did not exist and Queen Persephone was
your wife and priestess, she said you had no right to
name her and she had no right to accept the name."

"That is nonsense. The reason parents choose a
name before the character of the babe is known, before
a babe is shown to anyone, is to prevent another from
fixing an evil name on the child."

"You know it. I know it. All the world knows it—
but Demeter will not accept the truth. She has her own
fixed idea, that she would name her daughter Demeter
on her own deathbed and so live on. Nor would she
accept the right of a father, of blood or of adoption,
to give a daughter in marriage. A daughter is a
mother's, she insisted."

Hades shrugged. "I am sorry if Persephone is disappointed that her mother would not come, but Demeter's madness cannot change law and custom. I knew
she would be difficult, but I thought her desire to see

her daughter and offer her comfort—if she believed Persephone needed comfort—would overcome her fear and suspicion. You have done well enough. I cannot promise you a valley of your own, because none may be available until long in the future, but some reward I will find for you."

He waved Ixion away, but did not go to the temple himself or send anyone to fetch Persephone so he could tell her at once. In fact, he kept putting it off, until they were ready to get into bed, when he turned toward her abruptly and simply blurted out, "I sent Ixion to invite your mother to visit us, but she would not come."

To his intense relief, Persephone smiled brilliantly. "Was that what has been on your mind these past weeks, and most of all today? You looked at me so strangely."

"I looked at you strangely? Is it any wonder? Have you not been acting peculiarly? And you have done your share of looking too."

Persephone laughed. "I was a little worried. I guessed you had sent someone to bring my mother here. You said you would and, although you did not mention her again, I know you always do what you say. So when you did not mention mother again, I began to be afraid you had decided it would be the right thing to give me back to her if she insisted."

"What?"

The roar made her blink and then laugh again. "You are so careful of what is right, and you did abduct me—which, after all, is *not* right."

"I try to speak the truth and keep my word, Persephone, but I am not an idiot. I had your fath—Zeus's permission. Even so, if you were unhappy here, if you hated me, I might have considered letting you go, now that you have trained some priestesses who can train others. It would break my heart to part from you, but if *you* wished to leave me, I would set your good above my own. Your good. No one else's. No one will ever take you from me against your will. I swear, I would make the earth swallow Olympus or bring the mountains down upon it, before I would yield you to your mother or anyone else."

"No Hades!" She flung herself into his arms and buried her face in his breast. "Do not make such an oath!"

"I have made it already and long ago although I did not speak it aloud," he said, his mouth grim. "You are the dazzling brightness that has lighted my soul after a long, long darkness. I was not unhappy. To me the dark is comfortable and I had duty and sometimes satisfaction. But I never had joy. You are my light, my joy. That it is new to me makes it so much more precious. Do you think I would allow any man—or woman—to take you away from me and hold you against your will?"

Chapter 13

Demeter turned her back on the evil, deceptive thing that wore the lineaments of Ixion. She knew that Zeus had cast Ixion into Hades's realm with a blast of lightning for trying to make love to Hera. Had Hades sent Ixion as his messenger because he hoped she would listen to another Zeus had wronged? Then why had he not sent Iasion? She shuddered and told herself it was because Iasion, who loved her and loved his daughter, would have refused to carry such a message. But what had sprung into her mind with the question and lay behind everything she thought and everything Ixion said, was the terrifying knowledge that she would not have known Iasion's face. What if she met him by chance among the dead and did not know him?

Quite unaware of the fact that she was clutching Hades's ring in her hand, she fled into the sunlight. Behind her she could hear Ixion calling, begging her to return, begging her to listen and consider, promising to remain so that if she changed her mind she could return to the cavern. When she was beyond the sound of that pleading voice, she sat down on a stone to catch her breath. What a terrible fear Hades must arouse in the dead to make his messenger plead so eagerly. What a terrible fate he must have planned for her . . . What a terrible fate had overtaken her Kore!

Raising her hands to hide her face, she became aware that one was tightly clenched. She opened it and stared at the exquisite setting and the ruby, which in the sunlight glowed like pulsing blood. With a squeak of revulsion, she dropped the ring, but it lay winking at her, unchanged. It had not become a stinking turd netted in matted hair as had the rings on the hand Ixion had thrust across the trough. This was, indeed, from Hades's own hand. She remembered that when he stalked the streets in Olympus and brought a quick end to the dying, his jewels had glittered in the torchlight amid the rags and loathsome decorations of those who followed him.

After a moment, she bent and picked up the ring, holding it gingerly. But she sensed no magic in the thing. It was a beautiful ring, no more. Perhaps it only spread a spell in Plutos, but she was not going there, not even for Kore!

"But that is not for lack of love," she cried aloud to the empty countryside. "That is because I can be of more use to Kore, more able to arrange her escape to freedom, where I am than if I myself were a prisoner in the underworld."

Even spoken aloud the words held little comfort. She really had no idea what to do next. It had not occurred to her that once she discovered his abduction, Hades would refuse flatly to restore Kore to her. She had been shocked mute when Ixion said boldly that Hades had named her daughter. She shook her head in furious negation. A name of such power!

Demeter had expected Hades to set a high price, but

she was not concerned over the cost of redeeming Kore. She knew she could wrest virtually anything— even one of his daughters to replace Kore—out of King Celeus, who was in such awe of her now that the field she had blessed was ten times as fertile as all the others, that he probably would not have stopped her from dropping his infant son, whom she often held and fondled, into the fire. But instead of setting a price, Hades had refused to return Kore, had said Kore did not exist, and invited her to visit Queen Per—no, she would never accept that name!

The invitation was a trap. It must be. Demeter knew Hades's reputation. Even Zeus, who trusted no one, almost trusted him. Nonetheless, honorable men had been known to bend when the prize was great enough. Kore was so high a stake . . . Had Hades learned of Kore's Gift? If so, he would never give her up willingly. Someone would have to steal Kore, as he had stolen her. Demeter stared down at the ring. Kore was not completely out of her reach. Hades had invited her to Plutos with a safe conduct.

A violent fit of trembling struck her. No, she could not do it herself. He would suspect her. Behind the surface thoughts, behind the smooth, brilliant surface of the ruby that held her eyes, was a tall form that stretched his arms to her and called her name . . . but his face was blank and she could not paint features on it. Her hand closed over Hades's ring. She would find a hero to rescue Kore and give him the safe conduct.

The decision gave her renewed hope and she rose and walked downhill to where the Eleusinian guard waited to escort her back to King Celeus's country palace. When she told the king the excuse she had concocted—that she was prohibited from entering

Hades's realm lest her powers of fertility be contaminated by the sterility of death—and broached the plan of sending a hero in her place, he did not refuse, but he did not suggest any man, only stared at her hopelessly.

"So, great king," she challenged him, "is there none, not one man in your entire kingdom who would do my bidding?"

"Great lady, you can order that one of my warriors, even my eldest son Triptolemus, go. He or any other will obey your bidding, but to what purpose? Can you believe that even with the ring to bring him safely into Plutos my son or the strongest of my men could wrest your daughter from Hades's grasp? Hard and strong as stone is Hades. What man can match a god?"

She could not deny Hades was a god. Somehow the native peoples had lost knowledge of the Mother and worshipped strange animistic beings or, more and more often, the great mages of Olympus. Her own power over King Celeus rested on the fact that he believed she was a god.

"I did not expect a man to wrestle with Hades but to—" But to what? Trick him? She could not think of any plan herself, so what could she expect of these poor creatures? She shook her head. "No, I will bid no man do what he does not believe he can bring to a successful conclusion. I will reward any person who can convince me he—or she—can bring back my daughter, but I do not desire useless sacrifices that are only likely to annoy the King of the Dead."

If Demeter could have laughed at anything, she would have laughed at the expression on Celeus's face. Ungrateful dog! He had profited enormously from trade with Plutos and from extending his hospitality to her, yet she could read in his eyes that he wished he had never heard of either of them. And he looked down at the stone floor of his inner audience chamber with such horror that Demeter was suddenly stricken with a new realization. If she got Kore back by trickery, how was she to keep her? Hades could come up out of the earth at her feet wherever she fled.

It was that problem that occupied her mind more than whether King Celeus had indeed spread word of the reward she had offered to anyone who would bring her daughter out of Plutos. Certainly while summer peaked and passed, no one came to suggest a plan to her and ask for the ring that would provide safe conduct. Some small satisfaction warmed Demeter's heart when Celeus ordered that a handsome temple be built for her in the city. Another satisfaction came to her when the Eleusinians gathered their richest harvest in memory.

The temple was dedicated at the harvest ceremonies. The large stone porticos and storerooms were not complete, but the altar and Demeter's sacred chambers were liveable. Taking Iambe, who had been freed, and several other women in whom she had detected a Gift, Demeter moved into the temple. Her life began to approach the pattern she had established in Olympus, except that her acolyte and priestesses worshipped her instead of envying her.

She had not forgotten Kore. Sometimes she took Hades's ring out of the golden box in which she kept it and wept a little. But she had forgotten the problem she had created in Olympus, and even if she had remembered it she would not have associated the disastrous harvests in Olympus with Poseidon. Thus she felt nothing but a mild surprise when a temple servant told her that an aged seer called Nerus had begged audience with her.

In a moment the surprise was displaced by anxiety. What if Poseidon resented the fact that Celeus had built her a temple? She had, she now recalled, promised to teach the mysteries of the Corn Goddess only with his approval. What would Celeus do if confronted by a contest between her and Poseidon? No, it must not come to that. She had become very fond of the people of Eleusis.

"Bid Nerus come here to my private apartment," she told the servant.

Her mind raced madly, seeking explanations and palliations in the few minutes it took the woman to shepherd Nerus into her sitting room, and it was all wasted.

"Hermes has come seeking you in my master's palace," Nerus said. "King Poseidon thinks it unwise to say you did not stay after the spell brought you because that mischievous trickster is sure to winkle out the truth from some unsuspecting servant. The king is willing to deny he knows to where you took ship, since fewer know that, but he thinks it useless. Word of the crops that have been garnered in Eleusis will soon come to Zeus's ears."

Demeter stood up, tears of fury springing to her eyes. Zeus! Always Zeus who tore away her little comfort, even the shreds of peace she had patched together here. Her mounting rage was such that it wiped from her both fear for herself and consideration for the people who loved her.

"I do not care whether Zeus knows where I am or not," she spat. "The mystery of the Corn Goddess is mine to give, not to withhold, as Zeus himself told me.

And if he thinks to blast my temple and harm the people of Eleusis, I do not think the other mages will long endure his tyranny. I may be first to suffer his wrath, but who among them will believe he or she will not be next? Will he blast Hera's temples? Athena's? Ares's?"

"Forgive me, my lady," Nerus said. "In my eagerness to pass on my master's message and explain that he wishes only good to you, I have given you a false notion. Zeus has made no threats. Hermes only said he was asked to find you and bring you back to Olympus."

Zeus wanted her back? For one moment she was utterly bewildered, able to think only that Zeus begrudged her the worship of the Eleusinians and wished to deny them the rich harvest she had given them. Then she remembered that the harvest in Olympus must have been a disaster. Aglaia and Dorkas could not have properly quickened the seed. Zeus wanted her back to force her to restore fertility to Olympus.

"I will not go! I will stick a knife between Hermes's ribs if he tries to hold me close to transport me, and—"

"Please! I have no intention of forcing you, Demeter. That would defeat Zeus's purpose and make him angry at me."

Both Demeter and Nerus jumped. Just inside the door stood the tall, curly-haired Hermes, his lips curved just a trifle upward with the suppressed amusement of having appeared where he was not expected or wanted.

Demeter scrabbled on the small table beside the chair in which she had been sitting and caught up the little knife she used for paring fruit. "My Lady does not love magic," she breathed, her eyes staring with near madness, "but I know one spell that will dry up the earth past ever again bearing and wither a man's virility so that he is less than a eunuch."

"Demeter!" The laughter was gone from Hermes's mouth and his eyes were plain brown. "I will not move from where I am. And I will cast no spell while I am near you, none, for any purpose at all until you give me leave—I swear by the Styx, which never sees the sun and to which I will be confined if I lie. Just listen to me. I think you will be very glad of what you hear."

"I am glad of no message that comes from Zeus."

"He only wishes to speak to you, Demeter. He will give whatever assurance you desire that you come and go freely."

"But I do not wish to speak to him! I said all I had to say nearly two years ago. I want my daughter back. I know now Zeus himself did not take her. He sold her to Hades—for what, I do not know, perhaps the jewel-flowers that Hera wears. When Zeus buys back my daughter and gives her to me, I will listen to a message from him."

"But Demeter, Zeus cannot—"

"Go away, Hermes," Nerus said hastily as Demeter closed her eyes and began to whisper to herself, "quickly! She is beyond reason and will destroy us all." The young mage flung himself out of the door near which he had been standing, and Nerus shook Demeter lightly. "He is gone, my lady. Do not cast a spell that can do me little harm at my age, and will dry up all your power."

She opened her eyes and, after a moment, smiled. "I should have gone with Hermes and cast the spell in Zeus's court."

Nerus stared at her without reply, but apparently it

was not her threat that silenced him because suddenly his eyes glazed. "There will be no need to speak the spell of living death," he mumbled. "You will get back your daughter, but not Kore, never Kore, and Pers—"

"Wake up, old man!" Demeter snapped, stepping forward and slapping his face lightly.

She had heard Nerus called a seer several times and recognized instantly a moment of prophecy. Unuttered, it might be unfulfilled, and Demeter was not about to hear any worse than she had heard already, even if startling Nerus out of his trance killed him. Nonetheless, she felt guilty enough to steady him while his eyes rolled up and he jerked and shuddered. He shook his head dazedly when the fit was over and looked around the room, then sighed.

"I am sorry Hermes followed me here," he said. "I hope you will not blame my master. King Poseidon bade me take precautions, and I did, but it is almost impossible to hide anything from that master of mischief."

"No, I do not blame Poseidon," Demeter said slowly. "He has been a good friend to me."

She had only taken in what he said with the surface of her mind, and her reply was mechanical. She was thinking as she spoke of the first part of Nerus's prophecy—that she would get back her daughter—and remembering her fear when she first tried to think of a plan to steal Kore from Hades that the lord of the underworld could rise up out of the earth at her feet. Even if Zeus bought Kore back, what was to stop Hades from seizing her again?

The answer had come when she said the name Poseidon. Water! That would stop Hades. He was master of earth and rock, but not of water. He could not pass through water any more than Poseidon could pass through rock. If Zeus did get Kore back, they would both be safe on Aegina—if Poseidon would permit them to stay there. Demeter remembered all too well Poseidon's first refusal to ask Hades to return Kore and his hidden fear of the King of the Dead. But if he feared Hades, he must hate him too, and if Hades could not reach Aegina, Poseidon was safe from him—and might well enjoy keeping her poor Kore safe from recapture. Demeter smiled at Nerus and began to speak.

Having closed the door between himself and Demeter, Hermes was free of his oath not to work a spell without her permission. He pulled at his Gift, imaged a spot before Zeus's throne in Olympus, and gritted his teeth as a cold beyond cold leeched energy out of him. He barely had time to think that it was fortunate the spells he created to move others from one place to another took their energy from the one who used the spell, when he appeared at the spot he had imaged before the empty throne. His knees trembled slightly, having made two passages in so short a time, but he set off to find Zeus without delay.

Five days later Hermes appeared in a similar spot in Hades's great throne room. His legs did not tremble because it was the first passage he had made that day, but there were deep bruises under his eyes and his cheeks were hollowed by the heavy drawing on his power since he had first spoken to Demeter.

Hermes had chosen to arrive in Hades's great cavern at a time when the King of the Dead usually gave public audience. As he expected, the throne was occupied, and his arrival out of thin air caused some stir among the waiting petitioners. However, Hermes was almost as surprised as they. Beside Hades's throne was another chair, equally magnificent, which held a woman of ravishing beauty. Her hair poured like a gilded waterfall down over her shoulders and back, her eyes put to shame the glow in the best yellow diamonds, power was an almost palpable haze around her. That her quality was appreciated was evident: her gown was a diaphanous mystery and the brilliance and quantity of exquisite goldwork and precious stones that adorned her hair, brow, ears, neck, arms, waist— everywhere—was stunning.

"It is a long time since I have seen you, Hermes." Hades's deep voice was calm; he was not shocked by Hermes's sudden appearance nor in the least concerned about his purpose in coming. His black stare was level, compelling, as he continued, "Let me introduce you to my wife, Queen Persephone, who is also high priestess of the Goddess among us."

Hermes smiled—nervously—and bowed. The name probably meant "dazzling brightness," but there was another meaning for "Persephone" in the old language, with which Hermes's love for words, especially words with double meanings, had made him familiar. Persephone could also mean "brilliant destroyer." Either meaning seemed remarkably appropriate to the woman, and she looked at him as calmly as did Hades.

Hermes was never easy around Hades, not because he had any fears of being trapped in the underworld, but because Hades was indifferent to him. Unlike others, Hades did not fear Hermes's mischief; the quiet, dark power in him swiftly quenched any inclination on Hermes's part to practice tricks or tell lies. Hades was always patient, never angry, but every time a wicked notion flicked through Hermes's mind in Hades's presence, the young mage had a vision of a large, empty hole where his palace had once been.

"I bring a message from Zeus," Hermes said.

Without replying, Hades turned his head to look at Persephone. "Perhaps," she said, "it would be better to hear Zeus's message in private." She cocked a finger, and a big, strong man hurried forward and bowed. "Aktaion, would you be kind enough to take Hermes to the central audience chamber in the palace? Koios might wish to join him there while we finish our business here."

Hermes opened his mouth to ask if there were a new ruler in Plutos, but Hades had already turned his attention to a man with blackened face and hands who was saying something about a golden death that crept into a deep fissure. For one moment the woman beside Hades faded and looked uncertain and Hermes thought, *Kore. Mother bless me, that is Kore.* Then the woman's face firmed into a kind of disgusted hatred and Hermes shivered. *No,* he thought, *that was Kore. She is Persephone now without a doubt.*

He shuddered again as he followed the big man, who had bite scars on one cheek and one arm and shoulder, not because of the time he would have to spend with Koios, although the crippled steward made him feel sick, but because he feared he would be preaching a lost cause. He had counted on Hades having grown tired of his simpering captive, of a tearful and terrified little girl—not that Kore was any smaller of stature than Persephone, but that she seemed somehow *less*—begging to be allowed to return to her mother. He uttered a cracked laugh at the idea of

Persephone begging for anything, particularly for her mother.

Olympus would starve, he thought. With the crops they had and the secret importation of grain from the natives through the many temples where the Olympian "gods" were worshipped, they could eke out existence this year. But if they had no better crops next year, the cattle would have to be slaughtered because of the lack of fodder, and— The anxious thoughts were interrupted by a near hysterical gasp of laughter. Apollo would have a fit if his precious "golden" cattle were threatened.

Hermes caught his lip between his teeth. That might not be all bad. Perhaps Zeus could use the threat of slaughtering the cattle to convince Apollo and the other mages who controlled winds and temperature to alter the weather in the valley to provide grazing over the whole winter. No. Hermes shook his head. Such extended effort by the mages of Olympus would be seriously debilitating; it might not even be possible. He was already exhausted by the repeated effort of leaping between Olympus and Eleusis and Aegina. The thud and drag of Koios's approach was almost a relief.

The cripple struggled into the room and nodded as well as he could with his crooked neck. "You will not wish to eat here," Koios said, with a smile that made Hermes look away. "But sitting down will not bind you in any way, and I . . . find standing uncomfortable." He dropped into a chair and gestured toward another.

"I was not born when Kronos was Mage-King," Hermes said.

Koios uttered his rusty, gargling laugh. "I do not blame you for the damage done me. Nor did our lady intend to make you miserable by my presence. She is so kind and tender-hearted, she loves me because I love Hades. She does not think of how I look but enjoys my company and forgets that I make others uncomfortable."

That was true enough, but Koios knew Persephone had not sent him to join Hermes because she wished to give Hermes pleasure but because she did not wish to give Hermes any chance to get into—or make—trouble.

Hermes smiled blandly, but kind and tender-hearted was scarcely what he had thought likely characteristics of the woman Hades called Persephone. However, Koios's remark had given him one thread of hope. He had seen that something of Kore remained, and Koios seemed to imply that more remained than he had thought. Kore had been gentle and kind. Perhaps all was not lost. If he could play on what was left of Kore inside Persephone, she might pity her mother and the people of Olympus and induce Hades to let her go.

He had not intended to expose the parlous state of Olympus, simply to say that Zeus had changed his mind and wanted his daughter back, that he would supply another priestess to take Kore's place. That approach was hopeless. The idea that Hades could be indifferent to the magnificent creature who sat beside him—and to whom he deferred—was impossible. However, it was barely possible that Hades had bitten off more than he could chew and was regretting it. Persephone was rather overwhelming.

Hermes made some general answer to what Koios had said, adding his own praise of Persephone's startling beauty. He got from Koios a litany of the lady's perfections but the remarks were all so personally related to Koios himself that Hermes could not judge what Hades felt about so overpowering a consort. His hopes rose and fell during the conversation, but he was no wiser when Hades and Persephone joined them.

First his heart sank when he saw the possessive way Hades's hand rested on his wife's shoulder as they came through the door. His hopes rose again, however, when Persephone stripped off most of her jewels and dropped them carelessly on the table next to Koios as she bent to kiss the cripple's cheek and ask a low-voiced question. She was still lovely, but the incandescent beauty and aura of power that had startled him in the throne room were gone. Her expression was indeed kind and gentle.

Koios did not answer, only smiled and patted the hand she had laid on his arm, and she straightened and moved to a chair. Hades seated himself too, and they both faced Hermes.

"You may give me Zeus's message now," Hades said.

"It is about Demeter," Hermes said. "She knows where Kore—"

"There is no Kore!" Hades's voice grated like stone on stone. "Persephone is my wife and my queen."

"I beg your pardon," Hermes said. "I was thinking of Demeter, and she uses . . . ah . . . that word."

Although his attention seemed to be fixed on Hades, Hermes's eyes had flicked once to Persephone. It did not take more than that flickering glance to tell him that the lady was even less fond of the name Kore than Hades was. Persephone felt no longing to be again the nameless daughter of Demeter.

"We are aware that my mother knows I am Hades's wife," Persephone said. "Although he does not wel-

come the living of the outer world, my dear husband
was kind enough to invite her to come to visit me. She
did not choose to come. Perhaps she did not believe
what Hades's messenger told her. I hope you will tell
her that I am *very* happy here. You have seen for
yourself in what honor I am held." She glanced at
Hades and smiled. "You can also see that I am even
more indulged, cosseted, and pampered here than I
ever was in Olympus. My every wish is granted, almost
before I know I have wished it. Let her heart be at
ease."

Hades smiled and nodded. "And let her know that
my offer for her to come, stay as long or as short a time
as she desires, and to go when she will and where she
will, still stands. In fact, I will buy a spell—"

Persephone put a hand on Hades's arm and he
stopped and looked at her. She shook her head in-
finitesimally. Hermes barely managed to keep his face
expressionless. That little shake of the head said
clearly that Persephone did not want her mother to
visit. Hades had been about to offer to buy a spell from
him that would bring Demeter to Plutos and take her
back to Olympus at her own will—which should certainly reassure her if she was afraid of being trapped—
and her daughter had stopped him. But Hermes pretended he had not seen. His quick mind was leaping
here and there seeking some opening.

"I am sorry," he said. "I cannot tell her anything—"

"Is something wrong with my mother?" Persephone
asked, seeming concerned at last. She caught at
Hades's hand.

Hermes was extremely tempted to say Demeter was
dying and begging for her daughter on her deathbed.
The lie would not have troubled him, nor would trick-

ing Kore/Persephone. She was only a single person;
her happiness should not weigh heavier than the well-
being of an entire city. But Hermes felt Hades's black
gaze chill through his flesh to his bones. He looked up
and realized the salvation of Olympus meant very little
to him if he were not going to enjoy it, and though his
lips were parted to speak, no sound came out.

"Well, what is wrong with Demeter?" Hades prodded.

The lock on Hermes's tongue was broken, but he
did not like the taste of fear and he resolved to tell the
truth, or at least as much of it as would serve his
purpose. "She—she is mad," he said. "She will not
listen to anything anyone says. All of Olympus tried to
calm her. She does not desire hope or reassurance. She
only moans for her daughter to be returned to her."

To Hermes's intense disappointment, instead of
showing an increased sympathy for her mother's sad
condition, Persephone's expression cleared. "I am
sorry if she is making herself unhappy," she said, "but
I cannot see that there is anything more Hades or I can
do."

That door was closed, and Hermes had realized
when Hades sealed his lie in his mouth with a single
glance that no argument would convince him to yield
up his wife. Hermes had nothing left but one last bitter
truth. "Her unhappiness is somewhat more important
to us," he said harshly. "She has been wandering,
looking for you, since last winter. She was not in
Olympus to bless the fields and quicken the seed this
spring—and we have less crops than grow wild in the
natives' lands."

"But the temple—did not Aglaia and Dorkas—"

"They tried. Aglaia nearly died. The only reason we

are not starving already is due to what she blessed before she collapsed because Dorkas—she was worse than useless. I think the fields she blessed bore less than those that went without altogether."

"I am sorry to hear this," Hades said. "My people are accustomed to doing without, so I can trade some grain for . . . more pigs, I guess, or—" He looked at Persephone. "Would you rather take some sheep?"

"We can think about pigs or sheep later," Persephone said. "Surely now that she knows where I am, my mother will return to Olympus. And I know she will not withhold the blessing of the Goddess once she is there."

"She will not return. She is settled into a temple the Eleusinians built for her and threatened to stab me if I tried to come close enough to transport her. She says that Zeus sold you to Hades and that she will never set foot in Olympus again until you are there."

"Then Olympus is very likely to starve," Hades remarked coldly. "I suggest that you and Zeus bend your fertile minds to some ruse by which Demeter can be persuaded. It will be for a better purpose than your devices usually have, and the pinch in your bellies should be a fine inspiration. I know what you are hinting at, but that easy path will not be yours. Remember, Persephone has been eating the food of Plutos for nearly two years." His lips quirked, but his eyes were empty pools of darkness. "Have you not yet learned that the dead do not return?"

"Kore—Persephone is not dead," Hermes said desperately. In spite of Hades's frown, he struggled on. "I told you, Demeter is mad. She began the curse of the living death because I tried to stay and reason with her—"

"But that would destroy *her* power as well as blasting you, and the earth, and . . ." Persephone's voice faded away.

"I said she was mad!" Hermes cried. "That is why no clever device of mine or Zeus's is worth trying. She will destroy herself and the whole valley. I tell you, she will feed Olympus only if her daughter is with her. Hades, have mercy. You can have any or all of the priestesses in the temple. Only let me take Ko—Persephone back with me."

"No."

Hermes drew himself up. "Hades, we will not die without a fight. We are great mages also, and all our lives are at stake. Your powers are great, but against all of us—"

"No."

"Wait, Hades," Persephone said. "Yours is not the choice of whether I go or stay. Remember—the choice is mine." She turned her head to meet Hermes's eyes. "Come here, tomorrow at this time, and I will tell you what we have decided." She cast a glance back at her husband's face, which seemed carved in stone, and said to Hermes, "Go! Now!"

Hermes went on the instant—gratefully.

Chapter 14

There was only the sound of moving air as the spot where Hermes had been sitting was filled, then Persephone cried, "Hades, please!"

He rose slowly, then went and helped Koios to his feet. "Farewell," he said to Persephone.

"You are about to jump into a cave full of chrusos thanatos because you are too stubborn to turn back," Koios said, raising his crutch and blocking Hades's way to the door. "Perhaps there is no need to turn back. Stand still and see if you can avoid going deliberately to a lingering death. What can you lose by listening?"

"I do not *wish* to leave you," Persephone cried.

Hades turned to face her and Koios made his way to the door, went out, and closed it behind him.

"There is no need for you leave me," Hades said. "I do not see what there is to talk about. If you are still here tomorrow, after Hermes is gone, all will be well."

"No, it will not," she snapped. "We will all soon be dead."

Hades uttered a bitter bark of laughter. "We are all dead already, are we not?"

"I am not a fool!" Persephone exclaimed. "I know that no one who has really died is here. My father Iasion is not here, nor Adonis, nor Narcissus, nor many others that have truly died in the body. How long did you think I could work with the women in the temple and the men in the fields and not come to understand what you meant when you told me your folk were dead in the outer world but alive in the underworld?"

He walked a few steps away, half turning, as if to put himself at a safe distance. "You are cleverer than I thought you would be that first day. You believed the tale of the six pomegranate seeds, so I thought you would believe I had cast a spell that made the wraiths seem solid."

"For a while I did. When I first saw Koios, I did not believe anyone could live with such injuries. But Koios is not dead. No dead mind could be like his. Our people are the outcasts, the exiles, the scapegoats—dead only in the sense that they were driven out or escaped into Plutos. That is why they cannot return to the outerworld, and why they must eat and drink and have clothes to keep them warm. Did you think I would not notice that the children are not scarred or burned or broken, and that women bear children in a perfectly ordinary way—a strange thing for the dead to do."

"So you know. But above in Olympus, they do not. For all of Hermes's brave words, they will not attack Plutos."

"Hades," Persephone said softly, stretching a hand toward him. "Do you not see? They will not attack Plutos. They will attack you! And they will snatch me. You are not the only one who can abduct a woman."

Hades laughed again, but he had turned back to face her. "They will not take you by force if they do not want their pretty city swallowed up into the earth."

"That is why they will attack you first. They will kill you, Hades, to get at me." She ran to him and threw her arms around him. "I love you," she sobbed. "I do not wish to lose you when all I need is a few days or weeks to explain to my mother." She turned her tear-wet face up to him. "She loves me, Hades. She will not want to see me weep for you and cry day and night of my loneliness and desire. She lost a man she loved. She will let me return to you and then will do the Goddess's work at Olympus when she understands that Zeus did me the greatest kindness any man can do by giving me the perfect husband. I will tell her I am only happy with you."

"Would you cry for loss of me?" he asked.

"I love you," she whispered.

He loosened her arms from around him and pushed her away, but gently and only far enough so he could see her face. "You never said you loved me before— not once in all the time we have been together, not even when you begged me to enter you. Why do you say it now?"

She sniffed. "Because now I want you to be sure. Before, I wished to dangle the carrot of my confession to keep your big black eyes from looking elsewhere."

He shook his head. "If you mean that, you are as mad as your mother."

"You are a beautiful man, Hades, and a great mage—and you did not learn to make the kind of love that brings me to plead with you to give yourself to me without knowing other women." She shrugged. "I thought it could do no harm to leave a little doubt in you so I would have a small extra weapon. I have seen women look at you. If my charms should grow stale with much use—"

"You *are* mad. I grow hungrier and more in need of you each day. I can barely allow you to go to your duty in the temple and the far valleys—" He shook his head sharply and dropped the hand that had reached out to draw her close. "No, I cannot believe you. You have snared yourself in your own string of lies. If you were jealous as you claim, you would never leave me to console myself for your absence with Mother alone knows what bevy of beauties."

"I do not wish to leave you," Persephone shrieked, "but I would rather be jealous of a living man than sure of a dead one!" Her eyes filled and the tears ran down her cheeks, but she dashed them away and shook her fist at him. "But if I find that you have taken another woman to *our* bed while I am gone, I—I will cut it off!"

Mouth open to protest her denial, Hades choked and then began to laugh. He caught her to him and rested his cheek against her hair. His own eyes were full, but all he said was, "That is worse than cutting off your nose to spite your face."

She clung to him, trembling, frightened out of her wits because she realized her furious, if ridiculous, threat had somehow convinced him not only that she loved him but that he must let her go. Reason forced her along the path she herself had suggested, but she had clung to the irrational hope that Hades would propose a compromise, perhaps offer to come with her. She knew that was ridiculous. His presence would drive her mother into hysteria and convince Demeter that her daughter was only saying she loved him out of fear.

His arms tightened and then one hand slipped down her back to press her closer; the other rose, brushing the side of her breast, touching her ear, and finally lifting her chin so their mouths could meet. He touched her lips with his tongue, delicately, but broke the kiss just as her mouth opened in response.

"Before you cut it off," he murmured, smiling although there were two bright streaks on his cheeks and a sparkle of teardrops in his curly beard, "shall we use it?"

They made love for a very long time. Each unclothed the other bit by bit, kissing, caressing, fixing in memory the feel, smell, taste, and texture of the beloved. Long delayed, the climax that came upon them left them drained and weeping, but with the tears still wet, they reached for each other to begin again.

When they had driven their flagging bodies into a new response and into a climax as fierce as the first, Hades lay utterly limp, staring at the first image he had set in gems on those walls. It was in the far corner and showed a small, lonely figure staring up into the barely lit immensity of the great cavern. He remembered the utter desolation of that moment—to be all alone even in a world of such beauty was death to the soul. He could not endure it again. He could not!

With infinite effort, he lifted his hand and laid it on Persephone's thigh. His first effort to lift himself and turn on his side toward her failed; he simply had not enough strength in his arm, and when he tried again, Persephone whimpered, "We cannot make love forever. Tomorrow will come. Help me, Hades. I am afraid. I do not wish to leave Plutos and become nothing—a Kore—again."

His hand tightened on her thigh. "Then do not leave."

"Give me a plan—give me even a hope—of saving Olympus from starvation and keeping Zeus and his mages from attacking us and I will not go."

"I am not afraid of them."

She pushed him away. "Why should you be afraid? You will be dead! The dead are at peace. You will not be troubled by the knowledge that Plutos has fallen into chaos and all those we love are suffering. You will not care that I am a prisoner, racked with grief for loss of you and agony for our people. What have you to fear?"

"I might not be so easy to kill as you think," Hades said, feeling a little hurt at the way she dismissed his abilities.

"Is that supposed to make me feel better?" she shrieked, pushing herself upright. Do you think my slavery will be made more pleasant by the thought that before you died you managed to kill many people whom I liked? Do you think I will enjoy the thought of bright Apollo, clever Athena, or even wicked Hermes consumed by molten rock or entombed?"

"I see whom you value more," he said, also sitting up.

"Oh, do not be a fool!" She burst into tears and flung herself on him. "You could entomb them all—and my mother with them—for all I care, if I thought we could win. But we cannot, Hades. There are too many. Each we could defeat, even Zeus, but together they are too strong. I would drain myself dry to help you, but it would not be enough, and—"

"And a great many people beside me would be dead, not only men and women of Olympus." Hades sighed. "I could not keep my people out of the struggle. Many have power and would try to support me. Aktaion, Sisyphus—Mother help me, I can imagine Arachne and Koios trying to fight." He sighed again and stared over Persephone's head at the little, lonely figure in the great cave. "Are you sure you can make your mother agree to stay in Olympus and bless the seed?"

She looked up at him, eyes tear-drenched and lips down-turned. "She loves me, Hades. She was never cruel to me—nor did she oppress me in the sense you think. She was only trying to save me from"—her voice caught between a sob and a chuckle—"from just the kind of pain I am feeling now and will feel all the time we are apart. When she sees that pain and understands that her abandonment of Olympus is causing it and that you are the only balm and cure, she will agree to let me go and she will do her duty."

He was silent for several heartbeats, then asked, "How long must I wait for her to be convinced?"

Persephone bit her lip. "It will take a little time," she admitted. "Mother tends to understand only what she wants to understand." She found a watery smile. "But my mother also does not like to be uncomfortable— and I will see that she is *very* uncomfortable every minute we spend together. Still, in case she is too stubborn and unreasonable, we must have a set time when I tell her that I am going back to you no matter what she does. After that time you will come and fetch me back to Plutos."

The arm Hades had reflexively placed around her tightened and he drew a deep, deep breath, feeling as if an enormous weight had lifted. The doubt he had felt, despite all her protestations, the fear that she half wanted to return to Olympus and once there might well forget him and prefer to remain, was gone. Curbing his too-ready grasping at relief, he asked, "What set time?"

"It must be before planting time here, of course, near the spring solstice. That will give me four—no, five—moons to convince my mother. If I can bring her to reason sooner, I will either buy a spell from Hermes and come home myself or send him with a message." She frowned and then added, "Maybe it would be better not to trust Hermes or Zeus. Could I leave a sign in some cave near Olympus that you could look for? I could then go there and if the sign was gone, wait for you to come for me."

"I can make it even simpler. I can set a guard to wait in a cave not far from the temple. Any time you come, the guard can take you to a safe place and send me a signal through the caves. I will come at once."

"That is much better." Persephone nodded. "Just in case mother is more stubborn or Zeus more devious than usual. As it is, we are cutting the time for our own planting rather fine. Our seed must be in a moon or six weeks after the solstice. Some of my priestesses have real power, but I feel it is too soon to allow them to work on their own. And I do not think that without my feeding them the power granted to me by the Goddess, any of them is capable of opening new valleys in addition to her own, which we must do each year. No, I cannot give mother more time than the spring solstice—"

Hades's black eyes were bright with laughter. "Good! We will make an anniversary of it. I will abduct you again on the very same day, the spring solstice.''

"No!" Persephone exclaimed. "If I had not been allowed to leave on my own before then, I would be triply guarded on that day. I am afraid they would be lying in wait for you and hurt you. On the day of the solstice, I will make a public announcement that I have done my duty and now wish to return to my husband and my own realm."

"And if they will not let you go even after you demand your freedom?"

Persephone lifted her head and smiled very sweetly. "I think a little warning might be in order. I am not sure how much you can do without exhausting yourself or frightening them into an attack. Perhaps swallowing up part of the temple—*not* the part sacred to the Goddess—"

"I assure you I will not offend the Goddess," Hades said, also smiling.

Actually his smile was not nearly as poisonous as Persephone's because he was feeling more and more cheerful. He was not pleased about losing his wife possibly for as much as half a year, but compared with his first fears, her absence would not be unbearably prolonged. Having a particular day after which he knew she would return was soothing. He could go out each night and watch the waxing and waning of the moon so he would know the time was passing.

Beside that, he no longer felt helpless. By asking if he could cause part of the temple to be swallowed by the earth, Persephone had reminded him of a mighty weapon he could use against Zeus. When Zeus had convinced him to help overturn Kronos's rule, he had agreed to lead Zeus's army through the caves to the great cavern where Kronos imprisoned the slaves of Olympus. He had also agreed to bring his own army—a smaller one but much more dreadful, being made up of the dead—into Olympus "through a different way."

Zeus had, of course, assumed that Hades meant a different cave, and Hades did not contradict his devious brother's mistaken impression. Instead, during the moons while Zeus gathered men and brought them to the agreed-on entrance to the underworld, Hades had hollowed out many places beneath the city—several beneath the palace, one beneath the throne room itself.

Above those places, he had left a layer of earth and rock thick enough to support the buildings but thin enough for him to pass through—or bespell a small group of men to pass through—quickly. Now, while he waited for the spring solstice, he would have time enough to enlarge those hollows and thin the crust above them without exhausting himself and have his miners brace them so the braces could be destroyed all at once in widely separated places. The buildings would then collapse into the pits below. Oh, yes, they would return Persephone to him.

He laughed aloud suddenly, realizing that the work below Olympus would bring him near Persephone. He would not dare show himself, or everything Persephone had told her mother would appear to be a lie—and might betray his activities to Zeus—but the notion of being close delighted him. He crushed her to him, eyes alight.

"And if our little warning is not enough," he said, "I will bring down half the city." He kissed her hard before she could protest, which he knew she would do out of a fear of hurting anyone, then let her go and swung his legs out of bed. "Come love. I have just realized that we have not eaten and I have been working *very* hard. My poor stomach is clapping against my spine."

Hades's increasing good humor frightened Persephone. Despite her occasional fits of jealousy—which were, she had to admit to herself, not owing to anything Hades did but to the self-doubt bred in her over the years in which she was nothing but her mother's shadow—she did know how strong was Hades's devotion to her. She knew how lonely he had been in the past and the deep joy he felt in their companionship. Had he been grim and quiet, she would have been content; that was the reaction she expected once he understood the necessity of their parting and set himself to endure.

Merriment was wrong . . . unless he had thought of a way to keep her in Plutos. But would he not tell her that? Persephone tried while they were eating to think of a clever way to discover why he was so ready to laugh but she could not, and as he sat sipping at a final cup of wine, she asked him outright whether he had any hope of satisfying Zeus without letting her go. He shook his head.

"I wish I had. I did think of ignoring your mother entirely and offering to lend you to Olympus during their time of planting—but that would be too hard for you, my darling. You are very strong, but you could not feed their priestesses and then return to Plutos and feed ours."

"I never thought of that," Persephone breathed. "I could. Oh, Hades, I know I could. The Mother would support me. She would give me power, and I would only be parted from you a few weeks."

"Would the Goddess accept you in your mother's stead in her temple? She did not grant power to Aglaia. Remember, this would be year after year. No, my love. If it had been only this once, I might have taken the chance. We would survive in Plutos one more year with tight belts if you could not enliven all of our seed and soil. But I do not give my word and then withdraw it, and I do not believe you could, or would, cheat Olympus or Plutos by half measures. If the Goddess did not support our decision, you would be drained year after year until your power was gone beyond restoration."

"But that would not happen. I am sure it would not. The Goddess is good!"

Hades shook his head firmly. "Such trust is dangerous. We must try first to reconcile your mother. The Goddess *is* good, but She has Her own rules, and nowhere is writ what is a transgression until someone transgresses. That someone will not be you, Persephone. I would far rather die myself than permit you to be drained to nothingness."

Persephone blinked. Was that why Hades was so cheerful? Because if he could not get her back, he would drain himself utterly to bring down Olympus for revenge? He would not then need to face a long lifetime of loneliness. But what of her? Her lips parted to protest, and then she realized that he had already shown her the way to avoid the problem, but it was not a method she could admit to him she intended to use.

"Yes, of course we must try to convince mother first," Persephone said hastily to conceal her thoughts. "I had almost forgot that it is mother I must pacify. I keep fearing this is a plot of Zeus's, but that is ridiculous. It is mother who wants me, not Zeus. Mother did go all the way to Eleusis to ask for me, and Zeus gave me to you to be rid of me. Zeus could not want me back, except to satisfy my mother's demand."

She was babbling, covering the thought that Hades might be too honorable to go back on his word, but Zeus was not honorable at all. That, Persephone had decided, absolved her of any silly need to be like Hades. If her mother could not be brought to reason and Zeus planned to hold her, she would offer him her services for that spring, implying that the arrangement might be permanent, if he would let her go home to Plutos. That would not save Olympus from starvation forever, but it would show her whether the Goddess would support her, place her in no danger of being too exhausted if She would not, and give her another year to try to pacify her mother. She stopped speaking when Hades cocked his head at her and smiled at her nervous volubility.

"I believe it is true that Zeus wanted to be rid of you," Hades said, leaning across the dishes between them to kiss her. "But you have nothing to fear in any case. He will find any decision of his that keeps you past the spring solstice far too"—he grinned broadly—"earthshaking to cling to for long."

"Do not let my prejudice against Zeus make you act unreasonably," Persephone begged uncertainly.

Hades pushed back his chair and stood up, holding out a hand to raise her from her seat. "I have told you many times that I am fond of my brother. I have always believed he is fond of me. I do not expect to have to change that view and will certainly not allow your mother's prejudice—even when spoken through your beautiful lips—to change it for me."

He pulled her to him and kissed her again. His lips were firm and very hot and she clung to him hard, realizing how carefully he had not answered her plea. He would not allow her to change his opinion of Zeus, but if he learned that Zeus was not fond of him, had been using him . . . She pressed harder into Hades's body, chilled by her fears and needing his warmth.

"Now," he whispered into her ear, "I have just remembered the dreadful fate with which you threatened me, and I think I had better quench its desire so completely that it will hang its poor head all the while you are away and place itself in no danger of being cut off."

Persephone laughed shakily. "That is the silliest and most complicated way I have ever heard to say 'Let us go to bed.' I am very willing, but to speak the truth I do not believe 'it' can be so easily reduced to inaction."

"Not when you are the temptation," Hades murmured, leading her across to their bedchamber. "But with the taste of you in its mouth, it will be limp as a wet rag for any other."

Persephone was glad enough to be reduced to a mindless body aware only of physical sensation, and exhausted enough to sleep as if she had been struck dead when he had elicited from her a third, violent, culmination. Whether he slept she was not sure because when she woke, crying aloud that she was lost, lost, he was instantly ready to soothe her and seduce her into passion yet again. She would have been ready to spend the whole day before Hermes arrived in bed, smothering her fears under passion, but Hades reminded her that he had promised the miner to try to follow the seam of chrusos thanatos to decide whether he could burn it out or if he would need to seal off that section of the mine.

"I will go with you," she said. "We will burn it! Burn it all no matter how deep it goes."

"If we can," he replied, smiling at her fierce desire to destroy something.

In fact they were able to burn out the seam, tracing it up and out, always confined to an open fissure which was carefully enlarged as it was made safe, toward the surface where the ugly green-yellow growth emerged from a tangle of roots in the topsoil. Regretfully, for he did not like to damage living things, Hades slagged the entire area so that nothing would ever grow there again.

The work, delicate and dangerous, held their complete attention. Neither had a moment for fear or regret, and both were tired because Hades had to draw more than once on the power Persephone freely offered. They were surprised when they returned to the palace to find that the the great candle that marked time was over a quarter burnt away and Hermes would soon come again. That was an excellent excuse to bathe together to rid themselves of the chips and smears of black rock that soiled them, and such propinquity, when recollection of their imminent parting was so sharp a spur, could only result in making love. By then, when they found Hermes already waiting, their emotions were muted by exhaustion.

Hermes looked from one heavy-eyed face to the other. Neither seemed to notice him as they came forward hand in hand, although they must have been told he had arrived. Hades bent his head and Persephone raised hers. They exchanged a single, lingering kiss.

Then Hades looked at him. Hermes swallowed. Something was wrong. The black eyes in which he had feared to meet black rage had a glint that he could have sworn was amusement.

Hades said, "Queen Persephone has decided to allow you to take her to her mother. She wishes to assuage Demeter's grief and try, by convincing Demeter that she is very happy as my wife and has benefited greatly by Zeus's choice of a husband for her, to make peace between her mother and the Mage-King so that she can return to Plutos and need not be called to the outer world again."

"You agree to her going?" Hermes asked.

"I have agreed to her going but to no exchange. No other priestess will be accepted in Plutos. Persephone alone rules the temple."

This was too easy, Hermes thought. Hades had rejected any exchange, but he asked for no guarantees and Persephone was gesturing to Aktaion and two other men who were each carrying a substantial chest, apparently her possessions. Momentarily Hermes forgot Hades's unnatural agreeableness. That load would cost him! He might have to stay on Aegina for a day or two to gather back the power he would need to expend carrying everything.

He saw Hades glance at the chests, pull Persephone close once more, and close his eyes. Hermes swallowed again, this time a lump in his throat. Hades's love for his wife was almost a thing one could touch. Then the sympathy was swallowed up in anxiety. If Zeus would not free Persephone, doubtless it would be from him that Hades would seek to recover his lost love. If he brought her back as Hades demanded, Zeus would blast him; if he did not, Hades would entomb his palace, no doubt with him inside. Oh no, he would not! Hermes licked his lips.

"You understand that I am only a messenger. I do not wish to be blamed if Demeter will not be reasonable and will not release her daughter."

Hades lifted his head and regarded Hermes steadily. "I do not believe Demeter will wish to keep Persephone very long." His lips twitched. "My queen has eaten and drunk the fruits of Plutos. I think Demeter may find her . . . changed."

"That is between you and Demeter," Hermes said.

"No," Hades replied, and now the black eyes were cold and hard. "Zeus sent you here. You implied a threat to Plutos from all the mages. I would simply have pulled down Olympus around your selfish ears, but Persephone—a true priestess of the Mother—desires peace and plenty for all and dissuaded me. Whether she will go or stay and for how long is Persephone's decision to make, and I will hold every Olympian responsible for supporting her decision."

"Hades," Persephone said, touching his hand. "You are frightening Hermes and there is no need for that. My mother will let me go. I will return to you. Only . . . do not be impatient."

He smiled at her. "The dead are very patient."

She laughed. "But you are *not* dead, which is why I am warning you."

Then Hades laughed too. " 'It' is as good as dead, I promise."

Persephone put an arm around his neck and kissed him one more time, then pulled away abruptly and almost ran the few steps to Hermes. "Let us go," she said. "Before I change my mind and bid Hades to pull down Olympus."

Chapter 15

"Kore! Kore! My poor little girl! You are safe now. Mother has you safe."

Persephone was bewildered by the difference in passing through space with Hermes from the passages she often made with Hades. One passage was warm and slow and blind, the other full of flashing color and freezing cold with a terrifying loss of all sense of position. She had come to rest facing a throne as magnificent as Hades's, all irridescent with pearls of every color inlaid into designs of Nereids and fantastic sea creatures.

The man in the throne must be Poseidon. He looked a little like Hades—just enough to make her heart leap—but his hair, though dark, was softly curled, like Zeus's, rather than in tight springy knots like Hades's, and the look in his eyes startled her so much that she did not immediately associate the shrill cry of "girl" with herself. Realizing in the next instant that it was her mother's voice, high with excitement, she turned quickly—and felt a pull on her power.

Without conscious thought, her inner seal expanded into place. She saw the true joy in Demeter's face, the tears of relief streaming from her eyes—which suddenly widened with shock when no warm glow suffused her and gave her strength as in the past. Persephone saw it all, understood what Demeter felt, but locked inside herself, no echo of that emotion touched her.

"Kore?" Demeter whispered, trembling.

"My name is Persephone, mother."

"Mother? Mother?" Demeter withdrew a step, eyes still wide with shock, hands clasped tightly below her breast. "I am not *your* mother. You are not my Kore. You are some dreadful simulacrum—"

"I am not a simulacrum and you are indeed my mother, but I am no one's Kore. I was a girl when I went into the underworld, but I am a woman now—Persephone, Queen of Plutos."

Persephone hesitated as she thought of the proofs of her womanhood Hades had given her over the last night and day. Because her love for Hades was inside her, a warmth blossomed out, filling her and saving her from the utter isolation imposed by the shield that sealed in her power. She smiled and held out her hand.

"I am truly your daughter, but I am also Hades's wife and queen. I am very happy in that state. Hades is so good to me. I love him. Oh, mother, I am sorry if you grieved and worried. I should have sent you a message that I was safe and happy, but I feared that this would happen, that you would demand my return—and I did not wish to come."

"I do not believe you," Demeter cried. "I do not believe my Kore could have changed so much—to love stone-hearted Hades and change to stone herself. My daughter could not be happy to live in the dark surrounded by the dead. You are ensorcelled."

As her initial nervous excitement faded, Persephone's weariness returned manyfold. She felt as if more power had been leached from her; perhaps the cold of the passage with Hermes had drained her. She ached for the warmth of Hades's arms, the comfort of the darkness of their bedchamber lit only by the gleam of the gem image of falling water. But something her mother had said pierced that weariness and resonated with a hope. Ensorcelled? Why not? She had believed that story of the six pomegranate seeds; very likely her mother also believed it. She shook her head and smiled again.

"Not in the sense you mean, mother. Hades cast no spell—except the spell of his own love and need of me. But I have long eaten and drunk the food of Plutos. I no longer desire to live in the outer world."

"But you are not dead!" Demeter exclaimed.

"No, neither is Hades. I assure you he is very much alive," Persephone said, starting another smile, which changed into a huge yawn. "I beg your pardon," she sighed on the outward breath. "We were hard at work, Hades and I, until a little while before I left, and—" She uttered a gasp of laughter at the unintended double meaning of her statement—she had been thinking of the vein of chrusos thanatos they had destroyed—but even the memory of their restricted grappling in the tub could not keep her stimulated and she yawned again. "And I am very tired. Can we not talk later, after I have slept?"

The gasping yawns drew the attention of Poseidon, who had been talking very quietly with Hermes, and he heard her plea. He turned aside from Hermes, who had thanked him for an offer of hospitality but refused, saying that all the leaping he had done over the past few days must have strengthened him because he was not too tired.

"It is growing late, Demeter," Poseidon said. "You and . . . ah . . . your daughter will both be calmer and more able to hear reason in the morning." He raised his shell and blew. Nerus appeared. "Take the lady—"

"She can stay in my chamber, Poseidon," Demeter said. "There is room enough. She can sleep on the long bench—"

Poseidon's eyes flicked to Persephone just for an instant before he shook his head. The glow of her beauty had nearly taken his breath away at the moment of her arrival, and he had beckoned Hermes to him and asked some stupid question so that he would have to keep his eyes off her. But his second glance did not fulfill his expectations. She was lovely, but something was missing. Well, of course there was. She was exhausted.

"Do you think I am short of chambers and beds, Demeter? You cannot think that bench would be a comfortable place to sleep. Besides, I do not believe one accustomed to the quiet of the underworld would be happy on the sea-side of my palace. The sound of the breakers on the shore might be disturbing. Nerus, show the lady to one of the inner rooms."

"You can move me to an inner chamber," Demeter said. "I want to be with my daughter, so long lost to me."

"No, mother," Persephone said. "If I cannot lie with Hades, then I wish to lie alone."

She was not certain whether the words were really meant for her mother or for Poseidon, although he did not look quite so much like a shark contemplating a tasty tidbit as he had when she first caught his eye.

Nonetheless, she suspected his concern for her comfort was largely owing to his hope of putting her privacy to his own use.

"That is ridiculous!" Demeter exclaimed. "Poseidon, she is only a child. She has had a terrible experience. She may not yet realize it, but she needs her mother's comforting."

"I need no comfort but that of Hades."

"Demeter, listen to me—" Poseidon said, loudly enough to override Demeter's voice.

As he spoke Poseidon's eyes sought his steward's, caught them, flicked to Persephone, and then away. Nerus smiled and nodded, signalled silently to Neso—who had, as usual, followed him from behind the curtain—to arrange the transport of Persephone's chests, and gently touched Persephone's hand.

Dazed and angry as she was, Persephone instantly liked the old man and followed trustfully. It seemed like a long way. The throne room itself was huge, and by the time they passed through the large double doors, she was glad to lean on the arm Nerus offered. It was surprisingly strong for an old man, and the hand her fingers rested on was slick, but with regular, small raised ridges. She was too tired to be much surprised when she looked at it and saw that it was thinly scaled, the fingers webbed.

In the left-hand wall of the antechamber to the throne room was a door that opened into a corridor. The left-hand wall of the corridor ran along the throne room and was unbroken; on the right were several doors. Nerus opened the last onto a large room with a wide window, now blocked by a closed shutter. Persephone did not wonder what was behind the window. All she saw that interested her was the low bed backed with a fan of pearl-pink nacre. She released Nerus's hand, staggered to the bed, and dropped down on it. Vaguely, she felt hands undoing her sandals. She was almost asleep when a soft, light warmth covered her.

When Persephone opened her eyes, sun was streaming in the window. The sight startled her and she sat up, wondering whether she could have fallen asleep in the temple. The view beyond the window was of low hills rising to a distant mountain—as the view from the temple would have been—but it was somehow wrong and unfamiliar. Her eyes swept backward along the wall and over her shoulder to the glistening creamy gold and pink headboard of the bed; she remembered where she was and burst into tears.

"Do not weep, my poor Kore. Mother is here. You are safe."

Arms were around Persephone—a woman's arms. They offered comfort, but at the same time it was as if those arms were full of soft, open mouths that sucked at her. Before the ugly thought was truly formed, Persephone's shield was up. And even as the thought formed, she knew it was false; her mother was not deliberately draining her power. That very small taking, which could do her no harm because it absorbed only what flowed naturally from her, was part of Demeter's whole relationship with her. But it was too late now. She knew a love that freely gave to her and took only after asking.

Before Hades, before she had learned to resist all drawing on her power, she had received as much pleasure from giving as her mother got from taking. Giving had been the only way she knew of getting love. And Demeter had given love unstintingly, had given shelter from every harshness, protection . . . too much protection. She could not drop her shield; before she gave again, her mother had to be convinced she would get nothing from her daughter until she acknowledged her as Persephone, Hades's wife. In a strange, distant way—sealed off, Persephone could not respond to external emotion, not even to the pain she saw on her mother's face—Persephone knew she should feel sorry for Demeter. Now that she saw her again, she knew she should wish her mother could share her joy in her husband. But the only thing she felt, because it was inside herself, was her longing for Hades. She pulled away.

"Why should I not weep?" she cried. "You have taken me away from all I love. I agreed to come to you in Olympus so that you would return to live there and quicken the seed for them. I am not so cruel as you, and did not want the folk I knew all my life to starve. But we are not in Olympus are we? Was that not Poseidon I saw yesterday? Where are we?"

"We are on Aegina, dear child. We are far over the water, where Hades cannot follow. You are safe. He cannot rise up from the earth and seize you here. You need not pretend you love him and that dismal realm."

"Aegina?" Persephone shrieked, leaping from the bed and running to look out of the window. It was, indeed, no place she had ever seen, the crowning proof a glimpse from the extreme right of the window of a low, ugly mud-brick town at the head of a long inlet. She closed her eyes and turned her back on the scene. The panic, confined inside the shield, battered at her until she could think of nothing else.

"No!" she screamed. "No! Take me to Olympus." From Olympus she could have contrived an escape somehow. In Poseidon's stronghold of Aegina she was truly a prisoner.

"Child, be calm," Demeter said, coming toward her with outstretched arms. "You are safe here from Hades and from Zeus also."

"I love Hades!" Persephone cried, thrusting Demeter away. "I am not pretending anything. He is the best, the kindest man in the world."

Demeter shook her head sadly, dropping her arms. "Poor Kore, you are bespelled."

"No, madam, she is not," Nerus said from the door, which he had opened so Neso could carry in a tray of food.

His large gray-green eyes held Persephone so firmly that her need to scream and run wildly, anywhere, even into the ocean to free herself from this prison, diminished. They were quite inhuman eyes, Persephone realized, unable to be frightened or surprised, quite . . . fishlike—except that there was intelligence and kindness in them.

"Yes she is!" Demeter insisted. "If not a spell cast by Hades, then she has been changed by that poison which is the food of Plutos. We will stay here until it is all leached from her body and she is ready to give me the love she owes me."

"She is indeed changed," Nerus said. "And I know my master will make you welcome as long . . . as long as is necessary. But let her eat in peace now, Lady Demeter. She is too angry with you to listen to you now."

While Nerus and her mother had been speaking, Neso had come softly to Persephone's side. She put her arm gently around Persephone's waist. Subdued by Nerus's gaze but still boiling with terror, which begat hate and anguish that could find no escape through the impervious lining within her, and afraid to withdraw her shield, Persephone was hardly aware of the woman. She permitted Neso to draw her toward a small table on the other side of the bed, but she shuddered and turned her head away as she passed her mother.

What love did she owe Demeter, who had lied to catch her in a trap? She had lied about her Gift too. Persephone was sure now that Demeter had known about her Gift for a long time, even though Hades had not wanted her to hate her mother and had tried to soften the truth. Love! All her mother loved was her own comfort. She did not think of her daughter as a person, only as a well of power into which she could dip whenever she wanted so she would not have to draw on her own strength. Who could love a well? No wonder Demeter had refused to name her. Why bother to name something you used like a rag to wipe up dirt?

She heard the chair opposite the one in which Neso had seated her move and she lifted eyes containing nothing but hate. Demeter wanted power, did she? Well, she would give her power, enough to burn her or burst her. Fortunately, before her shield dropped she saw that it was Nerus in the chair, not her mother. Somehow the old man had gotten Demeter to leave the room. Now his strange eyes held her. Without any pull to resist, her shield thinned and softened and the rage inside her rebounded only sluggishly from the less-confining walls. Nonetheless, with no other emotion available to her, fury still dominated.

"Eat, Lady Persephone," Nerus said at last.

"Whatever is in the food of Plutos cannot be leached from the body or the spirit by the food of the outer world," Persephone snarled.

Nerus smiled. "I do not think it can be."

Lack of stimulus stilled the rage. She was walled off from everything except the warm glow that was her memory of Hades. She yearned to let that envelop her as it had in the past. Looking around, Persephone saw that Neso was also gone.

"Help me escape from here," she whispered. "I have seen that you pity me, and I know you are kind. I have chests full of gold and gems, gowns of such fabrics as you never saw and for which a woman would sell not only her body but her soul. My husband will give you anything you desire—"

Nerus had been shaking his head from her first word and at last she desisted. "What would your escape accomplish?" he asked gently. "Do you wish to bring down Olympus and see Hades die? I am sure you came to the outer world in the hope of convincing your mother to make her peace with Zeus. What difference does it make whether you convince her here or there?"

Persephone blinked at him stupidly. Not only was she sealed off from emotion, but words and ideas seemed to ooze only slowly into her isolation. "Hades believes I am in Olympus," she whimpered. "If he learns I am not—" Tears spilled over and ran down. "He will think I lied to him."

"Persephone, was he not with you every moment from the time Hermes came to you?" Nerus reminded her patiently. "You could not have conspired with Hermes while you were still in Plutos, and afterward you had nothing to offer him. Hades might blame Hermes for deceiving him, but not you."

Persephone stopped sobbing. "How do you know we were together every moment?"

Did Poseidon have a spy amongst the dead? And if so, how could that spy send news faster than Hermes's leaping? She felt very confused by such thoughts, but if Poseidon had a quick way to send a message to one of the dead, could she not use the same spell to tell Hades what had happened? Even as she wondered, Nerus's laughter proved the idea worthless.

"I am called a seer," the old man said. "But I do not need my 'vision' to know that. You are very much in love, my lady, and I do not believe even a man with a stone heart could resist you. Besides, Hermes told my master and your mother about Hades's reaction when he first suggested an exchange of priestesses."

The breaking of even so new and tenuous a thread that could have bound her to Hades crushed Persephone. Isolated as she felt, telling Hades where she was had seemed the solution to all her problems. Hades would know what to do. Somehow he would have managed to come for her, even if he could not travel through water. She felt even more desperate and alone now than before the idea had come to her.

She looked listlessly down at the table. The plate before her was a huge shell, fluted at the edges and whiter than snow. She had not the smallest inclination to touch the food in it; she hardly saw it. By then she had finally made sense of what Nerus had first said when she asked for his help to escape. He was right, of course. Even if she were more of a prisoner than she had expected to be, even if her mother was a liar and a leacher of power, she must try to reconcile her to Zeus.

She could not blast her—not her own mother, who

had kissed her and held her hand when she was unsteady on her feet long before her Gift could have been manifest. That impulse was not only born of a rage caught inside her shield but was the kind of ultimate stupidity generated by the dullness the shield generated. What good would it do to kill Demeter? she asked herself slowly. If Demeter were dead, who would bless the seed and the fields of Olympus? Would the Goddess manifest Herself in another of the priestesses so that Olympus no longer needed Demeter? More likely the Goddess would withdraw altogether from a place that bred a monster mad enough to murder her own mother. A mother was sacred no matter her faults.

Nerus was right, but time stretched before Persephone like a vast empty grayness. She now admitted to herself that she had not remembered just how singleminded, how selfish and closed into her own desires Demeter was—or had not wanted to remember. Now she was not sure whether she would ever be able to make her mother believe that she truly loved Hades, that he had done nothing to force that love—except offer her personhood and respect and show her the aching need within him, not for power but for a lover to share his life and the rare beauty of his realm.

Bleakly, Persephone rested her eyes on the strange curled things in the plate. They conveyed nothing to her. All she could think was that the only path left to her was to convince Demeter that the old Kore was truly lost to her, that she would never drink at that well of power again, that the longer she kept Persephone prisoner, the more the power would be withheld. That would take a long time. Demeter would not be easily forced to give up her dream. Persephone knew she had time. What she had forgotten was the horror of being shut inside herself, and as long as she was anywhere near her mother, she could not let down her shield.

Nerus, watching the horror grow in her, said, "You will be reunited with your husband."

Her eyes lifted to his. "How long?"

"That I do not see. I only see that you will reign long and happily in Plutos."

"If that is my fate, will you not help me send Hades word of where I am?"

"I cannot help you in any way. My master has the ability to make his servants sorry for irritating or disobeying him. He . . . does not love the King of the Dead. It will be his pleasure to keep Hades's beloved wife as long as he can."

"But you said I would be reunited with Hades, so Poseidon cannot keep me forever. I will be staying for several moons in any case. I only want Hades to know where I am."

"I told you what I saw because a seer cannot lie about his visions, but I see no more than what I told you. If you think some effort must be made to bring about the end you desire, you must decide what that effort should be and make it yourself. I will do what I can to make you comfortable on Aegina and, if you are interested, tell you what I can about the island, but I can do no more for you."

He smiled suddenly, a tight-lipped, mischievous smile, so that his last words stuck in Persephone's mind, not so much that he could do nothing for her as his remark about the island. At first she rejected the idea angrily. She wanted to get off Aegina, not learn about it. Pulling her eyes away from his gaze, they found the curled white things in her plate.

"You want me to accept Aegina and you fill my plate with grubs?"

"They are not grubs but a very lively fruit of the sea. Try one. I promise you will find the flavor enticing. And an empty stomach does not make for clear thought."

Unfortunately, although Nerus's promise about the flavor of the dish set before her held true, a full stomach did not help clear Persephone's mind. It remained clouded, ideas seeping through long after a conversation had ended. Three days of angry confrontations with her mother brought her no nearer her purpose. She had the uneasy feeling that she was doing something stupid, but the fact that her mother insisted more confidently each time they spoke that she was bespelled only made her angrier and more aggressive.

On the fourth day her mother did not come to her room, and when Nerus and Neso brought her breakfast, the old man told her that Poseidon wished to speak to her. Nerus was subdued and said little, but an odd glance or two from his strange eyes pierced the thickening wall inside Persephone and reminded her of what he had said, both about Poseidon's power over his servants and his dislike of Hades.

The warning was enough to keep Persephone from trying to enlist the sea king's aid by speaking of Nerus's vision or using the rational argument that he should want to help his brothers—one to restore fertility to Olympus and the other to recover his wife. Locked inside herself, she could feel nothing from him and could not guess what other argument or promise of reward might move him. She was puzzled by Poseidon's behavior: First he stared at her long and hard, then he rose and took her hand, seated her, and while he was making what seemed to her completely idle conversation—asking if she were content with her chamber and the servants' attentions and suchlike—he wandered about and looked at her from different positions.

She knew what he was doing should mean something, but inside her shield she felt not only unresponsive but dull. In fact, the wall inside her seemed to be growing thicker and harder each day. Suddenly more aware of that wall and unable to understand what Poseidon was saying to her at all, Persephone began to panic as she had the first time she erected a shield. She stared blankly at Poseidon when he came close and laid a hand on her shoulder, her mouth gaping open. She began to gasp for breath. Poseidon let her go and summoned Nerus. The old man's gaze and touch calmed her, but as soon as she was again alone in her room, she frantically tore open the hateful thing inside her and crumpled it away under her heart.

The relief was enormous. She ran about the room, examining the odd but attractive furnishings, comparing the chairs of polished bone to those of lightened stone and fancifully bent metal in Plutos. Although she was alone, she exclaimed aloud—for the pure joy of hearing a voice unimpeded by a barrier—over the dressing table with its top and drawer handles of mother-of-pearl. But the mirror, held between the halves of an enormous shell, was nothing—a small round of polished metal that discolored and distorted her face.

She wept a little over the memory of Hades's struggles to make the mirror now in her dressing room, which reflected a full-sized perfect image. He had never stopped trying until he found that a thin, thin melt of pure white silver onto the flat polished back of a cooled sheet of melted white sand would give the perfection he desired once the front of the sand melt was also polished flat.

The weeping ended when Neso came in bringing linens that she had received back from the washing women in the town. Glad to see anyone, Persephone smiled at her and said she would help fold and lay away. To make room, she lifted out a box of jewelry and an armful of her gowns. She laughed at the young woman's astonishment over her clothing and jewels, speaking with warmth of Hades's and Arachne's skill, and when Neso said she must go and they were packing away the gems, Persephone offered her a tiara of gold and pale emeralds that matched her sea-green eyes.

"I could not," Neso breathed.

"Why not?" Persephone laughed. "I have so much, and this piece befits you far better than it does me."

"It is so different," Neso said, stroking it. "I have pearls of every kind, strung and set in shell and bone, but nothing like this. Oh, will you take pearls in exchange?

"Why yes, I would be happy to have pearls," Persephone said, sensing—with a thrill that she could sense—that the offer was sincere. And then, again recalling Nerus's warning and suddenly concerned that her careless generosity would make trouble, she said, "Please tell King Poseidon what we have done. I would not want him to think I am trying to subvert his servants, and you have been so kind to me despite my sullenness."

"You were grieving," Neso said. "I understood. But one cannot grieve forever. I will tell Poseidon about the tiara."

No, Persephone thought when the young woman had gone, one cannot grieve forever. She did not miss Hades less nor long less for her home in Plutos, but the shock of his absence did not shake her so brutally each time she thought of him—and with her shield gone, her memory of him was not the only warmth in her life. She had enjoyed the time Neso had spent with her, and, she thought with some satisfaction, she had handled Neso well and had her goodwill. That might be valuable sometime in the future.

Not that she thought Neso would help her escape or get a message to Hades—nor would she ask it of her and bring Goddess only knew what punishment upon her—but ships must travel to and from the island. Neso might be willing to gossip about the ships and their ports of call. Persephone's heart jumped and she ran to the window and leaned out, straining to see more of the inlet below the town. Ships there were, and many empty jetties—

"Kore! Beloved! You have come back to me."

Persephone whirled around to see Demeter halfway across the room, arms open. Her shield exploded out, the tears she had made in it gone as though they had never been. She saw the change in her mother's face as Demeter stopped, mouth still parted to speak endearments. Persephone was not now so dulled as she had been in her earlier encounters with Demeter—first with fatigue and then with isolation—and she perceived what she had been doing wrong. Her behavior had made her mother believe some act or spell of Hades had stifled her power and that attempts to break that spell brought on spell-induced rage in her helpless and ensorcelled daughter. She walked past Demeter and carefully shut the door. She meant to speak gently and explain that she alone controlled access to her power, but bitterness welled up and, being confined, filled her.

"You told me I had no Gift," she said resentfully.

Her mother's eyes opened wide. "But my love, you have not, at least, not any Gift *you* can use."

Knowing she could not understand very well, Persephone carefully memorized that answer to reconsider later. "You are wrong, mother," she said. "Hades taught me just how to use my Gift."

Demeter froze for a moment, her lips thinned with anger, then she came close and grasped Persephone's wrist, speaking in a whisper. "That is dangerous! Very dangerous!" She softened her grip and stroked Persephone's face with her other hand. "Beloved, I never took more from you than flowed out freely. If you pour out your Gift into someone else, you could give too much and harm the mage or, worse, drain yourself to illness or death. And if knowledge of such a Gift was spread, every mage would try to seize you. They would fight over you, tear you apart rather than let another have you . . ."

"Yes, indeed, mother. That was the first thing of which Hades warned me, which you never did. And his first concern was to teach me to shield that Gift within myself so that no mage can feel it or draw upon it."

"Except him!" Demeter said bitterly.

"Oh no." Behind the shield a rich satisfaction welled and brought calm and more clarity to Persephone. "Hades has no more power over me than you. If he needs strength, he must ask. I am free to give or withhold as I please."

"Oh, you are allowed to think so, I am sure. I am equally sure that when he asks, you give whatever he desires."

Persephone was silent for a moment as she tried to understand the remark. When she did, memory was swift and she smiled. "That may be so, mother. I do not know how I would respond if Hades asked. I am only sure that I have lived with him nearly two years and he has refused my *offer* of power more often than he has accepted."

Now she freed her arm from her mother's grip, but gently. All the ideas she needed were inside her head already; she did not need the slow collection of outside thought and she was able to make a plan. Instead of pushing Demeter away as she had done previously, she took her mother's hands in hers.

"Mother, it is over. I am not your shadow or your tool any longer. Look at me. See me for what I am— Hades's Dazzling Brightness, a person, a woman."

"You are my Kore, bespelled but coming back to me."

"No, mother. I am Persephone."

"You are my child. My body was racked with the pain of bearing you. You owe me love!"

"Yes, and I am willing to love you—when I am treated as a daughter, a grown-up daughter, instead of as a prisoner. A prisoner owes her captor nothing, and I will give you nothing at all as long as I am confined to Aegina. Tell me that you will go back to Olympus and quicken the seed and bless the fields, and I will go with you gladly. Tell me I will be free when that duty is done, and I will help you as I used to do. I will even stay until after the celebration of the spring solstice. And if you need me, I will come each year for a few weeks at that time, so long as I am free to live the rest of the year with my beloved husband Hades in the underworld, which has also become very dear to me."

"Never!" Demeter shouted. "I will never again give you up to that stone-hearted monster who has changed you into a monster like himself."

Persephone caught the denial, although she did not yet understand the exact form. She had one more step to take in her appeal. "Mother, do you not wish me to be happy? Whatever the reason, I am truly happy as Hades's wife. And I must go home soon after the spring solstice. If I do not, Hades will swallow much of Olympus down into the earth. Surely—"

"You do not mean it?" Demeter's eyes were wide.

"Yes. I am afraid Hades means exactly what he says. He always tells the truth and always keeps his promises."

Demeter burst into crows of laughter. "I hope you will come back to me, my Kore, but if you do not, you have given me the perfect revenge. I could almost love Hades for what he will do. With good fortune Zeus will be entombed with his city and with all those who laughed at my pain when I searched and searched for you. What joy!"

Chapter 16

Even emotionless, Persephone had protested her mother's indiscriminate ferocity, pointing out that many innocents would be destroyed with the great mages, and that some of them must surely have sympathized with her. Demeter had laughed at her reasonings and her pleas. After her mother was gone and she dropped her shield, Persephone was stricken with horror at what she had done. First she blamed herself for thinking she could make a plan while her shield dulled her, but after she had wept herself dry she realized that sooner or later, shielded or not, she would have told her mother of Hades's threat. Until she had heard the words from Demeter's own mouth and heard her laugh, Persephone could not have imagined her mother could be so cold and cruel.

Later, as her guilt abated further, she began to hope that Demeter was only doing to her what she had tried to do herself—use a threat to induce compliance. Believing that her daughter cared enough about the people of Olympus to leave Plutos so that Olympus would have rich crops again, Demeter was using the threat of allowing the city to be destroyed to make her daughter agree to live with her. Well, Persephone would not agree, but Demeter was likely to drag out her resistance as long as she could. Persephone sighed.

She determined to wear her shield only in her mother's presence so that her mind would be clear and she would not be driven to senseless rages and panics. For several more days she spent most of her time in her chamber, trying to think of a way to induce Poseidon to help her if her mother continued to be stubborn. She asked many questions of Nerus and Neso about their master and both answered freely. Unfortunately, everything they told her was worse than no help.

Although they did not say so in words, Nerus and Neso implied that Poseidon envied and distrusted Zeus, and it was highly unlikely that he would be more concerned about the destruction of Olympus than Persephone's mother. She learned that the people of Aegina obeyed him absolutely, because his sea creatures could—and would on his order—sink their ships. Worse yet, he could raise such waves that the town would be washed away, the whole island, except for the high mountains, be drowned, which was nothing to the sea king, who could breathe water.

Thus, it was impossible that she would be able to bribe any of the people of Aegina, even with the marvelous jewels she had brought with her, to take her to the mainland. However, she also guessed from Neso's occasional frown and the word "ungrateful" that the townsfolk did not all love Poseidon, in particular the women whose men had lost their lives in storms.

"After all," Neso said, "Lord Poseidon has more important things to do than watch each and every one of their cockleshell boats. He cannot calm every single storm that rises. Sometimes he is far away, but they mutter among themselves that a god can be everywhere at once and refuse to understand."

Persephone was little interested in Neso's defense of her master, but she listened politely and made the appropriate responses. All that was significant to her at the moment was that she could not hope for help from Poseidon. She would have to work harder on convincing her mother.

Unable to believe Demeter was truly as unfeeling as she claimed, Persephone continued to plead with her and reason with her when she paid her morning duty call. She no longer avoided her mother's company. When Demeter insisted it would divert "Kore" and ease her loneliness to join Poseidon's court, she did not refuse. She did not enjoy herself because in her mother's presence she remained shielded, but after a few dinners and receptions she began to notice people that might be interesting. Through Neso and Nerus she met young men and young women with whom she could play games and talk and walk in the garden. This made her days pass a little more quickly and kept her spirits from utter despair, but brought her no hope of freedom.

The moon waxed and waned, waxed full again. In all that time nothing had changed, and Persephone began to feel desperate. She still started each day with a visit to her mother and wept each time, bemoaning the loss of her husband's love and insisting that the friends she had made and the kindness with which she was treated were nothing to her need for Hades and her own home. Finally, out of desperation, she used a weapon she had hoped to avoid. She reminded Demeter of how she herself had bewailed Iasion's death for many years and begged her not to force such sorrow on the child she said she loved.

Usually Demeter wiped away her tears and assured her that she was bespelled, and if "Kore" would give her mind to breaking the spell she would soon be free of it and loathe Hades. But when Persephone mentioned Iasion, Demeter's eyes did not fill with tears as they had always done in the past. Instead, she laughed very strangely and said, "Thanks to Hades's stealing you from me, I have recovered. I no longer desire Iasion. You will soon forget Hades's face too."

The oddity of her mother's laughter stuck in Persephone's mind. Later when she was unshielded again, Persephone reconsidered what her mother had said and wondered whether it was true that she would ever forget Hades's deep black eyes and mobile lips or the endearing way his tight curls peeked around his ears. And that led her to consider an even more unsettling idea. If she had been allowed to know the young men in Olympus and been free to choose among them, would she have so easily accepted Hades after he abducted her? Would she have chosen Hades if her choice had been free?

She did not need to wonder long. That very afternoon one of the young men whom Persephone had found particularly charming and amusing seized her in his arms as they walked in the garden and tried to kiss her. Without a single doubt or the smallest hesitation, she struck him as hard as she could, brought her heel down on his foot with all her not inconsiderable weight, and screamed for Neso, whom she had allowed to get out of sight.

Neso arrived, but her help was totally unnecessary. Shocked into releasing his hold both by surprise at

Persephone's violence and by the pain in his face and his foot, her admirer had then been felled by a sharp push. Persephone was instantly sorry for having used the young man so roughly, but she was accustomed to Hades's enormous strength and had expected a far harder struggle to win her freedom. Her push would barely have rocked her husband. Fortunately, before Persephone could offend the young man further by apologizing for being too strong for him, he had rushed away, furious and humiliated.

She spent the next two days in her room, thinking hard and practicing a new technique in front of her inadequate mirror. It was not easy to be sure of the result because of the natural distortion in the metal, but Persephone hoped her features were blurred into drabness. However, on the third day, after another fruitless visit to her mother, when she was wondering whether her new appearance would protect her, she realized what a fool she was. It was far, far too late to make herself look plain so men would not be attracted to her. Her young friends at the palace knew her, and to change her looks would be a dangerous admission of her Gift.

Then what was she to do? Sit in this room until Hades killed himself by draining his power dry to pull down Olympus? She had at least hoped to send him word that it was not Zeus who was holding her. But no one on Aegina would help poor Persephone.

Use of her name made her breath catch. It was true, no one would help Persephone, but an ordinary woman—a Gyne—with gold or jewels could buy many things in the town. Thinking of the townsfolk, Persephone remembered what Neso had said about some of the women. Ungrateful, Neso had called them. Did that mean some might hate Poseidon as much . . . more? . . . than they feared him? Perhaps there was a way she could send a message to the cave near Eleusis. She began to look through her chests and boxes of jewelry. Her preparations took two days more.

On the sixth day, after a very lachrymose visit with Demeter, which her mother ended by telling her to go cry herself out in her own room, Persephone walked boldly to the palace gate. Aside from her blurred face and a thick veil to cover her golden hair, she was wearing a warm gray cloak—in fact, it was the one she had worn in the caves when Hades had abducted her— and a plain blue wool gown, which Arachne had taken infinite pains to dye the exact delicate color of the twilight sky. She had patiently picked out all the decoration of precious stones and gold wire, covering the removals with simple, coarse embroidery.

Her unspoken reason for leaving was a broad basket that contained several inner garments she had deliberately soiled and hidden from Neso, who usually arranged the washing. In the plain purse attached to her belt, lay the bits of gold wire, several twisted together to make a handful of small lures. If she were not allowed through the gate, she would simply say she did not realize she needed to ask permission of Poseidon to bring her own washing into the town to ease her boredom. The plain dress, she would say, was because she was no fool and did not wish to tempt anyone to rob her.

Nonetheless, when the guard at the gate made no attempt to stop her, Persephone had great difficulty restraining herself from running down the road as fast as she could. She plodded grimly along, expecting every moment to hear a voice calling her back. Even after she was well away from the palace, she was not convinced that she was truly free. She planned to be very circumspect in what she did and said in the town. In any case, she knew it would take time to make herself a familiar figure and gain the confidence of the townsfolk.

That first day she did little more than wander about, stopping at this shop and that to examine the wares, until she saw a place where a merchant handed over small bars of silver for a larger number of even smaller pieces of copper. When he stepped out, Persephone walked in and asked if she could obtain copper for gold wire. The metalchanger looked from the few twisted pieces of wire in her hand to her gown, plainly guessing the one had come from the other, and nodded his head. Although her previous experience with using metal for barter had been limited to the times she had accompanied her mother to artisans' shops in Olympus, she thought the metalchanger had been fair, not that she really cared. She had gold enough in her jewelry, even without the gems, to buy the whole town. Cautiously, she used her copper only to buy a hot goat's-meat pie, which reminded her so much of hudorhaix pie that tears came to her eyes; a piece of braided bread; and a creamy cup of goat's milk.

She returned to the palace in time for the afternoon meal in case her mother should inquire for her, but she did not leave her room. The next day, although she deliberately quarreled with Demeter, she did not leave the palace. She spent some time in the garden, noticing that the young men mostly avoided her and the girls were rather more friendly, but they had all become very unimportant. All her hopes were now fixed on the town.

The moon had waned and begun to wax again and Persephone had spent many days in the town. No one interfered with her, but she was growing more and more certain she was being watched by scrying. For days she struggled with doubt, but finally she went to one of the few licensed magicians and bought a no-see-no-hear spell. It was good only for a few moons, a cheap, weak thing, which she was sure a good scryer could pierce—until she poured her own power in to strengthen it.

She did not use it for several days, but she was growing more and more eager to find a messenger, fearing her expeditions might be stopped. She had by then visited most of the artisans, made a number of small purchases, and discovered which shopkeepers were friendly. To those, she would admit she was a stranger come to Aegina with her father and ask innocent questions about how it was to live here, hoping to hear a note of bitterness or a tale of ill-treatment.

One of the friendliest was a potter from whom she bought a little glazed frog unguent pot that enchanted her. Her unfeigned enthusiasm had warmed the potter, who invited her, when she learned Persephone was a stranger who did not live in the town, to stop and rest in her shop whenever she wished. One day, her mind on a ship that would carry her token and her message, Persephone asked the potter about a good place to buy fish fresh from the sea.

Eulimine laughed and told her that all fish was fresh in Aegina, because any that was not sold for immediate eating was salted or pickled. Persephone sighed and said her father was old and very demanding. No matter that the fish was delicious, he had scolded her several times for not buying right from the ship, but she was afraid to go down to the dock to buy a fish herself—which was at least partly true. Persephone was certain that if she went near a ship, she would never be allowed out of the palace again.

As she "confessed," Eulimine looked thoughtful, then asked, "Would you like to use a woman who not only knows fish and will bring you the best but will give you the name of the ship, the captain, even the fisherman who caught the creature if you desire? Then you could tell your father all the details as if you had been to the docks yourself."

Trapped in her own tale, Persephone could only laugh uneasily and ask why any woman would bother to fetch one fish from the dock.

"Ah, that is a sad tale," Eulimine said. "Poor Pontoporeia will be glad of any task that will win her a bite to eat or a sliver of copper. She lost her father and brother when their boat capsized—not even in a storm, and all the others were saved—and her husband and sons on a different ship were swept overboard by a wave the very same day. Now all think she is accursed . . . ah! I should not have asked you to employ her. That was wrong."

"No, no," Persephone got out, realizing that her expression must have exposed the anxiety she felt and Eulimine had assumed the wrong cause for it. She had invoked the blanking spell, remembering that the magician had said it would be enough to blur a watcher's vision and hearing. "No, I am a stranger here. I would not be blamed. All I know is that she is a poor woman who was willing to do an errand for me."

"You have a kind heart," Eulimine said. "I am so

sorry for her. No one will give her work. Even I dare do no more than leave some food for her—in case she did somehow offend . . ." Her eyes flicked in the direction of the palace. "But perhaps no more than ill fortune dogs poor Pontoporeia."

"Oh, I am sure her losses were only a sad accident," Persephone said eagerly. "I cannot believe so mighty a lord would trouble himself with one poor woman. Tell me where she lives. Perhaps I can think of other errands for her."

"It is not far away," Eulimine said, rising from the table at which she had been working and walking to the door. "Go around to the back of my house. Beyond the garden you will see the road to the docks. Turn right onto that. It is—" She paused, clearly counting in her memory. "It is the fifth house on the left side of the lane, the last house on the hill that goes down to the docks. Likely she will be in the garden trying to find a few roots still in the ground. If she is not at home, I will pass a message for her and if you can come tomorrow, she will get your fish then."

"Thank you," Persephone breathed. "My father is not well at all. I was trying to screw up my courage to go among those rough men so he would not get excited. It will be a wonderful relief for me, if Pontoporeia is willing. Thank you."

Persephone all but ran into the garden. There, however, she checked her steps, cut the spell, and walked the rest of the way sedately in case an eye watched her in a crystal or scrying bowl. She hoped that if she were watched, the blurring would be considered a simple weakness in the vision, and she concentrated on keeping her expression calm and indifferent. This woman sounded like the answer to all her prayers. Pontoporeia was not only desperate and sure she was already accursed so that she had little to lose from Poseidon's anger, but she would be glad to leave Aegina and never return, no longer having friends or family to whom to return.

Persephone's heart leapt in her throat as she thought it might only be a few weeks before Hades came for her. How wonderful it would be when her lover and husband took her in his arms. And when she forced her mother to come with them, how Poseidon would grind his teeth . . . Persephone stopped—stopped walking, stopped breathing, as she considered the result of Poseidon's anger.

More likely than grinding his teeth, Poseidon would order Hades killed. Hades could not bring an army; they would have to come by ship, and no fleet of ships could come secretly to Aegina because Poseidon's sea creatures would bring him warning. Even if Hades came secretly for her, to where could they flee? There were mountains on Aegina; there might be caves, but those caves did not connect to Plutos. The ocean came between. Worse yet, they would be no better off than if she had refused to go with Hermes. If she could not bring her mother back to Olympus, the city would still starve.

In fact, Persephone realized, she dared not even tell Hades where she was or he would surely come, no matter what the danger. She would have to escape herself . . . somehow. Meanwhile, it was enough to know that Hades would not kill himself and destroy Olympus for nothing. She began to walk down the road again, counting the houses on the left. When she saw a bent back bobbing up and down in the garden of the fifth house on the left, she had to pause to recover from the dizziness of mingled frustrated disappointment and relief and tell herself harshly not to hope too much lest those hopes be dashed and leave her more desperate than before.

This time her long patience was rewarded. When she called to Pontoporeia and said she would pay her to do an errand, the old woman straightened slowly and said, "You do not wish to employ me. My ill-luck might spread to you."

"Oh, no," Persephone replied. "I do not think so, but I would like to hear of your trouble—if you are willing to tell me. May I come into your house? I am cold out here."

"You may come in, but it is not much warmer inside. I have no fire. I can offer you a blanket in which to wrap yourself. All fear the curse that befell me so much that they will not even buy my clothes and furniture, lest it spread to them from those things."

Persephone did not answer that directly, only went through the garden and stood by the door. Pontoporeia followed her, opened the door, and gestured her inside. As she entered, Persephone invoked the spell and poured her power into it. She could feel it spread, like a black coating over the inside of the old woman's house. She said, "I was asking Eulimine about obtaining fresh fish—"

"I have no fish. I have no boat—"

"No, I understand." Persephone repeated her fabrication about her cantankerous father and her fear of the rough sailors.

Pontoporeia shrugged. "I will take your copper and bring you a fish together with word of who caught it, if you will give me the head and the tail."

"Better buy two fish," Persephone said. "I dress

plainly when I am in the town because I am alone and afraid if I wore rich clothing that someone would rob me, but my father is not a poor man." She took a handful of copper pieces from her purse, and handed them to the old woman.

"That is too much," Pontoporeia said.

"You are an honest woman, considering your need." Persephone smiled. "Bring back what remains."

As soon as Pontoporeia left, Persephone began to have doubts. If Poseidon really did hate the poor woman for some unknowable reason and a scryer had seen her come here, Poseidon might order that Pontoporeia be seized and questioned. Still, Persephone felt she would have no better chance than this. Sooner or later she would have to make the next move toward freedom, and every day she waited was one day closer to the time when she might be prevented from acting at all or when her message might arrive too late to save Hades or Olympus. At least if Pontoporeia refused, she would have no one to tell about the crazy woman who asked her to carry a message to the King of the Dead.

That doubt temporarily quieted, Persephone began to plan how to introduce the fearful idea of dealing with the dead. She also realized she must be very careful about the message she asked Pontoporeia to carry. If her doubts had some foundation and the woman was questioned by Poseidon, nothing in the message must implicate Hades. She had barely decided what to say, when the old woman returned. Persephone had not realized quite how close they were to the docks. There was only the steep path down the hill and the short road past the buildings where the salting and pickling was done.

When Pontoporeia pushed both fish and nearly all the copper across the table toward Persephone, telling her to take the one she preferred, Persephone took the nearest without even looking at it and put it in her basket. She did not want the fish, but needed it to maintain the fabrication about her sick father. She pushed the copper back to Pontoporeia while she dutifully repeated the names of the ship and the captain who had caught the fish.

When she had those pat, she did not rise but said, "My father is not really just cross. He is very, very sick, and he has a task to perform. I was going to do it, but he is too sick for me to leave him now. Your life here is not happy. If I could arrange for you to leave Aegina and give you gold and jewels enough so that you could live out your life in ease on the mainland, would you take a token and a message to Eleusis for my father?"

"No ship will carry me," Pontoporeia said.

"No ship will carry Pontoporeia, but any ship will carry Lady . . . er . . . Halkyon of Eleusis, returning home after a visit to Lady Demeter."

The old woman laughed rustily, as if she had not laughed in a very long time. "Who would believe me a lady?"

"When you are dressed in a fine gown with jewels on your fingers and arms and a golden chaplet to hold down the fine veil that will hide your face from common folk, who will not believe?"

Pontoporeia stared at Persephone, then looked at her own work-gnarled hands, then back at Persephone. "Rings on these hands?" she muttered.

"If you hold your veil with the fabric over your hand only the glitter of the gold and jewels will show," Persephone said impatiently. "Are you telling me that you are willing to carry this message if such small matters can be worked out?"

"Yes, I am willing, but am I able? This must be an urgent and dangerous message. I am a simple woman. What if I make some mistake?"

"It is urgent, but not so dangerous or so difficult as you might think. Listen to the end before you deny me. My father has a message that must be delivered to the King of the Dead—"

"The King of the Dead?" Pontoporeia whispered.

"Please, I beg you to hear me out. I was just about to say that you need not carry the message to Hades himself. Near Eleusis there are caves in which the living may speak to the dead. I would prefer that you went yourself and gave the token, which is only a small wooden box, and delivered the message directly to the dead who will come to face you, but if you fear the dead, you may ask assistance from King Celeus in a private audience."

"Why should I fear the dead, I, whose loved ones are all dead?" Pontoporeia asked slowly, then shook her head. "But I have heard the seamen talk—before I became one of the outcast—and it was said among them that it is no easy task to find that cave. A king might be slow about granting a private audience, not to mention assistance to an unknown woman."

"Not if you ask in the name of the Lady Demeter, and say it is she who desires the token and the message to be delivered to the dead. King Celeus will send a messenger if you are afraid to go yourself, or send a guide with you."

At the mention of Demeter, Pontoporeia's expression grew less bleak. She said softly, "In the Lady Demeter's name? She is one chosen by the Goddess, and our farmers bless her name five times a day. I will serve in her name." She suddenly stood up and went to the cold fireplace, where a blackened pot sat on the tripod. She picked up the pot and brought it to the table. "Tell me your message," she said, "and I will go direct with it to King Hades and to all those I love, who are in his realm now. A spoonful of this draught brings me sleep for a few hours, but if I drink it all, I will never wake. I will not need your gold and jewels."

"No!" Persephone exclaimed, snatching the pot away. "I am not sending you to your death. The dead in the cave will do you no harm and Hades himself is *not* dead. If you died, who knows how long you might wander before he would get my father's message? I cannot take such a chance. You must swear to me by the Mother of All that you will faithfully do as I ask and try no short paths that may lead me and many others to disaster."

"What disaster?"

"The less you know the better, but I can tell you this. The King of the Dead has lost something, and he threatens to wreak great havoc unless it is returned."

Pontoporeia stared for a moment at the pot Persephone held and then around the room. Then she sighed. "You are real, and what you say is real. I had begun to think that I was finally mad. But I see the fish on the table. That must be real." Tears began to run down her face. "Can I ask about my menfolk when I speak to the dead?"

"So long as you first give the token and speak the message, you may ask anything you like. I cannot promise what kind of answer you will receive. I am not dead, nor my poor father . . ."

Persephone's voice faded as a new, wonderful idea came to her, an idea, if it were properly worked out, that might lead to her escape. She rose hurriedly and said she must go back to her father. If Pontoporeia could find out when a ship—with a captain honest enough not to steal her goods and drop her overboard—was leaving for Eleusis, she would bring the clothing and jewels and the token. As she left, however, she laid her hand on the doorframe and whispered the words that transferred the spell. Her power would fade from it if she left it too long, but she could renew it each time she came.

Chapter 17

Hades stared at the tiny jewel-flower that had fallen out of the thistledown packing in the small wooden box into his palm. "Tell me the message again," he said.

The messenger tried to steady his panting breath. He had run and climbed for nearly a full day, the last of a long relay that had started in the cave near Eleusis nine days earlier. "The words were: 'The sacrifice was not made to Zeus and cannot be retrieved from him whatever the wrenching. Be patient and the sacrifice will return of itself to you.'"

Hades nodded. "And who brought the message?"

He knew this runner could not have seen the person who carried Persephone's token and, presumably, her words, but the keeper of the cave at Eleusis should have been alerted by the mention of Zeus's name to examine the petitioner with care and pass along a description. Only the most devoted and cleverest men and women were allowed to serve as liaison between the dead and the living. They often needed keen wits to deal with half-mad lovers and parents who came to plead for the return of their dear ones, or fools who

thought the dead could predict the future or twist fate.
The devices used to try to bribe or befool the keepers
were myriad, but only rarely did one succeed and the
living pass the portal to wander the caves until death—
or one of Hades's patrols—ended the wanderings.
This keeper had not failed.

"A woman brought the message," the messenger
said, his breath coming more evenly. "The keeper said
she was old, but strong. Her dress was rich and her
jewelry, the keeper thought, was surely made by your
hand, but she was startled when she saw the keeper
and dropped the veil she had drawn across her face.
The keeper said her face and her hands were coarse
and worn, a woman who had worked all her life."

"Anything else passed along by the keeper?"

"For herself, the woman asked after a husband and
two sons, a father, and a brother, all lost at sea. The
keeper spoke the usual comfort about the dead being
at peace and unwilling to touch the world of the living
again because that caused them pain since she was sure
those four were not among the sacrifices made to us."

"That was right," Hades said, but absently, his
mind being elsewhere. Rousing himself momentarily
in response to the still-heavy breathing of the messenger, he added, "Go now and rest. I have no message to
send to Eleusis."

His eyes went back to the jewel-flower he was turning between his fingers. He thought it was the one he
had used to tempt Persephone, but he had made nearly
a score of the pretty trinkets and traded them to Zeus
for a herd of cattle. Zeus.

Hades got to his feet and moved restlessly around
the narrow confines of the small dead-end cavern he
had chosen as a living space for himself. He had to

turn sideways to pass between the chair and the small table, and there was just room for him to pass along the side of the narrow cot. Three steps farther took him to the curtain-hung entrance. He hesitated, tempted to walk down the passage to the larger cavern in which his miners ate and slept, but a freer space to pace was not worth the curiosity his behavior would awaken. He muttered an oath when his knee grazed the bed and turned again, reminding himself that he was usually too tired when he came here to do more than eat and drop into the bed.

When he came to the curtain again he stopped and stared at it, then lifted his hand and looked down at the jewel-flower he still held. Zeus. His brother had never yet betrayed him, but Zeus had an indifferent reputation. Hades had heard enough of his brother's deceptions to make him wary, and aside from the war on Kronos and Zeus's offer of Persephone—which was scarcely reassuring when considering Zeus's honor—they had had little intercourse of a serious nature. Usually their business was very unimportant, like the trade of cattle or grain for jewels or gold or metals for Hephaestus. Occasionally Zeus had asked Hades to take into Plutos a man or woman whom he did not wish to kill but had to be rid of for political or personal reasons—like Arachne. Only once had one of those made trouble. Hades had been forced to confine Tantalus and finally to kill him, but Zeus had warned him that Tantalus might be incorrigible.

Hades clenched his hand on the jewel-flower, opened it and clenched it again. This was different. He did not dare trust Zeus when Olympus itself was at stake. It was possible that the message he had received was truly from Persephone, but if it was and she was not in Olympus, why had she not said where she was? On the other hand, the woman who carried the message sounded like a native and it was not very likely Zeus would use a native and send her all the way to Eleusis. But perhaps it *was* likely. Zeus had a devious mind and might have counted on his brother making the assumption that Eleusis, where Zeus did not have a temple, was an unlikely place. And yet . . .

Uttering another oath as he caught his hip on the table, Hades took the three necessary strides, threw back the curtain, and started down the passage. The caverns he had chosen as a kind of camp while he was hollowing out the rock under Olympus, were a full candlemark's walking time from the city. In a way it was a nuisance, but the caves and passages nearest to the city were sometimes explored, particularly by the older children, and he had wished to be far enough away to be sure there would be no accidental sightings. Just now, he told himself as he set out, he was glad the distance was considerable. By the time he reached the workings under Zeus's palace, he would have had time to examine all the ramifications of the message he had received.

Unfortunately, neither the exercise nor the delay brought conviction that the message was genuine. In fact, each step he took made him more furious because he would not believe that Persephone had deliberately failed to say where she was. If he let himself believe that, he must also believe that she did not want him to come to her rescue and that would mean . . . she did not want him.

Hades suppressed the thought at once, which left him with the conclusion that the message must be false, a device to delay his coming to rescue his wife.

Persephone must have told whoever held her—
Zeus?—that if she were not released, her husband
would come for her. Indeed, an assurance that Zeus
was innocent and a vague promise of Persephone's
return would be typical of the first step Zeus would
take to fend off his brother's wrath. But would Zeus
have used such an infelicitous word as "sacrifice" in
referring to Persephone? Surely only she herself would
have thought in those terms. But if the word was hers,
then she had deliberately withheld information on
who was holding her prisoner and where, and that
meant—

No, it did not mean she did not love him. Hades
walked faster, recalling the last day and night they had
spent together. He could not doubt the warmth of her
kisses, the wild response to his lovemaking. But it was
now more than three moons that they had been apart.
If another man tempted her . . . No! She *was* a prisoner, and the message was false. It had to be, and the
only one who could profit from holding her was Zeus.

Usually Hades made sure what time of day or night
it was and where Zeus was before he decided to show
himself. This time he did not care. As soon as he
sensed above him the forms he recognized as Zeus's
palace, he caught up a ladder, wedged the hooks at the
top into the first convenient holds carved into the
stone wall, and climbed it, disappearing headfirst into
the rock above. He rose from the earth in the inner
courtyard of Zeus's palace with his bared sword in his
hand. The lone guard at the door only gaped with
voice-stilled fear, the whites of his eyes gleaming in the
darkness, his mouth a round black hole.

"Go and fetch Zeus," Hades said softly, because if
he released what was in him enough to shout, it would

escape altogether and melt the ground beneath his own feet, sending him, as well as Zeus's entire palace, to destruction. "Tell him his brother Hades has a few questions to ask him—and do not tell me it is not your place to disturb your master or I will bury you alive."

The guard turned and ran. After a moment Hades followed. He would be in greater danger inside Zeus's palace than in the courtyard, but he did not wish to give his agile-minded brother even the time it would take to walk from his bedchamber to think up excuses.

He heard the guard challenged. In the next moment the marble floor turned red and cracked under the challenger's feet, and he screamed and leapt away, dropping to the ground to tear at his sandals. The outside guard threw open a door and called, gibbering with terror. Hades heard Zeus's voice.

"Go away," he said, thrusting the man aside as he walked in the open door and slammed it shut behind him.

Zeus came from an inner chamber clutching a night robe around him just as Hades thrust the locking bar home. He gestured, and crystal lamps fastened to the wall—Hades's gifts—lit. "Hades!" he exclaimed. "I have been dreading this moment. I do not have her." He dropped heavily into a chair. "I seem to have been saying that for years. But I do not. I did everything that lying bitch Demeter demanded, but she did not keep her part of the bargain."

"And you expect me to believe that you do not know where she is or whether my wife is with her—"

Zeus looked startled. "Of course I know where they are. Demeter would not return here before Kor—"

"Do not—" Hades's voice, cold and quiet as death,

cut Zeus off and the tip of Hades's sword rose a trifle. "Do not call my wife by that name."

"I beg your pardon," Zeus said quickly. "I still think of her as a little girl. Well, Demeter said she would not return here before Queen Persephone joined her, so it was arranged—at least I thought it was arranged—that Hermes bring Queen Persephone to her mother, rest a day, and then bring them both here."

"But?"

Zeus shrugged. "Demeter would not come. She says that Queen Persephone rejects her and that her daughter's physical presence does not satisfy her demand that they be reunited. Until she and Queen Persephone become one, as they were in the past, Demeter will not come near Olympus nor do the Goddess's work here."

Hades sheathed his sword and his lips lost some of the grimness that had made them a hard gash in his face. Perhaps the message was true. If Persephone were still trying to convince her mother to return to Olympus, she might not want him to fetch her away, in which case she might not want him to know where she was.

"I am at my wit's end," Zeus said, running his hand through his hair and then scrubbing at his face as if he could wash away the tiredness in it. "Listen to me. If you will send a message by Hermes and say you desire Persephone to yield to her mother, I will give you Aglaia and the most promising of the young priest-esses, among whom you are sure to find one who will be strong enough to bring fertility to Plutos—and any other woman or ten women or fifty in Olympus that you desire to warm your bed, or any native woman—"

Hades laughed aloud. "I am not like you, brother.

I cannot exchange women as I do my clothing. For me there is only one woman, now and forever, and that is Persephone."

"Hades, be reasonable. We will live through this winter, but the next there will be hunger and I cannot swear what the other great mages will do—" Rage flashed in his eyes. "Nor would I try to stop them. They are not bound by my agreement with you not to meddle in Plutos."

"It is very difficult to frighten the dead, or to win any struggle against them," Hades said flatly, then he sighed. "But I do not desire any harm to Olympus. You know that. Only there is nothing I can do about Persephone, even if I were willing—which I am not. She is not the girl you knew or her mother knew. She is changed. There is something in her over which I have no control. But you need not starve. You say some of the younger priestesses are promising. I suspect Demeter did all she could to suppress their abilities because she would endure no rivals to her daughter. Let them be encouraged. In a few years—"

"We do not have a few years." Zeus's voice grated. "Olympus lives by the magic that brings abundance from soil and space that should not feed a tenth the people and herds we have. I told you. Next year we will need to slaughter our herds. The year after that we will starve—or fight."

"If you fight the dead, you will only join them." Hades's black eyes met his brother's bleakly, but then his lips twitched, and he added, "Frankly I do not desire your turbulent mages in my realm." He was silent a moment, so obviously thinking hard that Zeus did not speak. Finally he said slowly, "I do not like to make promises I cannot keep, so I will not promise.

But if I can get Persephone back, I believe she would be willing to bless your fields and quicken your seed for this coming year." He smiled grimly. "No, do not even think about keeping her. I will be with her."

"You are asking us to live from year to year on your charity."

"No. I am telling you that I *hope* to be able to provide one more year's grace in which you—and I, if I can help—will find a different solution to your problem. You cannot have Persephone. That is an absolute." Suddenly Hades burst out laughing. "Believe me, you would not want her if you had her. You think Demeter is trouble, but you have not yet known an unwilling or angry Persephone."

Zeus had listened closely to Hermes's description of Hades's relationship with his wife, and he looked at Hades sidelong under his lashes. "Is it love . . . or fear . . . that binds you to her?" he asked slyly.

Hades laughed again, easily, with true amusement at Zeus's attempt to prick his pride. Zeus did not understand the word "respect" as related to women. He knew only fear, as he feared the Mother and—when she had reached a certain level of rage—Hera, and a kind of indulgent contempt. Hades knew what existed between himself and Persephone would be incomprehensible to his brother.

"I would call it equal portions of lust and terror," he replied, smiling. "But Persephone is not your problem; she is mine. If I can get her back in time and she is willing to bring the Goddess's blessing to your crops, she may also be willing to see what she can do about awakening power in your younger priestesses. If they support Aglaia you should be safe. Or, once she is truly convinced she cannot break Persephone to her will, Demeter may return."

"I cannot say I like any of the choices," Zeus said, his mouth pursed as if he had tasted something sour. "Well, in the future I will leave the priestesses and all the avatars of the Mother to their own devices." He shuddered slightly. "Dorkas is dead. She was found lying before the altar." Then he frowned, rubbed his face again, and asked—as if he were truly awake at last, "Why did you appear here in the middle of the night?"

"I had a message from Persephone, and I am sorry to say, dear brother, I thought you had sent it to beguile me into patience."

"A message? But Hermes has not—"

"It did not come through Hermes but through one of those places where the dead may speak to the living."

"The message said I had K—er—Queen Persephone?"

"You are half asleep still," Hades said, smiling. "That would scarcely beguile me into patience. No, it said 'The sacrifice was not made to Zeus' and that if I had patience it would return to me of itself. That kind of vague promise . . . forgive me, brother, but it is in your style."

Zeus did not bother to deny it, merely shook his head, and Hades went on, "What made me suspicious was that Persephone did not say where she was so I could come for her. Now I see that she must have believed I knew already. Hermes had told us that Demeter had a temple in Eleusis, and the woman who brought the message carried it to the cave near Eleusis."

"Eleusis? But—" Zeus began.

Hades interrupted, adding, "I know she does not want me to interfere yet, but I cannot see any purpose in waiting longer. If Persephone has not been able to convince Demeter to keep her word to you in three moons, she will not succeed in time for the spring planting—which may be what Demeter intends, that both Olympus and Plutos be belly-pinched. But I think my presence might be more effective in convincing Demeter than anything Persephone says, so I will go to Eleusis and bring my influence to bear."

"But they are not at Eleusis," Zeus said. "I thought that was why you came to accuse me, because you had discovered they were not there and thought I had snatched them from Eleusis. Demeter may be mad, but she is clever. She is on Aegina, under the protection of Poseidon."

"Poseidon?" Hades breathed, his pallid skin taking on a sickly greenish hue. He fumbled for a chair and sank into it.

"So you know," Zeus said grimly. "I always wondered whether you realized how much he hated you."

Hades said nothing, staring down at his hands, clasped so hard that the knuckles showed white.

"Oh, you are an honorable man," Zeus remarked, his lips twisted into a bitter grimace. "Did you think I did not know that he had asked you to join with him to overthrow me just after we had deposed Kronos, and that you refused him?"

"You are both my brothers," Hades said quietly. "I was a long time alone in the caves. I value Poseidon even if he hates me. I understand how fear can breed hatred. It is sad for him that he never outgrew either the one or the other."

"Well, he did not, and he does hate you—and fear you. Knowing that, what will you do?" Zeus's clenched fist smacked into his free hand. "If I can help, I will, but I do not see what I can do. I do not think Hermes would be willing to try to bring Persephone back without Demeter's approval, and—"

Hades stood up. "I need to think," he said. "If there is any way you can help me, I will let you know." He found a very faint smile. "At a more reasonable hour of the day."

In fact he was saying the right things out of a kind of instinct for dealing with Zeus. Actually, his mind was nearly blank, as it had been since he heard that Persephone was in Poseidon's power. When he became aware of his surroundings again, he was almost back to his chamber. He did not have the slightest memory of leaving Olympus or how he reached the passage along which he was striding. Then he realized his instinctive responses to Zeus's question about what he would do had been totally misleading. He did not need to think, because his mind was already made up. He would go to Aegina and bring Persephone home. After that, if she wished, they could renew bargaining with Demeter, but first he would free his wife.

Did he want help from Zeus or Hermes? Hades thrust aside the curtain that separated his small living space from the passage, stood staring blankly for a moment, and then sat down on his bed. He found he was shaking his head. He would not ask Zeus for help. If they could have acted within the few moments following their conversation, Zeus would have done whatever he could. However, once his brother had time for second thoughts, Hades was less sure Zeus

would not try to keep his peace with Poseidon . . .
somehow.

Hermes. Hades bit his lip gently. He was so eager to
get to Persephone that he was sorely tempted to ask
the young mage for a spell to carry him to Aegina. He
was half standing before he quelled the temptation.
Hermes could only sell a spell that went from one
specific place to another and back, and he had to know
the place. Probably that meant Poseidon's throne
room, which would scarcely be safe or secret. Even in
the dead of night there would probably be guards;
Poseidon was not a trusting soul. Wandering around
his palace without the faintest idea of where Persephone might be was a recipe for certain disaster.

There was also the chance that Persephone was not
lodged—or imprisoned—in Poseidon's palace. In that
case, Hades thought bitterly, he would not only need
to get safely out of the palace, find her and rescue her,
but get back into the palace and into the throne room
to use the spell to return. He laughed softly. He did not
lack confidence in himself, but he knew what would
take a special miracle from the Mother and what he
could manage with his own strength, skill, and Gift.
Worse, if he were caught, every chance of rescuing
Persephone would be ended. He did not think Poseidon would kill him outright, but he might try to keep
him prisoner—a wooden ship in the ocean would be
quite effective—and in any case Persephone would be
too well guarded once Poseidon knew he was trying to
recover her to make a second attempt practical.

Hades gnawed on his lip a little harder. That last
thought was very troubling and virtually made help
from Hermes out of the question. There was no way
Hades knew to control the mischievous young mage.

Possibly Hermes could carry Hades to some place on Aegina outside the palace, but what then? Hermes would not be willing to stay for however long it took Hades to find Persephone and win her freedom by whatever method was necessary just to carry them back to Plutos. Not that he would want Hermes on Aegina. Mother alone knew what that young devil would be doing to keep himself amused.

That would mean Hermes would be loose in the world knowing he was on Aegina. Hades shook his head. Even if Hermes did not betray his presence to Poseidon purely for amusement, the young mage was very likely to tell the tale in Olympus. Hermes was an inveterate gossip and would be indifferent to the chance of the news getting back to Poseidon. And there were those who passed news of whatever was happening in Olympus to the sea king.

Hades did not blame Poseidon for buying information. There were as many, or more, who whispered news into the black tunnels behind the slave cave in the hopes of later finding worked gold or gems—a reasonably common reward. The sea king paid in pearls and nacre, and his creatures carried the news back to him through river and sea as quickly as the dead carried it through the underworld passages. That would not matter, Hades thought, if he could find Persephone immediately and flee with her at once. Then the rescue might be effected before the news reached Poseidon. But if he needed to spend much time searching for her, the fact that he was doing so might well be relayed to Poseidon before he succeeded, which would mean failure or confrontation.

Hades did not desire a confrontation. He did not wish to win and make his brother hate and fear him more; worse, he might not win. All the advantage would be with Poseidon while they were on Aegina. In fact, Hades thought, his only hope of getting Persephone back to the mainland without being sunk and drowned was for Poseidon not to realize she was gone. That meant no one—not Hermes, not Zeus, not even his own people—no one at all must know he was going to Aegina.

He stood up and drew a deep breath. At least time was not a pressing factor, except for his eagerness to see his wife. He had six weeks or so before Persephone would need to begin her blessing. He could travel secretly to the cave near Eleusis, take ship there for Aegina, and have all the time he needed to discover where Persephone was, how to reach her, and how to escape from the island. As he took a step toward the curtain, he realized he was trembling with eagerness and he stopped to steady himself. When he stepped out of his chamber and walked to the miners' quarters, his face might have been carved of stone.

The gang chief hurried forward, bowing. "My lord?"

"I must return to Plutos. I do not believe that it will be necessary to bring down the city, at least not immediately. Replace every third support with stone. That will give some greater security without making it impossible for me to change my mind. When you are finished, return to the home caves. Koios will have orders for your next task."

Chapter 18

Persephone's brilliant idea, well nurtured with hope and watered with tears, was about to bear a lovely fruit, which would soon ripen. It had taken her a week to move a suitable number of gowns and a good selection of jewelry to Pontoporeia's cottage. By then, the old woman had discovered a suitable ship and made arrangements with its captain. Persephone then told Eulimine that her father was growing weaker and she had purchased Pontoporeia's cottage so he could be nearer the port if he wished to sail home. And just before she sailed, Pontoporeia told Eulimine that with the metal Persephone had given her, she would try her luck in a village in the interior where she was not known.

For a week after Pontoporeia sailed, Persephone had made no attempt to leave the palace, praying fervently that her messenger had got safe away. She had watched her mother carefully but could see no sign that Demeter suspected what she had done, nor did Poseidon give her more than a glancing look or a polite, indifferent greeting now and again. Finally she had stiffened her courage, taken her basket, and gone to the gate. When she was allowed to pass without comment, she had at last believed that her ruse had succeeded. Hades would not destroy himself in an effort to destroy Olympus.

Her relief had been so great that she walked halfway to the town with tears pouring down her face. The realization that nothing could better forward her plans than tear-streaked cheeks had made her laugh with joy, but she had managed to arrive at Eulimine's house wearing a sad face. Her father, she had told the potter, had a violent attack of his disorder, which nearly killed him. He had recovered, but had changed his mind about being moved to the town. Instead, he had ordered that a special coffin be made for him so that he could be shipped home.

Eulimine shook her head. "Most ships will not carry a coffin."

Persephone sighed. "I know, but papa refuses to consign his body to a pyre. He insists on being carried to the cave near Eleusis where he can join the dead as he is. He was so sick and making himself worse. I promised. Do you not know of a clever carpenter who could build a closed litter that could serve as a coffin if . . . if need be?"

Eulimine stared at her for a moment, then remembered how happy Pontoporeia looked when she came to say goodbye. Pontoporeia had not suffered by being involved with the strange young woman. Eulimine nodded. "That I do know. Cyriakos could do it, and if he is well paid will do it without speaking of it, but I doubt he would be willing to work outside the town. He is usually too busy building and repairing ships."

"There would be no need for him to come to our house," Persephone said eagerly. "He could build it wherever he likes, and when it is finished, bring it to Pontoporeia's house. If my father grows strong enough to go home, I can send servants to fetch the litter. If I must take him, I can have his body carried secretly to Pontoporeia's house. Where can I find Cyriakos?"

As Eulimine described the way to Cyriakos's workshop, which was at the far end of the docks, near where the wooded hills sloped down toward the harbor, Persephone recalled that she must not have any open dealings with a shipbuilder or be seen near the docks. She fell back on her silly pose of fearfulness and induced kindhearted Eulimine to ask Cyriakos to meet her at Pontoporeia's cottage the next day.

She spent a restless night, fearing while she was awake that all was going too well and dreaming as soon as she fell asleep of Poseidon's heavy hand on her shoulder and her mother's shrill voice telling her that all was known. However, she left the palace as freely as ever and saw, as she was walking down the lane to Pontoporeia's house, a strong, squat old man accompanied by a taller but equally strong young one coming toward her. She paused by the gate and invited them inside, invoking and repowering the cloaking spell as she entered.

"I am Cyriakos," the older man said, bowing slightly. "This is my son, Cyros. He will build what you desire on one condition, that you do not take passage on a ship from Aegina with your father's corpse, if he should die."

"Oh," Persephone said, "yes, I will promise that. If my father grows stronger, we might need to take the first ship to meet a business obligation, but—but if he is dead . . . He will not be in a hurry and I will be able to wait for a foreign ship." Then, always wary of watchers, she added, "I do not have much time. Can you tell me quickly how you can satisfy my need and how it will be possible for me to learn about the progress of the work? I—I am afraid to go down to the docks."

The younger man started to laugh, then choked it back when his father glared at him. Persephone was puzzled, and then realized he thought her so plain that she had nothing to fear. She asked rather sharply whether they had any idea of how to build what she wanted, and Cyros, looking down as if chastened, described his plan, which amounted to a litter closed in by thin, light wood sliding panels with a much sturdier compartment below that could be made airtight by lining with metal if necessary.

"You could ride in the litter," he said, "if you do not fear what would be below you. And if your father recovers, the storage space will be useful. A panel can be dropped down so he can sit upright with his feet in the space below or you could carry clothing or other articles in it."

"That is exactly what I want," Persephone said, her pique soothed when she understood what Cyros planned to build. It flashed through her mind that the pair had devised the complex idea very quickly or, more likely, had built similar conveyances before. That hardly mattered to her, except that it almost guaranteed they would keep the work secret. "How soon can it be done, and what will be the charge?"

"Within a moon," Cyriakos said, and named a price.

The price was high, as Eulimine warned, but gold and gems were not precious to Persephone anymore.

She bargained because she was sure the carpenter would be suspicious if she did not. She pleaded for a more reasonable fee, saying her father would be angry with her for paying so much or might insist she find another carpenter, but she was so happy that her plain face grew less plain. Eventually they agreed and she said she would obtain her father's approval and pay one quarter of the fee the next day. To seal the bargain, she passed to Cyriakos two new twists of gold wire.

He felt the softness of the metal and smiled. "I will send Cyros at this time tomorrow," Cyriakos said. "He will bring samples of the wood and the stains so you can choose."

Persephone nodded. "I will come if I can. If my father is having a bad day, I will leave the key to this house and the gold with Eulimine. You can put the samples here, and I will send word to you of which I favor as soon as I can."

She went back to thank Eulimine for her help and to leave the key and a pouch she had concealed that contained some battered and broken links of a heavy gold chain. The links came from one of several pieces of jewelry she had pounded apart one night in a distant corner of the garden, knowing she would need metal to pay for the litter, for her passage, for servants to carry the litter—and perhaps for bribes. She gave several small pieces of gold to Eulimine: "to hold for her until she sailed, in case she might not be able to get what she needed herself, and to keep thereafter." What Persephone dared not say aloud until she could get Eulimine into Pontoporeia's house was that she would need her to hire porters to carry her "father" to a ship.

She had not intended to come the next day; she feared going to the town three days in succession might draw attention, but she simply could not bear to delay the work on the litter, which she realized must happen if she did not tell Cyros which wood and stain she wanted him to use. She had a fright when the guard at the gate smiled at her as she passed through, and she hurried back to the palace after drawing Cyros into Pontoporeia's house, choosing—almost at random—the wood and stain, paying him, and arranging to meet him at the same place a week later with the next quarter payment.

For the next few days, she spent her time with the young women who frequented the palace. She found it very easy to be silly and she laughed a lot to cover her difficulty in concentrating on their talk and amusements. Her mind was busy devising a plan to get her mother to come into the town with her. In the time Persephone had been on Aegina, Demeter had never left the palace, although she knew from what Pontoporeia had said that her mother must have blessed the seed and the fields the past spring. That, Persephone thought, must be her lever. She knew when she would have to use it—any day after the litter was finished and delivered on which Poseidon was away from the palace—but she could not yet see *how* to use it.

One thing she realized was that she must pretend to be on better terms with her mother or it would not be reasonable to seek her company when she needed to get her into Pontoporeia's house. Once there, she would have to find a way to make her swallow a spoonful of Pontoporeia's sleeping potion. After that, Demeter could be bundled into the bottom of the litter or perhaps, wrapped beyond recognition, be carried in the body of the litter itself, disguised as Persephone's sick father.

Persephone found the approach to her mother far easier than she expected; in fact, it was Demeter who showed the way by remarking—about the middle of the first week that Cyros was working on the litter—that she was very happy to learn from Neso that Kore was beginning to enjoy her friends in Aegina, in the palace and in the town. Persephone's heart almost stopped on those last words, but Demeter patted her cheek and said she was well content for little Kore to have her freedom. She had never intended, Demeter went on, to make a prisoner of her daughter but only to protect her from being made the tool of an unscrupulous mage. Since Kore had learned so well to conceal her Gift and had done nothing foolish, why should she not visit the town?

Fortunately, Persephone was so frightened that she did not flinch away from her mother's hand. She stammered something about seeking distraction for her grief over losing her husband, and Demeter laughed and told her not to be so stubborn and spiteful.

"You do not really miss him anymore," she said. "Only when you deliberately remind yourself to punish me. I do not understand why you find those coarse natives more attractive than the young folk in the palace—although I suppose none of the men will come near you now, after the way you knocked down Momos. I just wanted you to know, Kore, that I am tired of your weeping and blaming me and then, having assuaged your silly guilt—after all, you owe nothing to a man who abducted and raped you—dancing out and enjoying yourself."

Lowering her eyes to conceal the rage in them was another happy accident. Her mother immediately embraced her and murmured, "There, there, dearling. I do not mean to scold you, but I am jealous when I see you laughing with the maidens of the court and confiding in a coarse woman who makes pots in the town and I get nothing but reproaches and tears."

Demeter spoke just long enough for Persephone's anger to be completely wiped out by her realization that she had accomplished her purpose without even trying. Demeter herself had opened the path to Persephone's change in behavior and provided the reason for it. In the next moment Persephone recalled that before her mother had spoken those disgusting lies about Hades she had given her tacit leave to spend time in the town. With her head still bowed, she murmured, "Yes, mother," almost choking on her joy.

After that it was hard not to laugh all the time, to remember not to embrace and kiss Demeter out of the sheer happiness of knowing her mother's self-absorbed blindness would make escape possible. Within a moon or six weeks, Persephone was sure she would be back in Hades's arms. She reminded herself that too rapid a change of mood might arouse suspicion of its sincerity in her mother, but often the hope and anticipation leaked through and Persephone's eyes shone a deeper, brighter amber, her hair gleamed more golden, and her lips softened into a fuller, lovelier line.

She was too happy to realize that, even though she was aware that the young men were inching closer again. She ignored them, thinking she would spend little time with them. Since Demeter knew of her trips into town, Persephone felt she could go more frequently. The first time, although she remembered to wear her plain clothing and plain face so she would not shock Eulimine, the potter smiled at her after a moment and said, "Your father is better."

"Yes," Persephone said, also smiling. "How did you know?"

"You look as if a heavy weight had dropped off your back."

Persephone took a deep breath and lowered her eyes. First her mother and now Eulimine were saying and doing of themselves what she had schemed and planned to maneuver them into doing.

"I feel that way," she admitted. "Yet I must not hope too much. This has happened before, in fact before we set out for Aegina he recovered from a bad attack and was very well until he fell ill soon after we arrived. Still, he is much improved—" She hesitated, then leaned close to whisper, as one does when to speak of good fortune aloud might bring it to the attention of some malevolent power. "He feels so well that he has begun to talk of going home—alive. He is so eager that he has given me leave to offer Cyros an extra quarter payment if he will finish the work on the litter within two weeks more." She straightened, bit her lip, then smiled pleadingly and asked aloud, "Could you interrupt your work and go now to ask him to meet me at Pontoporeia's house?"

"If I do, this vessel will crack when I fire it. Wait until it is sound and I will go."

"Please, Eulimine?" Persephone was whispering again, praying her voice was too low for the scryer to hear. "I am being silly, I know, but I feel as if every minute is important. As if papa will get sick again just an hour before the litter is ready if I do not speak to Cyros at once. Oh, please? Let me buy the vessel, just as it is." She giggled faintly. "If we take ship for home, I will keep it always as a memory of this moment when my spirits soared."

Eulimine shook her head, but she laughed and rose to take the large, squat container and move it to the drying rack.

"Thank you," Persephone cried, embracing her as she wiped her hands. "I will meet him at Pontoporeia's house," she cried as she danced to the door, but she did not forget to put several bits of copper on the table as she passed.

With the full power of the no-see-no-hear spell invoked, she could speak plainly. It did not take long to convince Cyros to agree to put aside all other work to finish the litter after he weighed the gold she offered in his hand. He was somewhat more reluctant to agree to discover for her what ships would be leaving Aegina for the whole week after the date on which he would deliver the litter. He seemed suspicious, reminding her that she had promised not to take a corpse aboard any ship based in Aegina. She explained at length about her father's recovery and that he was completing his business as quickly as he could now that he was better, but she could not be sure of the exact day he would be ready to leave.

Cyros remained reluctant until Persephone was visited by an inspiration and asked about the cushions and padding for the inside of the litter. At that, Cyros brightened. She could see him thinking that one does not worry about cushions for a dead man, and he said he would see to those details too, for another quarter-bit of gold. And when she agreed to that, he said he would find out about the ships for her, but that she would have to meet him again in two more days to choose the leather or fabric for the linings. She agreed immediately, without showing any doubt that she would be free, and he left the house just ahead of her with a broad, satisfied smile on his face.

The next two weeks were so busy for Persephone that she had no time to be nervous or to think much about the fact that Poseidon had twice called her up to speak to him. Joy had not quite unseated her reason, so she remained withdrawn in his presence, eyes downcast, saying not a single word more than was necessary to answer his questions and keeping well out of his reach.

Her mother asked questions too, specifically about the people she met in the town. She answered with half-truths—mentioning a farm just outside of the town where she went to watch the pigs. She had indeed gone there several times so she could dose a young sow with differing amounts of Pontoporeia's sleeping draught, and see it, a few days later quite recovered, none the worse for its long sleep. She spoke most of Eulimine and how fascinating she found the making of pots. She even mentioned the metalchanger who had given her copper and silver for gold—but she never mentioned Pontoporeia's house or Cyros.

From knowing glances and a remark or two she gathered that her mother knew about the bespelled house but thought she was meeting a man there. She made no effort to deny this, merely laughing and shaking her head, delighted because it was clear Demeter believed the house was bespelled to conceal romantic meetings. If the idea had not served her purpose so well, she would have been furious at the notion she would betray Hades, but she was too amused by the fact that Demeter would likely fall into a trap of her own making. If she could not think of a reason relating to the Goddess to induce Demeter to come to Pontoporeia's house, Persephone thought, she could always ask her to come to meet her lover.

A few days later she met Cyros one last time. The litter stood against the back wall of Pontoporeia's house, at right angles to it, protruding into the room. They spent some time together, Cyros proudly displaying the beauty of his work and showing Persephone how to raise, lower, and adjust the panels that covered the lower carrying portion. Persephone was rather surprised at the size of the litter and Cyros said he had judged from her height that her father was a big man. Since she could not admit it was her mother, who was a smaller woman, that she planned to carry in it, she sighed and said her father had been tall once but was now sadly shrunken.

When at last he was certain the beauties of his skill had been duly understood and admired, Cyros relayed to her the names and berths of the ships that were expected to sail out of Aegina the following week. Thoughtfully, Persephone remarked that her father continued very well and might now linger in Aegina a few days or even a week or two longer. Would Cyros bring the shipping information the next week if Eulimine asked for it? Then she paid, and added still an extra bit above the bonus she had promised. Cyros looked at the metal in his hand and said he would be happy to pass any information the lady desired, and he walked out the door smiling broadly, pausing to bow before he turned away.

Persephone almost danced all the way back to the palace. Now she had only to wait until Poseidon would be gone for a while and get her mother to the town. In preparation, she asked Neso what she hoped would be considered innocent questions about Poseidon—could he really breathe under water? and could he really talk to the creatures of the sea? and did he truly live in the sea when he left the palace? and how long could he live there? Neso answered as freely as she always did when she felt her answers would enhance her master's power and prestige, but Persephone soon noticed the sea girl's speculative expression and grew alarmed.

"Oh, do not tell him I have been asking about him," Persephone begged. "It is none of my business, I know. He might be angry with you for gossiping and me for asking."

"I promise you he will not be angry," Neso said, smiling, but then, seeing that Persephone looked really frightened, she added, "I will not tell him what you asked."

Having what she thought was agreement, Persephone hastened to change the subject. She spoke about how much warmer it was in Aegina than in her home and asked if spring had yet touched the valleys away from the sea.

Neso shook her head. "I am of the sea," she pointed out. "I do not travel far from the water. You should ask your mother if you wish to learn of the land."

Armed with this remark, Persephone later reproached Demeter for going on excursions without her. Demeter laughed and pointed out that until recently her daughter had been in no mood to accompany her.

"But what do you do?" Persephone asked.

Demeter lowered her eyes and a small satisfied smile curved the corners of her lips. "I have taught the women to worship the Goddess again," she said softly, "and I have taught the Gifted to draw in Her power to give back to the earth and the seed."

"That is wonderful, Mother," Persephone said, taking her mother's hands. Then she frowned. "But She has no temple in the town."

Demeter sighed. "Nor will She. The sea king desires no rivals and will permit no temples to any god or goddess, even the Mother. He gives leave to a few weak workers of magic to sell small spells, but all who are discovered to be truly Gifted—men and women alike—he orders thrown into the sea where they are devoured by his creatures."

"That is horrible," Persephone breathed.

Demeter looked at her coldly. "More horrible than being driven into the underworld with stones and whips?"

"But—" Persephone cut off the protest and lowered her eyes. Hades's secret would not be safe with her mother.

A slight smile marked Demeter's triumph when her daughter did not persist in her defense of the underworld, but she did not labor the point. She went on, as if there had been no interruption, "Nonetheless, the women I have brought to worship Her have built shrines in secret places and I have blessed those shrines and felt the Goddess accept them. Would you like to see them?"

"Yes, indeed!" Persephone's eyes widened, and then she smiled and deliberately leaked a taste of power for her mother to suck in.

She felt Demeter deserved that for not catching her near admission that those driven into the underworld did not die horribly but lived long, productive lives in

Plutos. More important, her mother had also provided the answer to her last problem, so she kissed Demeter warmly and asked if they could go after the noon meal the next day. That, Persephone thought, should make them late enough in returning to miss the normal dinner hour.

Demeter raised her brows, and muttered what Persephone thought was the word "lust" under her breath, but aloud she only agreed to her daughter's proposal. That annoyed Persephone, who was effectively muzzled. She could scarcely defend herself against her mother's assumption that she was such a fool and slave to her body that she would put off a devotion to the Goddess to meet her lover in the town.

The irritation salved the slight pang of guilt Persephone had felt over perverting Demeter's real dedication to the Goddess to her own purposes. As she returned to her room, she resolved again that she would use the bait Demeter had provided. She would tell her mother that the reason Pontoporeia's house was bespelled was that a shrine had been built there. Then she would confess she had not told her mother sooner because she was trying to call the Goddess to the new shrine herself and had failed. Persephone was certain, after that admission, that Demeter would come to bless it.

Now, if only Poseidon would go away—or was that really necessary? If she and Demeter went into the farmland together and returned once or twice, especially if they usually came back too late to attend Poseidon's court dinner, would he notice they were missing at once on the day they took ship? And what if he did notice? Immediately an ugly question she had not faced before came into her mind. Was Demeter as much a prisoner as she? Would the sea king, as she had been assuming all along, accept her mother's departure with her or would he be angry enough to sink the ship on which they were traveling?

Persephone shuddered and then steadied. He might wish to keep her to spite Hades, and to keep Demeter to make Zeus and Olympus suffer, but he would not dare kill them. That would make both Hades and Zeus into such bitter enemies—not to mention Athena and Ares and all the other mages who would know there was no more hope of saving their city and their luxurious way of life—that they would join together to kill him. Poseidon was not likely to overlook the fact that even the protection of the sea could not shield him from all the great mages linked together in rage.

Hope buoyed her up; fear cast her down. Persephone hid in her room and got through the rest of that day, but the time dragged so horribly that she decided to fulfill her mother's expectations and go into town the next morning. At least it would give her something to do and keep new questions out of Demeter's mind.

By habit, she went to Eulimine's house. Once there, however, she found herself too fearful—with escape almost within her grasp—to make idle conversation lest she unwittingly betray herself. Glancing around in the hope something she saw would present a safe subjet, her eye caught the vessel she had prevented Eulimine from finishing, still on the drying rack. Persephone immediately insisted on paying for it, saying, when Eulimine protested payment was unnecessary, that she was taking no chances of bringing ill luck on herself for breaking a promise, no matter how silly.

Having paid, she carried her prize—with difficulty— away to Pontoporeia's house, setting it on the table.

The sun was still barely above the hills to the east, so she whiled away some more time cutting into strips for bandaging her mother's face and head—or for tying and gagging her if necessary—cloth she had bought over the past moon and concealed behind Pontoporeia's discarded clothes. When the strips were folded and hidden inside the litter, she left the house. As she stepped out, she stopped abruptly and looked out over the warehouses and storage sheds below the cliff toward the sea, certain she had heard her name. Who would call her from the sea? Cyros? What could Cyros want?

She scanned the road as far as she could see it, but it was empty. And then she swallowed hard. Cyros would not call her Persephone. He had never heard that name and called her "lady." Someone from the court?

Persephone ran to the edge of the hill, not wishing to be caught standing in front of Pontoporeia's house. Far out to sea was a ship making for harbor. She pulled her eyes away to scan right and left, looked down the hill again. No one. Then she caught her breath. Why had she come to the edge of the cliff? Normally she would have run the other way, toward the town. She snapped her shield tight. The pull on her, a hardly perceptible drawing, was cut. Someone wanted her down on the docks. Who? Why? Trembling with fear, she turned away from the cliff and hurried back toward the palace.

As she neared the gate, however, Persephone found herself walking more and more slowly, reluctant to enter. If she went in, would she ever be allowed out? Could her mother be so cruel as to let her expend so much care and thought to regain her freedom and snatch away her chance for escape at the last moment? But Demeter would not think it cruel; she would think of it as teaching her daughter a lesson. Persephone was tempted to go back to the town, but she knew that escape was impossible—or would only create a worse disaster in the long run—if she did not bring Demeter with her.

In any case, going back to the town would not solve her problem, Persephone thought, still walking forward slowly. If Demeter did know her plans and she did not come to the noon meal as she had promised, her mother would begin to look for her. She had no place to hide; the scryers would find her. And she did not know for certain that her plans had been exposed. In fact, she doubted Demeter would call her "Persephone" even to set a trap. All she had felt was her name and a pull on her—she drew a sudden deep breath. Yes, a pull . . . from the sea. Her eyes widened. Poseidon?

Persephone bit her lip. She had been noticing that he was looking her over again, less with real interest than with a kind of puzzled doubt. She had done her best not to draw his notice, but possibly her recent hope of escape had made her less careful. She gnawed her lip a little harder. If the calling had been generated by Poseidon, dare she go back to the palace? Yes. She was as safe there as anywhere else on Aegina since no one, except possibly her mother, who was in the palace, would dare protect her from him.

Her pace quickened. Whether her mother had sent that caller as some kind of trap for her or Poseidon had wished to lure her into a hidden cove along the beach, or whether she had imagined the whole thing, she must not give any cause for suspicion. She must go in; she must look happy; she must behave as normally as possible and try to discover who had tried to "call" her and for what purpose.

Persephone suspected that her pretense at ease and happiness did not deceive her mother, but instead of questioning her, Demeter looked rather smug. Persephone was now sure the calling had been part of some clever design of her mother's that she was too weak and stupid ever to understand. She had been played with, teased with the illusion of being strong and clever. She nearly choked in her attempt to eat and felt so worthless that she nearly wept with gratitude when her mother deigned to notice her and ask if she were ready to leave. She rose with alacrity, went to fetch her cloak, and met her mother at the northern gate, on the opposite side of the palace to the one she usually used.

As soon as they were well away, Demeter said, "You fool! Have I not told you a million times that men bring nothing but grief? I never thought my daughter could be such a slave to lust. Barely have I weaned you from craving that monster Hades when you entangle yourself with a—a clod of a native."

Open eyed, open mouthed, Persephone stumbled along beside Demeter without the smallest protest. In fact, she was so stunned by relief when she realized that her plan of escape had not been fathomed or betrayed, that her mother believed her fear and anxiety was owing to a lover's quarrel, that she had to be mute or roar with inexplicable laughter. All the way to the shrine, Demeter enlarged on her daughter's imagined quarrel with her lover. She pointed out in a double handful of different ways that what Kore called imprisonment was her loving mother's effort to shield her daughter against what she was now suffering. If

Kore had only taken to heart her mother's advice and remained a dutiful daughter, she would be happy now instead of hurt and grieved.

Persephone was far too grateful that her secret was undetected to object to her mother's scolding, even though it went on and on all during the long walk over the hill behind the palace, past the farms, and into the woods that clothed the lower flank of the mountain she could see from her window. After she was sure the scolding was genuine and not a lure to draw her into a confession that she did not have a lover, she hardly heard it. Her mind had gone back to her real problem and was full of new doubts about what she had felt outside Pontoporeia's house, whether she should try to avoid Poseidon until he left the palace or try to escape at once. When they came to the shrine, however, the scolding mother yielded to the dedicated priestess and Persephone's attention was suddenly fixed.

The shrine was no more than an open-sided shed housing a small wooden statue, roughly carved, but Persephone could see Demeter change. Even tight-locked within herself, she could perceive her mother's devotion and she gathered in her shield and opened herself. The Mother was here! Warmth and love bathed her and calmed her. She became sure she need not fear that call from the sea. The Goddess approved of her and would help and protect her. Beyond that, her mother, praying with rapt face, was all golden to her eyes. Demeter had her faults, but she was a true priestess and accepted by the Mother; she could not be evil.

Persephone's love poured out to the Goddess and the Mother's strength flooded back in. She heard a sharp indrawn breath and vaguely saw movement, but she was enwrapped in power and she drank and drank and drank and drank until she was fuller than she had ever been and the excess streamed out around her, making her skin tingle and her hair lift and crackle with energy.

The river of power washed once more around her. Warmth changed to dangerous heat; still Persephone stood in adoration, and before she was burned, the power was withdrawn. She was released. For a moment longer she stood adoring Her Lady. Then she blinked . . . and wondered why she had been filled to bursting when there were no priestesses to feed. And her mother, staring with dilated eyes, voiced Persephone's question and whispered, "Why?"

Since she had no better knowledge than Demeter, Persephone sidestepped the question and said, "I am consecrated to Her, even as you are, mother. I am Her high priestess in Her temple in Plutos."

"It is too soon for you," Demeter cried. "It was my place you were designed to take in the fullness of time. That was the purpose in my conceiving you."

Satisfied that she had diverted her mother from her original question, Persephone chuckled and shook her head. "Perhaps it was your purpose, mother, but the Goddess has Her Own purposes."

Demeter stared at her daughter, around whom there was still a glow of power. She half lifted a hand, as if to ward off Persephone's words, then her lips set. "How foolish I am to ask *you* why," she snapped. "I am Her high priestess and understand Her best. She gave to you because we were together, to show that we will both be enriched as long as we are one. You are unshielded now, not selfishly trying to withhold your Gift from me. That is why you were blessed."

Persephone's lips parted, but she did not speak. A sharp blade of doubt pierced her, but the knife was withdrawn in the same moment as she remembered how the Goddess filled her in the temple in Plutos. The memory brought soothing, the Mother's gentle hand spread a healing salve over the hurt of being called selfish. Then she felt, faintly, as if from a distance a command to be strong, to resist her mother's attempt to dominate her. The Goddess's assurance? But the touch was different somehow, darker and carrying a touch of a cold, black fury foreign to the Mother; Her anger, more dreadful when aroused, was scorching red. Persephone would have pursued the faint touch despite the warning, but her mother was talking again, and shaking her lightly, which broke Persephone's concentration.

"What did you say, mother?"

"That I do not know what to do with you. We cannot go back to the palace while you are glowing like hot embers. Even a common person could feel you, and to Poseidon you will shine like the sun."

"You have forgotten," Persephone said, smiling. "I have only to withdraw within my shield and my Gift will be locked inside."

"You would not dare close yourself off from me again," Demeter said. "Not after this proof of the Goddess's approval of our union in her service."

The doubt pricked Persephone again, because of the wealth of power with which she had been infused. Much more had been given her in her mother's presence—yet she was not denied strength when she was alone. And then she sighed as understanding came. The rich flood was the Goddess's promise that she would always have enough—enough to ease her mother's burden each planting season if Demeter were willing to make peace with Zeus, enough to feed the priestesses of Olympus as well as Plutos if Demeter refused to be pacified with the half-loaf of her daughter's presence for a few weeks each year. She smiled and held out her hand.

"The peace of the Goddess is in me. Until we come near the palace where I must hide my Gift from Poseidon, I will not shut you out."

Chapter 19

Persephone had indeed been granted peace. She replied with such smiling patience to her mother's jibes, threats, and promises on the long walk home, that after a time Demeter fell silent, glancing at her now and again with a troubled frown.

"You are like a sated beast," she burst out at last.

"I feel rather like one," Persephone replied agreeably.

In fact, her mother would have needed to hit her with a stick to break her calm. Her one doubt had been about the effect of the extra power when she closed her shield, but it seemed to mitigate the deadness she hated rather than distress her further by battering against the barrier. However, she did feel very tired when they reached the palace and not at all in need of eating. Within her, a presence urged that she sleep, and this time she was sure the touch was that of the Goddess.

She excused herself from her mother and made her way toward her chamber. Outside the throne room, she sidestepped a large figure without raising her eyes from the ground. Insulated both by the deadening her shield created and the sense of peace within her, she did not feel the attention that pursued her down the corridor and watched her door close.

"She is a very strange person," Poseidon said to Nerus. "Mostly she is plain as a closed oyster, but when she first came she glowed like a true pearl and even now I sometimes catch a glimpse of a glowing nacre." He shrugged. "When I have time, and when Demeter no longer cares—she has her doubts already, I know—I will force open the shell that encloses her daughter and see what is within."

"Lord," Nerus breathed, "you cannot keep Lady Persephone. I have seen that she will rule long by Hades's side."

"What?" Poseidon caught at the old man's shoulder and the strange, fishlike eyes rolled in agony.

"I cannot change my visions," Nerus gasped. "What you do not like is yet for your good."

"I did not mean to hurt you," Poseidon said, relaxing his grip. "I was only surprised by what you said. So, she goes back to Hades, does she? Do you see whether he wants her back or must take her?"

"She rules beside him. That is all I know."

"Rules? Truly rules?"

"Yes, lord."

Poseidon's bottom lip thrust forward. "So despite the fact he has done nothing to retrieve her for all these moons, Hades loves her. What else have you foreseen? Is there some danger in my association with her?"

"Nothing. I have seen nothing that shows any binding between you, nor any danger from her . . . nor from Hades."

"Good enough. I desire no bond with the woman, only a taste or two of her flesh and a solution to the mystery of why she has the glow of fine gold at one moment and the look of tarnished brass another."

Nerus said nothing. He felt no compulsion to volunteer any information that did not affect his master's safety, particularly when he suspected the information would be unwelcome and knew it could not affect the end result.

Poseidon was looking past him in the direction of Persephone's chamber when he suddenly laughed. "If I must give her up to my brother, I can at least sour his joy in her."

He started to brush past Nerus, but the old man caught at his arm. "Lord, if you do not start now, you will not come in time to keep your promise to Amphitrite to be there for the celebration of Rhode's birthday."

Not pleased at being reminded of a duty, even a pleasant one, Poseidon made no reply. Irritation momentarily heightened his impulse to work off part of his long-held grudge against Hades by seducing—or, if necessary, forcing—Persephone. With a toss of his head, he started down the long corridor, leaving Nerus behind. The old man watched him, his fishlike eyes intent, and by the time Poseidon reached Persephone's door, he had reconsidered. It would be a shame to disappoint his wife, who rarely left her palace in the sea and even more rarely interfered with him, and his daughter was a gentle creature who would take joy in his visit. Persephone could wait.

By the time Poseidon had reached the pool in his room, he had forgotten all about Persephone. Nerus, who had followed his master down the corridor, was the one who hesitated by Persephone's door, a slightly puzzled expression on his face. He did not linger, however, merely shook his head, wondering why he had taken such a foolish and dangerous chance as to tamper with his master's will.

Persephone slept peacefully, insulated against both hopes and fears, all evening and right through the night. She woke very early. Dawn was barely lightening the sky. She lay, everything that had happened clear in her mind, and then sat up and hugged her knees. What she had to do before she somehow induced her mother to come into the town so she could abduct her was arrange for passage off Aegina.

First she must make sure that the two ships Cyros named would sail the next day. It would be best if she herself could speak to the masters of the vessels and see whether either one had available a private cabin. But how? She did not dare go near the dock. Or did she? Thinking of booking passage reminded her of what she had said to Pontoporeia. An old servant woman could ask questions, even pay for a passage, for her mistress. And no one would see Persephone become the old woman inside the bespelled house. Heaven knew, after the Goddess's gift she had enough power to charge the spell for years.

Perhaps if she left now, before sunrise, which she had never done before, the scryer assigned to watch her might not yet be awake. Would that matter? Did the scryer search by appearance or by some other characteristic? The faint trace of her Gift? She had never worn her shield in town because there were so few Gifted she did not believe any could detect her power or dare report it if it were detected. But today she would. Persephone rose and dressed hurriedly. If she could get to Pontoporeia's house without being noticed, she could certainly change her outer appearance. With her shield up, the scryer might miss her altogether.

Because it was chilly, Persephone was able to pull the hood of her cloak well over her face and wrap the garment around her more closely than she had in the past few weeks. Fortunately two other women, also well wrapped, were waiting for the guard to open the gate, and she merely passed through behind them. The piece of good luck confirmed her intention of altering herself if she could, and she walked slowly, falling behind the other women and thinking hard about how she might accomplish such a purpose.

Ahead she saw the women start aside and make a wide pass around a huddled figure in a tattered brown robe on the grass verge. A beggar on this road? She had seen beggars in the town but never on the road, and she suspected that they were not permitted so near the palace. Full of her own hope, she fumbled in her purse for a small piece of metal determined to warn the poor creature that the palace guards might drive him away. Persephone had the metal in her hand, her arm already reaching out as she drew abreast of the beggar.

"Alms, great lady?"

The voice was hardly above a whisper, but the warmth that meant Hades inside the shell that closed her off from the world burst out of its little core and flooded her as his head lifted. The skin was brown, the hair grown into long tangled elf-locks, the beard now covered his cheeks and was longer and unkempt over his chin, but the great black eyes were his as was the love for her that poured out of him. The piece of metal she held fell from her nerveless fingers.

"Careful!" he whispered, scrabbling in the thin grass for what she had dropped.

He seemed to find it and rose, but not to his full height. Bent over a thick staff, he bowed and bowed again, meanwhile steadying her with the arm hidden by his body and hers. His caution brought back all Persephone's fears. A thrill of terror, sharp and hot, dispersed the numbness of a shock that had almost caused her to faint. If Poseidon sensed him and caught him all alone, unarmed, defenseless . . .

"Beggars are not permitted on the road to Lord Poseidon's palace," she said, struggling in vain to keep her voice from trembling. And then a murmur hardly above the sound of her breath, "Come to the last house on the hill above the road down to the docks." And though she felt as if her heart would be wrenched out of her body and left behind with him, she turned and walked away.

She heard an uneven step behind her and bit her lip, fearing that he would follow her closely and awaken the suspicion of the guard, who could still see them. However, the shuffling stride grew closer, and the bent old beggarman passed wide of her, shambling on down the road, making quite a good speed despite the crablike, sidewise gait. Despite her shaken state, Persephone had to smile. She had known that Hades had quite a turn for histrionics, but she was surprised at how convincing was his portrayal of an old cripple frightened out of his wits.

What was hard after that was restraining herself from running after him. Although she knew exactly how long it took to walk from the palace to Pontoporeia's house—she had done it often enough—and she was unable to resist walking somewhat faster than her usual pace, she still felt that years were passing before she turned into the familiar street.

He was not waiting by the house. Her heart sank. Were there other roads down to the docks? Other houses he could have mistaken for this one? She looked quickly at the house across the road somewhat farther back, but no one was near, and the house was still and dark. Unable to think what to do or where to look for him, Persephone opened the door. A dark bulk turned the sea-side corner of the house, rushed along the front wall, and swept her inside. The door slammed shut.

Poseidon woke in the great bed he shared with Amphitrite sated with sweet agreeableness. He felt a bit as if he had eaten nothing but honey for a week. A soft glow suffused the chamber, and when he lifted his head he could see his wife's lovely face. The faint green tinge of her luminous complexion, the darker gold-green of her hair spread on the pillow, which he had found so enticing when he first pursued her—and a long hard pursuit it had been—now added to his feeling that he was drowning in sweetness. She had been much more interesting when she resisted him, when he had believed there was something new and fresh in her cool, scaled skin, some mystery behind her dark green eyes.

The word "mystery" reminded him of Persephone. He snorted faintly. She would be no different. All women were much of a muchness once they were caught and tamed. And yet, from what Hermes said, Hades was utterly enchanted with her and he had lived with her for two years. Of course, Hades was a simple soul, a fool with limited desires. But that fool had denied him Olympus, had left him to rule fish and monsters. He owed Hades a bad turn, and what way to strike at him more deeply than to violate his wife? Nerus said she would rule beside Hades for many years. Let Hades drink the bitter cup of regret, as he had drunk the loss of Olympus, for all those years. Poseidon sat up abruptly and swung his legs out of the bed.

Amphitrite opened her eyes. "Do you desire my service, my lord?" she asked softly.

"No, go back to sleep. I have business in Aegina."

"Yes, my lord," she whispered, and obediently closed her eyes.

He stood staring down at her for a moment, exasperated, then shrugged and launched himself through the shimmering veil of water that made up one wall of the chamber. Beyond, he seized a twisted, glowing shell tethered to a frond of seaweed. When he put his lips to it, a mellow song echoed through the water. Not long after, a huge dark shape began to circle just above him. He rose effortlessly through the water, caught the tall dorsal fin, and lay down along the creature's back.

The sun was barely tingeing the eastern sky with gold, when Poseidon rose through the pool into his bedchamber. A maid uncurled from beside the pool where she had been sleeping and presented a large, soft drying cloth. He passed it over his body briefly—little water clung to his dark skin—and clasped around his waist the kilt she offered, waving away the tunic she held over her arm and the tray of ornaments for which she reached.

Without saying a word, he walked out, turned the corner of the corridor, and made his way to Persephone's room. He opened the door and slipped in, closing it softly behind him. The room was still dark, but he heard nothing and advanced quickly but silently toward the shadow he knew must be the bed. It was not until he reached out to grasp her that he realized the bed was empty.

He straightened up with an odd feeling of relief. On and off during the journey from the palace in the sea to Aegina, doubts about the wisdom of forcing Persephone had risen in his mind. He was almost certain Demeter would have no objections if he seduced her daughter, particularly since she would assume that if Persephone transferred her affections to him she would be content to remain on Aegina. Rape was another matter entirely. If Persephone held a grudge for that—and a surprising number of women did not accept it as a compliment and hated bitterly the man who forced them—Demeter might also take offense.

It would be stupid to annoy Demeter, Poseidon had thought. She could withhold this spring the fertility she had brought to his island last planting season. Worse yet, Demeter might be so angry, she would think Zeus the lesser offender and return to Olympus. That would spoil his revenge against Zeus. One revenge balanced against another, but that against Zeus might bring a substantial profit too. If the mages rebelled against Zeus because of the famine, and Demeter, who could end the famine, was his ally, he might be welcomed as ruler in Olympus. Revenge on Hades would bring no profit beyond his satisfaction in rubbing that pompous prig's nose in the dirt. But Hades . . . If Persephone told Hades she had been forced . . .

Poseidon suppressed that thought, but the *frisson* of fear that had run up the sea king's spine had made him very angry. He did *not* fear Hades. There was nothing Hades could do to him, no way that pitiful creature who had allowed himself to be content creeping about under the earth in the dark, could confront him. He would bed Hades's queen to show he did not fear his cowardly older brother.

That angry mood had carried him through the palace to Persephone's bed, but he was not altogether sorry to find her missing. Actually, he thought, as he left the chamber, his revenge would be much the sweeter if he seduced her. Nerus's vision said she ruled beside Hades. That meant that either she would never tell her husband she had found his brother more to her taste—or, she would tell him and he would be slave enough to keep her anyway. Out in the corridor again, Poseidon laughed aloud. *That* would be a true revenge.

He returned to his chamber, ordered food be brought despite the early hour, and summoned Neso. "Find Persephone," he said, "and tell her I would like her to join me. If she has not yet eaten, she can share my meal."

He would have grown irritable again, because Neso did not return as soon as he expected, but Nerus begged admittance and when he received permission, presented a problem of rising animosity between two island populations. It was a matter of fish changing their feeding grounds so that the two, who for years had fished separate waters, now came into conflict. While Poseidon was considering whether it would be best to discover what had caused the change in the habits of the fish and correct it so they would go back to their original areas, to introduce animals that preferred the new conditions, or to let the two populations fight it out, he forgot Persephone. Thus, when Neso returned to say she could not find her anywhere in the palace, Poseidon was mildly puzzled rather than annoyed.

When he had finished breakfast, he sent for Demeter and asked her whether she knew her daughter was missing. He was intrigued by the flash of irritation that she swiftly masked under an indifferent shrug.

"I suppose she is in the town," she said with a sigh. "I do not know where I erred with that child. She has the coarsest and most vulgar taste in friends. She turns up her nose at the suitable and elegant young folk of your court and has taken up with, of all people, a potter."

"A potter?" Poseidon echoed, thinking that if the little bitch were already unfaithful to her husband he would have a threat with which to seal her mouth and would not need to woo her.

"Yes." Demeter might want to slap Kore silly for rushing off to town to make up with her unsuitable lover, but she was not about to betray her daughter to Poseidon. "She is forever running off to the woman's house and sitting gossiping with her. They go to market together. Kore even buys things—I suppose to make herself seem more ordinary. She once brought home a fish! A fish!"

"How do you know where she goes?" Poseidon asked.

"When I first learned she had left the palace, I was afraid she was stupid enough to try to escape from Aegina. I did not want to warn her that you could easily bring her back if she tried because I did not want to put the idea of escape into her head if it was not there already. You remember that she had been bespelled by Hades and only wished to return to him. Well, that has worn off. I asked your scryer to watch her, but she never went near the docks or made the smallest attempt to speak to any person who sails."

"The scryer watches her constantly?"

"As long as it does not interfere with any task you set for him. That comes first, always, of course. And once she is settled in the potter's house or at some familiar occupation, he only calls her image now and again to be sure she is not doing anything new. I understand it is tiring to hold the spell at full strength for more than a few minutes at a time but no trouble to set it and invoke it periodically to see whether the subject has moved. After all, who could care what she said to the potter? It was all lies anyhow. She was afraid to admit she came from the palace, lest her low friends begin to fear her."

Poseidon laughed. This habit of Persephone's of wandering into the town would make everything much easier. He could try seduction, and if that did not work, pursue her to the potter's house and carry her off. He was sure he could find some indiscretion to use as a threat to prevent her from complaining to her mother—possibly he would only need to say that he would forbid her to go to the town if she did not yield. After all, she was scarcely a maiden who needed to guard the prize of her virginity. In any case, there was no great hurry in dealing with her. He had better see what had caused whole schools of fish to alter the behavior of many years. That might be significant even if he decided not to interfere in the affairs of the islanders.

"So long as you know what she is doing and are satisfied," he said to Demeter. "Neso told me she was missing from her chamber, so I thought I had better tell you."

"Thank you," Demeter replied, smiling sweetly. "You are always thoughtful of my well-doing."

Poseidon nodded gravely. "I wish you to be happy. It is good for me and for my people. In fact, the reason I disturbed you so early is that I must go out at once to discover why two islands are about to come to blows."

"Then I will not keep you," Demeter said, rising. "I am sorry Neso troubled you."

She left, returning a few minutes later to retrieve the scarf she had let fall when she rose. One of the maids always on duty admitted her and handed her the scarf. Poseidon was already gone from the chamber and Demeter saw with some relief that the margin of the pool was awash, showing that the water had been violently disturbed as it would be if a large man dived in. Poseidon had gone into the sea, which meant he had not sent for the scryer. She wondered uneasily what had aroused this sudden interest in Kore; he had never asked about what Kore did nor questioned the scryer before. Perhaps some power had leaked through Kore's shield and he had felt it?

He had not lied. Demeter did not doubt that Neso had told him Kore was missing. However, Demeter knew quite well that Neso would be most unlikely to look for Kore so early or report her missing to Poseidon without first telling her mother she was gone. Neso was fond of Kore, and would not voluntarily make trouble for her. Thus, Poseidon had sent Neso to find Kore—very early, before the sun rose—and Kore had already gone to the town. Little slut! Demeter was exasperated, but then she sighed. In this case it was just as well she was gone. What could Poseidon have wanted with her so early in the morning?

There could be no answer to that question—unless Kore knew? That thought irritated Demeter all over again, and she went to check with the scryer just to be sure Kore was where she thought she was. The man was barely awake, but he apologized, excusing himself with the fact that Kore had never before left the palace so early. Demeter agreed, soothing him, and said she merely wished to be sure her daughter was not in some unexpected, possibly dangerous, place or in trouble.

The scryer brought out the specially bespelled bowl and invoked the spell. "The shielding on the house is much weakened," he reported with some surprise, peering intently. Then he shook his head. "She is there. My spell found her, which it could not do when the no-see-no-hear was at full strength, but I cannot really see . . . Oh!" He glanced sidelong at Demeter. "She—she is with a man. They are—"

"That is what I thought," Demeter interrupted. She did not want a blow-by-blow description, and she did not want the scryer to watch either. "Please put the bowl away," she said stiffly. "I only wished to make sure my daughter was where she said she would be. You need not continue to watch her today."

Kore would be back for the noon meal, Demeter thought. That was why she decided to meet her lover so early. She will want to visit another shrine in the afternoon. Perhaps the Mother does not mind that Kore comes to her dripping the stench of lust, and lust with an unworthy partner—She is said to be lenient in such matters—but I mind. I will go out to the second shrine this morning. Kore can just wait until I get back, as she seems to expect me to wait for her. I can make clear how I feel then.

Filled with righteous indignation, which screened

the fact that Demeter was not too eager to see again the favor the Goddess showed her erring daughter, she returned to her chamber and sent for Neso. "I am going out to look over the fields near Khalas Méni to see that they are ready for blessing," she said. "Tell Kore I will not be back for the noon meal but that she is to wait for me."

Some time earlier, while Poseidon was still being carried swiftly from the palace in the sea to Aegina, Hades had limped crabwise along the road to the docks. He had passed Pontoporeia's house as if he had no interest in it, then carefully circled back and waited on the seaward side. When he heard the door open, he rushed forward.

Persephone gasped with shock as she was thrust into the dark interior of Pontoporeia's house. She would have fallen from the violent push, but arms were supporting her, turning her around. Lips fell awry in the dark and in haste on her temple and cheek before they found her mouth. Persephone kissed him back feverishly; she had not seen his face when he rushed her into the cottage, but she knew him—the taste of his mouth, the smell of his big body, the feel of his beard against her cheek and chin.

Too soon he lifted his head. Persephone clung, but he took her face in his hands, broke the kiss, and murmured, "Whose house is this? Are we safe here?"

"Yes, safe," she sighed, reaching for his lips.

He kissed her again, pulled back her hood and stroked her hair, then her back, but then he pulled away again and murmured, "For how long are we safe? Will the owner return soon?"

"No one will come," Persephone said. "It is my house. The woman who carried my message owned it. I bought it from her, and it is bespelled against scrying."

"I am so hungry for you."

"And I for you."

The touch and taste of him blotted out all else. She was one ache of longing, her nipples so hard and sensitive that the faint movement of his breathing against her set her breasts aflame and started a pulsing between her thighs. She scrabbled at his cloak, found the pin, pulled it and cast it aside. The cloak fell too, and she managed to unbuckle his belt, but it did not cover the familiar ties of his kilt. He was wearing a tunic, which defeated her blind effort, and beneath that there was something hard. Persephone whimpered with frustration.

"Let me, beloved," Hades muttered.

She hated to release him, even for the few moments he needed to undress, but her own clothing had become a burden and shedding it distracted her just enough to remind her of the bed. She doubted it was clean and it was certainly damp from being unused, but it would be better than the floor. She reached out to take Hades's hand and lead him, but she caught his hip instead and could not resist the urge to slide her fingers across his abdomen and touch what she wanted.

He dropped whatever he had been holding and caught her to him, holding her buttocks and lifting her a little. She took him between her legs most willingly, but the position did not give her the full satisfaction she wanted. And from the wordless exclamations Hades was making as he shifted her, he was also frustrated but enough caught up in the pleasure the pressure of her thighs was giving him to be unwilling to let her go.

"Bed," Persephone muttered, freeing her lips for a moment. "Behind me, a bed."

She felt him stiffen, then let her slip down. The sliding movement rubbed her along the top of his shaft and she moaned, but he was free before she could try to lift herself against him again and she remembered the bed. Nonetheless, he held her so close that each movement inflamed them anew, and they very nearly did not manage to take the few steps so they could lie down. Then the bed groaned so terribly when their weight came upon it that Persephone's mind was cleared of the fog of passion for an instant. She had a pang of regret for ever thinking of that bed. It would surely collapse, she thought, but just then Hades lodged himself and she knew it would not matter; she wrapped her legs around her husband and heaved.

"Wait," Hades gasped. "Wait. I am too eager—"

"Listen to the bed."

Persephone giggled as she heaved again and the bed creaked desperately. She ignored it, twisting her shoulders so that her nipples rubbed back and forth against her husband's chest.

Hades's choking chuckle mingled with the imminent sound of collapse, but the threat of being deposited on the floor cooled him enough so he could thrust. He hesitated as the warm, moist flesh sucked at him, but when Persephone's legs relaxed temptingly on his hips, he drew and thrust again. He could not endure a repetition of the heightened sensation and held his place then, but lifted and twisted so he could take her nipple in his mouth.

That was enough. As his tongue swiped across the engorged flesh, Persephone writhed frantically and then pressed her mouth against his shoulder to muffle her shrieks. The first convulsion of her climax triggered his. His body arched as he flung his head up and began to pump his hips violently for a few heartbeats, groaning and gasping, the movement intensifying Persephone's orgasm into near agony.

When Hades collapsed, the thrill subsided slowly, but they still lay together. Persephone embraced him with both arms and legs as if she feared he would disappear if she let him go. Hades lay motionless in her embrace, except for his lips, which clung to her throat in a lingering caress.

Chapter 20

Sated and exhausted, for he had spent a miserable, cold night crouched in the ditch, Hades was half asleep. The arm with which he had been embracing Persephone slipped away from her—and his elbow hit the frame of the narrow bed. The small pain reminded him that he was not safe in his own realm and he suddenly remembered the last thing Persephone had said. He lifted his head and levered himself up on one arm.

"Spelled against scrying?" he asked. "Why?"

There was now enough light seeping in through the cracked and uneven shutters that Persephone could just see he was staring down at her. But his echo of her words reminded her of her fear for him and how carefully she had worded her message so as not to betray her whereabouts.

"How did you discover where I was? I did not tell you apurpose. Why did you come?"

"You seemed glad enough to see me a moment ago," he replied, a touch of reserve in his voice.

Persephone laughed. "I cannot tell you how glad I am, but it is dangerous for you to be here, my love."

"Because Poseidon does not love me? Or because he loves you too well?"

"Thank the Mother, he has not troubled me in that way." Persephone's answer was easy and without hesitation. "When I first came"—she shuddered slightly—"he looked at me the way a shark looks at a tasty tidbit, but I have been very careful to appear plain since then, and he lost interest. I have hardly exchanged twenty words with him." She laughed softly, lifted herself on her elbow, and kissed Hades. "I thought *I* was the jealous one."

"You have nothing about which to be jealous," Hades said. "I have spent the whole time you were away under Olympus with an army of miners. But you have not said why this house is spelled against scrying—and why there is a bed here."

Persephone's mouth opened, but nothing came out because she was torn between amusement and irritation. Then she reached up and touched Hades's face. "Love, did I not just give proof that I was very, very hungry? And do not be so silly. The bed came with the house. It was not worth moving it, or the table or the chairs or any other thing in the place. And the house is bespelled because it is very difficult to plan an escape when every word you say is passed along to your gaoler."

"Plan an escape?"

"Did not my message say that the sacrifice would return of itself? Would I not have to escape in order to return?"

He smiled. "I suppose so, but I did not think of it. I am afraid I did not think at all because at first I was so angry. I feared the message was not from you but was a ruse to make me more patient. And . . . I missed you."

Persephone shifted so she could put her arms around him again. Hades sighed with satisfaction and rested his head against hers. After a moment he chuckled.

"Besides," he continued briskly, "I decided when I got your message that if you had not yet convinced your mother to make her peace with Zeus and abide by the agreement to return to Olympus when you joined her that it was time for me to try my influence. I thought you were at Eleusis, of course. When I heard you were in Aegina . . ." His voice faltered.

"Poseidon has done me no harm," Persephone said quickly. "I do not think he was ever interested in me, except to keep me here, away from you, and that only because you desired me, not because he did. Hermes told him you were enamored of me, I think. So he did not want me to escape. Still, I am almost sure it was my mother who set the scryer on me—although it may have been Poseidon's scryer and they may have shared the information. My mother certainly knew about my coming to this house—"

"Then her damned scryer may have seen me come in with you."

Persephone laughed. "I hope the scryer and my mother are both still asleep. This is much earlier than I have ever left the palace before. But if you were seen, it is all to the good. My mother knows that I have often come to this house to meet a man. She thinks I have taken a lover."

Hades jerked away from her. "A lover?" he echoed.

"Hades!" Persephone exclaimed, quite exasperated. "The man was Cyros, the carpenter, and he made—

oh, you cannot see it. He made the special litter that is standing against the wall. It was far better that Demeter think I had a lover than that she suspect me of planning to escape Aegina."

"For what did you need a litter in an escape?"

"Hades! Use your brain instead of your ballocks for a moment. How was I to get my mother aboard a ship? By sweet reason?"

"Your mother? Why bring Demeter on an escape?"

"I could not escape without her. First because if I do not go to her every morning, she comes looking for me. If she could not find me—and the scryer could not find me—she might try this house first. Hmmm . . . I wonder if—No, let me finish one thought at a time. But if she could not find me here, I am sure she would tell Poseidon I was gone. It takes two days to cross from Aegina to Eleusis and I am afraid he could fetch me back."

"But would he not do the same if you were both missing?"

"I hope he will not immediately realize we are missing," she began, and explained about going to the local shrine with Demeter and staying late. "Because my mother blessed his people's fields last spring and stayed in the countryside for as much as a week at a time, I hoped he would think we were both at the same work, especially since nothing would be gone from our apartments."

Hades nodded slowly. "That is possible—unless Demeter always told Poseidon in advance what she planned to do."

"I doubt it," Persephone said, "since she has been encouraging the worship of the Mother in secret."

"So Poseidon, too, wishes to be a god." Hades

shrugged. "I have burdens enough without trying to usurp the Mother's place."

"I think my mother is worshipped in Eleusis, but—" She swallowed. "Poseidon casts his Gifted into the sea and his creatures *eat* them."

He pulled her close and kissed her hair. "I am sorry, love, but there is nothing I can do. You know that I have spread the word as widely as I can that all Gifted are to be sacrificed to the King of the Dead by being driven into the caves. I have even managed to punish those natives who maim or kill their "witches" before they give them to us. But for those on an island—I cannot reach them."

"It is not your fault, beloved," Persephone whispered. "I should not have told you. Now you will worry yourself sick over it."

"Perhaps when I am safe in my own realm," Hades said with a wry chuckle. "For now, I have my own skin to worry about, and yours . . . and Demeter's too, I suppose." He sighed. "You are probably right about the necessity of bringing her."

"Yes, and not only because of the escape itself, but what good would it do for me to be free when my mother could just start the whole business over from the beginning? And she would, just for spite, even though she knows she cannot make me hers again. You do not know how tenacious she is. In fact, you had the right idea when you said it was time for you to use your influence. I am sure that is the only way we will ever bring her to reason. Think how much more effective you can be when she is in your power rather than in a safe haven."

"How can she be in my power no matter where she

is?" Hades asked testily. "What could I do to your mother?"

Persephone laughed delightedly. "Frown at her! Hades, you have no idea how—how *severe* you can look. Mother needs to be loved, to be appreciated. That is what I gave her and what she craves—and from what she hinted to me, that was what she got at Eleusis. I wonder . . ." She shook herself. "Let us win free of this place first. Then I can think about making her content so she will not trouble us."

Hades released a long sigh. "I can scarcely believe what I hear, that you are so eager to come back to Plutos, so cold and dark, after these moons on this bright island."

She kissed him long and tenderly, but when she pulled free her voice was light with laughter. "How could you doubt it? I am my mother's daughter after all. Am I not the dazzling brightness of Plutos? Where else would I be so cozened, so adored?"

"Alas," he murmured, "anywhere. The Mother shines through you, Persephone. You have become a dazzling brightness for all."

"But there is nowhere else I wish to be than with you, Hades. And as for the Mother shining through— oh, Hades, we need not fear! I can feed the priestesses of Olympus and Plutos both. When we went to the shrine, She gave me so much. It was a promise that I could help my mother and bless my own crops also."

"Are you sure?"

"Yes. That is what I planned to offer my mother, that I would come each spring to help her quicken the seed and bless the fields. You would not mind, would you, Hades?"

"I would mind. I mind when you are gone for an

hour to the temple or I go alone into the mines, but I would not interfere." He smiled. "Perhaps if I am sufficiently ingratiating, Demeter will allow me to accompany you."

"She might," Persephone said, also smiling. "If we can bring her to agree, she might wish to be generous." Then she sat up and said eagerly, "I must say, your coming is to me the final proof that we are favored by the Mother. I hoped to go tomorrow, and I had come into town to try to work out how to get down to the docks to buy passage without giving away my whole plan. Now you can do that."

"Tomorrow? Are you so far along in your plan?"

"Now that the litter is finished and you are here, all I need do is get my mother into this house. If you open the window you will be able to see the litter and we can plan better together," she said.

"The scryer?"

"The no-see-no-hear spell covers all openings or it would be of little use."

"A costly spell," Hades remarked, getting out of bed.

He found himself rather reluctant to rise and had to remind himself that when they were free of Aegina they would have their entire lives to play abed—and in a better smelling one than this. The thought made him laugh as he pushed back the shutters and light poured in. It was the final proof that his wife had not used it to be unfaithful. If she had, she would have aired it and had fresh, clean bedding. Apparently her thoughts had followed his—except, he hoped, for the last—and she was out of bed too.

There was enough light, the sun having risen, to begin collecting his clothes. Persephone, he saw, as he

straightened holding the linen tunic he wore under a
fitted, sleeveless leather garment, was looking around
bemusedly. Her surprise, as she identified her garments, strewn as widely as his, made him chuckle. It
reminded him distinctly of the first time they had come
together, which made him again regret getting out of
bed, but by then Persephone had pulled on her undertunic and was straightening her outer garment.

"Well, it was," she said, continuing to dress.

"What was what?" Hades asked as he drew on the
leather garment, having forgotten his last remark.

"A costly spell, but all spells are costly here because
Poseidon kills the truly Gifted and only grants li-
cense—at a high fee—to the weakest magicians." She
smiled. "You know you will be taking me back with
no more than I had when you first abducted me. I
cannot take the clothing—oh, dear, Arachne will murder me—and I have broken up nearly all my jewelry to
pay for that." She gestured toward the litter, standing
against the wall.

"It is rather large. Will that not make your escape a
trifle conspicuous?"

"I hope no one will think I am escaping," she reminded him, and then went on to tell him about the
long pretense of a sick father. "I had thought of getting my mother here by pretending a shrine to the
Goddess had been built but would not awaken and
beg her to come to invoke Her. She is truly devoted to
the Goddess, and is greatly beloved, I believe, despite
her faults—as I am beloved despite mine."

"You have none," Hades said.

"Oh, I wish there were some way I could set those
words into stone so I could point them out to you
every time you bemoan my shortcomings."

Large black eyes gazed at her with soulful innocence. "I am so glad you noticed I was very careful not to say it where you might ask me to do that—or have witnesses."

Persephone looked up from tying her belt, her lips parted in surprise, and then laughed. "Monster! When we are safe, I will make you suffer for that. First things first, however. When I was talking before about the need to bring my mother with me, I mentioned that if I did not visit her and the scryer could not find me in the town, she might seek me here. I will wait here until the afternoon. If she does not come, I will go back to the palace and leave a message for her, that I am staying the night in the bespelled house. She will think I am with my lover—and I will be, of course." She went and put her arms around his neck. "That might bring her. If it does not, I will go back to the palace again in the morning and use the tale of the shrine."

"Good enough," Hades said, "but I do not see how we can get her into the litter or make her stay there. If she sees me, she is likely to scream the town down— and there is that curse to blast all fertility . . ."

"She will not see you if you are behind the door. If she does, you will have to silence her." She dropped her arms and stepped back.

Hades looked troubled. "How can I silence her without violence? And how can I use violence against *your* mother?"

"Mother or not," Persephone said, her voice hard, "how did you think I planned to deal with her? Ask her sweetly: Mother dear will you not drink this sleeping potion so I can abduct you?" Then she shivered slightly and added, "But do not stick your sword in her."

Hades laughed. "That produces too profound and too prolonged a silence. But I might have to strike her—ah—rather hard."

Persephone sighed. "That will not endear you to her, but it cannot be helped, and perhaps by the time she wakes she will not be sore and will not remember."

"You meant what you said about a sleeping potion?"

"Oh, yes. And I have soft cloth to bind her and gag her—I did not forget that curse. She cannot say the spell if she is muted. When we have got that draught down her throat and she is bound and gagged, we can put her in here." She showed him the hidden section below the litter. "I had intended to pretend I was a daughter taking my sick father home to Eleusis. Now that you are here, it will be much easier. I can be the sick old man, you his servant. That way, there will be no women seen leaving the island."

"Do you have the sleeping draught?"

"Yes, and I have tried it on a pig about my mother's weight, so I know how much to give her." She closed the panel of the litter and straightened up. "What I do not have is any food in the house. I left too early to break my fast, and now"—she glanced sidelong at him—"with all that exercise, I am starving."

Hades laughed aloud. "I also. I went straight from the ship to the palace. Yesterday, in the late afternoon, before we came to shore, I had the feeling that you were frightened, threatened by something. I nearly jumped overboard—only I knew I could not swim faster than the ship could sail. I tried to send you the will to be strong, to tell you I was coming. I intended to come through the wall of the palace, but by the time we docked and I reached the place, I could not feel you at all. So I spent the night in the ditch in order to be close if you needed me." He pulled her against him. "And then you were there. Those other two women were afraid, but not you. You reached out to give a poor beggar alms and to warn him." He paused, pressing his mouth to her hair. "I do not know whether I can bear to leave you again, even to get food."

She hugged him back, began to laugh, stopped suddenly, and pulled away so she could see his face. "Hades, were you also thinking about me, perhaps midmorning, yesterday?"

"I thought about you all the time, but we first sighted the island at midmorning. I 'called' you. I knew it would do no good. I am not one with the power of calling, but—"

"Perhaps you cannot call everyone—but I 'heard' you. It nearly frightened me out of my wits. I never thought it might be you. First I thought it was my mother, trying to get me down to the docks so she could use that as an excuse to forbid me coming into the town. And then I thought it might be Poseidon, because the call came from the sea—"

"You said he had not troubled you." Hades's face went stiff, his voice cold.

"He has not," Persephone said with a shrug, "but I never trusted him, and after I thought about it I was sure the calling came from the sea, and the sea is his place." She smiled. "I was so frightened I did not stop to think it might have come from a ship. Ah, some good things come from the sea . . . oysters would be nice, and fried shrimp—I thought they were grubs when I first saw them, but they taste delicious, and fieldberries if they have them."

Hades shook his head. "I do not understand why

you do not weigh as much as a horse. You eat like one."

"I do not," Persephone said indignantly. "I never eat raw oats or hay, and I never saw a horse eat shrimp."

He burst out laughing and caught her into his arms again. "You are sweet in bed, my love, but I feel as if I have not laughed since you left me—and that is what I miss the most, the way you lighten my whole life."

"Yes, yes. I am very glad you love me in bed and out, but just now my stomach rules my heart. Do you have copper or iron with which to buy food? Silver and gold from a beggar man might be suspicious."

Hades hesitated, as if surprised by her answer, but he only said, "I am not going as a beggar man. I had no idea what roles I would need to play before I found you, and I think my contrivances very clever. If you will turn my cloak inside out, I will become a moderately respectable trader."

She did that, discovering a good, dark blue cloak that had served as a lining to the ragged, stained brown. When they were reversed, only a thin edge of the brown garment showed, looking rather like a decorative edging. Persephone realized that the patches and stains were all on the upper part and shoulders, invisible when the cloak was reversed and worn even if it should flap in the breeze.

Meanwhile, Hades had extracted a comb and a thong from a purse that Persephone guessed he had worn on a long cord, hidden under the back of the ragged tunic, which still lay on the floor. While he combed his hair and tied it back, she picked up the tunic and hung it behind the curtain with Pontoporeia's discarded clothing, thinking how clever he was. The purse was safe from keen eyes under the tunic and cloak and made Hades look hunchbacked when he bent over. Now he pushed his heavy belt through the double loops of the purse and fastened it. Then he combed out his beard so it looked full and glossy rather than ragged. Last, he wrenched at the staff, which he had dropped when he embraced her, and the top parted from the lower section, exposing a rather narrow short sword, which he slid through a loop of the belt.

"Well," Persephone said, "you are too tall and strong, but you are supposed to be a foreigner, so you should pass. Do not forget to bring back something to drink too. There is not even water in the house." She giggled. "I am sorry to ask you to do woman's work, but I dare not go outside."

"What if your mother comes while I am gone?"

Persephone glanced out the window at the angle of the sun. "It is too early. Sometimes I would join her and we would break our fast together, but more often I ate alone in my room. She will not think to look for me for some time yet." She laughed again. "And it would not matter. If she does come, I will tell her my lover will soon return and ask her to sit down and wait for him. Go now, dear heart, I am starving."

Finding himself almost thrust out the door, Hades walked up the lane, away from the cliff, below which lay the docks. He did not wish to believe it, but surely she was in haste to be rid of him. And if it were because she was hungry, why had she not bothered to tell him where he would find the market? Common sense presented the simple reason that the road he was on, coming from the docks into the town, would naturally pass through the market.

Oddly, the fact that the road did lead to the market only exacerbated his feeling of injury and his suspicion that his wife had thrust him out of the house because the time had come for her to meet someone else—and not her mother—there. He reminded himself of the damp and musty bed, which clearly had not been used in weeks or moons. That soothed him sufficiently that his mind was temporarily diverted by his stomach, which insisted he pay attention to a delicious aroma. It was when he began to bargain for the fried shrimp that Persephone had requested that he realized he had forgotten something essential—vessels in which to carry the food.

In the end, that was far from a disaster. The oversight not only identified him as a foreigner but provided him with a good reason for explaining himself. He was a merchant with two partners, one of whom had fallen aboard ship and injured himself and was now in a house near the docks being physicked. He needed a meal, or several meals perhaps, for himself and his healthy partner, who was with the sick man.

He bought the food and left extra metal for the pots, which would be returned if he brought back the vessels. One vendor passed him—and his explanation—along to the next, establishing the "truth" of his tale.

That was convenient in the market, but it raised the question of whether and how quickly the story would get back to the palace, and his description with it. No stranger could pass into Plutos without being reported to him, but he did not know whether that was true for Aegina. If it were, he could only hope that the brown dye he had applied to his skin and his plain clothes—his pallid complexion and the ornate and bejeweled accoutrements he normally wore when he visited

Olympus were well known—would be a sufficient disguise.

He was still thinking about whether he had been wise to say his sick partner was in a house near the docks rather than still on the ship as he started back. Naturally his next thought was whether he and Persephone should leave the house, whereupon he recalled that she said it was bespelled and she could not leave without falling under the observation of a scryer. And as night follows day, black doubts about her hurry to be rid of him overshadowed his mind again.

Chapter 21

Hades was not the only one who had fallen prey to doubt. Once he was gone, Persephone felt her confidence draining away. She felt imprisoned and wished she had gone with him. That was ridiculous, of course. If the scryer should mention that she was with a man and be asked to describe him, her mother or Poseidon might well recognize the description of a man with black eyes, hair, and beard, much larger than a native, and guess that Hades had come for her. The thought was unsettling and brought back all her fear. She wished he had gone as a beggar; no one would have suspected him in that form, but big and strong as he was, people would notice him.

For something to do, she pulled the bedding off the bed and spread it over the litter to air, then turned the straw-filled pallet that padded the leather straps. She heard voices and froze, her eyes on the window. A group of men was coming up the road from the docks. Persephone cowered back, though she knew they should see nothing if they looked in the window. If the spell were working, she could see out but only darkness would meet eyes looking in. If the spell were working . . . Breath held with horror, she pressed back against the wall.

In her confusion of joy and fear and lust, she had failed to feed power to the spell when she entered the house. The men passed, but none had turned his head, so she could not tell whether the interior of the room were visible. She swallowed hard. If the spell had failed and the scryer had found her, her mother would know that Hades was with her. Fool that she was, she had called him by name more than once. Persephone had no doubt that Demeter would tell Poseidon at once. She ran to the door and touched the frame. It seemed she could feel the magic, and she poured more power into the spell, but what good would that do now? And Hades had been gone so long—surely too long. But when she glanced at the window, the light had not changed at all.

She tried to fix her mind on what had to be done. She checked on the pot of sleeping potion she had carefully covered with oiled leather, checked on the cloth for wrapping and binding Demeter, looked out the window at the sun again. It still had not moved. She sat down with her back to the window and clasped her hands. She waited and waited and waited. And turned to look at the sun—and it had not moved.

No one could stop the sun, she told herself. Not Poseidon, not Zeus, probably not even the Goddess could stop the sun. Could She? But why should She? Had she been wrong and her mother right? Could that great gift of power have been meant as a warning?

"Mother," she prayed, rising slowly and lifting her arms, "if I have misunderstood and disobeyed, it is I who am at fault. Do not let harm come to my Hades."

Before she lowered her arms, a heavy thud came

from the door. Persephone gasped. The thud was repeated. She looked wildly around the room for a
weapon, then snatched up the bottom half of Hades's
staff. A third thud. She ran to the window—and
choked on laughter. Hades was kicking the door. He
was safe and sound, but too festooned with pots,
loaves of bread, and a skin of wine to knock—and
even such an idiot as she should have realized he could
not call her name. She dropped the staff and hurried to
open the door.

"What is wrong?" Hades asked tensely.

In the same moment he saw the cloth draped over
the litter and he flung away the large earthenware pot
he had been balancing in his right hand so he could
draw his sword.

Persephone leapt to catch the pot, which she barely
managed because she had not been far from him, crying, "Nothing is wrong."

The eyes he turned on her as he came forward as far
as the table were so black and cold that she was struck
mute with terror and could not even ask why he was
so angry. She merely stood, clutching the pot to her
breast, blank with shock, as he shifted his eyes back to
the bedding hiding the litter.

"I am glad all is well," he said, pushing aside with
his elbow the large unfired vessel standing on the table,
but his voice was colder than the look he had given
her, and Persephone still could not speak.

Meanwhile, his eyes still on the bedding, Hades
began to set down the chunk of ham, two loaves of
bread, and two small pots he had been carrying by
their handles. Last, he unlooped a skin of wine from
over his shoulder. When he was free of impediments—
eyes still on the litter—he smiled. Persephone shivered.

"Who is behind that draping?" he asked.

"Behind the draping?" Persephone echoed faintly.

Hades stepped softly around the edge of the table and past the end of the bed to make his way to the litter clear. Following him with her eyes, Persephone took in the bed and was reminded of his jealous questions. A huge breath of relief whooshed out of her. She had been imagining a whole new set of fears, the two most prominent that the Mother had driven him mad to punish her or that Demeter or Poseidon or both had cast a spell on him. She shook her head, wondering what had turned her loving and trusting husband into a jealous lunatic.

"There is no one there, Hades," she said, smiling now. "I just decided to air the bedding."

To her horror he only looked angrier, angry with that cold, black fury she had not sensed in him since she had refused to be priestess in Plutos on the day he had first abducted her. He took a step forward. Persephone shrank back, wondering again if he were mad or ensorcelled.

"I will ask you again, Persephone. Whom have you concealed from me?"

"You can ask me a thousand times." Her voice came out thin and high. "You will get the same answer. When you left I decided to air the bedding. Mother knows," her voice gained strength as her exasperation increased, "it was damp and musty enough to make me sorry we had not used the floor."

His eyes flashed to her, back to the litter, and with a swiftness she had forgotten he could use, he thrust her aside so hard she fell. The lid flew off the pot she was still holding and half the shrimp were catapulted all over her and the floor.

Unnoticing, Hades leapt forward and thrust his sword through the bedding. There was a crack as a panel of the litter split and the bedclothes fell to the floor. Hades jumped forward again and tore open the panel, bent to open the secret panel to the bottom section, and then rushed around to look between the litter and the wall. Even a thin mouse would have had a problem hiding there. Slowly, looking extremely sheepish, he sheathed his sword, came back, and looked down at Persephone.

She lay with the pot on her belly, speckled with shrimp, and looked up at him. "Well?"

"I am very sorry," he said.

She picked a shrimp off her shoulder and popped it in her mouth. "Pick them up," she said, "the ones on me, at least, and put them back in the pot."

He knelt beside her and picked up shrimp. When she was free of them, he took the pot and offered his hand. She ignored it and got to her feet. He put the pot on the table and repeated, "I am very sorry. I did not mean to knock you down, only to prevent you from leaping in front of me."

"You did not wish me to sacrifice my life to save the litter from being stabbed? I value fine workmanship, but not to the point of suicide."

He looked at her sidelong, then went and picked up the bedding, shook it to free it from the dirt of the floor, and rehung it over the litter. "It is less musty already," he remarked in a carefully neutral tone. "Your decision was very wise. Perhaps if you had come to the door as soon as I kicked it, I would not have had time to entertain such . . . ah . . . erroneous ideas."

"Perhaps 'outrageous' would be a better word."

He did not answer and looked meekly down at his toes, but Persephone had the feeling that he was more involved in an effort to hide incipient laughter than shame. A single shrimp had landed on the table in the general upheaval, and he picked it up and ate it. Persephone sighed.

"If you want to know why I did not come to the door, it was because I was frightened. I remembered I had not renewed the spell. I was afraid that I had betrayed us and that you had been seized in the market. When you kicked the door instead of knocking, I thought it must be guards sent from the palace to take me."

Hades's eyes, holding no amusement now, met hers. "How great is that danger?"

She bit her lip. "I hope not very great. When I touched the place where the spell is lodged, I thought I could feel it. Even if it had worn thin, it would garble the scryer's vision. He or she might have recognized me, since the scrying spell is fixed to me, but I doubt what we said would have been clear, or the vision of you." She blushed faintly. "Whoever watched would have known what we were doing, though."

Hades grinned. "I am not ashamed of that. I think we make love well."

She felt like asking, "Then why are you so jealous?" but she knew from personal experience that jealousy was not reasonable. She had scolded Hades more than once for looking at women she knew he would not touch, so all she said was, "The spell is fully powered now."

He did not answer sharply, as she had half expected, that powering the spell after they were betrayed was like locking the house after it was robbed. Instead, as if what was foremost in his mind was her association of the spell with their lovemaking, his eyes flicked from her to the bed to the bedding, but he did not suggest that the bedding had aired long enough. His eyes dropped and he asked, "When would the scryer usually start looking for you?"

"Not until after the household had broken its fast."

"Broken its fast," he repeated. His eyes moved to the food on the table and he suddenly swallowed. "That seems long enough ago to me that we would have seen some sign if anyone wished to come for us. Let us move the table to the window, where we can see the road in both directions, and eat."

Persephone was far less confident that enough time had passed to indicate that the scryer had not passed on news of Hades's presence, but she could not think of anything more practical to do than to follow his suggestion—and she was hungry too. She helped him move the table, and then sat down on the stool he solicitously presented. He fetched plates from a shelf on the wall and served her, asking anxiously whether his selection was satisfactory, apologizing because the berries she had requested were not available, nor any other fresh fruit; offering stewed fruit instead.

Persephone resisted as long as she could, but at last she burst out laughing. "Oh, sit and eat your own meal," she said. "You are forgiven. When we have eaten I will agree that the bedding has aired long enough. And you are a fool, too. You should know by now that I can never resist you."

"I know you have never refused me," he said, bringing another stool and sitting down. "But that is not the same thing at all."

She was somewhat startled at the grimness of his

tone, having thought he was playfully trying to "make up" with the overdone attentiveness, but all she said was, "For me it is."

She knew it was pointless to say more. Jealousy was not cured by words. At first she had been flattered; Hades had never shown a flicker of that demon, although all the men in Plutos fawned on her. Then she had felt somewhat indignant because he did not trust her. Her recollection of her own unreasonable accusations had cured that, but she knew she would soon grow very tired of having continually to pacify him. A flicker of sympathy for his exasperated denials touched her, but she dismissed that to wonder why he should be jealous now? Perhaps, she thought, it was really the outer world of which he was jealous, thinking that because she had lived in it all her life before he took her, she liked what it offered better than what she had in Plutos. If so, the quicker they were home, the happier they would be.

Persephone swallowed the rather large mouthful she had been chewing and asked, "If I can get my mother here this afternoon, can we leave tonight?"

"I do not know," Hades replied. "The ships' departures depend on the tides, and I did not inquire about the tides because I had no idea how long it would take me to find you."

He had been eating too, but after he spoke he glanced down at his plate with more interest and his voice sounded more relaxed. That boded well for a peaceful life after their return—at least peaceful personally. Life in Plutos was never as dull as life in the outer world; there was always a little thrill of danger to keep one interested, such as the exigencies of earthquakes, minor volcanic eruptions, and new incursions of chrusos thanatos into the deep mines.

"I would like to leave as soon as possible," she said.

Hades smiled. "I too, but we should also be careful not to wake any suspicion that we are fleeing."

"I will leave you to decide what is best on that score," Persephone said. "If we use the sick father excuse, that might be reason enough for haste. If he wished to be buried in his native land, he would have to take ship before he died because most ships will not carry a corpse."

"Yes, but would not the daughter be expected to travel with her father? Never mind, I gave a similar excuse to the food vendors when I had to explain why I brought no vessels to carry away my meal. I said I had carried an injured partner ashore to be physicked. Either tale will do—but not on the ship on which I arrived."

She told him then about Cyros's list of vessels that were due to sail that week, and they settled more comfortably together to eat . and plan. The detailed schemes for escape lifted their spirits, and the partially accidental touching of their hands as they both reached for the same dish soon came to intentional caresses. As one appetite faded, another rose, but the sharpest edge of desire had been blunted, and they lingered over their meal, taking bites of food from one another's mouths so that their lips touched, and drinking wine from one cup.

Later they spread the bedclothes, marginally less musty, and took a long time over removing their garments, with frequent intervals, half-clothed, to talk of extraneous matters. Persephone exclaimed over the weight of Hades's belt—and stroked his waist and hips to soothe away the pressure of the burden they had carried. He showed her—cheek to cheek while they made the examination—that between the two thin layers of leather was a thicker one of gold, so pure it was as soft and flexible as the well-tanned hide, from which pieces could be broken.

She laughed at his subterfuge, her warm breath teasing his ear, and exposed her own: the fine drape of her cloak was owing to the weight of all the jewels she had removed from the gold settings and sewn into the hem. She donned the cloak over her thin undertunic to show him, and when he took it off again, his fingers stroked the back of her neck and her now-bare shoulders.

Their lovemaking was as slow and easy as their foreplay, and their satisfaction as sharp and sweet as a sudden summer shower on a sunny day. It left them refreshed rather than exhausted, and after a brief contented rest closely embraced, they returned to their planning with renewed zest. By the time both were satisfied that all contingencies had been examined, it was time for the midday meal. They rose, half-dressed, and finished the food in a leisurely manner, talking now with serious contentment of affairs in Plutos. Both periodically glanced at the road, but without much fear.

Not long after, they were in bed again. It seemed the best way to while away the time and, being satisfied, this time Hades slept. Persephone smiled at him fondly, knowing he must be very tired. Having spent the previous night in a ditch outside the palace, he must have slept little if at all. For a time she went over in her mind all that they must do, and then she dozed lightly for a while. When she opened her eyes and saw the angle of the sun, she sighed. If Demeter had not come to seek her by now, she would not come at all, and Persephone was afraid that if she waited much longer, her mother might send guards to fetch her. She sat up, leaned down, and kissed Hades.

"It is time, beloved. My mother has not come. I must go back to the palace and leave a message that I will stay in this house for the night."

His eyes opened immediately, and such joy lit his face when he saw her that Persephone kissed him again. The enthusiasm of his response almost trapped her, but she was now so eager to begin their escape that she pulled away.

"It is growing late," she said softly, "and I fear she may send others to look for me. I must go back and lay my snare."

"Are you sure they will let you leave again?" Hades asked.

"Oh, how I feared that before you came," she said, and stroked his cheek. "Now, how can they stop me? If I do not return before dark, you need only walk through the wall, which is of stone, and then through the wall of my room, which faces the garden." She described, starting from the road, the face of the wall he must enter. "I will either be waiting in the garden, or if I am confined to my room, I will watch for you from the window and light a lamp when I see you."

Persephone left the house first, full of joy and completely at peace. If the scryer was watching for her at the house, the vision would follow her, at least until the watcher was certain she was coming back to the palace. Well after she left, but before the scryer would consider her destination a foregone conclusion, Hades would leave. He would first take the pots he had borrowed back to the market. Failure to collect the guarantees he had left might arouse comment or curiosity.

In addition, returning the vessels would give him the opportunity to mention that his partner was better, although still weak, and that they had decided to continue their voyage. Then he would go to the docks, check on when the tides would be right for departure, and pay for passage on one or more ships. That done, he would return to the house to wait for her. Persephone was so happy that she forgot until she was halfway to the palace that she had not stopped at Eulimine's house to say goodbye. She hesitated, but then laughed softly and continued on her way. She would have time enough for that when she returned, and she could leave all her metal bits and pieces with the potter, even a handful of jewels, because Hades had enough to pay for their passage and anything else they would need.

Her mind was busy with how she could convince Eulimine to take a suitable reward. Should she just leave the metal and jewels? Would it be safe to tell the potter who she really was? Could she bring Hades with her when she said goodbye? How she would enjoy Eulimine's surprise when she saw the King of the Dead. Surely when she had spoken to him and seen his kindness, Eulimine would never fear death again. Of course Hades had nothing to do with the truly dead, but for the short-lived natives, dying was a much greater shadow on life as one grew older than it was for the long-lived Olympians, who did not need to consider death for many hundreds of years.

Persephone put the idea aside rather regretfully as she approached the gate of the palace. Knowing the truth about her identity and Hades's could be dangerous for Eulimine. If Poseidon was angry about her mother's unannounced "departure," Eulimine, who must be known to the scryer, might be questioned. If she knew nothing beyond the lies Persephone had told, a truth-seeker would sense that, and the potter would be more likely to escape punishment.

Totally absorbed in her thoughts, Persephone did not notice the widening of the guard's eyes as she passed him. She met no one on the way to her room, from where she blew into the little shell that summoned Neso. The shell made no sound that Persephone could detect, but the maid arrived with her usual promptness, in fact before Persephone had quite decided what she was going to tell her mother. Her thoughts were fixed on getting Demeter down to Pontoporeia's house, wavering between the lie about the altar to the Goddess or a form of truth, begging her, now that they were on better terms, to come and meet her lover. She hardly looked at Neso, just told her to ask Demeter to come to her room.

"I do not think she has yet returned," Neso replied, looking down so that Persephone would not see the shock in her eyes. "The Lady Demeter told me this morning that she wished to examine the fields near Khalas méni to see whether they were ready for blessing. She asked that you wait for her."

"Oh, I cannot," Persephone cried, relief filling her with such a bubbling effusion of pure joy she felt she might float away. "I came to beg her to come to the town with me. There is someone I wish her to meet. It is very important. Will you tell her that I beg her pardon for not waiting as she asked, and also tell her that I will be spending the night in the town. If she is not too tired and can come—she knows the house where I will be staying—she will be very, very welcome."

"You are happy," Neso said softly, finding it hard to associate this glowing creature, her aura of power dancing and sparkling around her, with the plain, dull woman of the past months. "Very happy."

"Oh, yes, I am," Persephone said, laughing aloud. "And I want my mother to share my joy. Tell her that. Beg her for me to come."

"I will. I will, indeed," Neso said.

Impulsively, Persephone kissed the maid's cheek, then sighed. "I must go back now," she said. "If my mother cannot come, I will return to the palace in the morning."

She left the room on Neso's heels, turned toward the outer door rather than the inner chambers, and half ran, half danced, all the way to the gate. Resting on a bench in the garden, not far from the entrance to the palace, Demeter sensed her daughter's aura. She looked up just in time to see Kore disappear through the gate. She stood up, furious because her daughter had not waited for her as she had bid her, but it was too late to call her and Demeter was too tired to run after her. She sank down on the bench again, staring at the gate and wondering how she could bring the stupid girl to heel.

Her first impulse was to ask Poseidon to forbid her idiot daughter to go into the town. That would separate Kore from her lover, but Demeter did not wish to admit to Poseidon that Kore had taken as a lover one of the common folk of the town. Beyond that, Demeter had had a bitter taste of her daughter's anger and despair. She feared that to separate Kore from a second lover might have dire results. Would it be better to wait until Kore tired of her swain's bucolic charms?

If she did not interfere, she was reasonably sure that Kore would be content to remain in Aegina. On the other hand, she did not intend to remain in Aegina forever. She missed her temple in Eleusis and was concerned about the effectiveness of her priestesses in maintaining the fertility she had established. How long would it take this love to pall? More than a few weeks, Demeter feared. She began to examine other ways to break up the affair.

Inside the palace, Neso had watched Persephone disappear down the corridor and turned toward Poseidon's chamber. She did not wish to go to him but could not help herself. Like Nerus, she was bespelled to report to Poseidon at once any fact or incident that might affect him. Any Gift might do so, and Persephone had great power. How she had hidden it all these moons, Neso did not know. She had sensed a flicker of power in Persephone now and again, but the Gift had seemed so weak that the compulsion to tell Poseidon had not been invoked. Now she moved toward her master's chamber with dragging steps. She liked Persephone and knew how jealous Poseidon was of the Gifted.

Remembering Poseidon's usual response to a strong Gift, Neso shuddered with horror, but then she realized he would not harm Persephone. For one thing, she was of his own kind, not one of the native people or seafolk. For another, Persephone's Gift was probably the same as Demeter's, and Poseidon did not seem to regard Demeter as a threat. Neso tried to linger at the door but she could not, and with tears in her eyes she breathed her name to the shining plaque that would transmit it to a servant within. In the moment before the door opened, she remembered that Poseidon had left the palace in the morning and hope that he had not returned rose in her, but his own voice from the plaque bid her enter.

He was propped in the bed, holding a tall goblet—another item traded for salt fish to King Celeus, who got it from the dead—of a sweet purple wine. Before she had completed her bow, he asked, "Has Persephone returned?"

Neso's eyes widened with fear. "Yes, lord, but she has gone again. I did not know you still desired to see her."

"Left again? For where?"

"The town. She came to invite her mother to go back there with her, but Demeter had gone to look at the fields near Khalas méni and had not yet returned. Lady Persephone told me to ask Demeter to come and join her if she were not too tired."

"Join her where?"

"I do not know, lord. She was very excited, very happy, and she said her mother would know the house and that there was someone it was important for her mother to meet."

"Important for Demeter to meet?" Poseidon echoed.

Suddenly he smelled fish—long-dead fish. He remembered the odd expression he had caught on Demeter's face when he first told her her daughter was missing. He had assumed she was annoyed because Persephone was gone, but she had not been in the least surprised about it. Perhaps she had not been annoyed with Persephone but with the fact that he had discovered the girl was missing! That glib explanation about the potter— He had swallowed it whole, but was it the truth? What was that conniving bitch Demeter up to?

He leapt from the bed, thrusting Neso aside so violently that she tripped over the low wall that kept the water off Poseidon's rugs and shining floor and fell backward, striking her head on the edge of the flat area around the pool and sliding into the water. Poseidon did not even look toward her. She could not drown, and one of the maids would soon draw her out. She would be waiting for him when he returned.

A few moments later he burst into the scryer's chamber and bellowed, "Where is Lady Persephone?"

The man leapt to his feet, stammering, "I-In th-the p-palace. I-I looked in the b-bowl only a lit-little while ago."

"No, she is gone again," Poseidon said, but more quietly, and he gestured for the scryer to sit down. The worst of his fears, that the whole tale Demeter had told him was a fabrication to hide some plot she had hatched against him, was greatly diminished by the fact that the scryer apparently did have a bowl bespelled to track Persephone. "Look again for her," he said. "Where is she now?"

It took the scryer a little time to activate the spell, longer actually than usual, because he was so nervous, but he was able to report that Persephone was some way down the road toward the town and that if Poseidon wanted her back before she reached the place, he would have to send out guards at once.

Poseidon shook his head. "I am more interested in where she is going," he said.

"I cannot say for certain, lord," the scryer mumbled, his voice shaking. "There are three places most common: the market, the potter's house, and the bespelled house."

Poseidon had almost turned away when the scryer named the market and the potter's house as most probable goals for Persephone. The first two matched perfectly with what Demeter had told him and implied that his suspicions had no validity. The last words stopped him cold.

"Bespelled house?" he echoed. "Have you ever seen inside that house?"

"Before it was bespelled, once. Lady Persephone bought a fish from the woman who lived there." The scryer knew he had missed something very important that had taken place in that house—he had heard Persephone bargaining for a fish and turned his attention elsewhere; when he looked back she had been leaving, and the way she and the old woman looked at each other had sent chills down his spine—so he had never admitted the lapse and was not about to do so now. "And once after it was bespelled," he hurried on, his voice shaking again, "this morning, in fact—the spell was weakened for a while." The scryer dropped his eyes. "The lady was in bed with her lover."

"Her lover!"

The scryer huddled in on himself at the bellow. "She was in bed with a man," he whispered. "The vision was not clear because the spell was still working, just not strong enough to shut me out completely. I thought they were—"

Poseidon burst out laughing. So that was what Demeter was hiding, that her daughter was a little whore. "Where is Persephone now?" he asked.

"Still on the road, lord."

"Can you tell me where the bespelled house is?"

"Oh, yes, my lord. It is the last house on the road

that goes down to the docks, on the left side if you face the sea."

Poseidon laughed again. "Give me your cloak," he said.

He snatched it from the man's hand and strode out of the palace and through the gate, carrying the cloak in his hand. At first he did not see Persephone, but his stride was longer than hers, and before the first houses of the town appeared, he caught a glimpse of her on a straight stretch of the road ahead. His lips pulled back in a feral smile as he swung the cloak over his shoulders and pulled up the hood.

Poseidon did not want the townsfolk to recognize him just yet. Their awed cries and bows would warn Persephone. Then he laughed. It did not matter. He had her now! Even if she were going to the market or to the potter's house, he could seize her and drag her to the place the scryer had described. When he told her he knew she used the place to lie with lovers, the slut would not dare refuse him or complain that he had forced her. But he did not push off the hood. It would be easier, sweeter, if she went to meet her lover and he took her in the same bed, perhaps with the lover watching. He would enjoy watching her face when the churl would not defend her.

Still seated on the bench in the garden, Demeter had not seen Poseidon emerge from the palace; however, the stir at the gates—the guards drawing themselves upright, the shouted orders to make way—had drawn her attention. For a moment when she saw him pass through, without attendants or guards and clutching a shabby cloak, she simply stared blankly at his disappearing back. Then, suddenly, she connected Kore's hurried departure with Poseidon. She recalled that

Poseidon had sent for Kore before dawn—just at the time when a man woke with lustful urges!

Demeter leapt to her feet, all fatigue forgotten, as a surge of protective fury swept over her. Poor Kore, she was not running back to a lover but away from Poseidon! That lecher! She knew he was, of course, not only with human women, but with all sorts of creatures from the sea, Nereids and merwomen—but he would not have her daughter! She had come to him for protection, but he was worse than Zeus. She would see him dead or damned before she let him take Kore against her will.

She ran out of the gate and down the road, but Poseidon was well ahead of her and she soon slowed, realizing that she did not dare confront him yet. She had no proof of his evil intentions. He would laugh at her and lie. She would have to catch him in the act.

Persephone had not kept up the rapid pace at which she had started for the town for long. At first she had almost skipped along, savoring her conversation with Neso. She was virtually certain that the message she had left would bring Demeter after her in a fury, and she had not needed to tell a single lie! She giggled and actually did skip a step or two. It was, indeed, very important for Demeter to meet Hades and she *did* hope her mother would share her joy in her husband once she saw him without a bloody sword in hand and came to realize how handsome and tender and loving he was.

Too soon, she realized Demeter would not have a chance to think of Hades as tender and loving if he had to overpower her and silence her so that she could be forced to drink the sleeping potion. Her pace slowed to her ordinary swinging walk as she considered the ramifications of the situation. If they were able to leave at once, Demeter would wake on the ship in all the comfort that could be provided. But if the tides were wrong and they could not sail until the next day, her mother would wake bound and gagged in that cramped and airless compartment under the litter. Persephone shuddered as she walked. Demeter would be so terrified and furious that no amount of soothing or reasoning would propitiate her.

That must be avoided if at all possible, Persephone thought, and almost at once realized that they would not need to put her mother into the compartment until they were ready to leave. She would be able to watch for Demeter's awakening and explain what was happening. If her mother had not already seen Hades, he could keep out of the way or only appear to do something kind, like bringing food and drink.

Then Persephone began to wonder whether they would need to hide Demeter in the compartment at all. The dark and discomfort would add beyond measure to her fury over being abducted. Suitably bandaged—for a broken jaw and a cracked head, which would prevent her from speaking and explain any violent gestures or cries—her mother could travel in the upper section of the litter. She was large enough to be accepted as male if her features were hidden—a sick or hurt man accompanied by either his partner and an old woman to care for him or by two servants, an old man and an old woman.

A plain face and a gray cloak would not be enough to disguise her as an old woman, Persephone knew. She began to consider what she must do, and then she remembered that Pontoporeia had left nearly all her clothing in the little house. She was much taller than the old woman, but she should be able to devise something; she could walk with bent knees, which would change her stride to a waddle. Persephone began to walk more quickly. In her eagerness to try out her idea, she forgot she had intended to stop at Eulimine's house, and hurried past the potter's place.

The door was on the latch, which did not trouble Persephone. She and Hades had decided it was better to leave it unlocked than to take a chance on hiding the key and having the one who had not hidden it arrive first and be unable to find it. As a precaution, they had strung a line across and hung the bedclothes in front of the litter. She entered eagerly, hoping Hades was there so she could propose her new idea, but the light from the doorway showed the house was empty and the window closed.

This time she remembered to stop with her hand on the doorframe. The spell was still strong, but she poured more power into it anyway. The last thing she wanted was for the scryer to get even the dimmest view of her mother being overpowered and bound. She went and opened the window and then closed the door, but she did not lock it. Considering the message she had left for her mother and the likelihood that Demeter had already returned to the palace—since her mother's order to wait for her implied she would soon be back—Persephone thought the scryer might already be watching her. She did not want Hades to have to wait outside for her to open the door. The less time the scryer had to examine the man who entered after her, the less he would be able to describe her "lover" to Demeter.

From the door she went toward the curtain that hid Pontoporeia's clothing, removing and dropping her cloak on the bed. She took out one garment and then another, shaking her head when she realized that Pontoporeia had been too much shorter. A moment later she smiled with relief. When the clothing had been made, before poor Pontoporeia had lost so much weight, the old woman had been somewhat broader than she. Although the length of the garments made her initial idea of walking with bent knees impossible, she could still manage. She could wear one gown over the other, the skirt of one looped up in the belt to hide the fact that the top of the underdress was fastened around her hips.

The next step was to try out her idea. Persephone found two gowns of essentially the same color—no great feat when all the garments were black, brown, and gray—and lifted her outer tunic off over her head. As she pulled one arm clear, she heard the latch click.

"Oh, love," she cried, pulling her other arm out of the tunic and dropping it on the bed. "I have had the most wonderful idea."

Chapter 22

Cresting the rise on the road from the dock to Pontoporeia's house, Hades saw a man lift the latch and enter as if he knew the door would be unlocked. Anger and fury struck him such a blow that he had to lean on his staff until the pain subsided and he could catch his breath. With breath came reason. No matter how lustful or how much in love, no sane woman would arrange to meet her lover in the house to which she expected her husband would return at any moment. Still, for the man to enter with such assurance implied a very unhealthy familiarity. Hades bit his lip. It was too possible that a lover had come without an invitation to wait for Persephone at a time arranged before he himself arrived.

He started forward so choked with rage that he could not shout—and stopped again. A woman was coming hurriedly along the street, a woman head and shoulders taller than any native, blonde—not a golden glory like Persephone but the paler shimmer of a winter sun—and lovely. He had not seen her in a very long time, but surely that was Demeter. Hades stood frowning, suddenly realizing that the man's cloak had reached hardly to his knees and that he had to bend his head—just as Hades had to bend his own head—to enter the cottage door. Poseidon! That had been Poseidon!

Poseidon leaned back against the door behind him and replied to Persephone's exclamation that she had a wonderful idea, "Not as good as mine."

Shocked mute, Persephone whirled to face him, staring. Poseidon laughed and came away from the door, looking around scornfully. "I would have thought you could furnish your love nest a little more comfortably," he sneered. "But I suppose a straw mattress and bedclothes hanging to air suit your lover's primitive taste."

Still openmouthed, but now with relief as much as with shock, Persephone sidled away from the bed so she was on the far side of the table. Her mind was racing. Poseidon did not yet know that Hades had come for her or that she was planning to escape. Like her mother, he thought she had a lover. A flash of black hatred momentarily blanked all else from her mind—except that her mother had betrayed her to Poseidon. That was horrible. More horrible than anything else Demeter had done. Persephone gasped for breath. Poseidon reached the other side of the table.

"Come now, you slut, you must know you cannot act the stupid innocent with me any more." He cocked his head. "Well, you are a beauty. How in the world do you hide it?"

"It is my Gift," Persephone whispered. "When I am happy, I am beautiful. If you take me, I will become ugly as sin."

He roared with laughter as he leaned across the table and reached for her. "That will not trouble me. I can always close my eyes. What I stick my rod in is the same."

His hand closed on her wrist. Persephone had not even tried to avoid him. She was slow with indecision. To give him what he wanted was the sensible thing. If Hades returned before Poseidon was through with her, he would find her struggling and crying and would kill Poseidon; if he did not, Poseidon would go away satisfied and they could escape with even less danger of discovery—and Hades need never know. Good sense notwithstanding, when Poseidon began to pull her around the table toward him, Persephone could not act indifferent or compliant. She felt a sick revulsion, and began to fight him, snarling, "No! No!"

The door slammed open. Poseidon turned his head without alarm, merely so the lover would see with whom he had to contend. He was totally unprepared to hear a female shriek like the squall of a wildcat and have a wild woman, hissing and spitting with rage, launch herself at him with hands crooked into claws and teeth bared.

Demeter got in one good slash, her nails catching the corner of Poseidon's eye and scoring his cheek before he released Persephone to turn and grab for the fury attacking him. He caught her arm, but had misjudged her strength, and she managed to raise his restraining hand to her mouth and bite him. Roaring with anger, Poseidon let go of her arm, but only to strike her in the face with his full strength. Fortunately, it was his left hand with which he launched the blow and it was awkwardly delivered across his body or he might have killed her. As it was, Demeter flew bonelessly backward and lay still when she hit the floor.

Poseidon started to turn back to seize Persephone again, but he had misjudged her too, and it was too late. Unable to find another weapon, and filled with the insane strength of desperation, Persephone had caught up from the table the large, heavy, unfired vessel she had bought from Eulimine, raised it above her head, and brought it crashing down on his.

When Hades had seen Demeter put her hand on the door latch with the same unhesitating certainty that Poseidon had shown, he was shaken by new doubts. Was this some trap for him that Persephone had devised? As the thought came, he knew it was ridiculous. She could have no idea when he would return. He might have been in the house already. Could she have arranged a meeting with her mother and Poseidon in the hope of reasoning them into allowing her to leave?

As that second ridiculous idea came, a furious shriek echoed out of the open door. Clearly, reason was not being employed. Hades wasted no more time thinking but ran at full speed toward the house, wrenching his sword out of its concealment in his staff. Inside, he skidded to a halt at the sight of the body- and earthenware-strewn floor, almost colliding with Persephone.

"If I had known you were going to reason with them so forcibly," he gasped, "I would not have run so fast."

"Reason with them?" Persephone repeated, eyes wild with shock. But what he had said and even her own echo of his words had no meaning to her and she threw herself into his arms with a sob.

He barely got his sword out of the way before she

spitted herself, but he held her close with that arm and patted her with the other hand. "Never mind, love," he soothed, choking back laughter. "I will explain that stupidity later. Are you all right?"

"I am frightened out of my wits," she gasped, trembling with reaction but already so much restored by Hades's presence that she was able to feel indignant that Hades had found something to tickle his sensitive funnybone in the violence that had taken place.

Her husband sobered and clutched her tighter. "Did he hurt you? Why are you in your underdress?"

"I was—I was going to put on Pontoporeia's clothes to see if I could be an old woman . . ." Her voice wavered and then trailed away as the horror of hearing Poseidon's voice instead of Hades's momentarily overcame her. She buried her face tighter against Hades's shoulder.

He could not make head or tail of that remark, nor did he care. Persephone's assurance that honor would not require his brother's death restored all his joy. He felt sillier and happier at this moment than at any time since Persephone had first accepted him. No lovers, no plot—that was all his own sick imagining. Proof of his wife's loyalty was the unconscious bodies on the floor. He kissed Persephone's hair and then her cheek; he was about to try to lift her face so he could kiss her lips when Demeter moaned.

"Sit down, love, and rest," he urged, pushing Persephone gently toward the bed. "Your mother is waking, I think, and she should be restrained before she can make more trouble."

She braced herself against him and then pulled away. "I am better now. Let me bind her. If she wakes and finds you doing that, she will never forgive you.

You had better secure Poseidon in some way. Let my mother think it was you that felled him.''

"I would not wish to steal your honors," Hades said, grinning and bowing.

He could not remain serious. At this moment the world was bright and beautiful to him, full of laughter. Somewhere underneath his joy lay the cold knowledge of how dangerous a prisoner they had taken, but he would not yet uncover that trouble.

Her memory of fear turned insignificant by Hades's strong assurance and amusement, Persephone cast a clear eye on her mother. She saw at once how to deal with Demeter so that her mother might never know the indignities to which she and Hades would need to submit her. If her mother did not fully regain her wits until they were aboard the ship, she would never realize she had been carried aboard bound and gagged. Persephone then intended to remind Demeter that *she* had attacked Poseidon, making it necessary for them all to escape. Her mother would accept that, and would probably accept Hades as their savior, albeit grudgingly. Then there would be no need to restrain her for the whole voyage. She grinned back at her husband.

"We can—" she began, but her mother moaned again and stirred. She made a quick gesture toward Poseidon, and ran to the back of the room where she took the pot of sleeping draught from the shelf. One spoonful went into a cup, and a little of the wine, which they had not finished. She swirled the two together, then rushed to her mother and tenderly lifted her head.

"Drink this, mother," she urged, blocking Demeter's view of the room with her body. "You will soon feel better."

Demeter's hand lifted waveringly toward her head, not to push away the cup Persephone had brought to her lips but to feel her bruised face.

"Drink, mama. It will ease the pain," Persephone insisted.

Half conscious, more to moan again than in response to the words, Demeter's lips parted. Persephone tipped the cup. Demeter swallowed, coughed weakly, losing some of the liquid, but then swallowed more strongly. Her eyes cleared.

"Kore," she whispered, "did he—"

"No, mama," Persephone replied soothingly. "You held him off long enough. I was saved."

She bent and kissed Demeter, ashamed of how willingly she had embraced the ugly notion that her mother had told Poseidon she had a lover. Demeter's eyes had closed again, but she was not yet asleep. Persephone did not hide behind her shield, but let her mother sip at her power.

A glance over her shoulder showed her that Hades had found the strips of cloth she had stored in the litter and was busy binding Poseidon, arms behind his back and knees bent so his ankles could be looped to the wrist ties. The room was too small for Hades to hide. And, Persephone realized, there was no need to fear the scryer. If he were watching, who could he tell that a man he did not know had come out of the bespelled house? When Hades had tested the ties, Persephone put a finger to her lips, gestured to her mother, pointed at the door, and cocked her head questioningly. Hades looked puzzled for a moment but then nodded and went outside.

"Come, mother," Persephone murmured. "Try to get up. I will help you. You can rest on the bed for a while."

Demeter opened her eyes and looked vaguely at her daughter. "My head hurts," she said querulously.

"I am so sorry," Persephone murmured. "Poseidon hit you, but there is time to rest. Come, get up. You can lie in the bed until the pain goes away."

"Bed? Where?"

Her voice was already slurred, Persephone noted with delight. "Just a few steps," she assured her, putting an arm around her and tugging. To her relief, Demeter got up with only a little help and accepted her guidance to the bed. She lay down, not even noticing the worn, flattened pad, and closed her eyes. Persephone waited. In a very short time her mother's little whimpers stopped and she began to snore lightly. Persephone ran to the door and pulled it open.

"Hades," she called softly.

He came around the house from the sea side and hurried through the door. When he took in Demeter's totally relaxed form on the bed, he asked, "Do you have any more of that sleeping potion?"

"Yes." Persephone pointed to the pot she had left sitting on the table.

"I think we had better get some of it into Poseidon. I have him bound and gagged, but he is strong, and that cloth is old. I do not think he can break free, but I do not want to need to watch him every moment."

"A large spoonful for my mother. A spoon and a half or two spoonsful for him?"

Persephone did not wait for Hades to reply but got the pot and the spoon and knelt down beside Poseidon while Hades elevated his head. She pulled down the gag, pushed the spoon between his lips, past his teeth, and tilted it slowly. After considering for a moment, she poured another spoonful into him.

"It will not kill him," she said, seeing Hades's black eyes fixed on her face. "The sow did not die from three spoonsful, although she slept more than a day."

Hades stood up and looked down at his brother, his face bleak. "Was he trying to rape you, Persephone?"

"I think he had threat in mind more than force," she said slowly, not wanting anything she said to push Hades into an action he might later regret so bitterly that he would begin to blame her. "From what he said when he came in the door, he believed I already had a lover, in which case he would not be soiling his brother's loyal wife. Perhaps he intended to punish me for betraying you."

"A strange way to punish you," Hades said.

On the other hand, Persephone did not want her husband to think she was defending Poseidon, which might waken the senseless jealousy he had shown earlier. She shrugged. "I think so too, but he is very envious of you. I have no idea what caused him to follow me today. He has never shown much interest in where I went or what I did before. I thought my mother had told him I had a lover, but the way she attacked him—" She glanced at Demeter, who had turned her head and stopped snoring.

Hades looked from one to the other, ran a hand through his hair, and laughed shortly. "Well, there are your spoils of war. What do you want to do with them?"

She told him about her plans for her mother and he nodded and said they were in luck. One of the ships on which he had purchased passage would leave with the predawn tide.

"Thank the Mother for that," she said. "As for Poseidon," she added, "I have no idea what to do with him."

"I should kill him," Hades said, and closed his eyes.

The cold knowledge he had buried had risen. He knew that he and Persephone were holding a sauraima—a powerful beast with a long tail at one end and many, many sharp teeth at the other—by that long, flexible tail. He could sense Persephone, gone still and rigid, looking at him, but he could not meet what he thought might be reproach in her eyes.

"I cannot," he said, between set teeth. "Forgive me, love. Even to insure your safety I cannot kill my brother while he is lying helpless." He heard Persephone draw a harsh breath, and added hastily, "To delay our escape to let him wake so I could fight him—"

"No!" Persephone exclaimed. "That is insane!"

"Yes." Hades caught her expression and chuckled. "Particularly since I am not at all sure I would win." She shuddered and he put an arm around her and pulled her close. "I think I would. Between hunting and moving rock, I am hard and fit, and my sword gets frequent use against beasts and outlaws. I think Poseidon lives an easier life, but—"

"But I do not trust him farther than I could throw him," Persephone said tartly. "You might plan on a fair fight, but angry and humiliated as he would be when you released him, would he fight fair? Or would he summon to his aid his guards and even those sea beasts that can come to land?"

Hades smiled wryly. "There is always that. He has

given me cause to know he is not always trustworthy."

"The passage to the mainland takes two days or more," she said. "If he is free at any time before we land—we are dead. When I planned to escape, I was sure he would not dare drown both my mother and me because that would draw upon him the vengeance of Zeus and all the mages of Olympus as well as your anger. But after getting his head cracked and being tied up like a pig for slaughter, I am afraid he will be in no mood to worry about future vengeance."

Hades laughed without mirth. "How right you are. Well, if I took him two days up to the mountains and left him in a cave— No, those bonds are not so tight or so strong; he would get loose before long and it would take me almost as long to get back here as it took me to bring him there. And if I tied him more securely, I might be condemning him to a death far more cruel than just cutting his throat."

"We must take him with us," Persephone said. "When we are ashore, you can free him."

"What will we do with your mother? And we cannot take Poseidon on the ship that leaves tonight. The captain is from Eleusis, but he knows Poseidon. He mentioned meeting my brother when he commented that I was almost as tall, too tall for a native sailor's sleeping shelf. Even if we bandaged Poseidon's head so his face was hidden, I am afraid his size and weight would raise suspicion."

"No one will see any part of him," Persephone pointed out. "He will go into the lower compartment of the litter. My mother, with her head all bandaged, will go into the top part. But the weight will be a problem. My mother is lighter than I, but no wraith either, and that atop Poseidon—Wait. I have an an-

swer to that also. I will get the man who made the litter
to arrange to carry it aboard. You remember I told
you that I asked him to make the litter for my sick
father who might die?"

"Yes, I remember, but I do not see—"

"I can tell him I have lined the lower compartment
with lead. He will believe I have made it ready in case
my imaginary father should die on the journey and the
weight will be no surprise to him."

Hades nodded, then sighed. "I hope your carpenter
and the ship's captain do not have time to compare
stories. I took passage for myself, my injured master,
and his sister. I thought you would have your choice
of ages—my master might be young or old."

"I do not think it matters. Who is there to look for
us? Poseidon does not give to any of his servants the
kind of power that you allow me or Koios, nor does he
encourage them to think for themselves so they can
protect his interests even in his absence. Even if Nerus
or Neso should notice that my mother and I are missing, they would not institute a search for us themselves; they would wait for Poseidon. So long as the
captain does not refuse to take us aboard for some
reason of his own, I think we will get away without
pursuit."

"Perhaps you are right," Hades said, scrubbing fret-
fully at his beard. "I hope so, but I have this feeling
that it is all too easy."

A few minutes later he was both laughing and curs-
ing over having spoken too soon. Between them, he
and Persephone were able to pull the litter away from
the wall without any difficulty. It had been made carefully and was surprisingly light and strong. Fitting

Poseidon into it, however, was a kettle of entirely different fish.

They got him up on the top bed and opened the panel, but in his bent position there was no way the space would hold him. They could not lay him on his face, because his arms and legs, tied behind him, rose too high and prevented the bed of the upper compartment from seating properly. Nor could they lay him on his side, because his shoulders were too broad. The lower compartment had been designed to hold a corpse flat on its back and be inconspicuous.

Finally, using language that kept sending Persephone into giggles, and complaining bitterly that he thought he had crippled himself, Hades lifted Poseidon out again. Leaving Persephone with a heavy iron pot in hand, in case Poseidon should appear to be breaking loose, he went down to the docks again to a chandler's shop where he bought some thin, hard ship line. When he returned, breathing rather hard with haste, he pointed out that the sun was about to set and suggested that Persephone go to the market and bring back food, not only for their evening meal but for the voyage.

Having taken a large basket, two covered crocks, two small pots, and a selection of bowls and plates, she set off. By the time she returned, Poseidon had been retied in so intricate a webwork that she insisted on an explanation as she set out their meal.

Hades smiled at her. "I had to think of what he might do if he should come awake, and fix him so he could not. You realize, I hope, that we will not be able to do more than peep at him from time to time, and we not only have to keep him hidden from the captain but keep the identity of the captain and ship from him."

"Oh, sweet Mother, yes!" Persephone breathed. "I had forgotten about that. He would take dreadful vengeance, and that would be poor thanks from us for being carried safely away."

She ladled out a savory fish stew and broke pieces off a loaf of bread. For a while both were silent as they ate. Persephone looked at her mother now and again, but Demeter still slept. Soon the last of the light was gone. Hades shut the window and brought three long crystals out of his purse. He set them upright on the table, gestured, and they began to glow. Persephone pulled boiled crabs out of the basket, uncovered a bowl of cooked millet, and poured some savory-smelling sauce over it from one of the pots. Poseidon began to snore loudly. Both looked at him.

"That is one thing I did not consider when I tied him so he cannot move," Hades said as he wrenched a leg vengefully off an innocent boiled crab.

"I thought you would just wrap him round and round with cloth and rope."

"Too much rope, and I would not trust any of the cloth in this house against his strength. Believe me, Persephone, he cannot move. If he tries to put his feet flat on the base of the litter and push the top section off with his knees, he will break his big toes, which are tied together and fastened to his ankles—and it is impossible to lift the litter bed without bending his knees because he has no leverage. He cannot move his arms to raise himself or pull off his gag, because his wrists are tied together and fastened to his neck with a line down to his crotch and up his back. If he pulls his hands up, he'll saw off his balls and choke himself at the same time. That should discourage him." Hades grinned. "It would discourage me, and I am not nearly as fond of women as Poseidon." Then he shook his head again. "But short of strangling him, I cannot see how to stop him from snoring."

"It will not be so loud once the panel is closed, and we can always say it is the injured man who is snoring. Let us hope they do not do it at the same time." She got up and moved Poseidon's head. The snoring stopped. "I suppose if he does not move, he will be quite comfortable?" Persephone returned to the table, bending down to kiss her husband as she passed him.

"Well, not comfortable. No one can be comfortable tied and gagged, but I wished to avoid infuriating him more than necessary. You did buy enough food for all of us, I hope. We will have to feed him when he wakes."

"You sound sorry for him."

Hades did not reply for a moment and then shrugged. "I am. He was the one in the middle. My father was not so bad in the beginning; he just ignored me until he sensed my Gift. When he knew it would be strong enough to be a threat to him, he tried to kill me. So I was twelve, old enough to understand what was good and what was evil and that I *could* save myself before I had to escape. Poseidon was too young, only six. All he knew was fear and helplessness. Then my mother had to leave him with the ruler of this island."

"Poor child," Persephone said. "Why did Rhea have to leave him?"

"Zeus told me she was trying to save him; she feared that Kronos would trail her and kill the children. But she had to take Zeus because she was still suckling him. Perhaps Poseidon could not understand and felt abandoned. I had made my own life by then. I would have taken them into Plutos if I had known, but in those years we of Plutos were very few, and my powers had not reached their full. Mostly we hid as far from Olympus as we could get, so I heard no word of my mother's need."

"Is that why Poseidon carries a grudge against you? Did he believe you had deliberately withheld a sanctuary?"

Hades's face hardened. "No. That was another matter. I have just thought: How will we let your carpenter know we need him to shift the litter?"

Persephone felt a stab of resentment at the abrupt change of subject. She was not accustomed to being closed out by Hades, who was generally only too eager to share his thoughts and problems with her. Then she guessed that he might be avoiding discussion of something that would make Poseidon even more distasteful to her. She sniffed, but swallowed her impulse to prod him into disclosing what he wished to hide. That would hurt poor Hades and do Poseidon no harm, since she was in no doubt about the sea king's character without further revelations.

"Cyros made the litter, but he works in the shop of his father, Cyriakos. Their place is somewhere on the docks. Unfortunately I have no idea where, or where they live if they do not live at the shop. Most of their work is refitting ships—that is what Eulimine said. Oh, dear! Eulimine! I never said goodbye . . . Oh!"

Hades looked up from his careful dissection of the crab he was eating along with spoonsful of the sauce-covered millet. He had heard the change in her voice from controlled irritation, through concern, to revelation.

"Eulimine knows where to find them," Persephone said. "She recommended them and brought them to me. I was afraid to go near the docks because I did not want to give away my intention to escape, so I told her I was afraid of the rough sailors." She bit her lip. "She laughed at me, but perhaps she will feel differently at night."

Hades pushed away his half-finished crab and stood up. "If she is afraid to go alone in the dark, you can tell her I am your father's servant and I can go with her. Help me get Poseidon into the litter. Then let us cover your mother's face, bind her hands, and move her to the litter too. Those two will stay as they are for the little time we are both away even if they wake. Then you can come back here and watch them."

Chapter 23

In the plank shelter built on the stern deck aboard the *Thrasus Ichthus,* Hades and Persephone sat cross-legged on blankets beside the litter and stared tensely at each other. Both felt as Hades had earlier that night, before they had struggled to get Poseidon into the litter—that the difficulties they encountered had been too easily overcome, and disaster was about to overtake them.

What kept them rigid with anxiety was not all superstition. This little hint and that little suggestion of catastrophe loomed. The first suggestion of trouble was caused by the weight of the litter. Cyros could not lift the front alone and had to fetch his father to help. He had looked from Persephone to Hades, but he had not asked any questions. Nor had Cyros and his father said anything when Hades lifted the rear alone, and they had taken care not to look back at him while they got the burden down the hill; however, from the occasional looks exchanged between Cyros and his father, it was clear they believed the weight was more than a lead lining could create and that they did not really accept the identification of Hades as the "sick man's" servant.

The resonant snores that had twice started—and stopped when Hades tilted and straightened the litter (almost causing Cyros to drop his pole each time as the additional weight came on him) did not help. Although Persephone had opened the panel and pretended to move her "father's" head just before Hades shifted the litter, shaking Poseidon, the coincidence of his movement to the actual cessation of the snores was noticeable.

Another cause for concern was that the captain of the ship had looked with too-great interest at the struggle of the men to carry the litter up the boarding plank, and Persephone had noticed how he cocked his head at the thud when the men set their burden down. What he thought they were carrying she could not guess, but his disbelief that the weight was one injured man was plain.

"The question," Hades whispered, leaning close to Persephone, "is who will do what when?"

His eyes were so black, so brilliant with excitement in the light of the lamp that hung from the low ceiling, that Persephone had to smile. Now that they were together, Hades was enjoying himself. She did not find the question cryptic. She knew what he meant: Would Cyriakos report his suspicions to the guard or the palace, or would his fear of the trouble that might come upon him when she confessed Cyros had made the hiding place keep him quiet despite the hope of a reward for betraying an abduction or smuggling? And if Cyriakos did report them, would the guard act before the ship sailed? Or if they escaped that threat, would the captain's suspicions induce him to put them

off the ship before sailing, or was his greed stronger
than his fear of being caught smuggling?

Their great advantage was that neither Cyros and
Cyriakos nor the captain had long to consider and
reconsider the choices. Hades had set the hour for
Cyros to come to Pontoporeia's house at midnight.
That should have put them aboard the ship with considerable time to spare. However, the delay when
Cyros found the weight too much and had to fetch his
father, and their slow pace down to the docks, had
brought them to the *Thrasus Ichthus* only shortly
before the tide turned.

Persephone reached out and put her hand over
Hades's, which held his bared sword. He sat facing the
thin plank door of the stern shelter, unlocked because
to lock it would serve no purpose when a man could
probably kick it down with a single blow. In her other
hand she held the bottom of Hades's staff. It was hard
wood and would doubtless break a few heads before
the empty core caused it to shatter. Near the wall of
the shelter but well within reach were several sturdy
iron pots. They held food but could be used as weapons if necessary.

The captain called; Persephone heard men running
about and stiffened. Hades shook his head at her,
smiling. "He is ordering his men to cast off the lines,"
he said softly. "In only a few minutes we will be free
of the dock. After that, it is only the captain himself we
need worry about."

Not long after, when the ship was moving with a
longer heave and roll than the sharp jolts caused by the
choppy waves in the harbor, he took the staff from her
hand gently. "Lie down and try to sleep, love," he
urged.

"It would be better for you to sleep now," she said. "The captain will not trouble us until we are farther out at sea. If he intends to toss bodies into the water, he does not want them fetching up in Aegina. You will need to be alert then."

"Yes, but will not your mother wake some time in the morning? You said you wished to talk to her before she saw me."

Persephone frowned. "True. But you are very tired, my love. You have slept only a few hours in two days. Let us tie a line from the litter to the latch. If we hang two or three cups from the line, well spaced so the movement of the ship does not bang them against each other, they will still make a clatter when the door is opened and they fall to the floor. Then we can both lie down until morning."

Hades hesitated, plainly worried because the cups would not make much noise when they hit the wooden deck and also concerned about the amount of time he would have between the warning and the attack. Nonetheless, having made the noble gesture and having listened to Persephone's far more sensible suggestion, he sighed. Carrying that litter had taken more out of him than he liked to admit. His arms felt like lead and his eyelids seemed weighted with half a mountain each.

After looking around the shelter and seeing there was nothing he could use to block the door, he shrugged and nodded. Like Persephone, he did not expect any trouble until they were well clear of the land. She leaned back and reached to where Pontoporeia's worn mattress and bedding, carried down to the ship before Cyros came to help with the litter, lay rolled behind the pots of food. Hades levered himself to his feet, surveyed the space available, smiled suddenly, and then laid out the bedding right against the door. He handed his cloak to Persephone and lay down quite content.

Anyone who opened the door would have to do so against his considerable bulk. The door would hit him, and one of the cups should now drop right on his head when the line that supported it went slack. If that did not wake him before any attacker could get in, he would be dead already and of no use anyway.

Persephone put their two cloaks together, shoulders to hems to make a nearly rectangular blanket. Her attempts were somewhat impeded by the increased pitching and rolling of the ship, but she finally got them fairly straight and bent down to spread them. That effort was also defeated by the ship's movement. As she bent, the ship dipped, and she fell forward with such impetus that she would have gone head first into the door had not Hades caught her. She hit him instead, drawing an anguished "Ooof," and they rolled together first against the wall, then away, and back again.

"What a shame we cannot make love," Hades whispered. "We could just lie still and let the ship work for us."

Persephone locked one leg around his back and pushed the other between his thighs. "You are too tired," she whispered back, "even if we let the ship do all the work."

The increasing pressure she felt on the thigh between his legs gave her the lie direct, but before he could answer in words, a cold wind whistled through the cracks in the planking of the shelter. Persephone shivered, relaxed the hold she had on him, and groped for the cloaks she had let fall. "It is too cold," she said regretfully, "and I would not really enjoy it. If the wind can come through, so could our love cries. As long as they believe we are alert, they might think twice about attacking us. They know how strong you are. But it would be beyond imprudence to issue an open invitation by the sounds of our grappling."

It was a mark of how tired he was that he did not even offer a token protest. He sighed and helped her straighten the cloaks and was asleep almost in the moment that they were well wrapped. Fortunately their expectation that they would not be troubled was confirmed, which was just as well because Hades was still soundly asleep when a dull thudding and muffled cries woke Persephone. Her eyes flew to the door, but that was closed and her ears had already told her that the sounds were coming from beyond her head, from the litter.

She squirmed out of the lax grip Hades still had on her and then from under the cloaks as quickly as she could. By then she was certain the protests were too high-pitched to be from Poseidon. She hurried to the litter and pushed back the panel.

"Hush, mother," she whispered urgently. "I am sorry to have bound and gagged you, but Poseidon had hit you so hard that I feared you would try to fight or cry out as we were taking you aboard ship. If you will promise not to scream or utter any curses, I will take off the gag so you can have a drink and, if you want it, some food."

Demeter nodded at once, so quickly that she made Persephone suspicious. "I will hold the gag in my hand," she warned. "If you do not keep your promise, I will simply jam it back into your mouth."

She shrugged as Demeter shook her head "no" vigorously and fetched a small jug of watered wine, which she held between her knees as she undid Demeter's gag. Lifting her mother's head with one hand, she tilted the jug cautiously with the other, so that the liquid hardly reached the lip of the jug. The motion of the ship slopped some into Demeter's mouth—and some over her chin and down her neck.

After a few sips, Demeter raised her chin to push the jug away. "What happened?" she whispered. "How did we come aboard a ship?"

"Hades saved us," Persephone whispered back.

"Hades?"

"I told you I loved him and he loves me. I sent him a message more than a moon since and he came for me. Oh, mother, I never had a lover."

"It was not Hades you met in that bespelled house," Demeter said.

"No." Persephone smiled. "It was the carpenter who made the litter in which you lie, but he never touched me. I paid him with gold I broke from the jewelry Hades had given me. How could you think any common creature could content me after I had lain in Hades's arms for two years? He is a great mage and a great man. He made me high priestess and queen—and I am my mother's daughter. I desire to rule, as do you, mother, and like you I can love only one man."

"Love wears out," Demeter muttered.

"Perhaps after a man is dead for nearly twenty years, but my man is not dead. I longed for him more with each day that passed. All I thought about was how to send him word and how to escape to join him."

"Did he kill Poseidon?" Demeter breathed.

"Hades would not do that! He is good and gentle—"

"And a great fool!" Demeter snarled. "Poseidon will drown us all as soon as he comes to himself."

"No, he will not," Persephone said, but she did not tell her mother that Poseidon was with them. Angry as Demeter had been over the sea king's attempt to rape her daughter, Persephone did not trust her mother not to join forces with Poseidon against Hades.

Demeter stared at her and then said, "Let me free. Where can I go aboard a ship? I wish at least to have a chance to swim or to catch part of the ship when we go down."

"Not unless you swear by the Styx and by Her continued favor that you will speak no curses, nor try to harm my husband, nor join with anyone else who wishes to harm or constrain him or me, nor do anything at all in his despite for any purpose at all—"

"Have done! I swear by all I hold holy, by the Goddess whom I serve, and by the black Styx, that I will not curse and I will not interfere—while we are aboard this ship—with any desire or plan of yours or of Hades's, no matter how unwise. Now loose me and let me free or I will bepiss myself."

"Oh!" Persephone exclaimed and hurriedly rolled her mother over so she could untie the cloth that bound her wrists.

The binding was soft and the knot large, so that was quickly done. Nor were Demeter's arms or hands numb from pressure, because she had been rocked back and forth all night long by the motion of the ship. She pushed herself erect while Kore was untying her feet, and the first thing she saw over her daughter's bent back was Hades, sitting erect and gazing at her.

His eyes were obsidian, his features granite. Demeter shuddered slightly.

This was what Kore said was the kindest and gentlest man in the world? No, not Kore—it was Persephone, hard as flint herself, who praised Hades. Kore was sweet and gentle; sipping her power was like tasting honeydew. The power that leaked from Persephone was hot as peppercorns. Her daughter had been ensorcelled and the spell could not be leached out of her simply by the passage of time.

At the moment Demeter was too bemused—and too frightened—to consider whether the spell was beyond breaking in other ways. Her feet came free; Persephone helped her to stand and pointed behind the litter where the curve of the stern left a small space in which there was a large, wide-lipped pot and a box of leaves. She stumbled, but Persephone did not see. Her daughter had caught sight of Hades and turned to him at once, asking, her voice soft as Arachne's spider cloth, whether he was well rested and if he wanted to eat. Demeter lifted her skirts and used the pot, thinking that it would take the greatest of mages to break that spell, if it could be broken at all.

"I will just go outside and relieve my bladder," Hades said. "I did not want you to turn around and think I had been spirited away."

"Be careful, beloved."

Demeter stared at the wooden panel of the litter that hid Hades and Kore—no, Persephone—from her. It was sickening, she thought, the amused tone of his voice and the way her daughter fawned on him. What could happen to him, unless he were so clumsy she feared he would fall overboard? Demeter had no idea what kind of binding could produce quite the result displayed by Persephone, but that did not matter. Aphrodite would know. She knew every binding that existed.

As she stood up and rearranged her garments, Demeter's lips thinned. Aphrodite was in Olympus and was not one to look for trouble—except when it might bring her a lover. If she wanted Aphrodite's help, Demeter knew, she would have to return to Olympus and make her peace with Zeus. So be it. She would bind herself to make the fields of Olympus fertile if Zeus would command Aphrodite to seek for a way to unspell her daughter.

She smiled at her daughter as she emerged from behind the litter and Kore/Persephone made haste to take her place. She even found a tentative smile for Hades when he came back. His hard mouth did not curve in response, but he nodded acknowledgement. Persephone had promised to remain with her until the fields were blessed, Demeter reminded herself. Perhaps Aphrodite would find a spell of unbinding before it was necessary to let Persephone go back and give her Kore again. But even if she could not, Persephone would come back each spring. Sooner or later Kore would stay with her. She smiled with more certainty and said, "Good morning."

"To you also," Hades replied. Then Persephone came around the end of the litter and Hades's expression changed. Demeter bit her lip. "And to you also," he said. "May every morning until the end of time be a good morning for you."

"And so it will be if we are together," Persephone said, flashing a smile at him, and then with a lift of the brow, "How was it out there?"

"Quiet," Hades said. "Perhaps we have done the

captain an injustice and he means honestly by us. I did tell him last night that there would be a reward above his charge for passage if we came swiftly to Eleusis. Nonetheless, it will be well to be wary and keep weapons at hand."

Possibly the warning implicit in that little speech was taken seriously after daylight had clearly shown the captain and crew Hades's height and breadth, his steel weapons, and his determination to set a high price on any advantage they might try to take. Possibly she and Hades had held unnecessary suspicions about an honest man. In any case, no attack came. Demeter laughed at their concern, especially after breaking their fast when Hades took her out to walk a little on the deck to relieve her cramping and boredom.

Hades reported in answer to Persephone's anxious questions when they came in that no more than cautious curiosity was shown by any member of the crew. And Demeter said, "Now that they have seen us in the light, straight and tall—at least they have seen Hades and his "partner's" sister—you need not fear them. They are more likely to faint with terror if you speak to them than offer you insult."

"I think Lady Demeter is right," Hades said. "I might be one of them grown large, but Lady Demeter's size and coloring is too different from that of native women."

"Do they know who you are?" Persephone asked.

"I have a temple in Eleusis," Demeter said, and laughed lightly again. "They suspect, but they know they must not acknowledge a goddess who does not wish to be recognized." Her eyes flicked from Hades's face to her daughter's, but Persephone—not Kore—

looked harder and more threatening than he. Demeter shrugged. "You need not look at me that way. I will not break my oath not to interfere. I know if I commanded the crew to overpower Hades you would not come to Olympus to assist me. And now that I have enraged Poseidon for your sake, I have little choice. Without his protection, I doubt Zeus would long leave me in peace in Eleusis. So I must come to terms with Zeus. Having his brother thrown overboard would not pave the way to that goal."

Although she smiled at her mother's little joke, Persephone was uneasy. She felt Demeter had yielded too tamely and was planning to make trouble somehow, and she warned Hades when she walked out with him after the noon meal. "She is too agreeable. Do you think she knows we have someone hidden in the litter?"

"Have you heard him stir?" Hades asked eagerly. "I was beginning to worry about him." He glanced toward the door, which was close by, neither having enough faith in Demeter to do more than pace back and forth along the wall of the shelter. "Surely she would not be foolish enough to release him?"

Persephone did not reply, but with one accord they turned back. The panel of the litter facing the room was closed; of course, it was impossible to say whether it was still closed or closed again, but Demeter showed no signs of hurry or confusion. She was sitting quietly on the pallet, her face thoughtful but not spiteful. Persephone went to use the pot, as if that was why they had come in so soon. Hades heard the far panel hiss softly as she opened it and then a faint squeak. When she came out, she was carrying the blankets in which

Demeter had been wrapped. She folded them and sat down on them.

"If you dropped that ring into the space between the leather padding when you helped me lay my mother in the litter, it shifted its position," she said. "Do you want to look for it?"

Hades had worn no rings at any time since he had left his own domain, so what had shifted must be Poseidon. "I had better look," he said. "I do not want it to pop out of the litter at an inappropriate moment."

"Do not play childish games with me," Demeter said, her voice sharp but kept very low. "Rings do not thump and groan. Whom did you abduct? If you took Neso or Nerus as a hostage, you are worse fools than I thought. Poseidon does not care enough for them, or anyone, to keep you safe, and he can drown us without hurting them anyway. Both are of the sea and can breathe in water."

"Not Neso or Nerus, whomever they are," Hades said with a faint smile. "We brought someone Poseidon loves more than any other being." The smile changed to a frown. "But you are right about drowning us. I had forgotten that person could breathe in water." He looked at Persephone. "Should we pour more of that sleeping draught into him?"

Persephone looked stricken. "I did not bring it," she whispered. "When we ate, I put it back on the shelf so it would be out of the way. And when I packed up the food for you to take to the ship, I forgot it. Oh, love, I am sorry."

"Never mind," Hades said, putting an arm around her. "In a way I am glad. I was a little afraid to give him more lest it do him harm. If I need to do so, I can always knock him on the head again, but truly, I do not see what harm he can do bound and gagged. For the first setting, a spell must be said aloud with the appropriate gestures. Afterward it may be used or transferred with only a token, but the token must be given."

Somewhat uneasily Persephone agreed. She had had to touch the doorframe to transfer her no-see-no-hear spell, and Hades's had kissed her forehead to transfer to her the spell that lit crystal. But she could pass strength to him without a touch or a token, only by her will, so it seemed to her that Poseidon might be able to do something without words or gestures. She did not voice that concern aloud. She thought Hades had spoken more to calm and console her than because he was overconfident about Poseidon's helplessness. As if to confirm her thought, he went to the litter, removed the bed of the upper compartment, and stared down at his brother.

Poseidon's eyes were closed and his breathing was slow and even. Hades thought his hands were in a different position than when he had closed the panel on him and that his knees were slightly more flexed. Persephone came to stand beside him.

"Has he wakened?" she asked.

"I cannot tell," Hades replied, "and he surely will give no sign to help us decide. I moved the litter sharply twice when we carried it here. It is possible the shaking shifted him. Do not worry, love. I do not think it possible for him to break free, but I will check on him now and again."

He did so throughout the afternoon without any positive result. Once he thought he saw a finger twitch, and he said over his shoulder to Persephone, "I wish he would show that he is awake. He must need to piss and be very thirsty, perhaps hungry too."

"Let him alone," she replied. "It is possible the potion is still affecting him, and as far as needing to piss, he has had nothing to drink and may have little to void."

Hades waited another moment to see if Poseidon would respond and when he did not, covered the compartment. "I suppose it will be safe to leave him as he is until we come to land."

"And what do you intend to do with him—and me—when you come to land?" Demeter asked.

"I will take you both to the caves of the dead," Hades said.

Demeter shrank back and Persephone said, "My mother must go to Olympus and I with her. I promised."

"So you shall," Hades replied. "There are ways to Olympus through my realm, as you well know."

Persephone glanced at him and then down at her hands, which were folded in her lap. She understood that Hades did not wish to leave his hostile brother and her stubborn and unreliable mother behind when they went ashore. Poseidon had considerable influence with the native kings along the coast and Demeter was worshipped in Eleusis. Together they might easily be able to organize a party to pursue them. On the other hand, getting the oversize and overweight litter to the cave of the dead might prove difficult. As she understood it, the entrance was not close to the town or the port but some leagues away in the mountains. How were they to control their captives without the sleeping potion?

A silence fell and lingered. When worrying at the

details of the problems brought her no closer to a solution, Persephone glanced again at her companions. The look afforded her little satisfaction. Hades was staring at a crack in the wall as if he could see something faintly amusing through it. Demeter was also looking at Hades, trying not very successfully to hide her growing consternation. Persephone wished Hades had been less frank or looked less as if he were happily contemplating the death throes of enemies.

Finally, afraid that fear of the underworld might force Demeter to break her promise and try to interfere with their escape, Persephone moved over beside her mother and began to assure her she would find Plutos beautiful and fascinating, not at all dreadful. And when Demeter protested that she could not exist for long without food and drink, but that she would rather die than be condemned forever—as poor Kore had been—to a living death in Hades's realm, Persephone did not angrily reject the name Kore but gently assured her mother that food and drink would be brought to her from the outer world so she need not fear being trapped below.

Persephone had just turned to Hades to urge him to confirm her promise and add his assurances to hers that Demeter would not be forced to remain in Plutos, when the ship creaked and jolted as if it had hit something. Demeter cried out and Persephone gasped. Both began to rise, but the ship lurched violently sideways, quite out of pattern with the movement to which they had become accustomed, and they were thrown together. Simultaneously, there was a huge thrashing of water, an ear-splitting keening of animal pain or fear, a bellow of warning, and a chorus of shrieks of human terror.

Hades leapt to his feet and rushed out of the door, his drawn sword in his hand. With a cry of caution, Persephone thrust Demeter away and ran after him, snatching one of the bread knives from a basket of food. More shouts and shrieks brought Demeter to her feet just as the ship lurched violently again, throwing her against the doorframe with stunning force.

Around the ship, the sea was boiling with life. As she emerged onto the deck, Persephone saw Hades strike out with his sword at a thing, huge and white with gaping jaws, that was leaping from the water. Had he been wielding his own long sword, he might have touched it, but the shorter, thinner blade he carried whipped by, short of its goal. The beast fell back into the sea, causing an enormous wave and a spume of water that drenched the deck.

The ship heeled over and Hades staggered back, colliding with a cowering sailor. As he steadied himself, another creature rose, seemingly all mouth filled with rows of teeth attached to a long, sinuous neck that stretched over the deck. Hades struck with all his strength and the sword bit. A long arc of red appeared behind the head, followed, as Hades wrenched his sword free, by a cascade of blood, spouting like a pulsing fountain. The creature howled, and the head, dangling to the side, jerked away and disappeared.

By the bow of the ship an animal like a squid, only ten times as large, rose from the sea as if propelled by a catapult. It shot up high enough to clear the rail of the ship and came down with spread tentacles right above a sailor who was helping a mate repell something Persephone could not see. An extra-long tentacle snapped out and caught his neck; the remainder embraced him. A shout of surprise and fear was immediately followed by a shriek of agony. The captain ran forward with a long fish spear and stabbed the squid as the mate attacked it from the other side. It heaved and released its prey. Persephone screamed. The man's head was gone.

The white thing with the gaping maw appeared again. Hades snatched another fish spear from a sailor and cast it right between the jaws so that it lodged in the throat. Contracting with agony but silent, it fell short of the deck and into the sea, its huge tale beating the water to froth.

No one noticed. On one side of the ship another squid thing had risen. This one had come down on the rail and was clinging there with some tentacles while it snatched blindly with others. One sailor slashed back with a club, another stabbed with a long knife. One of them shrieked, but by that time shouts from the other side of the ship had drawn Persephone's attention.

Something else, long and thin, had thrust its head over the ship's rail. Hades hacked at it and another man tried to help with a knife. The snakelike head whipped around and the teeth fastened on the man's arm. As soon as it had him, the creature began to slide backward, dragging the screaming sailor with it. Hades raised his sword.

"Be strong, Hades. Be strong," Persephone muttered.

She felt the burning power pour out, heard Hades shout as it seared him. But then Hades's sword bit again, bit deep, and was torn from his hand as the spine severed and the flesh tore. The body slid down into the sea with the sword. The man fell backward, the head still attached to his arm.

Backed against the wall of the shelter where she was

out of the way of the struggling men and frantic creatures, Persephone looked down at the knife in her hand, wondering if she should run forward and give it to Hades. But the paltry weapon was useless. Her power beat at her, burning, but she knew no way to use it as a weapon herself and she dared not thrust more at Hades. He had caught up a cargo hook from the deck and was fighting another of the long-necked beasts, the iron hook glowing red and the wooden haft in his hand beginning to smoke where it met the metal. The thing shrieked and shrieked again as the hot metal seared it, but it pressed forward, snapping and slashing at Hades, rocking the boat, driven by a force greater than its own will.

Behind her, from the roof of the shelter, a thin, high voice—the ship's boy—screeched, "Leviathan!"

The power of that word was great enough to tear Persephone's eyes from Hades's desperate fight. At a distance ahead, but clearly approaching, were the flukes of a tail so huge that they nearly covered the horizon from edge to edge. The smallest tip of one could crush the ship into splinters.

Chapter 24

The certainty that there was no escape, that they were all dead, cleared Persephone's mind of the immediate horrors surrounding her. As soon as thought returned, she understood that a sea boiling with monsters of the deep was no natural event. One might be disturbed and rise or be hungry and go hunting, but the creatures Hades and the crew were fighting did not eat, or seek to eat, men, and they lived far too deep in the sea for any boat to disturb them. They had been summoned!

On the instant, Persephone knew what to do with the knife. She rushed back into the shelter, tore open the panel of the litter, and pulled off the covering of the lower compartment. She grabbed Poseidon's arms and yanked them up. The cord bit into his genitals. His eyes snapped open and he bellowed with pain behind the gag. She dropped his arms and he choked as the cord sawed at him once more.

Persephone yanked the gag from his mouth. "Bid your creatures go!" she screamed. "Send away leviathan!"

"You will die before you can unman me," Poseidon snarled.

Persephone set the blade of the knife at the base of his throat and leaned on it, just enough to draw a bead of blood. The ship lurched. The knife cut deeper. Poseidon stared up into eyes that changed from gold to burning copper and then glowed red, at hair that stood away from her head and snapped and crackled with blue sparks.

"You dare not!" Poseidon yelled. He sought authority of tone, but the words were half a scream of fear. Hades would never have driven home that knife. Even as the ship sank, he would have been too much a coward to spill his brother's blood. But not this mad bitch. She smiled.

"I have just thought," she cried, laughing above the noise of the battle, "when you are dead they will all go anyway. They are creatures of the deep and come at your summoning, but they are in pain. Your death will release them to their natural place."

"No!" Poseidon shouted, but he knew it was too late.

"If they do not go"—her lips pulled back; she leaned closer, red eyes glaring, as if she intended to tear his throat out with her teeth—"you will be dead before Hades. That will be my joy."

Panic lent strength and immunity from pain. Poseidon screamed two liquid words as he shoved his heels against the litter and straightened his knees in an instinctive effort to shrink from her, but he could not shift himself. "Wait!" he bellowed. "I have loosed their bonds."

"You are too treacherous to trust," she snarled.

She would have pushed the knife home on the words, but the ship heaved, tipping her backwards. She caught at Poseidon's bound hands to steady herself, bringing another shriek of pain from him, but she did not let go of the knife.

"They are gone! They are gone!" Poseidon yelled as she raised her arm.

"Kore! Stop!" Demeter screamed, staggering toward her, and then shrank back as the glaring red eyes fixed on her. "Persephone, I acknowledge thee," she cried. "But do not kill!"

"Why?" Persephone asked, the knife still poised.

"A priestess of the Corn Goddess does not kill," Demeter pleaded.

Her mother's voice was softer now, broken by sobs, but Persephone could hear her. She realized that the noise outside the shelter had almost died away. Where was Hades? Had he lost his battle before she forced Poseidon to call off his beasts? That question filled her, mind and soul, but her voice responded not to her fears but to what Demeter had said and asked harshly, "How is this different—except that this is quicker and more merciful—from what you planned for the people of Olympus?"

Eyes and mouth round with shock, Demeter stared into the merciless face that was her daughter's—and was not her daughter's. Persephone was almost as surprised as her mother by the words that had come out of her mouth. But if the Goddess had spoken through her, She was immediately gone and, oddly, left no reluctance in Persephone to take revenge for the loss she feared and to remove permanently any threat Poseidon could create. Persephone's arm tensed to strike.

"Persephone!" Hades said sharply from the doorway. "Please do not slit my brother's throat."

"I did not intend to slit it," she snapped, but her eyes were pure gold again as relief at his safety drew the heat of hatred out of her power. She lowered her arm. "I intended to push the point right through it . . . slowly," she added, smiling at her husband. "Does he not deserve it?"

Hades was all spattered with blood and his clothes were burned where the hot metal he had been handling had touched them, but he laughed rather breathlessly, closed the door, and leaned against it.

"Not if you look at it from his point of view," he said. "He might not have known, until you threatened him, who had taken him prisoner. And even if he did, he might feel being swallowed by sea monsters was a deserved punishment for someone who hit him on the head and trussed him up in a particularly undignified manner when he had only wished to offer you—and me—the compliment of rape."

"It was a mistake," Poseidon said. "I thought she had betrayed you. The scryer told me she was lying with a man, and I thought you still in Plutos."

Hades came away from the door, walked to the litter, and stood looking down at his brother. He did not speak, and Poseidon swallowed audibly. After a long moment had passed, Hades said, "You must be hungry and thirsty and need to piss too. I will help you, but will not loose you. I am sure you understand why. I will tell you, too, that I wish you no harm, despite your 'mistake.' I doubt you will make another mistake with Persephone, even if she should come into your power again."

Poseidon glanced toward her and saw only a smiling woman of breathtaking beauty. And then he noticed she still held the knife and he remembered vividly those glaring red eyes. He shuddered. "You may be sure I will return her to you with all the haste I may make."

"That is not very flattering," Persephone said, laughing. "Would you not even offer me three days of guesting?"

"Tchk," Hades remarked reprovingly. "Did you not realize that no one wants a guest who first hits him on the head and then threatens to shove a knife into his throat . . . slowly? Some day I will have to discuss with you the proper behavior for guesting."

Persephone laughed again. "Well, I will listen, my lord, but I think it a great waste of time. I have no desire to leave my home in Plutos to go guesting, and I do not think the rules of proper behavior apply to those made guests against their will."

Hades looked from Poseidon to Demeter. "I doubt you will be troubled again in that way, my love."

"No," both assured him in chorus, with deep sincerity.

Despite those assurances, neither Hades nor Persephone trusted their captives. Without a word spoken, they agreed a strict watch must be kept on Demeter and Poseidon. With a single kiss and a hand on Hades's cheek, Persephone indicated that he should sleep first. Even with the power she had given to him, he had fought nearly to the end of his strength and he needed rest.

Persephone sat near Poseidon with the naked knife in her lap. She did not threaten, but the sea king knew that he would be dead before the first cry of alarm faded away—even if he were not guilty of summoning the trouble. He could do nothing while the slow hours passed and the sun sank slowly in the west except pray the waters would be quiet, for he could not control those without being in their midst, warn the denizens of the sea away from the ship, and hope that no mariner would, out of nervousness, cry a warning for a nonexistent danger.

Persephone lit the lamp as soon as the shelter darkened so that she could watch his expression, which offered him no comfort. How could he tell what such a madwoman would consider dangerous? Poseidon hoped he was not sweating. The lamplight would catch the sheen of moisture and she might take that as an excuse to kill him, saying she feared he was sweating with concentration in an effort to destroy them.

Oddly, he was not as relieved as he expected to be when Hades woke and took Persephone's place. They had all eaten before Persephone went to sleep, she and Hades alternately holding morsels to his mouth and carefully raising his head so that he could drink while the cord around his neck and between his legs neither strangled nor threatened to bisect him. There was something about the way Hades kissed his wife when she lay down, and the absolute absence of expression on his face, that warned Poseidon his brother would no longer hesitate to kill him. If *she* were threatened in any way, Poseidon knew he would be dead before he could open his mouth to plead innocence.

For a long time the thought of being a victim of circumstances beyond his control occupied Poseidon's mind to the exclusion of all else. However, as the night passed, the near paralysis of fear that had held him ebbed. Not that he was fool enough to try any more tricks while they were aboard ship, but he was able to remember that he was not powerless on land either.

They were going to Eleusis and Celeus, who ruled there, feared him for his power over wind and wave; Celeus would do his bidding, but Celeus could not "hear" him. A messenger must be sent to Celeus—but only the creatures of the sea "heard" him. Yes, but there was one sea creature who could come onto land and manage as well as in the sea, the triton. Moreover, once they were ashore, Hades and that destroying brilliance of his would relax their guard.

This time, however, Poseidon did not send out his silent summons at once. Tritons were strong, but simple and mischievous. Left to their own devices they would forget his purpose and ravage the land for amusement. Thus, he did not send out his search call until afternoon, and it was early evening before a few dark shapes slipped through the water of the bay of Eleusis and came to rest on the rocky shore to the west of the town. One and then another crawled ashore and, whimpering with pain, slowly changed to a sleek-haired male creature with flat sea-green eyes and slightly scaled skin.

When the first to arrive was recovered, he walked along the beach until he came to the road and then followed that boldly through the town. He met no opposition. Twice he looked toward a stall left vacant by the merchant, who had hastily fled inside and barred the door at the first warnings of his approach, but his head turned back to the road to Celeus's palace as if pushed by some outside force, and he snarled at nothing each time.

At Celeus's palace he stopped by the barred gate. A hand stretched out to seize the gate and shake it loose, then paused. His great green eyes looked at the hand with dumb amazement, and then widened still more with surprise as his voice cried out, "My master, the sea king, sends a message to King Celeus," sounds he had never before made in his life and which he did not understand. Then he stood, snarling with impatience but leashed by another's will, until a wicket in the gate opened.

"I am King Celeus," a man said.

To the triton the sounds were meaningless; nonetheless, his mouth opened and noise came out: "A ship comes to Eleusis. You are bid to give the litter on the ship to the tritons and kill those accompanying the litter."

On the other side of the gate more noises were made, but the triton knew he would not be allowed to break the gate so he turned and ran down the road toward where the others of his kind waited. In the town again he swerved and stretched an arm to snatch at a woman cowering by a wall, but again his hand stopped before it reached its goal and he was driven along toward the shore. Angry at the frustration of all his attempts to play, he tried to slide under the weight that restrained him and slip back into the sea. In that, too, he failed, and he joined his grumbling fellows, who nonetheless all stood looking out toward a darker speck against the darkening sky, which was a ship approaching.

Unknowing, Hades and Persephone had by mutual consent arranged the conditions that permitted Poseidon to use all his strength to manage the tritons. At the first hail sighting land, they had hastily fed him and let him drink and relieve himself. Then they had bound his eyes and gagged him. Neither cared that the cloths obscured his expression. The litter was still open, and both Hades and Persephone were close enough that a knife stroke could finish Poseidon should there be any alarm. But neither noticed the beading of sweat that formed on the slivers of cheek, chin, and forehead which showed around the gag and blindfold. In a moment the beads were gone, absorbed by the cloth, leaving only a faint sheen where more sweat formed and was swallowed up.

Both were more concerned about Demeter. The closer they drew to land, the more frantic her pleas became not to be dragged down into the underworld. All their assurances went for nothing.

"I am afraid of the dark, the terrible, unending dark," she cried.

"But we do not live in the dark, groping about like moles in the earth," Persephone said, smiling. "Our palace is alive with the light of crystal. Indeed, mother, I am not trying to punish you. I wish you to be at peace, knowing how beautiful is the world in which I live."

"Among the dead!"

"But—" Persephone began.

"You will not see the dead," Hades interrupted. "I will ward them away from you, I promise."

"I will feel them," Demeter whimpered. "I cannot bear it. I cannot! I swear I will wait for you in Eleusis."

"You will be within Poseidon's reach in Eleusis," Hades pointed out.

"You can hold Poseidon in the underworld," Demeter said.

"It is not reasonable for us to travel to Plutos and then for me to come back to Eleusis, mother. We can reach Olympus in a few days from Plutos, whereas travel from Eleusis may take weeks, and if we do not come soon to Olympus, the crops will be late there and I might not have time to bless those of Plutos at all."

"Then you go to Olympus. You do not need me. The Mother will give you strength—you said so yourself."

"Lady Demeter, you must go to Olympus until you can come to some arrangement with Poseidon,"

Hades put in. "I cannot keep my brother in Plutos for long. He did me no real wrong. As soon as Persephone and I are safe, he must be returned to his own realm."

"And I cannot be high priestess of two temples. You must make your peace with Zeus, as you said yesterday you would," Persephone said. She looked at Hades and he shrugged slightly. "If you will bind yourself beyond any hope of breaking that oath to be reconciled with Zeus and go to Olympus with Hermes when he is sent to fetch you, we will not force you to accompany us to Plutos."

"Zeus did wrong when he gave you to Hades—" Demeter began.

"You may think he did you a wrong," Persephone interrupted, laughing and reaching for Hades's hand, "but he did no wrong to me."

Demeter made an impatient gesture. "So you say, but I had not finished. I was about to acknowledge that I, too, did wrong when to spite Zeus I would have let Olympus starve. So if he will allow me to live in peace—"

"I have assurance of that, Lady Demeter," Hades said. "When I went to ask him where was my wife and we spoke of the possibility of your return to Olympus, he swore to me that in the future he would leave the priestesses of the Corn Goddess and all the avatars of the Mother to their own devices. Zeus will not seek to meddle with your temple again—and if he does, you need only send me a message and I will remind him of his promise."

"Why should Zeus fear you?" Demeter asked, her head atilt.

They had been working too hard to remove her fear, Hades thought. She was taking him too lightly. With

Demeter that could be dangerous. She would try again to keep his wife from him. He knew there was no way she could do that, not in Olympus, but it would breed less bitterness for her to remain too afraid to try than that she try and fail. He did not answer her question at once, merely looked at her until she shrank away and shuddered.

Then he said mildly, "There is no reason for Zeus to fear me. He is my youngest brother and I love him." Demeter shuddered again, and Hades was satisfied and smiled slightly as he added, even more gently, "But even the Mage-King of Olympus knows it is unwise to ignore the advice of the King of the Dead."

Persephone blew lightly in his ear. "Only the Queen of the Dead can be that silly."

"Quite true," Hades admitted. "Why not, since it is my feet that get burnt carrying her away from a pretty spill of lava she wished to see closer—against my advice."

His face and voice had remained unchanged; no one, except perhaps Persephone, could have guessed he was so happy that he had to wage a fierce struggle not to caper around the tiny shelter like an idiot. He had had a doubt when he set out to frighten Demeter that Persephone would not understand and would try to make his words seem less threatening. But she was closer to him than the one flesh and blood and bone a wife should be; beyond that, they were one mind and one soul. She had left the threat intact and yet proved that it did not apply to her so her mother's fears for her would not be awakened anew.

He came suddenly back to earth from the place where his spirit was dancing in the sun as the captain shouted and the ship changed its motion. Persephone was already leaning over Poseidon, knife in hand, but he signaled her to wait. There had been no alarm in the captain's voice and he could hear the sound of breakers.

"I think we are coming ashore. I will go out. If I do not call a warning, close the litter. Either bind and gag your mother or take from her an oath that will hold her to the promises she has made."

"I will give any oath you like," Demeter said crossly, "but you are wasting my time and yours. You cannot get to the caves tonight. It is almost dark already. You will get no bearers to go up that road in the dark. Why do you not take me to the temple and start out in the morning?"

Hades stopped at the door and blinked at her, then nodded. "You are quite right, Lady Demeter," he said. "But I fear no bearers would carry the litter to the caves even in the daylight. I will ask the captain to give us one of the carts sent down to carry the cargo to take the litter up to the temple. After what he has seen on this voyage, he will think that a most reasonable request."

He started to open the door, hesitated, and turned back, coming close enough to speak very softly. "Lady, you played a game with me that has cost me dear. Because I, too, love your daughter, I understand your desire to keep her with you—although that is unnatural in a mother—and I am willing to forgive the hurt done me. I beg you, for your own sake, because my wrath is very long and very cold, play no more games."

There was a long silence after he stepped out of the shelter, broken by the calls of the sailors and the groaning of the oars driving the ship to land. Then Persephone said, "He is very patient, very slow to anger, and very indulgent to me, but I think I have reached the limit of my influence with him. Do not press your luck with Hades further, mother."

"I will not. I have told you already that I will help rather than hinder your safe arrival at the temple. I swear that by the black Styx which will cover me and by the favor She will withdraw from me if I do not keep faith."

Persephone wished her mother had not been so specific in her oath, but she no longer feared Olympus would threaten Plutos. She could, and would, provide fertility for Olympus until a new priestess was trained and accepted by the Goddess. Still, everyone would be much more at peace if Demeter publicly accepted her as Persephone, queen and high priestess of Plutos, and took her own place as high priestess of Olympus. She tried one more warning.

"Mother, for me the underworld is a place of exquisite beauty and great pleasure and excitement. It is the best of all possible homes. I may choose when I wish to play in sunlight or make love by cavelight, but there are places of eternal dark and painful punishment deep under Plutos—and Hades is master of those places too. He is merciful—but I have heard of prisoners confined in the depths. I—"

A muffled sound from the litter made her jump to her feet and jab Poseidon with the knife. "Be still!" she hissed. "Another sound and you are dead."

To make sure that no one would hear if he did not obey her—he must realize that once the litter was closed her knife could not reach him—she heaped blankets around him, muffling his head. His feet moved feebly, and with tight lips she pulled the blankets aside to make a narrow space for air to reach him before she closed the secret compartment of the litter. Hades would never forgive himself (and perhaps never forgive her) if his brother suffocated.

Poseidon had been listening to the arguments of Hades and Persephone and the promises of Demeter with considerable amusement. All that effort expended to calm Demeter into willingly going to the under-world where she was headed will she nill she. After a while he listened with only half an ear, wondering petulantly whether Hades and Persephone would still be King and Queen of the Dead after they, themselves, had become one of them. Or would the furious wraiths reject their once-fleshly rulers, perhaps out of resentment at past bondage, and eternally torment them?

That would be only just after the way they had treated him—bound like a sacrificial animal to be released at their pleasure. That the tritons should tear them apart would be a sweet revenge, which would have the additional benefit of bringing down Zeus and Olympus. With no fertility goddess to enrich their poor valley soil, they would have to abandon their shining city and live in their temples cheek-by-jowl with the stinking natives as he did. And no one would blame him. If Zeus wanted a target for his lightnings, he had provided Celeus, whose men would outnumber the tritons.

His attention was drawn more fully to the others by the signs of the ship coming close to the shore. The soft warning Hades gave to Demeter came to his ears too, and he felt a chill creep slowly down his spine. He told himself it was impossible for the tritons, aided by Celeus's men, to fail. Hades did not even have a sword with which to defend himself. But he might get one from the captain or crew before they left the ship and

. . . and he had heard how Hades fought when Kronos fell in Olympus.

Who knew whether those tales were true, Poseidon told himself. Besides, in Olympus Hades had been surrounded by the dead, and they had struck such fear into any who met them that a ten-year-old girl with a stick could have defeated Hades's opponents. But what Persephone said of the depths of the underworld he knew to be true. He had been one of those who condemned Tantalus, and he himself had seen Hades's face when he agreed to the doom. Involuntarily, Poseidon cried out in protest, felt the prick of Persephone's knife, and then the smothering folds of the blankets around his head.

Poseidon's hold on the tritons wavered. They had been coming toward the town from the uninhabited coastline to the west, where they had been hidden among the rocks fallen from the cliffs. Now they began to hesitate and mill about. One looked toward the sea but another, who had carried the message, remembered the woman he had not been able to touch and some bright shining things on the merchant's table with which he had wished to play. He called to the others and they all continued eastward at a quicker pace.

Aware of his creatures' new purpose, Poseidon struggled with himself. Fear that Hades would again make the impossible come true and escape urged him to send the tritons back into the sea. But the knowledge that he would never have another chance as good as this to free himself of the threat that some day Hades would betray him, to have revenge for all the years he had felt a sinking in his gut when Zeus smiled at him, drove him to seize control of them again. They were now headed a little north of east, into the heart of the town. He must force them south to where the ship had come ashore.

The litter tilted and jerked as it was lifted. Panic at the thought of being taken into Hades's dark world seized him. He was so shaken by the realization that he would be completely at his brother's mercy that he lost all contact with his creatures. As the litter swayed across the deck, his hands moved and the cord cut at him. Rage burned in him, intensified by his sense of helplessness. Where were Celeus and his men? Why were they not down at the shore seizing the litter? Had Celeus failed him?

Let the tritons come, he thought. Let them ravage the town. It was no more than Celeus deserved. The litter jerked upward as the ropes of the pulley lifted it over the ship's side, swayed more wildly as a sailor drew it outward toward the waiting ox-drawn cart. The mass of the blanket shifted, closing the fissure Persephone had arranged to supply air. Poseidon tried to shout and struggle free, gasping for breath out of fear of lack of air rather than because he could not find air to breathe. The muffled sounds he made were completely swallowed up by the groan of the pulley and the creak of the cart as the weight settled into it. The ox protested too as its driver applied the goad. By the time its grunts and low moans had been stilled by resignation, Poseidon had lost his senses.

In fact, Celeus's men were on their way. It was inevitable that they should come upon the tritons in the center of the town wreaking merry havoc, bashing doors and seizing whatever caught their eyes within, dragging out women, whose screams of fear and pleas for mercy they did not understand at all. To them the

cries and writhings were no different from the playful
shrieks and struggles of the merwomen they pursued
in the sea.

Because twilight was rapidly changing to full dark,
it took a few minutes for the captain to take in what
was happening. His first thought was that the tritons
were angry because they had not been given the litter
as soon as they came out of the sea. The captain began
to shout an explanation, but before he was finished
one of the men screamed, "That is my sister!"

A triton had playfully released his hold upon a girl,
who fled toward the armed troop, wailing with terror.
The triton, laughing gleefully, pursued, intent on his
game, ignoring the men who were momentarily motionless with shock. Whether the captain would have
tried to hold his men to their original purpose was
never put to the test. The brother had leapt to intercept
his sister's pursuer. He struck the triton with his
sword. The triton picked him up and threw him away.
His body collided with the captain, who fell, hit his
head, and was stunned. Without contrary orders the
men fell upon the triton, who had dismissed the attack
on him as that of some puny rival and returned to his
merry pursuit.

The triton was very strong and his scaled skin was
hard, but twenty armed men were too much for him.
When the first blow really hurt him, he shouted with
surprise, and though several swords pierced him immediately thereafter, he still had time to cry out to his
fellows for help.

The four remaining tritons abandoned their amusements and rushed into the crowd of soldiers. Battle
had been joined in earnest when Hades with Demeter
and Persephone walking beside the cart came up the

eastern road from the shore. Because of the irregular placement of the houses, making the road twist and turn, and the increasing darkness, the small party did not realize a battle was taking place. They had emerged right into the market square just north of the thickest of the fight before they could see enough to understand what the babble of shouts and cries meant.

"Back!" Hades snarled at the ox driver. "Go back!"

The man was only too willing to obey him, but an ox is a slow and stubborn beast. His efforts to make the animal back up resulted only in a dead stop, and his second attempt, to get the beast to circle around, had brought the cart broadside across the road, blocking it. This new position exposed the litter to the eyes of the captain, who was just regaining his senses. He was still half stunned, only just struggling to his feet and standing, sword in hand, staring at his men being mauled and thrown about by the enraged tritons, who were bleeding and battered, but far from subdued.

While the springless ox cart was traveling up the rutted street, the heavy jolting of the litter had caused the blankets around Poseidon's head to flap up and down, uncovering his face. His own semiconscious state had eliminated the panic that had earlier made him struggle senselessly for breath. He was almost fully aware, although still somewhat confused, by the time the cart encountered the fight. The violent emotions of the tritons flooded into him, restoring both his energy and his sense of panic and helplessness.

"To me!" he demanded silently. "To me!"

Such was the strength of his will, fueled by his terror and need for freedom—freedom to move, freedom to breathe—that even the fighting rage of his creatures was overwhelmed. As one being, the tritons thrust away the men with whom they had been struggling and rushed to the cart.

"Out! Get me out! Set me free!"

The will of their master tore at them, his need lanced into them like hot knives, but they did not know how to fulfill his desire. Poseidon was himself too confused by their emotions echoing back his own violent need to visualize to them how to take the litter off the cart and open the secret compartment. All they knew was that he was confined and must be brought out. They smashed the cart to bits and then ripped and tore at the litter, scattering wood and leather and then the enveloping blankets until Poseidon was exposed.

Although the tritons were strong, tearing apart the solidly constructed cart and litter took considerably longer than opening the panels. Poseidon was no longer confused by the time they reached him, but his need to be free of the shameful and painful cords binding him was no less overwhelming. Forgetting Hades completely, he concentrated on mental images to show the tritons, who had no knives, how to bite through the cords without hurting him.

When Hades saw the ox stalled and the cart blocking the road back to the shore, he had swept Persephone and Demeter behind him as close to the buildings as they could get and begun a strategic retreat up toward the temple on the hill beyond the palace. He had got his party free of the men and tritons and on the road out of the market square before the captain remembered the second part of his instructions—to kill those who accompanied the litter.

He had seen them escaping, but at that moment was still dazed and trying to absorb the sudden way the tritons had abandoned the fight. By the time they went for the litter, the captain's head was clear and he remembered Celeus's order to give the litter to the tritons. His men, however, were caught in the heat of battle and about to attack again when they saw the tritons begin to destroy the cart.

It took the captain a little while to convince them that what the tritons did with the litter was no business of theirs. Their orders were to give the litter to the creatures, no more. That the tritons had taken it on their own was satisfactory; certainly it would be stupid to fight them to get it back so they could give it to them again. It was then that he recalled the fleeing figures, connected them with the second part of his orders, and bade the men follow.

The pursuit was not as swift as it might have been and only twelve of the original twenty could follow at all, the others being crippled by broken bones. And even those who could pursue were sore and bleeding from their encounter with the tritons. However, they were less hindered than Hades, Persephone, and Demeter by the full dark because they were more familiar with the road, and they came up with the party just below the entrance to the temple.

"Stop!" the captain shouted. "Do not dare enter the sacred temple. It will not save you. I do not wish to soil the holy precincts with blood, but I will pursue you within if I must. My orders from King Celeus are to take you."

He did not say "kill," because to take away all hope would merely make his prey more desperate. They would certainly run into the temple to try to find weapons or hiding places rather than yielding tamely in the expectation of gaining their freedom from the king. However, they neither fled nor yielded. The taller of the two women stepped forward and placed her hand on the big man's shoulder; the shorter, who had been closest to the temple, whirled around and returned to face him.

"You are mad!" she shouted. "I am Lady Demeter. How dare King Celeus give such an order."

The captain stood open-mouthed; the men, who had readied their weapons, paused in consternation. All were certain a dreadful mistake had been made. Their king would not order the death of the Lady who had brought them such plenty. But before the captain could excuse himself and beg Demeter to come with them and explain the confusion to their master, the man spoke.

"Your king has mistaken us for others," Hades said. "I am sure he does not really desire a visit from the King of the Dead."

As he spoke, a strip of the road about a handspan wide right in front of them heaved, spat steam, and then began to glow—first red and then yellow, sinking a little as it started to bubble like thick mud. All shouted in terror and jumped back, the men shrinking away from the melted, boiling earth. They were too frightened to take their eyes off Hades and were backing down the road when a huge voice roared, "Stand your ground. I am the sea king, and I will drown Eleusis and wash it all into the sea, including Demeter's puny temple, if you do not follow King Celeus's command and kill these three."

Poseidon did not wait for the men, paralyzed with horror, to act. On the same breath he said to the tritons, "Take them! Rend them!"

His will lashed them, but the sea creatures did not leap forward over the glowing, molten earth. Even stronger than the sharp prod of Poseidon's will was their terror of fire. The fear that held them frozen made them even simpler and unable to understand that, although their master's will drove them directly forward over the molten earth, they could obey by going around the burning area. Poseidon's fury at their lack of response made him slow to understand as well, and by the time he realized what the trouble was, the bubbling yellow had stretched to nearly an arm's length in width and was curving around to form a protective moat.

Poseidon laughed. "Fool!" he said. "How long do you think you can expend so much power? All I need do is wait."

In reply a thin, molten tendril leapt across the space between Poseidon and the glowing moat and lashed out over his bare feet so that he screeched with rage and pain. Then Persephone handed Hades something and he threw it. The rock reddened as it flew, turned bright yellow, glowed white, and began to drip just as it struck and lodged in the flesh of one of the tritons. The creature shrieked and tore at his breast, then wailed and ran, his intense physical pain breaking the hold Poseidon had on him. His keening floated back as he raced for the cool quenching waters of the sea.

The threat was clear, and Poseidon, seeing his revenge escaping him, roared with rage and gathered himself, seeming about to launch himself at Hades over the widening area of molten ground. Hades had just reached back for another stone and his eyes, fixed on his brother, showed that the next white-hot rock would not be a threat or a weapon against the terrified tritons. In that instant, before personal combat and crippling injury could generate irrevocable enmity, a blinding blue flash arced over Hades's head and struck the ground at Poseidon's feet.

Everyone's hair stood on end and a long spark shot from Persephone's hand to Hades's, making them both cry out with surprise and drop the stone she had readied. Poseidon was so shocked that the last bond he held on the tritons was severed and they, screeching in horror as the lightning flickered and spat all around them, fled.

"You mortal men, begone!" a voice like a brass gong bellowed. "I am the servant of Lady Demeter, the guardian of this temple. Only her will holds on these grounds, not that of your king or of any other god. Go!"

They did not need a second invitation. The sound of running and cries of fear and pain when a man fell and was helped to his feet and dragged along by his fellows diminished into the darkness. A brief pause followed while the lightning Zeus had used sparked and crackled away the last of its energy. Then in a slightly plaintive voice, Zeus said, "Hades, please. Turn off the heat."

"I cannot," Hades said, equally plaintively. "I can only heat it. It has to cool by itself. Can you not draw up a nice gushing spring, Poseidon? That would wreath us in steam and provide a truly godlike exit for us."

"For whom to see?" Poseidon growled—but he was no longer incoherent with rage; indeed, his voice sounded more long-suffering than indignant, betraying the relief that lay under his belligerence when he added, "Who asked you to interfere in our affairs, Zeus?"

"Actually, Hera. She has been so worried since

Hades's visit to me that she had an unusually clear vision of this confrontation, which is how I knew where to come and when. She is very fond of both of you, you know." He laughed. "A good deal fonder than I am at this moment. I was sorely tempted to fry both of you, but I need you. There is no one but Hades that can keep the dead confined, and no one but Poseidon who can rule the creatures of the sea. However, I *will* take oath of both of you that this will end here now and for all time."

"Given," Hades said promptly, "by the Styx and under the authority of the Mother of All. I am sincerely sorry for the insult and injury done you, Poseidon, but powerless as I was in your realm, I could think of no other way to protect myself and my wife."

"Given, by the Styx and by the Mother."

Poseidon was less gracious and offered no apology for the near rape of Persephone, but he was not sorry to be bound to forgo any revenge on Hades. He had not realized just how powerful Hades's Gift was or how it could be used as defense and weapon and not only in the underworld. However, in the future he would not forget the way that white-hot stone seared its way into the triton's flesh or that the next was meant for him and would have found its mark.

"And you, Persephone?" Zeus asked.

"Poseidon did me no harm," she said softly. "What happened was a mistake, and I am sure will not happen again. I owe him no ill will and I am sorry for the poor triton who was hurt."

Carefully, Zeus did not ask what had happened. He said instead, "Hermes is here, Poseidon, and will spell you back to Aegina if you wish—at my cost."

"Good enough," Poseidon said.

Zeus gestured and the young mage stepped out of the shadows near the temple wall into the dimming orange glow from the still-molten ground. He flew across the hot trench, murmured, and pressed a finger to Poseidon's brow and to both arms. He nodded. Poseidon spoke a single word and was gone. After a minute pause to be sure no failure in the spell would bring him back, everyone sighed with relief.

"With your permission, Demeter, we will enter the temple where we can find light and places to sit."

Demeter started when Zeus spoke to her, but she nodded a gracious acceptance of the courteous, almost apologetic tone. "Of course," she said, hurrying into the building and calling for her priestesses.

Cries of relief came at the sound of her voice. In moments she was surrounded by scurrying priestesses, who had been huddling in the darkest corners. They wept for joy at her return. Lamps were lit, wine and cold meat and rounds of bread and cheese were laid out. Demeter kissed them and blessed them and sent them away, and they went at once, but looked backward with adoring eyes.

Persephone recalled the less harmonious atmosphere of the temple in Olympus and the frustration of the priestesses, who felt themselves to be Demeter's equals held back by her from honor and power. That would not happen in Eleusis. These native women, although Gifted, would never aspire to Demeter's power. If her mother had Eleusis to refresh her spirit, she might be happier in Olympus during the time she spent there and would not miss her daughter so much.

"Demeter," Zeus said. "Olympus will starve if the crop is not good this year, but I cannot give your daughter back."

"You should not have given her away."

Zeus shook his head. "I cannot say I am sorry for that. My brother, whom I love, is happy. My daughter, whom I was not allowed to know but who I felt needed her freedom, is also happy. I can say that I am sorry what I did caused you so much pain, but that is all."

"Mother—" Persephone said.

Demeter made an angry gesture, but it did not have the force of full conviction. She was remembering how Zeus had said he was her servant, the guardian of her temple. He had not tried to usurp her power in Eleusis. She knew both from what Hades had told her and from Zeus's manner that he would not again meddle in temple affairs in Olympus either. But after a struggle that had stretched over nearly three years, she hated to give in so tamely.

"You will have your crop," she said. "I will return to Olympus, with you if you desire, but I will enliven no seed nor bless any field until my daughter joins me."

"Demeter—" Zeus began.

"That is what we promised, brother," Hades said. "Persephone will come each spring to bless the seed and fields of Olympus with her mother. Then she will return to me."

"You are generous, brother," Zeus said.

Hades grinned. "I am an enslaved husband, brother, and do my wife's will."

"You are my good and gracious lord, always indulgent."

Persephone leaned forward and kissed Hades's lips, and what was between them filled the room so that Zeus looked away, his lips thin with envy, and Demeter's eyes brimmed with tears.

Epilogue

The seed had been quickened, the fields blessed. So strong was the fecund power that the first fields already showed a mist of green shoots. In two days more, Demeter would need to accompany her daughter to the entrance of the great cave where the sacrifices to the dead were sent and yield her up to black-eyed Hades.

Demeter hesitated, then entered the door, held open by a smiling and cherubic boy-child who led her swiftly down the wide corridor to another door that opened onto a large chamber painted in the likeness of a lovely garden. Beyond a small pool into which tinkled a tiny fountain, soft cushioned couches were drawn into a close semicircle. On the central couch, Aphrodite reclined.

Demeter felt surprised as she always did when she saw Aphrodite, despite the many years she had known her and no matter how often she saw her. Each time, Demeter still expected a sensual, knowing woman, with a voluptuous body, full breasts, rounded hips and thighs. Instead she saw the figure of a barely nubile girl, a perfectly modest gown, and an expression of innocence that wrung the heart.

"We are so glad to have you back, dear Demeter," Aphrodite said.

Again Demeter was shaken. The voice was sweet, low, musical, full of sincerity and conviction. Demeter gathered her wits and reminded herself that it was part of Aphrodite's Gift. It was neither true nor false—just part of her.

"Zeus has spoken to you as he promised?" Demeter asked.

"Oh yes. He is very eager to avoid any other misunderstanding. He asked me to break the spell that causes your daughter to love Hades—but that is impossible."

"I thought you could make and break any love spell."

"And so I can," Aphrodite said, "but I know no spells that can change true love into hate or indifference—and if I did, I would not use such an abomination."

"But if she is bespelled to love him—"

"Demeter, Persephone is not bespelled. I have seen her, heard her, touched her, smelled her, even tasted her. No spell was ever used. She loves Hades for what he is, for what he has given her, but most of all for his terrible need for her." Aphrodite shrugged. "I can make and break a false loving. I can paint a garish image of love over the dull or ugly truth of hate or indifference—but when love comes of itself, the truth gives color to life, and I cannot change that. And so it is with Hades and Persephone."

"Then I must yield her to him?"

"Only until next spring, Demeter."

"For a few weeks, and then I must give her up again."

"Because he needs her more than you do, Demeter. He has only Persephone and will forever have only Persephone. Will you not open your eyes and see the many daughters that wish to love you and learn from you?"

Demeter turned away, but she was not scowling nor was her jaw set in the ugly, mulish line that had so long marked her unshaken determination to regain control of her daughter. She looked back over her shoulder at Aphrodite.

"I knew it when we parted in Eleusis," she said, "but I had to make sure." Suddenly she smiled. "These have been sweet weeks, with more love and kindness between us than has been for years. I will be content."

Author's Note

This book is a fantasy. Unlike my historical novels, in which I strive, although I do not always succeed, to obtain accuracy in every detail, in this book I have tried to carry the reader into an entirely different reality—the reality in which myths were the lives of all-too-human people. Although I have written a fantasy, I have taken few liberties with the major outline of the myth of Persephone and Hades; thus I feel no guilt over minor deviations because all myths in themselves are layered with millennia of changing accretions over some nugget of fact. For example, dragons, so prevalent in myth, may have been built on the folk memory of the lingering remnants of large saurians.

The differences between my tale and that found in versions in Edith Hamilton's *Mythology,* Bulfinch's *Mythology,* or summaries in such works as the Larousse *Encyclopedia of Mythology,* with which the reader may be familiar, are largely differences in characterization. I have not wantonly deformed the myth to suit my plot, however. Actually, the mythological characters have been deformed over the years to make pretty adventure stories for cultures that no longer believed in them as gods. Thus I have felt free to go back to earlier renditions of the characters, as described by Farnell and others, and have built my Hades and Persephone not only on the single myth of the "rape of Persephone" but on many other myths that also mention Hades, Kore/Persephone, Demeter, and the others.

I have consulted many scholarly works and read everything I could find about Demeter, Kore, and Hades (all of whom have many other names). I have also read whatever original sources I could find in translation—my Greek is a one-letter-at-a-time affair, so I could not use untranslated material. Some information I have used; other information I have discarded. For example, I ignored research that suggests that Kore and Demeter were different aspects of the same being—that would have required a plot entirely different from the best-known version of the myth. However, I used aspects of both that are adaptations of separate goddesses of different native populations, which were overrun by the tribal migrations of the people who became Greek, and were adopted into the Greek pantheon. From this material I have garnered images that I have developed into the characters of this book.

It is clear from the many myths that mention invasion of the underworld by various heroes, such as Heracles, that Persephone is no pallid, shrinking, homesick girl. She is, indeed, sometimes the dominant figure in the bargains made with the invaders. Nor does Greek art or ancillary myth support the notion that Persephone spent only the three months of winter with Hades. On every vase and in every myth, she is in the underworld, seated beside her husband—often the figure in more prominent view.

The Greeks, like many other peoples, were very superstitious about the chthonian (underworld) powers and did not worship them directly. Pausanias says that there was only one temple where Hades was worshipped, at Elis. However, the god of the underworld was worshipped over a wide area, appearing under various forms and names, such as Plouton, Klymenos, Trophonios, and even Zeus Chthonios. The Hades I have described comes from "this 'nether-Zeus,' [who] is not merely the grim lord of the dead but the beneficent god of fruitfulness . . ." (quoted from Lewis Richard Farnell, *Cults of the Greek States,* vol. III, *Ge, Demeter/Kore-Persephone, Hades-Pluton, Mother of the Gods and Rhea-Cybele,* The Clarendon Press, Oxford, 1909).

If any reader is particularly pleased, particularly offended, or simply wishes to comment on my work, I would be very glad to hear from her or him. I can be reached at Box 483, Roslyn Heights, NY 11577-2452. I do answer mail, but sometimes not for a very long time, so I beg patience and indulgence from those who choose to write to me.

RLG
Roslyn Heights, 1994